Slave
to
Fortune

The memoir of the adventures of Thomas Cheke Esq, AD 1629

Set as a novel by
DJ Munro

First edition, June 2015

Second edition, June 2018

ISBN-13: 978-1512022117
ISBN-10: 151202211X

Please visit www.slavetofortune.com for more information and to comment on the book.

Cover image: *Crescent Moon* by Montague Dawson.
Copyright © Felix Rosenstiel's Widow & Son, London

Dedications

'We are all chained to fortune: the chain of one is made of gold and wide, while that of another is short and rusty... Apply reason to difficulties; harsh circumstances can be softened, narrow limits can be widened, and burdensome things can be made to press less severely on those who bear them cleverly.'

Seneca

Contents

Chapter 1: Kidnapped

I was asleep when they came; we all were. They came in the dead of night.

A splintering crash woke me. For a dazed moment I thought I had dreamt that dreadful sound but a chilling draught confirmed the truth: our front door had been forced open. Downstairs I heard voices, furniture being overturned, crockery shattering, tankards and pans clattering to the flag-stoned floor. From out of this tumult came the thud of footsteps upon the stairs. They were coming up to the bedrooms. They were coming for us.

I was now wide awake but I lay stock-still beneath my blanket, my breath held, my heart pounding. I heard the footsteps cross the short landing towards my bedroom. For a second the world stopped. Then the door to my bedroom was kicked open and two burly figures burst in. I remember those men, strange and terrifying: their faces half-lit by a lantern in the doorway; their voices foreign and savage.

'Get out,' I shouted as I struggled to sit up.

One of the men grabbed my shoulder. I raised an arm to defend myself but he landed a punch in my face so hard that it sent me reeling backwards. Together they dragged me from my bed, across the floor and out of the room.

I remember the screaming next – though it may have started before – piercing, desperate cries that scar my memory. The screams came from my ten-year-old sister, Elizabeth, who slept beside my mother in the room next to mine. As I was shoved down the stairs, powerless to help them, I saw a man with a lantern at their bedroom door. The top of his head was wrapped in white cloth. I knew this to be a turban. I knew what it meant.

Moments later my mother and sister were being hauled down the stairs. They were both sobbing. Elizabeth was struggling to wrench herself free. Between her sobs, my mother was begging for mercy. 'In God's name, leave us alone,' she pleaded. I saw that she clutched the remnants of her rosary, which had hung over a bedpost. She must have grasped it as she was pulled from her bed; amber beads rolled down the wooden stairs.

The room downstairs was dark and crowded with the strange men. I was pushed face-down over a table. Strong hands clamped my arms behind my back. My hands were bound, the rope biting into the skin at my wrists. I made no move, my bruised cheek pressed upon the cold table top, blood trickling from the corner of my mouth.

From this skewed position I was able to make some sense of the nightmare before me. I counted eight men including the one I had seen with the turban who was coming back down the stairs. He held the lantern in one hand and a clutch of my mother's jewellery in the other. He was tall, his height exaggerated by his turban, with blue eyes set in a face of creased leather. His clothes were extravagant: a crimson jerkin; blue pantaloons; and around his waist a broad, silk sash in which he carried a pistol and a long dagger.

Most of the other men were bald or shaven-headed. They were armed with pistols, daggers and cruel, curving swords. All had moustaches on their sun-beaten faces. They wore coloured pantaloons and short-sleeved jerkins that left their muscular arms free to ransack our possessions: trinkets; lace; cutlery; even cheese and cured meat; fruit and vegetables – all were being stashed into pockets. The wreckage of plates, bowls, bottles and jars was strewn across the floor.

This looting was interrupted by the man with the lantern when he reached the bottom stair. He spoke in Dutch or Flemish of which I understood barely a word, except that he seemed to say 'no' as he gestured towards my mother and sister. In any event, my mother and Elizabeth were forced down upon two chairs that had been pushed against a wall. My sister buried her face in her shaking hands. My mother beseeched the man with the lantern to spare us.

'In the Lord's name, have mercy,' she cried. 'We've done you no harm.' Her eyes were imploring, her fingers grasping at his clothes.

He ignored her as he placed her jewellery in the pocket of his jerkin and motioned to the two men standing over me to take me out of the house.

At this point I recall feeling terror; until then all had been confusion. Now the reality struck me: I was being separated from my family. If truth be told, I thought I was about to meet my death but I had neither the wits nor the courage to offer the least resistance. Instead I cried out like a small boy: 'Mother, help me.'

She thrust out an arm towards me and shouted: 'Leave him, I beg you. He's just a boy.' She made a vain attempt to stand but the brute standing over her pushed her back down. One of his comrades threw him a length of rope and he began to tie her to the chair. I did not see that cruel work finished as I was bundled out of the house.

'Tom,' I heard her cry, 'no, please, no; not my Tom.'

Outside the air was cool and still. It was a late summer night; autumn was close at hand. A crescent moon had shone brightly earlier that evening but a band of clouds had since rolled in and smothered the land in oppressive darkness. I could not tell the hour: I sensed it was well after midnight but there was as yet no hint of dawn.

A strong hand gripped my arm and pushed me forward so that I struggled to keep my balance. I cast a forlorn glance up the lane towards the village, Mottistone: little more than a church, a manor and a dusting of old stone cottages, blanketed with thatch and huddled around a small green. All seemed quiet. There was no bark from an unsettled dog, no peal of the church bell to signal the alarm.

The knowledge that the village lay undisturbed removed any hope of immediate rescue from that quarter, not that there were sufficient local men to take on my well-armed captors. A few old muskets, pikes and swords were kept in the manor but they would be no match for this mob. As my eyes grew used to the darkness, I picked out a dozen more men loitering in the shadows of the hedges in the lane. It was for this reason that I did not cry out for help. I knew that any honest soul coming to assist me and stumbling into that crew would pay dearly for his efforts. Nor did I seek to run, fast runner as I was, for my bound hands would have encumbered me. Rather I accepted, perhaps rather meekly, that my fate now lay in the hands of my captors.

I was forced to kneel in the dried mud at the side of the lane, pressed against the hedgerow so that its brambles scratched my cheek and tore at my nightshirt. I remember the smell of the wild garlic rising up from the undergrowth, the song of a lone grasshopper. I knelt there, firm fingers gripping the back of my neck, until all the men had left the cottage. The man with the lantern came last, extinguishing the flame within it before he closed the broken door behind him, muffling the heart-rending cries within. Then I was pulled up by my hair and pushed bare-foot down the dusty lane, away from the village and towards the sea.

The lane where we lived runs in a zigzag fashion along the edges of the patchwork of fields separating Mottistone from the sea. It leads to a narrow gully, which we islanders call a chine, that spills out into the sea in a broad bay. We processed down the lane in file, myself in between two of the brutes. As we walked we picked up more of their comrades, who had been stationed at intervals along the lane. We approached two cottages, where the lane altered its course at a right angle, but we filed past them in silence – they were either undisturbed or already ransacked, I could not tell which. All was quiet. Even the branches of the trees and the leaves in the hedgerows seemed to cease their rustling as we passed.

Further down the lane, a little set back from the wayside, lay one of the manor barns. I was surprised to see activity outside it. Half a dozen men were waiting there with their spoils, which appeared to consist of a score of small barrels. Following a brief discussion with the man with the lantern, the men from our file picked up a barrel each before falling back into line. In different circumstances I daresay that I would have paid more attention to this intriguing scene than I did at the time. It was only when I had cause to reflect later that I recalled that this barn, to my knowledge, had only ever been used to store hay for the livestock in winter, nothing more. As I was shoved onwards I paid scant attention to those curious little barrels. My thoughts were consumed by my plight.

Beyond the barn, a fair distance further down the lane, one more isolated farmhouse lay between us and the beach. This was the home of the Leigh family, yeomen farmers in these parts for generations. A dozen more members of the sinister crew were positioned at the entrance to the farmyard. As I approached I could make out two little figures crouching in the darkness at the side of the lane. Like me, I could tell that they were in their nightshirts, their whiteness emitting a faint luminescence. My group filed past on the opposite side of the lane from them and I saw their small bodies, shivering or sobbing, side by side. I knew who they were – the farmer's children – George and Catherine. They were some years younger than me but I knew them well. Some quick words were exchanged between the men in my group and those waiting at the farmyard. Then the children were hauled to their feet, though less harshly than I had been. They must have fallen into our grim procession some way behind me.

As we filed past, I saw that things were by no means quiet at the Leighs' farmhouse. The horse in the stable was agitated, the cattle and oxen were stamping and lowing in the adjoining fields, and the farmer's dog was yelping. The farmhouse was remote enough for this racket to disturb no neighbour's sleep – neither in Mottistone nor in Brighstone, the next village along. I wondered what had become of the farmer and his wife and surmised that they had met a similar fate to my mother and sister, though I felt sure that the farmer, Henry Leigh, would have shown more spirited resistance than I had mustered.

I became aware at this time of the tears running down my cheeks. My mind was still in a state of disbelief and despair with no room yet for anger. I took little comfort from the gradual realisation that I was being kidnapped and was not about to be slaughtered. Every child in England had been told what it meant to fall into the hands of 'the Turk' – and how that was a fate far worse than a swift death. With my hands bound I could not wipe away my tears.

From the Leighs' farm it was but a short walk down through the chine to the beach. We followed the sandy path beside the brook as it tumbled down to meet the sea. I recall the sobering taste of salt in the air and the sound of the waves breaking upon the shore. I felt cold grains of sand between my toes and sensed a newfound swing in the step of my captors.

When we reached the beach the tide was high, leaving only a thin strip of dark sand below the cliffs that edged the shore. Three large rowing boats had been pulled up on to the beach, alongside the brook. More men had been stationed here, I presumed to keep watch over the boats and to collect fresh water from the brook in casks. At the sight of our arrival these men began to haul the first of the boats down towards the water.

The men from our procession joined in this task, dragging the other boats down into the sea. They led me out into the cold water and helped me into one of the boats, my treatment now less rough than it had been earlier. George and Catherine were prised apart and placed in separate boats, their pitiable cries audible over the breaking waves.

The boats were laden with the casks of fresh water from the beach and the small barrels from the barn. Then men in each of the boats took up their oars. I crouched in the centre of my boat, jostled by the legs of the oarsmen and by the casks and barrels, my hands still bound behind my back. The oarsmen settled into a rhythm under the measured orders of the helmsman. We slipped through dark, lapping waves and out into the bay. The two other boats in our small flotilla were heading in the same direction. A glistening trail of moonlight spilled from a fissure in the clouds and stretched out across the water as far as the great white cliffs that arced around the bay to the north.

Ahead of us, half a mile offshore, I saw that a ship lay at anchor. The sight of her invoked both curiosity and dread. By the shifting light of the moon I could make out some of her features. She looked like a three-masted merchant vessel.

When we neared the ship the oarsmen began to talk more freely in their strange language – the odd word sounding familiar to my ear but the whole sense meaning nothing to me. As the other boats closed in I heard the despairing sobs of a child above the rhythmic creak and splash of the oars.

Two rope ladders were thrown down from the main deck of the ship as our boat and another drew alongside. The first of our crew clambered upwards, carrying one of the small barrels deftly upon his shoulder. I wondered how I would be able to climb the ladder with my hands tied but then strong hands pushed me forwards and untied my bonds. One of the oarsmen pointed up to the main deck far above, indicating that it was my turn to climb.

At this point you may wonder whether it had not crossed my mind to dive from the boat and attempt to swim to freedom. In truth, that thought engaged me for only a moment: the cold, black depths of the sea, the distance from the land and the likelihood of pursuit were sufficient to extinguish any courage that might have been kindled inside me. Instead, with a final glance back towards my benighted island, I placed my hands upon the ladder and climbed.

As I clambered over the bulwark on to the deck of the ship, one of the crew on board was waiting for me. He was young, perhaps a little older than myself, and was not one of the men that I recognised from the shore party. He laid his hand upon my shoulder. 'This way,' he said pulling me in the direction of a hatchway in the centre of deck, near the main mast. His English words caught me by surprise.

I followed him down a wooden ladder to the lower deck. This was lit by several swaying lanterns and was crowded with men, hammocks, cannon and various stores. Though the fresh sea air permeated through the port holes, the lower deck reeked with the odour of unwashed men, mixed with the smell of the timbers and the sickly scent of exotic perfume.

The English youth picked his way through the clutter on the lower deck to another hatchway. This was covered by a wooden grille and locked shut with an iron bolt. Peering down through the hatchway I could see the top of a ladder, its lower rungs disappearing into the impenetrable darkness of the hold. A damp, nauseating stench wafted upwards. The youth drew back the bolt and raised the grille. At this point I must admit that my troubled mind was almost overcome: I felt my legs weaken and there must have been such a look in my eyes, such a pallor in my face, that a firm hand gripped my arm to steady me.

'It's down again for you,' said the youth. 'It ain't as bad it looks.'

I took one step forward, to the brink of the void. I swallowed hard, bent down and placed my trembling hands on the top of the ladder.

'Mind how you go,' he said, 'I'm sure you'll find somewhere to make yourself comfortable.'

I put a first, tentative foot on to one of the rungs of the ladder.

'Keep your fingers out of the stores,' he added, 'or the purser will chop 'em off. And don't worry: you'll have plenty of company.'

I wondered whether by 'company' he was referring to George and Catherine, or to some other desperate souls detained below, or to rats.

As I edged myself down into the void I heard the grille being shut and bolted above my head, imprisoning me. Rung by invisible rung, I climbed downwards. When I reached the foot of the ladder, the rocking of the ship and the blackness that enveloped me made me reluctant to let go of it. I must have stood there silent and still for a few minutes, trying to compose myself and to gain a sense of my surroundings, alternating my gaze between the grille above, through which only the faintest light passed, and the dark confines around me.

At length a man's voice called out from the darkness: 'Welcome aboard! Your hammock's waiting for you over here.' This sudden outburst prompted a snigger from elsewhere in the shadows.

'That'll be the one made of silk,' another voice added, eliciting more laughter. I noticed that both men spoke with a strong, West Country accent.

I mustered all my courage, let go of the ladder and took a few, tentative steps in the direction of the bow, my hands groping ahead of me to detect any obstruction. As I edged along, almost blind, my fingers traced the shape of wooden barrels and felt bulging sacks of foodstuff. After a while I found a small gap among the sacks and reckoned it as good a place as any to stop.

I sat down and put my head in my hands. My mind swirled with emotions: fear, little short of abject terror; utter despair at the helplessness of my predicament; and bewilderment at what had just come to pass. Barely an hour earlier I had been fast asleep in my own bed, unaware of the bitter twist of fortune that was about to befall me.

Some moments later, the first man spoke again. 'So who are you then, friend? And where is this place? We've been at anchor for several hours, so I daresay you weren't captured at sea.'

I pondered for a moment how full and honest a response to give. I concluded that I had nothing to lose from telling the truth; my situation could hardly get worse.

'My name is Tom, I mean Thomas Cheke,' I replied. 'And I was taken from my home. This ship now lies off the west coast of the Isle of Wight. Who are you, sir? And what is this ship?'

'Pleased to meet you Master Tom. My name is Jacob, and over there you'll find Silas.'

'That's me,' said the other voice.

'Somewhere yonder, over by that bulkhead,' Jacob went on, 'fast asleep I don't doubt, you'll find young Will and Adam. I'm afraid they didn't wait up to greet you.'

'No manners at all,' laughed Silas.

'And this here ship,' Jacob continued, 'is a corsair ship. Her name I could not tell you. But her captain is one of the most pitiless scoundrels that ever roamed the seven seas.'

'What age are you, Tom?' asked Silas.

'Fourteen,' I replied.

I sat for a minute or two, tears running down both cheeks. I did not speak lest my voice should falter, revealing my lack of fortitude. The stillness was broken by the dull clanking of metal against wood.

'That'll be the anchor,' said Jacob, 'they'll have hoisted the boats aboard by now and must be ready to make sail.'

'I'll wager they're putting out to open sea to avoid being spotted at dawn,' said Silas.

'Where do you think we're heading?' I asked.

'Can't say for sure,' Jacob replied, 'but the north coast of Africa is my reckoning.'

'He means we're heading to a slave market,' added Silas.

'Hush now, Silas,' Jacob replied with a loud tut, 'there's no need to scare the lad out of his wits.'

'How did you end up aboard?' I asked, in a pretence at maintaining my nerve.

'Taken at sea,' replied Jacob. 'Tried to out-run 'em but they were just too fast for us. And with all those guns up there pointing down at you, only a fool would resist 'em.'

'We're fishermen,' added Silas. 'They sank our ketch once they'd taken what they wanted from our catch and our possessions, including our good selves.'

'This is our second night on board,' said Jacob.

I heard the timbers around me groan and felt the rolling movement of the ship through the water. I pushed my head back into the firm sack behind me, which wasn't too uncomfortable. My body was drained but sleep did not consume me.

My thoughts continued to pitch and toss. I was fearful, of course, for the safety of my mother and sister, who I presumed were still tied up in the house. I tried to console myself that it would not be long before someone noticed the broken door and came to their aid. My fear was that they would not be found for days, by which time... I could not bear to think further on that prospect.

My thoughts turned back to my own plight. I recalled our parish vicar's fiery sermons about the perils and depravities of 'the Turks' as he called them. For years they had been the terror of the southern coast of England: the bogeymen that parents threatened their naughty children with. The vicar had tormented us with tales of the torture of poor Christian slaves – men, women and children – who had been captured by the Turks. We had all duly given generous alms to raise money for ransoms in the hope of bringing some poor souls back home from slavery.

Based on these sermons, and on the circumstances of my own capture, I was left in little doubt about the barbarity that awaited me at the end of this voyage, were I to last that long. What had confused me was the presence of white men amongst their crew, but then I remembered the stories of *'renegados'* – Christians who had 'turned Turk' during their captivity and, in the process, consigned their souls to eternal damnation – so said our vicar. I curtailed this depressing line of thought by telling myself that I should trust in God's Providence, however hard that might seem.

Snoring from behind the ladder, towards the stern, reignited my curiosity about my new, unseen acquaintances. The first two seemed tolerable enough and in truth I was already glad of their company. I shuddered at the thought of being locked down here in the foul darkness all alone. I felt that I needed to find out more from them about the ship and her crew, like the morbid interest that a patient has to discover his ailments and how serious they might be. As I pondered how best to restart the conversation, wondering whether my fellow captives had fallen asleep, I was pre-empted by Silas.

'So, how many others did they take tonight?' he asked.

'Just two that I saw,' I replied, 'two children.'

'Only a meagre catch then,' said Silas.

'Hardly worth the effort,' added Jacob.

'They also broke into a barn – one of the manor barns – took away quite a few barrels.'

'Sounds like they were taking on provisions,' said Silas.

'Well they didn't bring them down into this part of the hold, did they?' said Jacob. 'What kind of barrels were they?'

'They were small,' I replied, remembering them jostling at my feet in the boat.

'Remember anything else about 'em?' asked Silas.

'Well, they had a hole in the top with a bung in it, and some strips of wood, saplings I mean, wrapped around them in bands at each end.'

'Did they have any kind of stamp on them?' asked Jacob.

'Not sure; a crown maybe. It was dark.'

'They sound like powder kegs to me,' said Silas.

'Stolen from the navy, I don't doubt. Lot of that goes on round here,' added Jacob.

I blushed in the darkness at my ignorance; of course they were gunpowder kegs. That revelation sent my tired mind spinning off down a new line of thought: what were those kegs doing in a barn in Mottistone of all places? My village was not the kind of place that lends itself to danger and intrigue. And yet it seemed impossible to conceive that the corsairs had stumbled upon the gunpowder kegs by chance. The barn and, for that matter, all the manor estate now belonged to a gentleman named Robert Dillington, who had purchased them from my family after the untimely death of my father. My poor widowed mother had been obliged to sell up and Dillington had been good enough to buy at a fair price and to provide us with a decent cottage on the manor estate. Dillington, I reasoned, had no more use for gunpowder than we had, and certainly no need for a secret store of it in one of the manor barns.

As I tried to make sense of it all I concluded that my capture, and that of the Leigh children, were incidental to the prime target of the corsairs, which must have been the gunpowder store in the barn, howsoever it had arrived there. Little did this notion ease my mind; rather it gave me even more reason to curse my family's fate, which – to compound our earlier woes – had seen us located by such ill-fortune in one of the cottages close to the barn; close enough to attract the attention of marauding corsairs.

With these troubled thoughts preying on my tired mind, I fell at last into a fitful sleep.

Chapter 2: Barbary Corsairs

I guessed it was morning. I was awake but my nightmare persisted. A trickle of light seeped through the grille overhead. From this I began to put some shape to my surroundings.

The section of the ship's hold in which I had the misfortune to find myself was about fifteen yards in length and about eight yards wide at its broadest point, where a bulkhead separated our section from the rest of the hold. The planks forming the underside of the deck above looked just high enough for me to stand upright for most of its length. Space in the hold was limited as the ship was well stocked: sacks of foodstuff, barrels, earthenware pots, planks of wood, rolls of sailcloth, coils of rope – all arranged upon several tiers of shelving. I saw that, following my arrival last night, I had managed to edge about five yards from the foot of the ladder towards the ship's bow. In the darkness of the night it had felt like fifty.

To my right, at the bow, I saw two men, who appeared to be asleep. One, like me, was nestled among some sacks. The other lay outstretched upon the damp planks, having made a makeshift pillow from his jacket. It was from this direction that the voices of Jacob and Silas had emerged from the darkness, so I presumed that these must be their persons. Jacob's voice had sounded the closer, so I figured he was the one nestled amongst the sacks. I could appreciate now how, with their eyes accustomed to the darkness, they would have been able to see something of me as I made my descent into the hold.

I leant forward to gain a better view of what lay to my left. Beyond the ladder, two young men were sitting, their backs propped up by the sacks that lined the bulkhead. I deduced that these two must be Will and Adam, of whom the older men had spoken last night. Though they were silent, their eyes were open and they were awake. One had noticed me when I moved my head forward and seemed surprised. He caught the attention of his fellow, pointed in my direction and said, 'Here, Will, looks like we've got a visitor.'

Will rubbed his eyes and craned his neck to get a better view of me around the ladder. I realised that I had been well concealed among the sacks. 'I wonder if he speaks English?' he asked in a half whisper.

'Friend,' said Adam, 'can you understand me?'

'You daft mackerel: of course he can understand you,' replied Jacob from the bow, one eye half open. 'His name's Tom and he decided to drop in on us last night while you young fools were away with the fairies. He's a young gentleman, mark you, so treat him proper.'

Will got to his bare feet and walked towards me, his balance unaffected by the rolling of the ship. As he approached he extended his right hand towards me. 'Pleased to meet you. I'm Will – William Dart.'

He looked to be in his early twenties and had a friendly face, which was well tanned but fresher than those of the corsairs I had seen last night. He had fair, close-cropped hair, a light beard and brown eyes. He wore a coarse woollen shirt and breeches.

I shook his hand. 'Tom Cheke,' I replied.

'I guess they captured you too then?' asked Will, clearly thinking for a way to start a conversation.

'No, he volunteered for a life at sea,' chipped in a wakening Silas, 'what kind of a daft question is that?'

Will shrugged his shoulders. I interceded on his behalf.

'Yes, they took me and a couple of kids; no one else. They broke into our homes in the middle of the night.'

Will raised his eyebrows and let out a quiet whistle. 'Well, we'll look after you now,' he said.

'You'll have a hard enough time looking after yourself when we get to the *bagnio*,' replied Silas.

A shiver ran down from my neck to my spine. I had heard on good authority all about the *bagnios* – the pits of despair in which Christian slaves were locked at night, having endured a hard day's labour under the unrelenting African sun. Our vicar had given us lurid descriptions of the harrowing conditions within the *bagnios*, drawn from the accounts of those who had survived them and who now roamed the parishes of England, raising money to ransom the fellow captives they had left behind.

Will frowned and went on, 'Do you want some water? That's one good thing about being stuck down here in the hold: we can help ourselves. They think we can't open the barrels but we've managed to prise a couple of the standing ones open. You look like you could do with a bit of a wash and a drink.'

I looked down at my tattered nightshirt, saw a large blood stain and realised that my face must also have been in a state. I nodded to Will and attempted to smile, though my mouth was swollen. He strolled towards Adam, plucked an empty pot down from one of the shelves above and gave its inside a wipe with his sleeve. Then he lifted the lid off one of the barrels, filled up the pot and brought it to me.

'Thanks,' I said as I took the pot. Will smiled and returned to his corner. I poured some of the water into my hand, partly to check that it was drinkable but also to apply it to my face. I rubbed flakes of dried blood from my cheek. Then I took a sip, swilled it around to wash away the bloody residue from inside my mouth and swallowed. I would rather have spat out that first mouthful but I worried that this would have seemed uncouth. Thereafter, the water was bearable and indeed revived me in both mind and body. I hadn't appreciated the extent of my thirst.

As I drank, Silas pointed and called: 'Don't drink from that barrel over there, cos we use it as a latrine. That'll be a pleasant surprise for the crew someday.' The others sniggered.

I lowered the pot from my lips, my stomach convulsing at the thought. 'Aren't you worried about the purser chopping your fingers off when he finds out?' I asked.

Silas laughed. 'No, young master: they'll need me to have all my fingers in tact if they want me to fetch them a good price. We've got to look hale and hearty come the slave auction.'

'Thankfully that means they feed us too,' said Will.

'They'll toss us down some bread soon, if yesterday was anything to go by,' said Adam.

'They gave us bread when they were buttering us up,' said Jacob, shaking his head, a grim expression on his face. 'Now that we've declined their offer, they may not be so generous.'

Silas turned to address me. 'Has the captain made you his offer yet?'

I shook my head.

'Well then, you can expect your summons shortly. He'll tell you that if you help out on board, he'll let you sleep upstairs and you'll get rations like the others. If not, you'll stay down here in the hold with us, being let out once a day to relieve yourself over the side with half the crew gawping at you.'

I took another sip of my water and thought about how I would respond to such an offer. I had no wish to fraternise with the corsairs, but nor did I relish the prospect of a long spell of confinement in this fetid, airless hold. I imagined bilge water swilling over my feet and rats creeping around my ears. My thoughts also turned to George and Catherine; I felt duty bound to keep some kind of watch over them, if I could.

'It's the devil's choice,' said Jacob. 'But it'll not be long till we get to Algiers. That's where the captain told you we were heading, didn't he?' The question was directed at Silas.

'Yes. He told me that he would have a consignment to deliver to the ruler there and that we would end up in the *bagnio* unless we made ourselves useful as members of his crew and were willing to turn Turk.'

Over to my right, Jacob stood up and stretched out his arms with a yawn that infected us all. He walked over to the clean barrel of water and took some handfuls to wash his face and slake his thirst. I reckoned he was around fifty years old. His skin had been scoured by the elements; his hair and beard were whitish-grey.

Silas, meanwhile, had levered himself up into a sitting position and had propped his back against a barrel for support. He was of a similar age to Jacob, a little stouter perhaps. He was also weather-worn but his hair was still pure black. His eyes were dark brown and narrow giving him a furtive look.

A short while after Jacob had retaken his seat, the smell of fresh baking began to waft down from the deck above. It lingered tantalisingly in the suffocating air of the hold. The others must have smelt it too, though no one mentioned it. I saw them glancing upwards towards the grille. Doubtless all were wondering if we would be given any bread today. After what seemed like an age, I heard the sound of a bolt being drawn back. The hatch was opened and half a dozen pieces of flat, round bread were thrown down, scattering on the damp planks around the foot of the ladder. Then the hatch was closed and locked once more. Though my stomach heaved with hunger, I made no move towards the bread, not knowing how these scant rations were to be divided.

Will took it upon himself to share the bread around. He passed me a piece, which was still warm, then handed a piece to each of the others. He then made a further circuit of the hold, dividing the final piece equally amongst us. Everyone devoured his meagre portion.

After this, it was Adam's turn to refresh himself with the water and finally Silas's turn.

On his way back to his makeshift seat, Silas began to sing a shanty. When the chorus came round, Adam and Will joined in, while Jacob seemed to mouth the words. The song was about a sailor who went a-roving. None of them had the most musical of voices, indeed at another place and time the sound would have been grating, but here in the rolling depths of the hold their song was moving.

When Silas had finished, Will piped up with another shanty. And after him, Adam was encouraged to follow on but he only managed a couple of verses before he forgot the words. This prompted a round of hearty laughter and Silas explained in a loud voice that Adam had never once finished a song, something which the lad, for I could see that he was only about the same age as me, disputed with vigour.

Some minutes after the singing had died down, leaving a more upbeat mood in its wake, the grille overhead was unlocked and opened again. This time someone began to climb down the ladder and I could see two wide-eyed faces peering down through the hatchway into the gloom. The person climbing down turned out to be the youth who had met me when I boarded the ship. Silas muttered something about him under his breath to Jacob. As he reached the bottom of the ladder, the youth looked around, trying to spot something in the darkness. Eventually his eyes alighted on me.

'The captain wants a word with you,' he said.

I hesitated for a moment then got to my feet and went to follow him back up the ladder. As I went I heard Silas call after me: 'Be on your guard, lad. You can't trust any of them, least of all the captain.'

As I reached the top of the ladder, I felt an overwhelming sense of liberation at leaving the cramped darkness behind; light was filtering through the port holes into the lower deck. The grille was not closed immediately behind me and I noticed that several of the men were poised to carry the barrels of water that had been replenished on the island down into the hold.

The lower deck was a hive of activity and I was able to take in much more than I had done when I had passed through during the night. At the bow there was a small, brick-lined galley, from where the smell of the baking must have emanated. A couple of yards in front of the main mast was the grilled hatchway through which I had just climbed, and next to that a ladder leading up to the main deck. Behind the main mast was another hatchway opening into the stern section of the hold. Cannon were stowed along the lower deck and the personal possessions of the crew were crammed into every available nook.

I followed the young Englishman up the ladder on to the main deck. This likewise seemed a changed place from where I had boarded the previous night. There were plenty of men at work as the ship was in full sail. A fair wind was filling her sails and I saw that we were cutting through open sea.

I was led up some stairs towards the stern. The youth told me to wait as he knocked on the door of a cabin located beneath the poop deck. Having received some positive response from within, he told me to step inside.

The door opened to reveal a spacious cabin with a bed, a table and chairs and a gallery of windows facing out over the stern. There was a large chest in one corner and shelves bearing books, various weapons and navigational instruments and what looked like a set of large rosary beads.

A man was seated at the table, his turbaned head bent down over a map. He looked up as I entered. At once I recognised him as the man with the lantern, the one who had given the orders to the mob in my home. He now wore a more modest turban but his tunic was just as flamboyant, decorated in golden brocade. My heart began to beat fast and hard. A mixture of hatred, anger and fear surged inside me. I tried to remain composed.

He looked me up and down with his shrewd eyes, inspecting me.

'Thank you, Jack, you may leave us now,' he said to the youth in a Dutch accent, so that he said 'shank' instead of 'thank'.

The door closed behind me.

'So, Tom, welcome aboard my ship,' he said with a flicker of a smile. 'I trust you had a comfortable night's sleep?'

I looked at him but gave no answer. I was startled that he had addressed me by my name but reasoned that either my mother or sister must have called out my name in the house last night.

'In time you will come to terms with what has happened to you, and accept it as God's will,' he continued, lifting his eyes upwards.

'What is to become of me?' I asked.

'In some ways, the answer is out of my hands,' he replied. 'My ship is bound for Algiers. There you and the other captives will be sold as slaves. After that, I cannot say.' His tone was matter-of-fact.

I said nothing in reply. I could only think of how much I hated him for what he had done and of the vengeance I now wanted to wreak upon him. My fists were clenched.

'Until we reach Algiers,' he continued, 'I offer you the chance to be part of my crew. I see you are no mariner, so you would help out in the galley. Jack, the lad outside, is our cook – you would be his mate. As a reward, you would live and sleep on deck and be with the other children we took from your village.'

'And if I refuse?'

A fleeting expression of anger crossed his face, furrowing his forehead. 'Then you will keep the company of the others down in the hold. It makes no difference to me one way or the other. It's your choice.'

Conflicting thoughts rushed through my mind. I was torn between, on the one hand, my desire to escape the dark, putrid, airless hold and to meet up with George and Catherine and, on the other, my reluctance to assist the captain and his crew in any way or to break ranks with my new comrades down below. As Jacob had said: it was the devil's choice. My breast heaved with resentment. The captain raised his eyebrows, awaiting my answer.

'All right,' I said at last, 'I'll help out in the galley.' I felt like a traitor.

'Good,' replied the captain. 'Ask Jack to provide you with some decent clothes; my orders. Now you may leave.'

With that he returned to the study of his map, pulling a pair of compasses out of a drawer in the table. I let myself out of the cabin.

Jack was waiting outside, hanging over the port rail, between a pair of swivel-mounted guns. He turned to face me, expectation in his eyes.

'I'm to help you in the galley,' I said.

'Great,' he replied with a smile, giving me a hearty slap on the shoulder. 'I could do with some help.'

'The captain said you'd be able to find me some clothes,' I added.

'Of course I will; right away. Then there's a little time before dinner for me to show you what's what in the galley. Follow me. If you like, I'll tell you some of the other things you'll need to know on board the *Sword* as we go.'

'The *Sword*,' I replied, 'is that the name of this ship?'

'Yes. Although in fact she's really called the *Saif al Din*, which means the *Sword of the Faith* in Arabic. But we all just call her the *Sword*.'

Jack was slight in build, a little shorter than me, and light on his feet as he crossed the deck. He wore knee-length breeches and his short-sleeved tunic revealed fore-arms that were mottled with red scars. He led the way across the deck and down through the hatch. We climbed down and I followed him along the lower deck and up into the bow.

'So here's the galley,' he said, pointing with pride into an alcove at the foremost part of the lower deck. Inside there was a brick-lined furnace with copper pots hanging over it. Beside the furnace stood a table for preparing food. A cauldron was stowed beneath it, ingredients upon the two shelves above. Various cooking utensils – knives, forks, ladles and spoons – were suspended from hooks. Just outside the galley there was an opened sack of grain and a barrel of water.

'This,' he said, pointing to a patch of deck adjacent to the galley, 'is where I call home.'

There was a small chest containing his few possessions and a couple of bundles of clothes. He rummaged around in one bundle and extracted a pair of knee-length breeches and a cream-coloured tunic, which he handed to me. I put them on there and then, glad to be rid of my blood-stained night-shirt. They felt a little tight and were well used. Jack looked me up and down with an air of admiration, which I sensed was directed more at his clothes than at myself. Either way, I felt more at ease in my new attire.

'Come on,' he said, 'let me show you some other things you'll need to know.' He skipped forward, clearly relishing his new, guiding role.

At the step down from the galley to the rest of the lower deck he paused. 'This is where we dish up the grub: three times a day. The men line up this way – some will try it on and come back more than once, so be watchful. When the meal is all served up I throw the scraps down into the hold or out of the porthole – to feed the fish.' He grinned, revealing a couple of missing teeth.

We next stopped beside the grille opening into the fore section of the hold and I was stung once more by the guilt of betraying my newfound comrades. I could not help but glance down into the darkness; I was sure that I could feel their disapproving eyes upon me.

'Down there you've got your barrels of water and your sacks of flour and grain. You'll need to help me carry stuff up from time to time. The steward rations the water three times a day but, to be honest, there's plenty to go round, particularly since we took some more on board last night. We lower the prisoners a bucketful on a line of rope so they don't die of thirst.'

He walked a few paces beyond where the main mast passed through the lower deck and pointed into the hatchway over the stern section of the hold. 'And down there is where we keep all the stuff that we don't want any prisoners to get their sticky fingers into, including the grog. You probably won't get to go down there. The steward keeps it well locked up.'

I followed him up a ladder on to the main deck. He led me towards the stern and up the stairs I had taken earlier on my visit to the captain's cabin.

'This is the quarterdeck; only the officers hang about here,' he explained with a look of pride, 'I'm allowed here because it's my job to polish the ship's bell.' He gestured towards a shining brass bell. I had heard it ringing in stages over the course of the day, with varying numbers of chimes. I had even heard it faintly from the hold during the night.

'The bell rings every half an hour to mark the different stages of the watch,' Jack explained, without my asking. 'The quartermaster's mate measures each half hour with his time-glass and then rings the bell. As the ship's cook, I'm excused from watch duty, and I reckon you will be too. Breakfast is at seven o'clock, that's six bells for the folk that are about to go on the forenoon watch. It's at eight o'clock, that's eight bells, for them who've just finished the morning watch. Dinner is at eleven, that's six bells, for folk on the afternoon watch, and it's at noon, eight bells again, for everyone else. And supper is at five o'clock, that's two bells, for them that's on the last dog watch and it's at six o'clock, that's four bells, for everyone else. You and me get to eat once everyone else has been served. Get all that? Easy ain't it?' He laughed.

I thought that sounded anything but easy to remember but before I had a chance to protest or to question him, Jack was leading me up a narrower set of stairs to reach the small poop deck – the highest section of the ship's deck, directly above the captain's cabin. The 'mizzen' mast, the shortest and aftermost of the three upright masts on board, protruded from the centre of the poop deck. Unlike the other masts, this one was lateen rigged, which meant that the yard-arm, from which the sail was hung, was set at a slanting angle some way off the horizontal. We reached the very end of the ship where a flag cavorted in the wind. I noticed with surprise that it was the flag of France.

'Is this a French ship?' I asked.

Jack smiled. 'Today we're a French ship; tomorrow we'll be Spanish, and when we reach the Straits we'll reveal our true colours!'

I held on to the rail at the stern with both hands and gazed out over the cobalt waters racing past beneath us. The smell and feel of the salt-laced wind under the broad blue sky lifted my soul somewhat from the depths in which it was languishing.

'How long have you been on board?' I asked over my shoulder.

'Since I was just twelve years old. I'm sixteen now,' he replied with a look of pride. 'I was taken at Poole, plucked right off the street. They took me and a few others. I only came outside to see what was going on.'

After some moments of reflection, he continued with laughter in his voice, 'I guess you could say we were 'pressed,' except that we weren't pressed into His Majesty's navy, hell no! We were taken into Captain Murat's service. Before we reached port – it was Sallee we were heading for back then – I'd made myself useful on board and been offered a place in the crew, provided I converted to the true faith, of course.'

'You turned Turk?' I asked without thinking, surprise overcoming tact. Jack blushed. It hadn't occurred to me for a moment that such an ordinary lad – like any lad you'd find in any English town or village – would be a *'renegado'*.

'Yes, they cut me down there,' he glanced down to his groin, 'it hurt terrible, I can tell you, but just for a few days. After they've cut you, you just say the words and you're a fully-fledged convert. I can't say I regret it,' he added, 'it spared me from hard labour or worse. They treat you a lot better once you're, well you know, like them. And I daresay I wouldn't still be around today if I hadn't done it.'

He turned, his bearing a little less light than it had been, and walked back down on to the main deck. He stopped and placed a hand on the sturdy timbers of the main mast in the centre of the ship. This mast was crossed by a long horizontal yard-arm, from which hung the massive, billowing main sail. 'Up there,' he said, squinting into the sunlight, 'is the crow's nest. There's one on the foremast too. You get a fine view, I can tell you, especially when you're in the midst of a battle.'

Just then, from the direction of the bow, I heard a familiar voice: 'Tom, Tom'. There was a rapid patter of feet as George Leigh, with his sister Catherine in tow, ran across the main deck to greet me. Both were still clad in their dishevelled nightshirts. Catherine threw her arms around my waist, burying her tear-stained face into my chest.

'They told us that they'd taken someone else from the village, but we didn't know who,' said George, glowering at Jack, unfazed that the cook was a fair bit taller than him. Jack said he would head down below deck to get things ready in the galley and that I should come down and help in a few minutes.

'Yes, they took me,' I replied, once Jack had gone. 'They kept me down in the hold last night. There are some other captives down there too: fishermen. Come and show me where you've been hiding out.'

George turned and headed back up towards the bow. He was unsteady on his feet as the ship rolled to and fro. I had to take Catherine by the hand; she was reluctant to let go of my waist.

'Last night we were down on the deck below. I kept guard and didn't sleep a wink,' said George.

I knew George well enough that, despite being only twelve years old, his fearless attitude didn't surprise me in the least.

'Then in the morning,' he continued, 'we tucked ourselves away in a corner here.' I saw a spare piece of sailcloth which I guessed they had been huddling under.

'Have you eaten?' I asked. Both shook their heads.

'Catherine was really sick,' said George.

'But now I'm really hungry,' she added.

'Well, I can soon put that right. I have to work in the galley, preparing the meals for the crew.' George glared at me. I tried to justify myself. 'If I hadn't agreed to do it they would have kept me locked up in the hold and I wouldn't have been able to see you two.'

'Do you know where we're heading?' asked George.

'Somewhere in Africa, I think.' I was not keen to elaborate.

'Why did they take us? And why did they hurt papa?' asked Catherine.

'I don't know,' I replied. 'What happened to your father?'

Catherine pressed her face back into my side; her small hand gripped mine very tight.

George looked down at his bare feet for a few moments, then he looked up and answered, tears in his eyes: 'He fought back, punching and kicking them, shouting at them to let us go. They stabbed him and he fell. Then they took us away.'

I caught his eye for a moment but couldn't hold his gaze. I looked out to sea instead, feeling Catherine's small body shuddering against mine. We stayed like that for a minute or two.

'Where's Elizabeth?' Catherine asked, without releasing her grip on me. Catherine and my sister were of a similar age and had been close friends.

'They didn't want to take her or my mother. They tied them up and left them behind. I think they're safe. We'll be all right too,' I added, 'once we get ashore, I'll get word back home about paying a ransom. I'll write to Mr Dillington – he's got money and has always been good to my family, ever since my father died.'

George frowned. 'Papa and Mr Dillington don't get on. I've heard them arguing. He may help you, but I don't think he'll help us.'

'Well, let's just see once we get there.' I tried to sound as reassuring as I could, mainly for Catherine's sake; George seemed to have his mind made up on the matter.

'Tom,' I heard my name being called again, this time from a short distance behind me. I turned and saw Jack's head peeping out from a different hatchway, closer to the bow than the central hatch. 'Get a move on, it's nearly time to start dishing up.'

'I need to go,' I said, prising Catherine's arms away from me and putting her hand into her brother's. They made a moving sight: he standing fiercely, his eyes still wet; she with her head hung low, her long hair falling down like tears. 'Come down soon and get some food,' I said as I began to turn and cross the deck, 'I'll keep some back for you.'

Down in the galley, Jack had the cauldron simmering. He had made a pottage using grain from one of the sacks, boiled in water from a barrel. He had also baked another batch of the unleavened bread that I had eaten in the hold that morning. He told me that he had just taken the captain his meal in his cabin.

'Here, give me a hand moving this cauldron over there,' he said, eyeing the step down to the main section of the lower deck. He had wrapped rags around the handles to prevent them from burning our hands. We carried the cauldron over and then set up a makeshift serving table upon which we laid the trays of freshly baked bread. I noticed that the scarring on Jack's forearms must have come from burns as he reached into the oven. I looked down at my bare, unblemished skin.

Above us I heard the ship's bell ring six times. Moments later, a line of men began to assemble, carrying an array of tin or pewter bowls and cups in which to receive their portion. They were dressed alike in short-sleeved shirts, breeches and bare feet. Jack explained that these were the men who would form the afternoon watch, which meant that they ate before the rest of the crew.

I stood beside Jack and watched as he served out portions of the pottage with a ladle to the men who shuffled past, about a score in total. Most, if they offered more than a grunt of acknowledgement, thanked Jack in what sounded like Dutch. A couple, whom I took note of, thanked him in English and exchanged a few words. I handed each of the men a piece of bread and they sauntered off, some congregating around a table further down the deck, others retreating to their own private corners. When the last of them had passed, I helped Jack return the cauldron to hang above the furnace in the galley, where it would simmer until the eight bells.

I paid close attention as Jack made another batch of bread, mixing flour and water with a splash of olive oil. He kneaded this dough into thin circles and placed them on to a large metal plate over the furnace. After a couple of minutes on one side he flipped them over. As soon as this batch of bread was done he removed it and made another batch in the same way.

After the bell had rung eight times, the rest of the crew assembled. I counted around two score men in total. Again, most seemed to be Dutch, though there were a few Englishmen scattered amongst them. When they had received their portion they either sat at one of the communal tables or retreated to their own corners. The whole deck was soon filled with boisterous conversation and coarse laughter.

Once the last of the crew had filed past and Jack was serving out our own portions, I mentioned that the two children upstairs needed feeding. I climbed up the ladder and through the fore hatchway, finding George and Catherine tucked under the sailcloth. Waves were breaking against the bow, showering foam over them. Cold water sluiced across the deck and out through the scuppers. I tried in vain to persuade them to come down to the lower deck to join us. In the end I had to bring up the meals for the three of us. I wasn't sure whether that was in breach of the rules but no one stopped me. Jack had managed to find three spare pewter bowls and rough wooden spoons – he was good at finding things. The two children ate their meals in silence; they both seemed too miserable for words. When we had eaten, I told the children that I'd come back when my work was finished and that I'd see if I could lay my hands on some proper clothes for them.

Back on the lower deck I helped Jack to rinse the cauldron, clean the utensils and wash down the surfaces in the galley. In truth, Jack struck me as being quite self-sufficient in his work – he only needed a hand to carry some of the heavier loads. He nevertheless seemed pleased to have both the company and the assistance that I offered.

Before our work was over, we had to venture down into the fore section of the hold to bring up two sacks of flour. It was with trepidation that I followed Jack down through the hatchway into the void. The fishermen below could hardly be expected to approve of my decision to desert them to work for the corsair crew. One of Jack's comrades dangled a lantern through the hatchway to illuminate our descent. Its guttering flame flickered light and shadow into the gloom below.

As I climbed down it was Silas that piped up, 'Well if it isn't the prodigal son returned. Our company not good enough for you, Master Tom? That's a fine new outfit I see you're wearing.'

I tried not to meet any of their eyes and followed Jack over to the sacks.

'Leave him be,' replied Jacob. 'He had to make his choice, just as we made ours.'

'I'm sorry,' I said, 'I had to make sure the children were all right.' I felt embarrassed about my deceit: the well-being of the children had not been my only reason for seeking to escape from the confines of the hold.

'You'll be one of them before you know it,' said Silas.

'No,' I replied, 'the captain told me that I'll be put ashore at Algiers, just the same as you.'

'Then I'll see you in hell,' replied Silas.

'Hold your tongue, man,' said Jacob, 'The lad must account for his actions to the Lord Almighty, not to you.'

'Come on,' I said to Jack, 'Let's get these sacks up the ladder.'

At that point, Will got to his feet. 'Here, let me help you,' he said. With Will's assistance, we formed a chain up the ladder and hauled the two heavy sacks up through the hatchway.

Before I followed Jack up, I turned to Will and whispered: 'Thanks. If I can bring any more food down for you all, I will.'

In the half-light from the retreating lantern I saw Will smile. 'I know you will,' he said.

After I had clambered back up through the hatchway, Jack closed and bolted the grille and I let out a heavy sigh. 'Miserable lot,' he said as he started to drag the first of the sacks along the deck.

I spent about an hour and a half with George and Catherine during that afternoon. Talking was all that we could do to pass the time. We talked about recent events back home, as if they still had some relevance. I thought this put them in better spirits. Then Jack called me down again and I helped him prepare the evening meal in much the same way as dinner had been prepared. The only difference was that we added diced fish into the pottage, to give it some kind of flavour.

After both sittings of the meal had been served, I took some bread down into the hold, clambering down the ladder into the hostile gloom. I handed the bread around, rather than tossing the pieces down from above. I did not linger for conversation.

With Jack's permission I again took my own portion and two additional ones up on to the main deck to eat with George and Catherine. By the end of our meal the light was fading and I managed to persuade the children to come and sleep beside me next to the galley, explaining that it was set a little apart from the rest of the crew and that it would at least offer protection from the elements. They reluctantly agreed.

As I led Catherine by her trembling hand down the ladder to the lower deck I realised that she was still terrified of the crew, a fear that – perhaps of necessity – I had already overcome. George was as feisty as ever, ready to square up and defend himself and his sister against any new danger, but of course none came. The crew had other things to occupy them, like playing at cards or engaging in raucous conversation, mostly in loud and doubtless foul-mouthed Dutch. Howls of laughter reverberated in the smoky lantern-light. Despite the noise, the children were soon sleeping, curled up in each other's arms.

I stayed up a little longer, talking with Jack. It was clear that he loved to recount stories about the ship and her crew. He told me about the *Sword's* recent voyage to Amsterdam, where the captain had met up with his real, Dutch wife and their children – he had since found himself a new Moorish wife. It had not been a fond reunion. Jack also delighted in telling me about the sea battles he had been in, though from his accounts it appeared that he had witnessed these battles from the relative safety of the crow's nest rather than from the midst of the action.

Six bells had rung, signifying eleven o'clock, before I put my head down upon some rolled up sackcloth that Jack had found for me. I lay beside George and Catherine and slept.

Chapter 3: The Prize

I have often had cause to wonder at mankind's ability to persevere through the worst ordeals and hardships inflicted by Fortune. Somehow people find the strength within them to endure; they find ways to cope. I too resolved to make the best of my wretched circumstances and, after that first day at sea, my life aboard the *Sword* settled into a tolerable routine.

I would help Jack to prepare and serve out three meals a day, each in two sittings. After each meal time, we would clean the galley, the pots and pans and cooking utensils. We never knew when the unforgiving eye of the bosun would inspect our work. Before long the skin on my fingers began to blister and break from all the scrubbing and scouring.

We obtained our own supplies: hauling up heavy sacks of foodstuff and wood for burning from the hold, straining the muscles in my limbs and back and driving splinters into my hands.

When the sea was too rough to light the stove and risk a fire, the meals consisted of weevil-infested biscuits instead. The crew would pull the weevils out and use them as bait on the end of their fishing lines that hung over the ship's side. These provided a welcome supply of fish that we diced and added to the communal pot.

On rare occasions the steward would instruct us to cook some meat for the evening meal. This involved steeping hunks of salted meat for hours in a tub of water, to extract the salt that had preserved it. I still recall the sting of the salt upon the broken skin of my hands. The end result was still far too salty for my palate.

Jack would polish the ship's bell once each day, a privilege that he never shared with me, though I often watched him do it.

I ate my meals with George and Catherine. After each mealtime, I would take food to the fishermen in the hold, often smuggling down some additional left-overs. This was a marked improvement for them: before my arrival they had only been given bread twice a day, thrown down through the hatch on to the damp floor. I reckon even Silas came to appreciate my efforts.

In between meals, particularly in the afternoons, I would while away the time with George and Catherine. As the days passed, little by little and in their own ways, the two children adapted to life on board. For a long time, they remained wary of everyone save me, even of Jack, who always treated them with kindness.

George, in particular, began to find his sea legs. So far as I knew, he had never set foot on a ship before this enforced voyage. At first he had been tormented by sea sickness, especially once we had departed the Channel and entered the untamed waters of the Atlantic, whose storms whipped up waves that pummelled the hold and exploded over the main deck in torrents of foam. One day, however, George ventured to climb the rigging. He clearly had it in mind that he would visit one of the crow's nests, and he was the type of person who, once he had fixed on an idea, would never let it rest. Inch by vertiginous inch he had scaled up to the dizzying height of the crow's nest on the main mast, where he stayed for a good hour. He later admitted that it took him most of that time to work up the courage to climb down but, after he had done it once, there was no stopping him.

Catherine, by contrast, would pass the hours beside the galley, chatting to me as I worked. We would talk about things she used to do with my sister, the games they used to play and the places she knew round about our village. Often this would bring a tear to my eye, though I never let her see it.

With both Catherine and her brother, I liked to talk about our home. In hindsight, this must have had a soothing effect on my mind, perhaps on theirs too. Reminding ourselves of home gave us something to cling on to. It was somewhere that, deep down, we knew that we would not see again for a long time, if ever. Talking helped to keep our spirits up, to retain hope.

We talked about the beach, about the shells and boulders strewn across its fine sand, about the shipwrecks that revealed themselves at low tide. We talked about the crumbling red-grey cliffs that turned to clay where the water oozed from within them, trickling down like blood to stain the sand below.

They spoke with tenderness about their farm, with its fields stretching down to the cliff tops. They knew all their animals by name. They told me that the earth in their fields was seasoned with the salt blown in on the westerly winds, that you could taste it in their crops. Every now and then a stretch of field would collapse in a landslide on to the beach and uncover stones with peculiar markings. They brought the best stones home to show their parents, who reckoned they had been buried beneath those fields since the creation of the world.

We spoke about Mottistone, our village: the green with its well, the old church with its rickety wooden steeple; the leafy lanes; the time-worn houses and the families that lived in them. I liked to talk about the ridge, known as the down, which wrapped itself like a great arm around the village and overlooked the sea. I had spent many adventurous days in my childhood rambling over the barrows on top of the down, where our ancient forebears lay entombed. The children loved it when I told them frightening stories about the Longstone – the ancient standing stone that kept watch like an eerie sentinel over our village.

We also talked about the manor, which had a special significance for me, as I had lived there until the age of twelve. The Leigh children had loved coming to visit us. We remembered how we used to play games together in the manor garden, playing hide and seek among the vegetable patches and the flower beds and the secret groves.

Their father and mine had been good friends and neighbouring landowners. The Leighs owned the land by the shore; we had owned the hinterland, including the village and a good stretch of the enfolding down. That was before my father died and we had sold the manor to Robert Dillington and moved into our little cottage. Since then, George told me that his family had not visited the manor, as their father and Mr Dillington did not see eye to eye. George thought it was because his father had refused to sell his land to Mr Dillington: 'I'll not sell an inch to such a man as he, whatever his price,' he had heard his father say. 'This is our land, and we're keeping it.' I could imagine Mr Leigh's immovable expression as he uttered those words.

George also told me that people in the village, including his father, blamed Mr Dillington for what had happened to my family. My cheeks reddened at some of the words George said he had heard villagers mutter about Mr Dillington. I had heard the rumours of course: my friends had not been shy about telling me. The villagers didn't take to newcomers like Robert Dillington; they liked things the way they had always been and could not accept the misfortune that had beset my family. 'Never trust outsiders,' they would whisper. 'That man's made his money through avarice, you mark my words.'

I did my best to explain to George that Robert Dillington was an honourable gentleman who had treated my family well. He had looked out for us after my father's death and was always kind to my sister, Elizabeth – often bringing her some toy or trinket or some fine material for a new dress when he visited our cottage. Her face used to light up in a beautiful smile when he arrived with his gifts. But I could see in George's unflinching eyes that he was having none of it. 'Don't trust him,' he would mutter.

It was too much for a young mind like his to grasp but I knew the truth of the matter. My mother had explained everything to me once I was old enough to understand. Heaven knows I had raked over my family's ruin often enough, searching for any justification for our fall from grace. During the boredom of my chores in the galley, my thoughts would sometimes stray to the sequence of events that had been our undoing, an undoing that had been made complete by my kidnapping but had begun some years before. While it was true that Dillington had been entwined in those events, his actions were for good, not ill.

Dillington, a man of significant wealth, had been a joint investor with my father in his ill-fated foreign venture, the failure of which had crippled my father with debt and broken him in mind and body. After his death, his debts needed to be honoured. Much to our regret, the manor had been pledged as security for the loans that Dillington had made to my father to fund his investment. As the manor had become forfeit, Dillington was entitled to take possession of it. His own wealth had doubtless been dented by the loss of the ship; he stood to lose not only his own stake but the money he had lent to my father too. However, the worthy gentleman paid us a price for the manor which covered the debts. He allowed us to rent one of the better cottages on the estate at a reasonable rate, so preserving a degree of status and standard of living which our incomings could never otherwise have afforded. In this way Mottistone Manor and all its estate had passed from my family, who had held it for generations, to Dillington.

When I reflected on these events, I confess that I found it hard to keep faith in divine judgement, to believe that everything that comes to pass has been pre-ordained by God's will. Whenever I caught myself slipping into such thoughts, I remembered my mother and her unshakeable faith. 'Mind Tom,' she used to say, 'what scripture tells us about the depth of the wisdom and knowledge of God: how unsearchable are His judgments, His ways past finding out.' I drew solace from her strength and forced myself to think of happier times.

I would spend the evenings in conversation with the English members of the crew, always accompanied by Jack. George and Catherine never joined us. We would gather around one of the tables, under a lantern. Most of the men would smoke their clay pipes; all would drink their grog. We often played at cards or dominos as the banter ebbed and flowed.

It was on those evenings that I learned much about the ship and how she was sailed, as there was always someone willing to show off his nautical knowledge by answering my questions. I learned of past skirmishes at sea and of raids on land, led by their cunning captain, Murat Reis, whom the crew held in the highest esteem. Many of them told me their own life stories and about how they had ended up aboard a corsair ship. Some, like Jack, had themselves been captured by corsairs and had turned Turk to join the crew. Others had volunteered, often in some faraway port and sometimes as fugitives from their homelands.

These conversations were too long and too many for me to describe in detail. However, there was one conversation that is worth recounting as, though I did not know it at the time, it would come to be of particular significance.

Half a dozen of us were seated around one of the tables. We had been playing cards as usual – I think the game had been All Fours. We were playing with Jack's deck of cards, his most prized possession – the finest quality, printed in Rouen, with the four suits depicted in vivid colours. Overhead the lantern was swinging and the air was thick with pipe-smoke. A couple of the men fingered their prayer beads as they waited to play their cards, a custom they had picked up since their conversion to Islam.

Jack had just won a round, as he often did, and there were many jovial accusations of cheating levelled in his direction. I had joined in the fun declaring: 'A monkey could have out-played us all, for all the skill we showed in that last round.' Everyone laughed.

In response, one of the older mariners named Jeffers, who had a pock-marked face and rotten stumps for teeth, piped up: 'I'd expect nothing less than cheek from you, young Tom.'

This prompted raucous laughter, as the other men recalled my surname and understood the play on words.

'Tom Cheke indeed,' continued Jeffers, with the wind in his sails, 'I fancy I might call you Tom Powder instead.'

There followed another eruption of laughter but I for one had not grasped the meaning of the joke.

'Why Powder?' I asked. A couple of the others chipped in, echoing my question. All eyes turned to Jeffers.

'Because that was your bounty, Tom, and a strange one at that. Most of us have a price on our head that's payable in coins. But as for you, young Tom, you and your friends, your price was powder!'

With that he reached across the table, gripped my shoulder and shook it good-naturedly, his ear-ring glinting in the lantern light.

'Tom Powder, Powder Tom' he said with a loud chuckle, perhaps expecting the nickname to catch on, but it didn't. Instead, I caught one of the other old tars in our group casting a stern look at Jeffers. The laughter dried up and Jeffers changed the conversation, pressing Jack to get on and deal the next hand, since he had been victorious in the last.

Nothing more was ever said on the subject of the powder. I knew that the powder Jeffers had been talking about was the gunpowder kegs taken from the manor barn. Though my curiosity needled me to ask him more about it, in the end the opportunity passed me by.

Over the next week we sailed through calm waters and rough seas, though fierce winds and the faintest of breezes, heading in a south-westerly direction. The officers of the crew used a variety of instruments – compass, backstaff and astrolabe – alongside the captain's charts and their knowledge of the movements of the sun and stars to navigate the ship by day and by night. They passed orders up to the men who trimmed the sails and down to the helmsman. It was his job to push the whipstaff to port or starboard, shifting the tiller below and at its end the rudder that angled the ship through the water.

I was up on deck, near the bow, with Jack early one afternoon cleaning out the cauldron and watching an officer on the quarterdeck as he calculated our position. He was facing the stern, attempting to hold his backstaff level and capturing the angle of the scorching sun. His efforts and ours were both interrupted by a shout from the crow's nest on the foremast: a ship had been sighted on the horizon.

At once, the crew surged into action. Sailors scaled the ratlines and either clambered into a crow's nest or else clung to the rigging to gain a good view. The captain himself appeared on the poop-deck, armed with a spy-glass. He was out of my earshot but I could see that he was in discussion with the quartermaster. An order was given and the French flag at the stern of the ship was gathered in; in its place a Spanish flag was hoisted up.

Jack glanced up, but continued to scrub at the cauldron. 'So we'll be chasing a Spanish ship,' he said. 'A galleon laden with gold bullion would give us a nice bit of booty.'

He said this in a matter-of-fact way, as if affecting a lack of interest, but I sensed his excitement. I admit that I too felt my pulse quicken, but my over-riding feeling was one of trepidation, rather than anticipation. I looked up to the crow's nest on the main mast and saw George peering out across the sea, shielding his eyes from the glare of the sun.

I squinted at the ship, still miniscule on the horizon. 'Looks to be heading towards land,' I said. I knew that we had been heading south-west through the Bay of Biscay, and the ship ahead of us seemed to be traversing the horizon on an easterly heading, perhaps destined for one of the Basque ports.

'So she must be on the return leg of her voyage then,' Jack thought aloud, 'heading back from the Spanish Main, her hold filled with gold and silver and all manner of precious stones, I'll warrant.'

The chase was on. The order was given for all hands on deck. I wondered how long it would be until the Spanish vessel became aware of our pursuit. I noticed that we had changed course at the same time as we had changed flags. We were now heading south east, so that if both ships remained on an unaltered course and we were able to sail at a sufficient rate of knots then our paths would intersect.

The rush of activity continued in the rigging above my head and on the deck around me. The crew were trimming the sails to make the most of our new windward direction. With a stiff westerly breeze behind us, the sails billowed and the *Sword's* timbers creaked and quivered with tension.

Within quarter of an hour it became clear that we were closing in on our quarry. With my naked eye I could now see that she was a three-masted ship, like our own, with a crimson and gold flag fluttering from her stern mast. She seemed to be a stouter vessel than the *Sword*, more rounded and less graceful. Jack said that was a good sign as she was more likely to be a merchant vessel, less well armed and laden with a valuable cargo.

I wondered what was going through the minds of those on board the Spanish ship. They must have spotted us by this time, and had presumably seen our Spanish colours. I wondered whether that would breed complacency in her crew, whether the thought of meeting a compatriot out on the high seas would be reassuring. The chase continued in this way for half an hour, during which time I scrubbed the kitchen utensils until they gleamed. With every passing minute, the gap narrowed between the two ships. I continued to watch with morbid fascination. I could now make out the individual sails on the other ship – she was slipping through the waves without exertion. The *Sword* was slicing through them.

Another quarter of an hour passed by. I helped Jack carry the pots and pans down to the galley but then slipped away to my previous position just behind the bow. George joined me, red-faced and breathless. He had been told by one of the crew in the crow's nest that he would be safer below deck, much to his annoyance. The Spanish ship was now less than a mile ahead of us. We could see members of her crew busy about their work. A couple of figures were watching us from their poop-deck, pointing back at us. Sometimes, we could even hear faint snatches of conversation, though for the most part the wind was carrying their voices away from us.

Then there was a sudden change, as if a wave of energy had broken over the Spanish ship. Men swarmed up into her rigging. Her sails were braced as her yard-arms turned to capture more of the wind. The whole ship began to swing round to a new course, heading south towards the unseen coast of Spain beyond the horizon. It was now a straight race between the two ships, with the Spaniard having a slender head start.

'Must have guessed who we really are,' said George.

'My money's on our crew,' I said.

George nodded in agreement

'We should go and make sure that Catherine is all right,' I added.

We retreated from the bow and waited beside the fore hatchway for a chance to descend: the crew were busy to-ing and fro-ing on the ladders between the decks, bringing up grappling hooks and gang planks in readiness for boarding the other ship. When the chance came we darted below and back to the galley. We found Catherine darning a hole in the breeches of one of the sailors – a pastime she had taken up of late, earning the appreciation of many of the crew, who looked upon her with fatherly affection.

I spotted Jack beside the grille above the aft section of the hold, in conversation with the steward. He beckoned me over to help him fetch some biscuits up from the hold while the steward took care of the grog. Next the steward sent us down into the fore hold with a couple of other men to bring up some barrels of water.

The fishermen down below were keen to find out what was happening. They knew something was afoot. They had felt the bracing of the timbers as the ship strained under full sail, had heard the rush of footsteps on the deck overhead.

'We're closing in on a Spanish ship,' I said as we heaved the first of the heavy barrels upwards. Even in the scant light I could see the anxiety in my friends' faces.

'Spare a thought for us, Tom, if the ship should founder,' Adam entreated, a pitiable look in his eyes. If the ship went down then this airless prison would become their sunken grave.

'I'll make sure the grille is open if it's the last thing I do,' I said.

From the top of the ladder Jack called back, 'There'll be no need for that. No Spanish ship will ever sink the *Sword*. Not while the captain's in command.'

When the water had been brought up, Jack gave me one pot of biscuits and kept the other. He told me to hand them around, one apiece, to each of the men on the lower deck. Then he darted up the ladder to begin distributing his weevil-infested treats to the men on the main deck and up in the rigging.

I started my round of the lower deck, handing the biscuits out. Along the starboard side, men were assembled in teams of six about each of the five guns. I knew that each of the men had an assigned role in the gun team as I had watched them conduct a well-drilled rehearsal only two days before, blasting imaginary foes out of the water.

The leader of the gun team nearest the galley was fidgeting with the powder horn that was slung around his neck. This powder was for priming the gun. Beside him stood a man with a bag of powder and a long ladle whose job it was to push the powder along to the inner end of the gun's barrel. The next man held a cannonball ready, which he had to put down to take his biscuit. His job was to load the ball into the barrel and, when the time came, to place a match into the touch-hole that would fire the gun. On the other side of the gun stood a man with his hands full of wadding – old rags mixed with hay – which was used to pack the powder and the ball inside the barrel. I placed his biscuit in his pocket for him and wondered if the weevils would wriggle out. Another man stood holding a rod, which was used to ram the ball and wadding down the barrel. The last member of the team held another rod, this time with wet rags attached to the end, a bucket of water was at his feet. His job was to dampen the barrel after firing to ensure that there were no smouldering embers. If he didn't do his job properly then the gun could discharge early, killing or maiming himself and his comrades. Jack said he had seen that happen once: 'not a handsome sight'.

I finished handing out the biscuits to the other gun teams, all formed in the same way as the first, all just as tense. I climbed the ladder to the main deck and spotted Jack clambering down from the crow's nest on the foremast. He told me he had already seen to the gun team manning the bow chaser, a smaller gun than the cannon below. He told me to carry on handing out biscuits to the men and officers on the deck. He would take care of those up in the main crow's nest. This was a relief to me as I had developed none of George's agility in scaling the rigging. I squinted upwards and saw that there were four men in each of the two crow's nests, each bearing a musket.

As I strode towards the quarterdeck, I saw that grappling hooks had been placed behind the bulwark on the starboard side. Men were grouped in fours around the three swivel guns mounted on the bulwark. These men carried scimitars and daggers; some also had wheel-lock pistols tucked into their belts. They wore leather over their tunics as a basic form of armour. Arranged below their swivel guns were what looked like tankards full of powder and grape shot, ready to reload.

Up on the quarterdeck I handed biscuits around to the captain and officers. Murat Reis was surveying his quarry; she was almost within his merciless grasp. He was wearing the magnificent outfit that I had last seen on the night of my capture. A scimitar now hung from the sash around his waist, sheathed in a jewelled scabbard with strange inscriptions.

I returned to meet Jack on the main deck, our job done. Behind us an order was given by the captain and was relayed forward by the men on the main deck, triggering a loud explosion from the bow that made my bones all but leap out of my body.

'That's the bow-chaser,' said Jack, 'just to let them know we're in earnest.'

A cloud of smoke swirled upwards from the bow, filling the air with a sulphurous odour while the team manning the bow-chaser raced to reload their weapon.

All eyes were now on the Spanish ship, to gauge her reaction. I saw men on board her running around as if in blind panic. She stayed on her course.

There was a further shout of orders from our quarterdeck, which was relayed down to the lower deck. I heard the gunports banging open and the heaving of the gun-teams on the tackles as the cannon were rolled forward into position. I imagined the terror that sight would implant in the hearts of the Spanish crew.

The *Sword* adjusted her course so that her starboard side faced on to the Spanish ship. Once in position, a further order was given. This unleashed a terrible series of explosions from below, each one reverberating through the ship's timbers and shaking her rigging. I watched the battery of cannonballs hurtle towards the Spanish ship. They all fell short, crashing into the water between the two ships. Smoke swept over the starboard rail and billowed up through the hatchways. It made me cough, made my eyes water.

'They missed,' I remarked over my shoulder.

'We always fire short on the first volley,' replied Jack, 'it helps us find our range, and it might just scare the life out of 'em and bring on their surrender. We don't want to damage our prize any more than we have to.'

For the time being, the Spanish ship seemed determined to evade us. This seemed a futile effort, given the distance we had already made up on her. There was frantic activity upon her rigging as the sails were trimmed to harness every last breath of the wind. I saw that the Spaniards had a couple of swivel guns of their own, which were now pointing in our direction. Below me, I could hear the various orders of the gun-team leaders, as they damped down the barrels and reloaded.

'Right said Jack, I'm off up there.' He looked up to the main crow's nest and then handed me his near empty pot of biscuits, weevils squirming among the crumbs at the bottom.

'Take those back down to the galley,' he said and with that he was off to scale the starboard shroud that connected the quarterdeck to the main mast. I noticed as he climbed that the butt of a pistol and the handle of a dagger were sticking out from the top of his breeches.

As I returned to the smoke-filled lower deck, I caught sight of George and Catherine huddled up beneath a porthole next to the galley. Catherine clasped trembling hands to her ears and pressed herself close to George. She was crying; the noise of the guns had clearly terrified her. George, besides doing his best to console her, was peeking out of the porthole watching the action unfold. I offered them both a biscuit and tried to say a few words to reassure Catherine, but they seemed to make little impression.

Along the deck the gun teams were completing their preparations for the next volley: balls, powder and wadding were being rammed home and the guns were being hauled back into position. I joined George at the porthole, through which I could see that the *Sword* was now back on a course to intercept the Spanish ship.

Suddenly there were flashes of light and puffs of smoke from the Spanish swivel guns. Instinct made us duck down. At once we heard the roar of the Spanish guns' discharge and the rattling of grapeshot spraying across the *Sword's* timbers, just feet away from where we were crouching.

George was the first to dare to peep out of the porthole again. I followed and saw that we had again shifted our course, ready for another broadside assault. The gun teams were adjusting the angles of their barrels to place the fleeing Spaniards in range. From above came another order that was relayed along the lower deck. Matches were lit from the port-fuses and placed in the touch-holes of the guns. Seconds later the whole deck erupted in an inferno of noise and smoke as one after another the guns discharged their shot and recoiled. The men with the wet wadding rushed to dampen down the barrels.

As I watched the gun teams, George kept looking out from the porthole. 'We hit them,' he said, coughing on the smoke. I looked out but struggled to see any damage to the Spanish ship.

'We hit their rigging,' said George pointing. As I peered I now saw that a section of the Spaniard's starboard shroud had been shredded and there was a gaping hole in her main sail. Another sail flapped like a flag. A jubilant roar went up from our gun teams, so loud that it must have been heard by the Spanish crew. The *Sword* once again adjusted her course to intercept.

There was another flash of light from one of the Spanish swivel guns and we ducked down again. This time the grape-shot didn't hit the side of our ship but sprayed across the main deck. After the pitter-patter of that lethal rain, a shrieking broke out from one of the *Sword's* crew. I pressed my body further down into the deck, as if trying to make myself as small a target as possible. Catherine's wailing grew louder. The thunderclap of a discharge from the other Spanish swivel gun followed, almost lost in the cacophony of yells from our gun teams as they reloaded. Again the Spanish grapeshot must have rained carnage upon the main deck as a further anguished cry went up but then fell silent.

George and I both inched our heads upwards to look out of the porthole. We were now only about thirty yards away from the Spanish vessel which was labouring under its damaged rigging. Above us, I heard a different order being shouted and then, for the first time, the discharge of our own swivel guns. I saw their grapeshot cut through the air and across the main deck and the lower rigging of the Spanish ship. One man fell from the rigging and at least two collapsed upon the deck, which was now a scene of utter confusion.

The *Sword* continued to close in. A further order was given above that was relayed along the lower deck. Excited shouts erupted around me as the men of the gun teams put down their tools, gathered up their small arms and rushed up through the hatchways on to the main deck.

'They must be going to board her,' I said to George. He nodded.

We were now almost within touching distance of the Spanish ship and it was becoming difficult to see what was happening from our present vantage point. I saw a succession of grappling hooks fly out overhead, ropes uncoiling behind. Most managed to catch hold of the rigging or the bulwark of the Spanish ship. As the crew of the *Sword* above us heaved on the ropes, the Spaniards hacked at them. Their efforts were in vain; the two ships were being pulled together in a mortal embrace.

I told George that we should take shelter in the galley, which felt more protected than the rest of the lower deck. So the three of us hid ourselves away in there. George and I kept listening, trying to make sense of the manic confusion of sounds overhead. Pistol and musket fire punctuated the howls of the *Sword's* crew as they rushed forth onto the Spanish ship and were met by the shouts and screams of the Spaniards.

After what must have been just a couple of minutes but seemed far longer, further orders were given and the sound of the fighting began to subside. We waited, huddled together, peering through the acrid gloom of the deserted lower deck, the ship bobbing in a strange way, being fixed to the Spanish vessel. Catherine had managed to regain some composure, though her body still shuddered and her tears still flowed. Above, we could still hear incessant shouting and movement upon the main deck.

Some minutes later, Jack appeared through the nearest hatchway; there was a swagger in his step and a broad smile on his lips.

'We got her,' he said. 'Shot one of 'em myself, right between the eyes.' He placed his right hand proudly upon the butt of his pistol.

'Is it over then?' I asked.

'Certainly is. Our lads boarded and the Spaniards put up a bit of a fight but they soon realised the game was up. We had 'em split up - some pushed back on to the quarterdeck, others towards the bow. Then the Spanish captain, up on their poop deck, ordered their surrender. Them that's left, which is most of 'em, are being rounded up and searched before we lock 'em up. Them that's dead or nearly dead, well, they go over the side. But we kept most of 'em alive, to increase our booty.'

As he said this, the first of the Spanish sailors was pushed down the hatchway from the main deck and along the lower deck towards the grille over the fore hold, a dagger held to his back to ensure compliance. His posture betrayed his bewilderment and despair. Others followed, each escorted by a triumphant member of the *Sword's* crew.

'We'll keep a few of 'em here,' said Jack, 'to give those whining English ones down below some company. Most of 'em will be locked in their own hold, once they've been searched and relieved of their valuables.'

'What will happen to their ship?' asked George.

'Some of our lot will form a prize crew, and we'll sail down together to Algiers. That'll mean longer watches, but it'll be worth it when we get our share of the booty. We'll flog the whole lot – ship, cargo and crew, when we get to Algiers. The captain will see to it that we get a good price and a fair share, you mark my words.'

At this point, Jack's high spirits were punctured as one of the injured members of the *Sword's* crew, a Dutchman, was carried down to the lower deck by two of his comrades. The man was unconscious; his right arm and leg were drenched with blood. He was carried away towards the stern.

'What will happen to him?' whispered George.

'We'll bandage him up, as best we can,' replied Jack, 'and give him plenty of grog. If he makes it to Algiers, there are surgeons there who may be able to save him – though it's not much of a life once they've taken your leg or arm off.'

'How many others were lost?' I asked.

'From what I could see from up in the crow's nest, we lost a couple of men stone dead. And then there's poor old Jaap back there, who probably won't make it. They lost about four times as many, including the one I got.'

That night there was a jubilant atmosphere aboard the *Sword*. The captives had been locked away. The Spanish ship – which was called the *Santillana del Mar* – had been searched and its contents recorded by the purser of the *Sword*, a no-nonsense Fleming with an eye for detail. As it happens, Jack's hunch had been more-or-less correct. The *Santillana* was laden with silver bullion from the Americas. Short of a shipful of gold or diamonds, it could not have been a better haul. The one regret was that the *Santillana*, nearing the end of her intended voyage, was not better provisioned with food and water, which would restrict the rations on our voyage south.

After a couple of hours, the two ships were separated and we returned to a south-westerly heading with the *Sword* in the lead and the *Santillana* in escort, manned by the prize crew.

Murat Reis had given the order for double the usual measure of grog to be issued from the stores to each member of the *Sword's* crew. The laughter and singing carried on well into the night and I must admit that, once I had left George and Catherine fast asleep in their usual spot next to the galley, I partook of that revelry. I sat beside Jack on the main deck as celebratory pistol shots fired and joyous cries rose up into the still night air.

Jack delighted in explaining to me about the complex rules by which the prize money would be divided up. The grog clearly went to his head though, and by the third time he explained it to me, he so confused himself that he had to give up. He told me instead about how he planned to invest his share to secure a decent living for himself once he had settled down to bring up a family. His elation infected my spirits, despite my sympathy for the Spanish crew.

That night we continued our voyage in a leisurely fashion, reflecting the drunkenness of the crew. The *Sword's* carpenter and his men had transferred over to the prize crew on the *Santillana*. He and his comrades were having their own celebration aboard the Spanish ship. They had been tasked with making repairs to the *Santillana's* damaged rigging and splicing the rents in her sails in the morning. Until then, we drifted together across the moonlit sea.

Chapter 4: Algiers

We crossed the open sea. I imagined the long Atlantic coast of Portugal rolling by beyond the horizon. I never laid eyes on it though, and I am sure the captain was keen to keep it that way, to proceed unseen. I sensed that the hunt for prizes was over and that his sole aim now was to deliver the spoils and reap the reward.

I continued in my role as cook's mate, helping Jack with his daily routine. Jack had thought that I would be transferred to the *Santillana* with the prize crew, to cook for those on board. Thankfully I was spared that task, which would not only have taken me away from my friends but would have involved trying to make sense of the *Santillana's* food stores and galley. Instead, the first lieutenant from the *Sword* – who was now in command of the *Santillana* – had co-opted the Spanish cook into his prize crew along with a few others from amongst the cook's less scrupulous compatriots.

As a result of the reduced crew on the *Sword,* our galley chores became slightly easier, though we had to cook a little more bread to feed the extra mouths in the hold. This was in marked contrast to everyone else aboard, who now had to continue to work the entire ship with fewer hands. This meant that the duration of each watch was increased, such that not one of the remaining crew, not even the captain, slept for more than four hours at a time. Not that this extra work dampened spirits: though the raw elation that followed the capture had dissipated into the cool night air, the crew remained buoyed by their prize, ever visible off our stern. The presence of the prize ship reminded the crew of their forthcoming share in the spoils; the effect fanned by the expectation that they would soon be on land to enjoy them. The sight of the *Santillana* also reminded them of their personal heroics in her capture – feats which seemed to escalate in bravery and prowess with every passing day.

Speculation on how much each man's share of the spoils would be was a constant topic of conversation amongst the crew. This provided scope for endless and often violent debate over the value both of the prize and of the various stakes different people, including the Pasha – the ruler of Algiers – would have in it. According to Jack, whose enthusiastic explanation seemed as reliable as any other, there was a prescribed method for dividing the spoils, once the captured ship and her cargo – both people and goods – had been sold off. On the basis of his own arithmetic, Jack was quite sure that he would be handsomely rewarded for his work. 'I'll get more than I'd have earned in a year back home,' he assured me.

I learned much from Jack during the voyage. Although he was similar to me in age and had received much less schooling, I was aware that he had seen much more of the world. I was envious of that. He could tell stories of adventures and sea battles as well as anyone else in the crew. In truth, I suspect I learned as much from Jack about the real ways and workings of the world during my short time aboard the *Sword* as I had from the best of my teachers or from our vicar in all his lengthy sermons.

There was one particularly interesting thing that I learned during the latter stages of the voyage that is worth recounting. I have already mentioned that Jack's most prized belonging was his deck of cards. After that, his next most treasured possession was his set of prayer beads – or *misbaha*, as he called them – which were looped around the belt at his waist. Often, when his hands were free from his chores, I would find him fingering through those beads. One time curiosity got the better of me and I asked him about them.

'Those beads of yours, what are you doing with them?'

'Oh,' said Jack, blushing at being caught unaware that he was fingering them. 'They're for counting the prayers of the *tasbih*.'

'What's that?'

'It's a set of prayers; I guess it's a bit like saying the rosary, like the old wives used to do back home.'

'Yes - the old women in our village often pray with rosary beads. My mother had a set, but our vicar doesn't approve.'

'One of the old tars gave these prayer beads to me, they used to be his. He was a good man, old Pete, died from an infected chest wound a couple of years back. Still, during the last few nights before he went, I used to sit with him and he said he wanted me to have his beads after he'd gone. He taught me what to do with them and made me promise to pray every day using them.'

'And did you?' I asked.

'Yes, I did. I guess I still do, but sometimes I do it as much out of habit as on purpose; I don't really think about it that much anymore.'

'Does it feel different, you know, not saying Christian prayers?'

Jack laughed. 'Well, you say them in Arabic for a start. I can teach you if you like.'

I pulled a face.

'You don't even need a set of these beads,' Jack continued. 'I actually learned how to pray the *tasbih* even before I got my own *misbaha*. There's a special way of counting on your fingers, right up to ninety-nine, the number of prayers in the *tasbih*.'

I must have looked incredulous so Jack demonstrated, using different parts of each finger, and duly counted to ninety-nine. For a flawed scholar such as I, with a preference for mathematics over anything written, this method of counting was a fascinating revelation. It involved combining his fingers and thumb, each of which could be in one of three positions – down, half up, or fully extended. I didn't quite follow his demonstration first time, but I made him repeat it several times and, after a fair bit of practice, I too had mastered it and could count to ninety-nine on the fingers of just one hand.

As the crew's spirits had warmed following the capture of the *Santillana*, so the temperature had risen as our voyage progressed ever southwards, heading towards the midday sun. Jack seemed to grow more excited with each passing day. As he laboured over his pots and pans, he told me about Algiers in tones of fond recollection. He had been there with the crew of the *Sword* a couple of times, as the captain maintained strong connections in Algiers, having lived there for some years previously. Murat Reis, and by consequence all of his crew, were now settled in a port further west along the North African coast, the notorious Sallee.

On several occasions during those last days of the voyage, Jack and others among the English-speaking crew would come and slap me on the back seemingly unable to contain their high spirits. I was regaled with tales of the sordid delights of Algiers. Often, however, I observed that these tales would be cut short, prompted by an elbow in the ribs or a glaring frown from another of the crew, never so subtle as to evade my notice. An awkward silence would ensue before the topic of conversation changed. I knew why of course. Some of the crew had forgotten the different fate that had been decreed for me when we disembarked. When they were reminded of it they stopped short because, I should add, most of them had taken a liking to me and took no pleasure in my prospects – whether the price on my head increased their personal spoils or not.

None of the crew ever spoke about what was in store for me in Algiers. No one had even mentioned the subject since my conversation with the fishermen down in the hold on my first night on board. As a result, I was left to develop my own thoughts, fuelled by recollections of the sermons I had heard on the desperate plight of Christian slaves in Barbary. For my part, I too avoided raising the topic with George and Catherine, not wishing to trouble their poor little minds further but wracking my conscience about whether it was right to leave them unprepared for what lay ahead. I presumed that they too would be sold into slavery. There was always the off chance that George might be invited to join the crew, but I knew he would never agree to that, both in a principled rejection of who they were and what they had done to his family, and also because he would never volunteer to leave his sister, for whom there was no place in the crew.

The first and only landmarks that I recognised during our whole voyage were the Pillars of Hercules, the great rocks standing guard over the narrow strait of water that marked the western limit of the Mediterranean Sea. I had read about them in an old book at home that had once belonged to one of my kin, who had taught Greek up at Cambridge to no less a person than the king. As we sailed towards the strait, it became impossible for the ships to remain out of sight of the coast. I watched from the bow with George at my side as the coastline on both sides drew itself in – Africa and Europe, both straining to touch each other, but never quite reaching.

Within these narrows we sighted a few ships, but whether because we steered clear of them or they of us, there were no close encounters. The captain took the threat of attack seriously. He stationed himself upon the poop deck with his spyglass, scanning the coastline on either side for hidden dangers and examining any passing vessel. No man slept for our whole passage through the narrows. Extra men were placed up in the crow's nests to watch for potential threats while the gun crews were in a state of constant readiness down below, which meant that Jack and I were once again tasked with distributing those weevil-infested biscuits.

Once through the straits, we struck an easterly course that for a while kept us within sight of the African shore. A long green pennant now streamed from the main mast of the *Sword*, declaring our affiliation with the various Barbary potentates who I imagined were surveying our progress from their coastal strongholds.

Our passage from the Atlantic Ocean to the Mediterranean Sea marked a change in the climate. While the swell in the Mediterranean remained heavy, it was tame in comparison with the unfettered rollers that had battered us in the Atlantic. Less encouraging was the heat, which began to impose serious discomfort. It was pleasant enough to be on deck at the times when a cooling breeze caressed the sails, but the winds blowing off the African shore were warm and dusty and not in the least refreshing.

At night I was often too hot to sleep. I had by this time been given and had mastered the use of a hammock, which I slung up each day beside the galley – a parting gift from one of the crew who had fallen in the capture of the *Santillana*. During these searing spells of wakefulness, my guilt would remind me that those held down in the hold must be enduring far worse torments. To salve my conscience I made a point of taking additional rations to the captives below, who now included a half dozen Spaniards. Now that we were on the last leg of our voyage, the steward was more liberal with the remaining rations. He seemed to want the captives to be fed, watered and in tolerable health.

I also set aside some minutes each day to talk with the English fishermen, mostly with Will – thereby leaving the hatch open longer in an attempt to let more clean air in and some of the increasingly foul air out. I would update them on our progress, which they were always keen to hear. For their part, they were often good enough to reassure me that I had no need to worry about their condition down in the hold. They claimed that being confined in the shade with access to water and not having to labour under the blazing sun for a rogue's crew was a merciful relief. I half believed them.

The rest of the crew now treated their prisoners with more sympathy, allowing them to stay up on deck for longer each day and sometimes to come up more than once. In hindsight, perhaps, their prime motivation was to keep their prizes alive, rather than see them suffocate in the hold.

It was on the third day following our passage through the straits that I first laid eyes on the city of Algiers. I recall the sudden excitement that swept through the crew as word was passed down from the crow's nest that our destination was in sight. I downed my utensils and followed the rest of the crew up on to the main deck, muscling my way to a vantage point along the starboard rail, next to Jack.

My memory of that first sight is vivid. Beyond a retreating headland, a white finger of civilisation reached upwards from the blue haze, clinging to a hillside. As we rounded the headland, the finger broadened until it formed a shimmering white triangle.

'Ain't she a picture?' Jack asked, letting out a soft whistle of admiration.

I nodded. Despite all my trepidation, a part of me longed to set foot on firm ground after so long at sea.

We stood there, the whole crew, assembled at the rails, on the ratlines and in the crow's nests, watching the city reveal its treasures. Jack, as ever, was my guide.

'That's the mole you can see, the breakwater sticking out into the sea, protecting the harbour. It was built by slaves. They built it right out to where the old Spanish fort used to stand – see there, at the end of the mole.'

'Why was it a Spanish fort?' I asked.

'They used to control the port, till the Barbarossa brothers turned up and gave 'em the boot nigh on a hundred years ago. Back then most of the guns in the fort pointed in towards the city. Now the fort's part of the city's defences and its guns point out to sea, just in case the Spanish ever come back.'

'They'd have to be bold to try,' I said.

'Yeah, and they'd have to take more than that fort to regain the city. See the walls there, running up the hill on each side. And that part up at the top is known as the Kasbah. It's like a whole fortress town in its own right. Anyone trying to take Algiers from the sea would have to deal with a hundred cannon and culverins raining fire down from all over the city. Not to mention the combined arms of the corsair fleet – see their mast-tops there, beyond the mole?'

Following the direction of his extended finger, I screwed up my eyes and could just make out perhaps a dozen ships, their masts bristling in the haze that lingered over the bay.

'And then there's the mountains protecting the city from attack by land. The people round here say that Algiers is protected by God,' Jack concluded.

As we continued our approach, I began to discern features in the city: towers, domes and row upon row of white-washed buildings – brilliant in the sunshine.

The captain gave orders for the final preparations to be made for our arrival. The crew at the rail dispersed in a wave of frantic activity. The decks had already received a vigorous scrub that morning; all the metalwork had been polished. Jack had discharged his responsibility for polishing the bell with extreme solemnity. We had given the galley such a thorough clean that even the bosun had grudgingly commended our efforts. Pennants were now flying from all three masts and from the flag-pole at the stern. Below deck, hammocks and possessions had been stowed into chests.

The final preparations involved one last trim of the sails before the orders would be given to furl them. From my station at the galley, I watched the gun crews preparing their cannon.

'It's for our salute,' Jack explained, noting my curiosity. 'We'll fire our guns, then the city will return the compliment.'

'Let's hope they miss then,' I replied.

Our work was all but complete in the galley. We made ourselves look busy to match the rest of the crew whilst keeping watch through the nearest port hole. When we were about a mile from the harbour, one of the officers and half a dozen of the crew descended from the upper deck carrying weapons and lanterns. They encircled the hatchway leading down to the hold. The grille was unlocked and raised and four men with lanterns were sent below to round up the prisoners from the hold.

I watched the prisoners' faces as they appeared, one after another, through the hatchway. Their expressions ranged from outright dread – on the part of most of the Spaniards – to apprehension or nervous anticipation – which best described Will and Adam – to a stoical look in the eyes of Silas and Jacob. They were all led up to the main deck escorted by their guards. I realised with a shudder that it could only be a few moments before they came back for me.

When they came, I was standing beside George and Catherine, who stood hand in hand.

'It's time,' was all that the officer said.

I looked across to Jack and he nodded.

'Good luck,' he said.

With the Leigh children at my heels, I followed the officer, climbing the ladder to the upper deck for the final time.

We were told to stand in a line with the other captives on the quarterdeck, facing the harbour on our starboard. Crowds had gathered along the mole that protected the harbour. They were watching our approach, pointing and waving.

Behind me I heard the captain give the order to fire the salute. From below us came the roar from each of the cannon in turn, each one shaking the timbers of the ship like an eruption. In reply, through the mist of acrid smoke, I saw the guns of the fort spit fire. A moment later I heard the thunder of the responding salute. This prompted a great cheer from the crew all around us, who punched the air with their fists or raised their muskets or sabres, polished steel glinting in the strong sunshine.

'They're parading their booty.' It was Silas at my side who spoke. 'Lining us up like prize cattle. We're the small fry, of course. All of their heathen eyes will be on that Spanish ship behind us – figuring out her worth – crew, cargo, ship and all.'

I held on tightly to Catherine's hand; she stood bravely on my other side, next to her brother.

The *Sword* and the *Santillana* paraded into the harbour and the captain gave the order to drop anchor. The harbour was crowded with ships of various types and scores of boats earning their living on the waters. There were ships that looked like the *Sword*, which I took to be other corsair vessels. There were ships that looked like the *Santillana*, suggesting they too were prizes or were honest merchantmen doing business in the port, if it were possible to conduct honest trade in such a place. Then there were strange vessels, the like of which I had never seen before. They seemed to have only one deck, open to the elements and lay low in the water. They had slanting lateen rigging on every mast, like the *Sword* had on its mizzen mast. And where they were unfurled, their triangular sails were brightly coloured in greens and reds, often in a striped design.

'Is that a slave galley?' I asked Silas.

'Aye. They call 'em *chebecs*. And if we're out of luck then we might be on one of 'em tomorrow. They're always on the lookout for a mariner who knows how to pull an oar.'

The crew of the *Sword* were now in the process of lowering her three boats, ready for disembarkation. Tackles consisting of ropes and pulleys were ready to winch the heavier loads down to the boats. Captain Murat boarded the first boat, climbing down the rope ladder. He was followed by a couple of his officers and then by a shore-party to row the boat. The quartermaster, who remained on board, directed the first three Spanish captives to climb down to the second boat, along with their armed escort and other members of the crew to work the oars.

First the captain's boat and then the boat with the Spaniards aboard were rowed the short distance across the harbour to the crowded quay. It was the first time any of the corsair crew had set foot on dry land since their night-time foray on my island. I watched Captain Murat go first. As he stepped up on to the quayside he was embraced by several of the waiting men. The animated discussion that followed was well out of my earshot. I saw the captain pointing down to the second boat, which triggered a flurry of activity; various men were summoned and then dispatched in various directions. He also pointed towards the *Santillana* before departing with a man dressed in a purple robe and bulging turban. I saw them enter one of the buildings that lined the quay.

A few minutes later I watched the Spanish captives and their escort climb up on to the quay, not far from the point where the captain had alighted. A very different welcome awaited them. They were lined up in front of a table set up on the quayside. A man sat behind it. One by one the Spaniards came forward, each tailed by a guard. There followed a brief conversation, after which the man at the table wrote something down. Then the captive was led away by his guard.

I turned to Silas, making no attempt to conceal my apprehension. He, like every man in our wretched line, was watching proceedings on the quayside. He was frowning in the fierce sunlight, so that his eyes were invisible, concealing any emotion. He noticed my look when I turned to him but said nothing. I glanced down at George, who was also surveying the developments on the quayside, and I too said nothing. In a small mercy, Catherine's attention appeared to be captured by the colourful pageant of boats in the harbour.

After quarter of an hour, the two boats of the *Sword* returned to the ship and the quartermaster signalled that it was our turn to disembark. I and the two Leigh children were assigned with Will and Silas to one boat; the remaining Spaniards, Jacob and Adam were directed to the other.

I followed Will and Silas down. As I clambered over the rail to begin my descent, a couple of the crew of the *Sword* bade me farewell, others nodded in a friendly way. And Jack, who had come up unseen on to the deck behind us as we waited in the line, ran forward and gave me another hearty handshake. As he did so he pressed something into my hand. I looked into his face. His eyes were moist but sparkling. I looked down and saw his pack of cards in my right hand. I whisked them away into a pocket in my breeches. Then I looked back up; Jack was already pacing back across the deck, in that light-footed way of his, over towards the hatchway leading down to his galley. That was the last I ever saw of him.

First Catherine then George followed me down the rope ladder to the waiting boat. We sat together, flanked by oarsmen and with the escort keeping watch over us from the bow and stern. With measured sweeps of the oars, the boat glided across the harbour. I longed to dip my hand into the glistening water. Despite having been at sea for what seemed like an age, it had never been within touching distance; for now it remained tantalisingly out of reach. As the sun beat down I dreamed of diving in, not so much to escape as to cool down in the clear water. We moored and followed a couple of guards up on to the quayside; the remaining guards brought up the rear.

We lined up on the quay. A small crowd of locals gathered round us, inspecting us, sometimes pointing right into our faces. I remembered Silas's words: 'lining us up like prize cattle'. There were men and boys in the crowd, all dressed in exotic clothes. The men wore turbans and beards, long robes of red and brown or beige and pointed slippers. I saw George on my left put a protective arm around his sister, defiance in his eyes.

As we waited there, my gaze was drawn towards the table I had seen from the ship, at which the man sat with a ledger and quill. He had no shade and had to wipe the sweat from his brow to avoid it dripping upon his paper. My eyes were drawn to a couple of other men, who loitered around the table, their appearance distinguishing them from the crowd. They were dressed in a style not dissimilar to that of the more fashionable gentlemen I had seen back home. I wondered at their presence in this godforsaken place.

The man at the desk seemed to be some kind of registrar. He called out to our guards and we were brought forward one by one. Will was ahead of me in the line and I heard most of his exchanges with the man at the desk. He was asked – in a variety of languages – for his name – to which he eventually replied 'William Dart'. Once the man had ascertained that Will spoke English he asked him a few further questions in English including his age and his home town. These details were written down in a most curious way. At first I thought the man was left handed. Then I realised that he was writing from right to left in his ledger book. As he made his entries, one of the gentlemen behind the registrar called out to Will in perfect English, 'Young master, a word.' The registrar waved Will onwards and beckoned me forward, looked me up and down, and asked my details directly in English. I told him that I was Thomas Cheke of Mottistone, and that I was fourteen years of age. As the registrar wrote these details down in his ledger the English gentleman who had finished talking to Will called for my attention in just the same way: 'Young master, a word.'

The registrar waved me away and I stepped towards the gentleman, shadowed by my guard. The gentleman looked a pleasant and decent fellow, in his doublet, breeches and knee-length boots. He was red-faced and sweltering in the midday sun, beads of sweat trickling down into the large ruff around his neck.

'Did I hear you say it's Master Cheke?'

I nodded.

'My name is James Frizell. For my sins, I'm His Majesty's Consul in this city. And if you are a young man of means, I might be able to provide a useful service to you.'

'Sir,' I replied, 'I am a gentleman's son but I am of little more worth than what you see before you.'

'That is a veritable shame, young sir,' Frizell replied, 'for I can discern that you are indeed a gentleman. But unless you may call upon the means to aid your departure, by which I mean to pay a ransom for your deliverance, there is little I can do to assist.'

I thought about this for a few seconds and then answered. 'Mr Frizell, though my family is no longer blessed with fortune, since the death of my father, yet the gentleman who has taken on our former estate is of a good income and has looked kindly on my family in the past.'

'I pray you sir, tell me his name, so that I might convey a message to him and petition him for your freedom.'

'His name is Robert Dillington. He holds the manor of Mottistone on the Isle of Wight.'

Frizell produced a small piece of parchment from his breast pocket and a graphite pencil and proceeded to note the details I had given.

'Master Cheke, I shall petition Mr Dillington on your behalf by the first ship back to England. I shall come and find you when I receive correspondence from him.'

'Thank you, sir, for your kindness,' I said with a quavering voice, tears welling in my eyes.

'Not at all, not at all,' he replied, putting his pencil and parchment away in his breast pocket. 'And I trust you too were taken at sea?' he said, his gaze shifting away from me and on to the two Leigh children, whom he eyed with a look of concern. They were being dealt with together by the registrar. I presumed that George had not relinquished his hold on his sister.

'Not at all, sir,' I replied. 'I and those two children were taken from our beds at home.'

Frizell's attention snapped back on to me. 'From on land, in England?' he exclaimed.

'Yes, in a night time raid.'

'Preposterous,' he said, shaking his head and withdrawing his parchment once more, ready to note down the details. 'And can you tell me the date and whereabouts of your taking?'

'Yes, it was on the night of the third day of September, from our village of Mottistone.'

'Outrageous,' he added still jotting down his note. 'I shall refer to this assault on His Majesty's sovereign territory in my next dispatch to London.'

'One more thing,' I said.

'Yes, what's that?'

'That same Mr Dillington may also come to the assistance of these two children. Their father is a free-holder and a neighbour of Mr Dillington's in Mottistone. Their names are George and Catherine Leigh. L – e – i – g – h.'

'Thank you, Master Cheke, I shall make a careful note of that. And I hope to speak with you again soon when I have received some good news.'

Once the consul had finished writing he turned away from me and returned to hover behind the registrar, waiting to see who else had been washed up, starting with George and Catherine.

One of the guards behind me gave me a prod in the back and I trudged over towards a squat, grimy building, one of several that crouched on the quayside in the shadow of the city wall that lined the harbour. The building had a wide entrance with two doors wedged open. As we approached I could see that the interior resembled a smithy, with a furnace and various metal-working instruments both hung upon the walls and propped up on the floor. My guard, who did not speak English, signalled to me to wait outside.

Inside, I could see Will, with a guard at his shoulder. Will had his bare right foot up upon a low stool. The blacksmith, his familiar apron at odds with his exotic turban, was clamping an iron fetter around Will's ankle. Attached to the fetter was a chain, about three feet long, at the end of which was a heavy looking iron ring. With a deft stroke, the blacksmith hammered home a rivet to seal the leg iron. I watched Will flinch as the hammer fell, but he appeared uninjured. The blacksmith nodded and the guard led Will out of the smithy by the arm. Will's steps were awkward as he dragged the chain behind him. It was a sharp contrast to the ease with which he had traversed the rolling deck in the hold of the *Sword*. As he passed me he looked up and winked. 'Think it suits me?' he asked as he was led away.

I felt the prod in my back again and was motioned towards the stool beside the blacksmith. Inside the smithy was dark and hot and hazy with the smoke of charcoal. Sweat poured down my brow and stung my eyes. As I raised my right foot upon the stool, I looked down on my ankle, pale and fragile in the flickering fire-light from the furnace. The blacksmith came forward, never making eye contact, and clasped an iron fetter around my leg, a little above the ankle. Attached to the fetter was the iron chain, snaking across the dusty floor. I remember the feel of the metal on my skin: a cool sensation amidst the perishing heat. The smith picked up a long rivet from the many lying beside the stool and raised his hammer. I closed my eyes as the rivet was rammed home. The smith tested that the fetter was secure and then gave a nod and a grunt to my guard. This time I was tugged by the arm rather than prodded and I took my right foot down from the stool. As I dragged the chain forward the ring at its end caught the leg of the blacksmith's stool and up-ended it. I heard him curse behind me and I received a hard cuff on the right ear from my guard.

I walked out into the sunshine, my right leg labouring so that I hobbled along. My guard gestured to me to pick up the chain. I did so and found my movement eased somewhat, though I still needed to come to terms with the fact that my right leg was now attached to the iron ring in my right hand.

I was pushed to the back of the line that was reforming along the quayside. On the landward side, a crowd of onlookers, men and boys, had again come to gawp at us. They were pointing and laughing and seemed to be taunting us, but the language was wholly foreign to my ear. Our guards now seemed more relaxed and joined in the general merriment. On our seaward side, I caught my first view of the *Sword* in the daylight. She was resplendent. Her sails were tightly furled but her pennants fluttered in the warm breeze. I watched one of her boats being loaded at her side. It looked like the crew were bringing ashore those same kegs that had been taken from the barn in Mottistone. One by one I saw them being carried down the ladder and placed into the boat. They were transported to the quay and taken into the building that I had seen the captain enter earlier.

We waited for an hour or so on that sweltering, shadeless quayside as one by one the captives from the two ships were assembled in their leg irons. I was relieved to see that George and Catherine were treated with leniency. George had been fitted with an iron ankle fetter but no chain. True to form, he seemed indignant at being treated differently from the older captives, as if he would rather have suffered the inconvenience of the chain than the ignominy of having just the leg iron. Catherine meanwhile had not been constrained in any way, save that her hand was implanted in her brother's.

Once the last of our sorry company had been placed in irons, the registrar left his table and joined us, carrying his ledger book. Captain Murat reappeared soon afterwards. Accompanied by his officers from the *Sword*, he led our procession into the city.

Chapter 5: The Auction

A fortified gate led from the bright, open harbour into the cramped, shaded interior of the city. We snaked in a miserable file up a narrow street. Ramshackle buildings loomed on either side, their upper floors jutting out in tiers and almost meeting above the street to block out the sun.

Gated doorways and grated windows, high in the walls, concealed the inside of the houses. As we passed I could feel eyes watching me from within. The doorways were arched and decorated. Their doors had curious, fist-shaped knockers resting on the studded wood.

In between the houses were shops and workshops. We passed an array of butcher's shops. Raw meat dangled from hooks in unglazed windows, trickling blood into the centre of the street and feeding a gory stream running downhill as if through a ravine. I did my best to avoid it, but soon felt the gore coating the soles of my feet.

The going became increasingly tiring, even as the shade protected us from the full heat of the sun. On several occasions I saw men ahead of me stagger, perhaps wilting from the heat under the weight of their chains or stumbling on some uneven cobble stone. The gradient of the hill increased so that the street broke into flights of steps. Narrow alleys darted off on either side and small, shaded squares revealed themselves in ivy-clad recesses. In those squares, I saw men idling around water fountains, which bubbled and splashed, exacerbating my thirst. The men were inhaling or imbibing from curious instruments; their heavy eyes watched us pass.

At the end of the street we turned right into a long, wide concourse, running parallel to the harbour below. This broad street was awash with sunshine. It bustled with shops and market stalls. At one end I could see a great gate in the city wall. As we filed into the street, crowds of people thronged towards us, pointing, laughing, shouting. Some even reached out and grabbed at me; I saw Will fend off some unwanted attention with his unencumbered left arm.

The captain paused to receive the acclaim of the gathering crowd, shaking hands all around and being clapped on the back. I felt myself begin to swoon, either from the heat or from the overpowering of my senses. Almost before I knew what was happening, Will was at my side, propping me up.

'Can't be far now,' he said.

Perhaps it was the aroma wafting out from a nearby coffee house that revived me. In any event, I was steady on my feet as we set off again. In a small mercy, we were led along the broad, level street rather than up one of the streets that branched from it to continue the climb up the hill.

We passed beside a great Moorish church, which the Muslims call a mosque. As we passed beneath its lofty tower I heard a man up in the rafters begin to chant a strange, repetitive song. His song was echoed by voices elsewhere in the city. As his song continued I saw shops and stalls begin to close. The people milling in the street began to stream away, disappearing into the labyrinth of side streets and alleys. Captain Murat and a couple of his officers left us to join the crowd entering the mosque.

We pressed on and soon reached a large square around which the dust swirled in low clouds. Facing on to the square was an imposing building, its entrance flanked by arcaded galleries lined with columns of shining marble. I guessed that this was the Pasha's palace. One of the officers from the *Sword* instructed our guards to escort us to a fountain at one side of the square. We were encouraged to drink and wash ourselves. We needed no encouragement. The water that I splashed over my skin and hair felt like a divine blessing. We waited for around an hour until the captain rejoined us. He paused only for a moment to exchange a word with one of the officers before crossing the square. The great doors of the palace were opened for him and he disappeared inside, the registrar hot on his heels.

A few minutes later, the palace doors opened once more. A lone figure emerged and strode towards us, dust billowing around his slippers. He beckoned to our guards to follow him inside. They duly herded us across the square and into the palace. The heavy doors clanged shut behind us.

We congregated in a shaded courtyard paved with marble. I looked around. Sculptured arcades lined each side of the courtyard, their arches supported by graceful, spiralling pillars. The walls above and between the arches were decorated with blue and white tiles in floral designs.

George came up to me, still clutching Catherine's hand. 'Where are we?' he asked.

I shrugged my shoulders. 'Inside a palace by the look of things,' I ventured, not wishing to elaborate.

Jacob overheard and came to join us. He knelt down on one knee, to put himself more on a level with Catherine.

'We're in the Pasha's palace,' he said gently. 'He's the ruler of this place, rather like a king.'

'What does he want with us?' asked George.

'Well,' Jacob inhaled as he formed his reply, 'my friend Silas there reckons that he'll be choosing a few of us to work for him.'

'Will he choose us?' asked Catherine.

'That, I can't say little lady,' Jacob replied. 'Though whatever happens, I'm sure that someone will find a home for every one of us before this day is out.'

I tried to reassure Catherine with a smile but it was a weak effort. I knew I had no reassurance to offer.

'What if we don't like the person who chooses us?' asked George.

'Well in that case we must bear our lot with dignity and remember that we are all in God's hands,' replied Jacob.

Behind me, I turned to see the English consul, Frizell, slipping into the courtyard after a brief exchange with one of the guards at the door. He skulked over to one of the arcades. I watched him pace up and down in its shadows.

After a while a door opened from the interior of the palace. A company of guards issued forth and took up positions around the courtyard. The guards wore scarlet jackets and baggy pantaloons. They all had thick moustaches and dark eyes that flashed beneath large turbans. They carried curved swords, their cruel blades exposed.

The guards were followed some moments later by a man whom I took to be the Pasha. He was dressed in a very fine outfit consisting of a collar-less shirt of blue, embroidered silk, calf-length pantaloons and a long cloak of brown velvet. On his head was a bulging white turban with what seemed to be a small hat protruding upwards from its centre. His jewel-encrusted slippers advanced at a slug's pace, as if every step was a matter of the utmost gravity. After the Pasha, maintaining a respectful distance, came Captain Murat on one side and the registrar on the other. One of the Pasha's escort barked an order and the guards from the *Sword* began to push us and pull us so that we formed two rows, shoulder to shoulder. I was in the second row, a couple of yards behind the first. Silence descended upon the courtyard.

Of a sudden, from behind a column in the arcade, the English consul emerged and edged towards the Pasha and his small entourage. Frizell straightened up before bowing low to the Pasha with a flourish of his arm. 'Your Excellency,' he said, 'may I be so bold as to suggest that, amongst these captives here assembled, you have some English subjects taken in error.'

The Pasha's face was expressionless as the registrar translated for him. Captain Murat fixed a steely, unerring stare upon the consul. I glanced to Will on my left; his eyes were open wide, as if in newfound hope.

'I might add,' Frizell began to falter, 'that some of them, at least, were not captured legitimately: they were taken from the peace of their own homes.'

The registrar again translated. The Pasha's eyes betrayed a flash of anger. The Captain leaned towards him and offered some quiet words of advice.

The Pasha looked up to the sky above, a faultless blue, as he offered his opinion on the matter. The registrar interpreted his words in patchy English.

'His Excellency has listened to the advice of Captain Murat. He is assured that these are all legitimate *tutsaklar*. He would like to know whether you also now agree, consul?'

All English eyes now turned to the consul. It was only later that I learned the meaning of that harsh word, *tutsaklar*. It meant 'prisoner of war', and such prisoners were generally used as slaves. Frizell clearly understood the word. He bowed low, said 'Of course, Your Excellency,' and retreated back into the shadows, our hopes disappearing with him.

The Pasha then proceeded, at his very slow pace, to inspect the captives, followed by the registrar and the captain. He carried an ornate stick, rather like a sceptre, in his right hand and used it to prod at some of the men he passed – their arms, their legs, their bellies. At intervals the Pasha, without turning his head, passed an instruction back to the registrar and pointed with his stick to a man. The registrar would in turn pass the message back to the captain, who made a slight bow each time.

The Pasha drew level with me and looked me up and down. My heart was beating fast. I was terrified of making some false move that would be my undoing. For a second, I dared to meet the Pasha's eyes. I saw disdain in them. He did not think me even worth the effort of a prod and moved on, leaving an exotic scent trailing in the air behind him. He passed George to my right as if he did not notice him at all and spared only a fleeting look of surprise at Catherine before continuing.

Our inspection lasted for about a quarter of an hour, after which the Pasha retreated with ponderous steps into the interior of his palace, taking around four of his guards with him. The heavy doors closed after him and the calm in the courtyard ended.

The registrar now burst into action, signalling to the guards to pull to one side all the men that the Pasha had chosen and herding the remainder of us over towards the exit. I saw that Will's friend Adam was among those selected. I glanced at his face and saw a look of bewilderment before I averted my eyes. All the other men chosen, four in total, were Spaniards.

Our guards from the *Sword*, led by the captain, now herded us out of the palace and into the adjoining square. Our re-emergence dislodged a flock of starlings that had alighted upon one of the arcaded galleries that flanked the square. We were lined up once more in the blistering heat amid the pestering flies. Then we filed back along the same broad thoroughfare, to which the crowds had returned after their prayers.

After a couple of hundred yards we branched off and proceeded a short distance along a narrow street. Thereafter we passed through a gated archway into a much broader street, or elongated square, which was wholly enclosed by buildings and populated with men, standing in pairs and small clusters. As we entered, all eyes were drawn towards us. I heard the gates close behind.

We were made to line up along one side of the square, all except George and Catherine who were ushered to one side. The registrar walked up and down our line, consulting his ledger book, confirming our names, and instructing our guards to rearrange us into a particular order. Meanwhile, the groups of men loitering around the square advanced from their various corners and coalesced in front of us. I watched the captain stroll towards an arcade on one of the long sides of the square. On his way he stopped to converse with one of the men, who was dressed in a purple cloak and wore a large turban, quite possibly the same man whom he had met on the quayside earlier. Then the pair of them disappeared inside one of the rooms leading off from the arcade.

The registrar, having contented himself with our ordering, removed himself to a shaded table where a couple of other men were already waiting. From out of the same door that the captain had just entered an old man appeared. His white robe gleamed in the afternoon sunlight as he approached. He twirled a long cane in his right hand and beckoned to our guards with his left as he started talking in a voice that was loud enough for all the assembled onlookers to hear.

The guards brought forward the first man, one of the Spanish mariners, from the end of our line. They placed him in the centre of the square, in the gap between our row and the assembled onlookers. The guards retreated, leaving the Spaniard a solitary, dejected figure with nothing but the stub of a shadow for company. His head was bent down, his chain wrapped over his right forearm.

The registrar called out something, reading from his ledger. Then the man with the cane strutted up to the Spaniard, talking all the while as he approached. Without hesitation he grabbed the Spaniard's shirt at the neck and ripped it open down the middle, before pulling it off to reveal his torso. This act elicited a cheer of approval from the onlookers. Quick as a flash, the old man slashed with his cane at the left ankle of the Spaniard, who let out a cry of surprise and pain and jumped backwards, clanking his chain. This gave rise to a further cheer from the crowd. The Spaniard gave a quick glance behind him to his compatriots, perhaps looking for reassurance that could not be given.

Now that the Spaniard's head was raised, the man with the cane – speaking all the time in his rapid, ringing, foreign tongue – lifted up the mariner's left arm and showed it to the onlookers. Beads of sweat glinted on the Spaniard's bare back. Some of the onlookers looked serious, fingering their beards and moustaches; others were laughing and aping the Spaniard's pose. I now understood the old man's constant talk to be his sales patter, such as I had heard from auctioneers at livestock markets back home. Some of the onlookers approached right up to the Spaniard; a couple grabbed his biceps. One had a word with the auctioneer who first threatened the Spaniard with his cane then pulled down his jaw so that the enquirer could look inside his mouth.

Once the more inquisitive onlookers had withdrawn into the shade, the bidding began. Though I could not understand what was said, I understood that the auctioneer had now begun the familiar process of proposing a starting price and taking bids from the onlookers, who raised their hands or nodded when they caught the auctioneer's eye to signal their bid. The bidding concluded and the victorious bidder sidled over to the registrar's table while the bewildered Spaniard was led away. He was taken first to the registrar's table. One of the men who had been sitting alongside the registrar came forward with what seemed to be a pot of paint and a brush. He painted what appeared to be a number on the mariner's bare chest. Then the poor man was taken away to the opposite side of the square and made to sit down alone in the dirt.

The auctioneer beckoned the guards to bring forward the next in line, another Spaniard. The registrar called out what I guessed were the scant personal details he had collected from this man at the quayside. This provided the cue for the auctioneer to restart his sales pitch.

This process continued, with man after man being brought forward to be auctioned, until it felt like a ritual. I noticed that the bidding was more intense for some men – the younger, stronger looking ones – than for others. For a few of the men, the auctioneer worked hard to muster any interest at all. Those few who were not sold were at least spared the ignominy of having a number painted on their chests; they were sent to sit in a separate patch of dirt. Silas and Jacob were both among their number.

I was situated near the end of the line that the registrar had arranged. More than an hour had passed before my turn arrived.

That time had elapsed with painful slowness, particularly it seemed during the bidding for the man who preceded me. As my turn approached my pulse began to race; I was fearful both of my impending humiliation and of my fate at the hand of an unknown master. I surveyed the faces of the onlookers, trying to ascertain which were most likely to be in the bidding for me, which looked kindly and which looked like those to be avoided.

When my turn came round at last, I felt the prod in my back from the guard behind me. I knew where I had to go. Like others before me, I removed my shirt as I walked forward, to avoid having it ripped from me, and dropped it at my feet.

I was able to make some sense of the registrar's opening remarks, making out my name and nationality. The auctioneer's patter was already in full flow when I heard the hiss of his cane before it bit at my left ankle. As with the other captives, he raised my left arm. I cannot imagine that potential bidders were much impressed with what they saw, though I was fit and lean and above the average height for boys of my age. The auctioneer led me around for a few steps, my left arm still raised. He pulled open my jaw and seemed to draw particular attention to my teeth, which were in good condition compared to others I had seen on my voyage. He also took my wrists and held up my hands – first one then the other – revealing the blisters on my palms and fingers before continuing his patter. Then the bidding commenced.

I watched as various men in the crowd signalled their bids. I counted as many as eight in the bidding at the offset, but this soon whittled down to two bidders as my price increased.

One of the bidders was a stout, barrel-chested man with a thick moustache. He wore a long cloak which descended almost to his slippers. A broad, crimson sash served as a belt for his baggy trousers. A large feather protruded from his heavy turban. With his hands wedged against his hips and his stomach pushed forwards he looked like a jovial fellow. He signalled his bids by nodding his head under his turban, ruffling his feather.

The other bidder was tall and lean and considerably older. Beneath his cloak he wore an embroidered vest with jewelled buttons up the front. His sash and turban were more subtle than those of his rival bidder. His moustache was slender and grey, and he held his right hand to his chin, stroking his beard and signalling his bids with the merest tilt of his head and lowering of his dark eyes. He had a more serious demeanour than his rival, which made me fear him the more.

As the bidding continued, I heard snatches of numbers. I reasoned that the auctioneer was announcing my asking price in both the local language and in *sabir*, the curious language that had been spoken at times on the *Sword*. I stood without moving, entranced by the bidding contest. After several rounds it seemed that the jovial bidder had secured me. There followed a long pause suggesting that my auction had concluded. I stooped down to pick up my shirt. As I did so there was a shout and I caught the flash of the lean man's eyes signalling his new bid. My heart sank. I looked across to the other bidder, but his face had turned sour. He shook his head from side to side, hands still clamped to his hips, to indicate that he was out of the running. This time, the bidding really was over. I was sold.

I picked up my shirt and my chain and walked over to the registrar's table. A number was daubed on my chest in some kind of brown paint. Then I walked over to join the others who had been sold. I sat down next to Will, who was picking up handfuls of fine dust and allowing the grains to slip through his fingers. We sat together in silence for a while as the next auction got underway.

'What do you think will happen to Silas and Jacob?' I asked.

'They told me that unsold slaves become the property of the city,' Will replied, 'which means they'll be put to work mending the roads or the city walls or digging in the quarries.'

'Will they be ransomed?' I asked.

'Depends on the price. They ain't got much money. And much of what Jacob did have was invested in his boat, which the corsairs sank to the bottom of the sea once they'd plundered it.'

'How about you?' I asked.

'No. There's no one who'll pay a ransom for me.'

'There's the missionary orders,' I ventured, trying to sound upbeat. 'We used to give money to them at church to free the Christian slaves.'

Will tutted. 'How much of that do you think actually makes it over here?'

We watched the next auction conclude without a sale. The man, an ageing Spanish mariner, slouched over to join the rejected men beside Jacob and Silas.

'Another one for the *bagnio*,' Will muttered.

I had heard of the notorious *bagnios* in which most of the slaves lived: the lice, the beatings, the over-crowding, the plague – our vicar had relished describing their awful details.

We watched as the last of our sorry company was auctioned off. The jovial bidder got his purchase at last. As the man was duly painted and came over to sit alongside his compatriots I gathered in my chain ready for the order to move. The day's auction was not, however, complete.

A shout went up from behind me, then a child's cry. I turned my head and watched as one of the guards dragged George by the hair from the arcaded gallery. George was thrashing at his captor with his fists and feet, kicking up quite a cloud of dust. This caused much amusement among the onlookers. Meanwhile, another guard restrained Catherine, who cried out in desperation from the arcade as her brother was dragged from her. When they reached the centre of the square, the guard held George fast, his arms pinioned behind his back.

The auctioneer appeared revived by this turn of events and restarted the bidding process with gusto. As was his custom he whacked George on his calf with his cane. George spat in his face and received a cuff round the ear from the guard for his pains. I feared that he would receive worse but a sale was still to be made and the potential bidders seemed to be enjoying the spectacle. The auctioneer retained his professionalism, wiped the spit from his face and began his patter.

Though there were many in the initial round of bidding, most did not seem keen to invest significant money in such a troublesome youth. As the auction concluded, I noticed that my new master was standing next to the man who had just won the auction for George. I now recognised the latter, with his hooked nose and protruding eyes, as the same, purple-cloaked man who had left the square earlier in conversation with the captain. I had not noticed his return. He and my new master stood aloof from the other bidders and exchanged occasional words. George was led away still kicking and shouting to the registrar's table. The assistant cast a nervous glance at the boy as he painted the price on George's small chest. George did not come to join us; his guard kept him restrained at the side of the square.

Catherine was the finale of the auction. A guard led her sobbing to the auctioneer. In truth she made such a pitiable sight that the auctioneer seemed unable to dispel a sense of anti-climax among the bidders. When he held up her chin so that they could have a good look at her, what they saw was a red, tear-stained face with little appeal. Most seemed reluctant to enter the bidding and some began to saunter off, their interest in the day's auction over. Only the stout, jovial bidder seemed willing to meet the auctioneer's opening price, and even he had lost his mirth.

I watched as my owner exchanged another few words with his companion. Perhaps moved by pity, the man who had purchased George entered the bidding which lasted but a minute longer. The stout man seemed relieved to have some competition and the opportunity to bow out. No other bidders came forward and Catherine was sold to the same buyer as her brother, though neither child seemed composed enough to register this development. Catherine was led over to the registrar's table. He was now on his feet, preparing to depart, ledger in hand. The assistant painted Catherine's selling price on her shirt and her guard led her away, his grip on her arm as much to prop her up as to pull her along.

The auction now over, those men who had made purchases hung around in the shade while the others dispersed. I saw the auctioneer receive some coins from the registrar and then retreat into his shaded room in the arcade, which prompted the reappearance of Captain Murat.

We captives remained in our two distinct groups – those who had been purchased and those who had not - with separate guard details. I had supposed at this point that we would be assigned to our new masters but this did not happen. Instead the group that had been sold, myself included, were led back out through the gate by which we had entered, in a procession that now included the captain and registrar at the front and the new owners in a loose group at the rear, with our guards from the *Sword* still escorting us on each side.

We processed back along the broad, main street and I was surprised to see that we were returning to the Pasha's palace. This time we were not invited to drink and refresh ourselves at the fountain in the square. We were led straight back into the inner courtyard and once again made to line up in rows while the captain and registrar disappeared into the interior. I was positioned once again in the second row. George, who had by now calmed down, and Catherine, still sobbing, were made to stand apart from the rest of us, their guards right behind them. The purchasers from the slave market loitered in the arcade facing us, talking in low voices.

After some minutes, the captain and registrar returned, not with the Pasha this time but with one of his officials. The official inspected us, a much shorter process than before, taking into account the additional information painted upon our chests. He walked up and down our lines with the registrar in tow.

The official stopped in front of one man, one of the Spaniards, prodded the number on his chest with a stick and exchanged some brief words with the registrar. The registrar took a quick look in his ledger before replying to the official and beckoning one of the purchasers to come forward from the arcade.

'What's going on?' I whispered to Will, on my right, fearful that my words would attract a cuff from a watchful guard.

'Not sure,' Will whispered in reply, without turning his head. 'When we spoke about it back on the ship, Silas reckoned that the Pasha always gets a second chance to buy any slave for himself at the price raised at the auction, to make sure we ain't been sold too cheap.'

That explanation fitted what seemed to be happening, with the Pasha's official now negotiating with the man who had bought the Spaniard at the auction. In the end the previous purchaser shrugged his shoulders with a frown and walked back to the group in the arcade. The official gave a clap and two of the Pasha's guards rushed forward and forced the confused Spaniard off to one side.

The official continued his inspection. He finished the first row and started to inspect mine. In my head I was weighing up which fate held better prospects: remaining alone with my new, severe-looking master or being picked out by the official, which might see me reunited with Adam and possibly Silas and Jacob too.

The official lingered in front of Will; he inspected his hands and inside his mouth before losing interest. My turn arrived. He looked me in the eye then up and down, considered the price on my chest and then moved on. He made no further purchases from the second row and showed no interest at all in the scowling George and red-faced Catherine. Before disappearing back into the interior of the palace, he pulled out a silk purse from the sash around his waist and passed a few gold coins to the registrar.

Once the official had departed, the registrar moved over to the group of purchasers in the arcade. I could not see all that then passed given the bodies and columns that stood in between, but it seemed that various transactions were being completed. As each was concluded the purchaser stepped forward from the arcade to take delivery of his new stock. Gradually our number depleted as we were led singly, or sometimes in twos and threes, out of the courtyard through the external gate of the palace. I watched my new owner settle his transaction with the registrar. I turned to my right and caught Will's attention, extending my right hand.

'Good luck,' I said.

'God speed you back to England, Master Tom,' he replied with a smile, gripping my hand.

Then I stooped down and gathered up my chain ready for my new master's signal for me to follow. I looked over to George and Catherine, who were now together again, waiting for their new master. George caught my eye and I nodded my farewell to him. Then I followed my new master out of the gate.

Chapter 6: Servitude

I followed my new master across the square towards one of the arcades that ran along its side. It was a struggle to match his pace; the chain clanked at my side. We were heading towards another man who sat on a shaded step between two columns. He scrambled to his feet when he spotted our approach and gave a respectful bow to my master.

A brief conversation between the pair ensued, of which I understood nothing except what sounded like my first name and that I had been consigned to the custody of this other man. Then my master left us. I watched him walk across the square, his cloak catching the circulating breeze, before I lost sight of him in the throng of the main street.

The man to whom I had been entrusted was more plainly dressed than my master. He had neither cloak nor turban but wore neat breeches, a sash belt, and a long-sleeved shirt. He had a swarthy complexion and his black hair was streaked with grey. He surprised me by addressing me in broken English, pronounced with a thick French accent.

'My name is Pierre,' he said, choosing his words with difficulty. 'I am the steward of your master's household. You come with me now. You are Tom, yes?'

I nodded.

He led me through a warren of alleys and streets twisting back down the hill. We passed through the marine gate back on to the quayside. From there I could see the *Sword* and the *Santillana*, both resplendent in the bright blue water of the harbour. I noticed how low the Spanish ship squatted in the water, compared to the graceful *Sword*. The two ships remained a magnet of activity with mariners milling about on their upper decks and boats ferrying people and goods to and from the quayside.

Pierre led me back to the smithy where I had been fastened to my chain. Once more I was directed to place my right foot upon the blacksmith's stool, taking care to avoid further antagonising him. Fortunately he did not seem to remember me. The blacksmith, under the watchful eye of Pierre, unfastened the chain but, to my disappointment, left the iron fetter in place around my ankle. Pierre gave him a small, square, silver coin for his efforts. The blacksmith grunted in acknowledgement and returned to his furnace.

We proceeded back up the hill into the city, following a steep, narrow street similar to the one we had taken this morning. The going was now made much easier both by the reduced heat at this hour of the afternoon and by the removal of my chain. As we walked, Pierre pointed out various buildings of note, though most of the names were in a language which meant nothing to me and so were impossible for me to recall. We passed a collection of tallow-makers followed by a row of tanners, recognisable anywhere by their stench.

We crossed the main thoroughfare once more, which Pierre called the Grand Market, further along from where we had joined it earlier that day. It was still bustling: hundreds of people vied for space with donkeys and carts, horses, cows, sheep and other livestock. All were jostling through a thicket of market stalls selling fruits and vegetables, spices, pottery, shoes, clothing and materials in every colour. No one stopped to point and laugh at me now. It was as if I had been absorbed into the city.

We left the main street and followed another that climbed upwards. As we walked, I heard the air begin to ring once more with song, as if from the heavens. The call to prayer echoed along the street and into the cramped squares and alleys that stole away on either side.

After a row of goldsmiths' shops, Pierre directed me into one of the side alleys. He ushered me into a barber's shop and exchanged a few words with the barber. I sat down warily on a stool as the barber sharpened his blades. He proceeded to shave my head with firm but skilful hands such that I winced at the prospect of cuts that never came. I noticed that my brown hair had been bleached fair as it fell across my lap and littered the floor around me. He shaved my head almost to the skin and so exposed my reddened scalp, sore from itching during the voyage. The shave was over in a matter of minutes; Pierre produced another square silver coin from a purse concealed in his shirt and paid the barber, who muttered as he pocketed his earnings.

We continued along the alley before turning uphill at a right angle into another of those long, narrow streets that climbed the hillside like ivy on a wall. This street emptied into another broad concourse, running in parallel to the Grand Market below but neither as wide nor as bustling. The houses here were larger and less cramped than in the lower quarters of the city. From over their walls came the scent of jasmine and other exotic plants.

Further uphill, beyond the rooftops of the houses, I could see a high wall with towers and the tops of serried buildings behind it. Pierre spotted the direction of my gaze. 'The Kasbah,' he said, and I remembered that Jack had pointed out the fortress-like upper quarter of the city from the deck of the *Sword* during our approach.

We walked a little way along this broad street before taking a final branch off to the left into a dead-end street. We came to a stop outside a whitewashed building, similar to many we had passed though larger.

'This is the house of your master,' said Pierre as he banged the knocker several times on the studded door.

'Please, sir,' I asked, 'who is my master?'

'His name is Ibrahim Ali, but you must only call him "master". He is the *Hazinedar*, the Grand Treasurer of this city, a man very important, very important.'

I resisted the temptation to make further enquiries. The door was opened by a youth, who looked a little older than myself and whom I took to be a servant. We stepped into a small room like a vestibule. The air inside was cool. On the opposite wall, Pierre pulled back a curtain of embroidered velvet to reveal the entrance to an inner courtyard, rather like a cloister. He instructed me to wait in the courtyard while he conversed with the youth at the door. It was a pleasant enough place. An arcade lined each side, horse-shoe arches resting upon columns of carved marble. Each arcade supported a covered gallery on the upper floor, again lined with arches and columns, more slender than those below. An ornate wooden balustrade spanned the gaps between the columns.

The walls facing on to the courtyard were decorated, like the Pasha's palace, with tiles in intricate, floral designs, mostly blue and white but with occasional red flourishes. The floor was paved with white marble. Pruned plants added a dash of green and life. Numerous doors and grilled windows opened on to the courtyard but I could see nothing of what lay behind them. A fountain gurgled in one corner and I took the chance to refresh myself there while I waited.

Once he had finished his conversation with the lad in the vestibule, Pierre led me into one of the ground-floor rooms that opened on to the courtyard. It was narrow and dark, with no exterior windows, drawing its meagre light from the shaded inner courtyard. The tiles of the floor were cold underfoot, a merciful relief from the hot dust of the street. There were a couple of plain wooden chairs and a table, a chest, a wardrobe and something that looked similar to a dresser. In the corner was an unlit stove with a couple of pots hanging above it.

'This is where you sleep,' he said, pointing to a bed of straw on the floor in one corner. I looked around in the half light and saw two other crude beds in the room. 'Wait. I bring you clothes,' he said.

I sat down on the bed, resting my limbs. I ran my fingers over the unfamiliar fetter clasped around my right leg while Pierre rummaged in the wardrobe and in the chest. A couple of minutes later he threw me a bundle of clothes and then headed out into the courtyard. The clothes matched his outfit, except that I lacked the sash. The youth from the vestibule brought me a bowl of water. He grinned as he set the bowl down and gestured that I should use it to wash.

I stood up and peeled off the clothes that Jack had given me on board the *Sword*. They were soiled and wet with sweat. I retrieved the pack of cards from the lining of the shirt and concealed them in the straw of my bed. I washed all over, which was a much more pleasant experience than washing with sea water. Then I donned my new outfit, which was a little on the large side, though I considered that this would be a blessing given the heat in this place. The breeches, though baggy, were not long enough to conceal my ankle collar, even when standing.

When I had finished dressing, I sat down again on my bed, damp in my new clothes, my back against the cool wall. A few minutes later, Pierre returned. I stood to meet him and to show that I was ready.

'Better, it is much better,' he said, looking me up and down in the half light. 'You go to the market now to buy some... *chaussures*,' he paused, trying to remember the English word.

'Shoes,' I interjected.

'Ah yes,' he said with a look of pleasant surprise before repeating 'shoes'.

I thought this an opportune moment to enquire further into my new situation.

'Please, sir, what am I here for? What must I do?'

'You are the property of Master Ibrahim now, so you must follow his rules. You must do what your master and I tell you to do. If you do well, you have nothing to fear.'

I nodded, wondering if he could detect my apprehension.

'For the first days, you follow me and the other boy, Joaquin, so you can learn what you must do and learn some words in Turkish. Sometimes the master has messages for you to deliver in the city. Other times you must buy some things from the market or you must help in the house, washing clothes and cleaning or serving the master and his guests, many things like that.'

'Does the master live in this house alone?' I asked.

'No. His – how you say? – daughters live here too but you must not go in their rooms; never. Come, I will show you where you may go.'

We walked across the courtyard, through a door and up a staircase leading to the upper floor. We stood on the gallery and he pointed to several doorways which were either closed by doors or by curtains. 'You must never enter these doors: only in this one and that one and that one. And only when you are instructed to do so.'

I followed him into the first of these permissible doors which led into a large room. Its walls were decorated with tapestries; fine rugs lay on the marble floor. A large window filled the room with light, catching the golden hues sweeping the sky before sunset. The window looked down over the city to the harbour and the sea beyond, stretching out in a gilded blue across the horizon.

On one side of the room were two long chairs, of the kind I had seen in paintings of antiquity. In the centre, several plump, silk cushions were arranged around a low table. On the other side of the room stood a pair of bookcases, sagging under the weight of their tomes. Between the bookcases a purple curtain concealed what I guessed was a doorway leading to another room. A well-ordered writing desk and accompanying chair occupied the corner beneath the window such that the writer could sit and gaze out across the harbour when he lifted his eyes from his papers.

'When the master is in here, you wait by this door for his instructions,' Pierre explained, pointing to the doorway through which we had entered.

I followed Pierre back out on to the gallery overlooking the courtyard. He pointed at another of the doors. 'This is the kitchen,' he said. 'Sometimes you go there to carry some things. And up here,' he said, withdrawing the curtain from the final permissible doorway and proceeding up another staircase, 'is the terrace.'

The terrace proved to be a roof garden and a spectacular vantage point. 'You may only come here when the women of the house are not here.' I followed Pierre across the terrace and over to the parapet overlooking the city and the harbour. He stood with his hands placed on the parapet, gazing out. 'Sometimes, if you are lucky,' he said, 'you attend to the master here.'

I looked down and saw the white city sweeping down to the sea, with its labyrinth of narrow streets and intersecting alleyways, small squares and grand open spaces, towers and domes. From here I could now appreciate for the first time the city's defences, as I could see large stretches of the great wall of red stone that surrounded the city. In the harbour far below I could make out the *Sword* and the *Santillana* and a score of other ships under the protection of the outstretched mole. Spread out on either side of the city, beyond its imprisoning walls, lay a green landscape of farmland and low hills.

Pierre did not linger. As we turned to return down the stairs I surveyed the fortress quarter of the Kasbah. It was encircled by the perimeter wall of the city, with turrets and bastions running along its length, and by the inner wall that set it apart from the main part of Algiers. The Kasbah formed the highest point of the city, beyond which the ground clambered up to the hilltop above.

Pierre led the way down to the ground floor where we found Joaquin waiting in the vestibule. Pierre gave some quick instructions to the youth, in a language that sounded like the *sabir* often used by the corsairs on board the *Sword*, and passed him some coins.

'Go now with Joaquin,' he said to me, pointing at Joaquin's feet. 'Buy some shoes like the shoes of him.' They looked like comfortable beige slippers. I noticed that Joaquin also had an iron fetter around his right ankle.

Joaquin spoke no English but seemed pleasant enough. He led me down to an alleyway branching off Grand Market Street. There we found an array of shoe-makers' and cobblers' shops. I had no difficulty in finding a pair of slippers that suited, as the design seemed very common. I could just about follow the conversation as Joaquin haggled with the shopkeeper over the price. There seemed to be some concern from the shopkeeper about the silver coins Joaquin was offering.

Once we had left the shop, I tried to ask Joaquin where he was from, using the best of my schoolboy French and Latin, and established that he was from Spain and, counting on fingers, was sixteen years old. I told him that my name was Tom, which he repeated to himself, nodding.

'Hambre?' he asked, pointing to his mouth then stomach. He used the copper coins he had received as change from the shoes to purchase a couple of pieces of bread and meat from a small shop in the Grand Market. He handed me my share and I wolfed it down, not only because it was my first food since breakfast but also because it was the first real bread and the first fresh meat that I had eaten since my capture. Joaquin smiled at me with satisfaction. We drank from a large public fountain on the main street and I ran water over my shaven scalp which felt wonderful. We sauntered back to the master's house.

'Very good,' said Pierre looking at my new shoes as he let us in. 'Now you are ready to do some work for the master. Joaquin will show you what to do.' He continued to give what sounded like detailed instructions to Joaquin, who nodded as he took them all in.

'As I already say to you, the master is the *Hazinedar*. Now you must to go to the houses of the *hocas* and bring back their reports.'

'Sorry, I don't understand,' I replied.

'The *Hazinedar*, the Grand Treasurer, is an official very important,' Pierre explained. 'He is responsible for the finances of the city and also for many other affairs important. The *hocas* are the officials who work for the *Hazinedar*. Some of the *hocas* must give reports today. Joaquin will take you. Remember who they are and where they live so you can go alone the next time.'

Joaquin led me back out into the city. The temperature was cooling; a light breeze wafted in from the sea. The darkening streets still teemed with people of all sorts. There were men with dark skin and others with swarthy complexions. Some had skin that must once have been as fair as mine but had been tanned in the unrelenting sun.

The range of costumes was also varied in both colour and style. Many of the men and boys were dressed in a long outer garment reaching down to their ankles, often with a hood or scarf wrapped around their shoulders. The men wore turbans, in various colours and sizes, or small caps, which were usually red. Slippers, such as those that I had just acquired, were the norm.

I noticed several men dressed in black. They too wore turbans or skullcaps and one man that I passed wore the Star of David on a pendant around his neck, from which I took him to be a Jew. There were Jewish women too, also distinguished by their black dress. They sat talking in their doorways as we passed them.

I saw European men dressed like those on board the *Sword*, some with turbans, others without. And, once or twice, Joaquin and I pressed our backs against a wall to allow a company of soldiers, in a blaze of red jackets and blue pantaloons, to proceed unhindered. 'Oçak', Joaquin whispered as the first company strode past, bristling with curved swords and muskets.

It struck me that it was largely men and boys that I saw walking past. There were occasional women, drifting by in small groups, shrouded in white garments that covered them up to their veiled faces. I noticed that Joaquin looked down whenever he passed them so I did the same.

My legs were already weary before we set off on this errand. By the time we had visited the half dozen places required, which were scattered across the city, I was exhausted. At every building, Joaquin knocked upon the door, was recognised and given a roll of paper, which he passed to me to hold before taking his leave. By the time we returned to the master's house darkness had taken hold of the city. I passed the rolls of paper to Pierre who instructed us to remain in the vestibule to watch over the front door as he disappeared into the courtyard.

Joaquin and I passed the time in the vestibule, attempting to communicate as best we could given our limited common language, which was a source of mutual amusement, easing my apprehension. He seemed to be conversant in *sabir*, which meant that I could pick out certain words and phrases that I had heard on the *Sword* and that were close to French or had an obvious Latin root. I established that he had been a captive in Algiers for three years, having been captured whilst out on a fishing boat with his father, who seemed to have been killed in the encounter.

After around half an hour there was a knock at the door. Joaquin opened it and the master walked in. He gave me a glance up and down, as if inspecting his purchase once again now that it had been spruced up. He nodded to me then entered into the courtyard where Pierre greeted him and the pair engaged in conversation. I listened and reckoned that the impenetrable language they used must be Turkish, as Pierre had mentioned.

The master proceeded upstairs and Joaquin gestured that we should follow. We both stood and waited in silence beside the doorway in the living room, which was now illuminated by several lamps. Through the window, far to the west, I could see the embers of sunset in the night sky.

The master was already sitting at his desk, unrolling the scrolls of paper that Joaquin and I had collected for him and glancing over their contents. Pierre stood a few, respectful paces away. I noticed the master tut and sigh as he read some of the reports; others he passed over without so much as a blink. On the final report he again tutted, then picked up a pen, dipped it in ink, and wrote a few words, in the curious manner from right to left, passing a comment to Pierre as he did so. This marked the end of the master's paperwork. He stood up from his chair and clapped his hands once. Pierre scooped up the rolls of paper while Joaquin indicated that it was now time for us to leave.

As I followed him down the stairs, Joaquin gestured that it would soon be time to eat, saying '*mangare*', and we returned to our room. I noticed that the small stove in the corner was lit and that one of the pots was bubbling away. The smell was appetising and I went to investigate. Joaquin accompanied me and pointed at the contents of the pot, saying '*kuskussu*'. The contents looked similar to a spiced rice dish I had once seen Jack prepare for a special occasion on the *Sword*. I had seen great cauldrons of the stuff simmering in shop fronts along Grand Market Street. Joaquin placed a shallow pan above the stove, added a little oil and then unwrapped some balls of what appeared to be minced beef, which had been placed upon the side, wrapped in leaves. When the oil was hot, Joaquin placed each of the three meatballs into the sizzling pan. He used a long fork to push them around in the pan to prevent them from burning; as he did so he looked at me with a smile and said 'kofte'. I nodded and returned the smile.

I glanced over to the corner beside my bed and noticed that my old clothes had gone. Partly to reassure myself that they were still there, I retrieved my pack of cards from where I had concealed them in the bed. I sat down on one of the chairs at the table, shuffling the cards to while away the time. Joaquin brought out some tin plates and forks from the dresser and laid them on the table.

Pierre entered the room and was drawn towards the stove to inspect the food. He prodded at the meatballs with the long fork. Then he came and sat beside me at the other chair with a weary sigh. He picked up the little wooden box that housed my playing cards and raised his thick black eyebrows in pleasant surprise as he discovered that they had been made in Rouen.

'The best quality,' he said with a small chuckle to himself. 'Do you play at cards?'

'Yes, I like to,' I replied.

'Très bien, very good. This night, we play.'

Joaquin laid out the food and we all ate. It was a small meal but far better than anything I had eaten during my voyage.

During the meal, Pierre enquired about where I was from and how I had been captured. His eyebrows rose again when I explained the manner in which I had been taken captive along with the Leigh children. 'Mon Dieu,' he muttered to himself. Joaquin listened and Pierre would translate occasional words and phrases for him.

I asked Pierre where he was from and he said he came from a little fishing village called Pornic on the Atlantic coast of Brittany, near the town of Guérande, which he claimed produced the finest salt in all the world. He had been one of the crew on a fishing boat that had plied the English Channel, or La Manche as he insisted on calling it. He had been many times in 'the English Cornouaille' and had learned to speak English there. His whole crew had been captured around ten years ago by corsairs. He had left a wife, two daughters and a son behind.

Pierre said he had been in his current employment for the past three years, since the master had arrived from Istanbul to take up his position. Before that he had been a servant in the household of another official, but had clearly cared much less for him, only ever referring to him with a sneer as *l'idiote turquois'*.

After the meal, Pierre insisted that we play cards. I discovered that he knew how to play whist and so we played several hands of that, with Joaquin watching on.

At the end of our game of whist, Pierre retrieved a small bottle of cognac from his chest which he poured into a small glass. He offered me some but I politely declined, as did Joaquin. The drink seemed to raise his spirits and ease his tongue. He began to teach the pair of us words and phrases in Turkish, and took great delight in our error-prone repetitions.

Pierre taught us his favourite card game, *Piquet*, and I taught him games that he did not know such as All Fours and Cribbage. As we played, I took the opportunity to enquire some more about the master's business.

'What were the papers that we collected today?' I asked.

'Oh, they were the reports from the *hocas*. They show how much money comes to the treasury each day, from taxes and so on. The treasury must bring in enough money to keep the Pasha content.'

'And why was the master unhappy this evening?'

'He is not happy with the *gümrük emin*, the *douanier*, you know?'

'The Controller of Customs?'

'Yes, the Controller of Customs. Your French is good, *n'est-ce pas?*'

'My school teacher always told me that it was not good enough,' I laughed. 'I always preferred numbers and logic. I was much better at those – my teacher said I was uncultured.'

That made Pierre laugh out loud. 'Well here, in this town, you will hear many, many languages – from Europe, from Africa and even from the Indies. And you must learn Turkish, the master's language. He thinks the Controller of Customs is not collecting enough money, or perhaps he is keeping too much money for himself, eh?'

'So what will the master do?'

'Tomorrow, you must take the report of the Controller of Customs back with a question for him from my master – asking him where all the money is.' His laughter was so infectious that even Joaquin joined in, though I doubt he understood why.

So began my period of servitude in Algiers. It was the start of a hard, new life: a daily grind of mundane chores laboured through the blistering heat of summer and the bitter cold of winter. Lest you believe otherwise, I give you my word that the hot sun does not glare down every day upon African soil. For months in the winter it retreats before the cold winds that stir up from the great desert to the south and howl in from across the bay.

When I was working alone during these dark times I often shed silent tears for the gentle world and innocent freedom that had been taken from me. A dreadful homesickness gnawed at the pit of my stomach: I longed for the touch of my mother, the chatter of my sister, the company of my friends. I wrote to my mother several times in those first months, enclosing the letters in my missives to Mr Dillington, requesting his support for a ransom, both for myself and for the Leigh children. The consul, Mr Frizell, promised to send them but I never received a reply. I took a morsel of comfort from the knowledge that Mr Dillington would be looking out for my mother and sister during my absence.

But just as dawn follows even the darkest night, so the light began to come back into my life. This did not happen all at once but came gradually, like the slow rise of the sun on the longest day. Mostly that light came from the new friends that Fortune had bestowed on me. Two of them lived and worked in the same house as me. I learned much from Pierre and also from Joaquin, who was as fluent as anyone in *sabir* and had an intimate knowledge of the city.

After a few weeks I had learned enough Turkish to follow basic instructions from my master and enough *sabir* to be able to converse with the market traders and shopkeepers. This equipped me to conduct most errands by myself. Often Pierre would send me to buy bits and pieces from the stalls in the Grand Market or from shops across the city. As if the language was not difficult enough to master, every time I was sent to make purchases the prices of the goods seemed to have gone up and I would return to the house to meet Pierre's displeasure. At first I thought it was just me, that the shopkeepers were having some sport with an incompetent foreign slave, but soon I realised that the prices were going up for everyone. I did not need to understand every word to understand the bitterness this caused amongst the people.

I soon learned the lie of the city: its streets and alleys; its mosques and palaces; its squares – great and small; its *hammams*, where the people bathed; and the infamous *bagnios*, where the slaves who belonged to the state were lodged.

It was in the one of the *bagnios* that I eventually tracked down Silas and Jacob. They seemed in good spirits even though their bodies displayed the sinister effects of gruelling work, far harder than mine. They had welts on their faces, where the sun had burned their skin raw, and weeping blisters on their hands. Since they worked by day and the gates of their *bagnio* were locked at night, I could only meet them in the evenings or between my chores on a Friday, which was the day of rest in the city. I thank God for the Grace that enabled me to find these two old fishermen, steadfast lights amid the darkness. I look back with warm memories on the times we shared together, talking and laughing; they with their clay pipes and all three of us with our dreams of escaping home.

Chapter 7: Learning

It is not possible for me to detail every aspect of my life in Algiers over the next six years, during which I served my master faithfully. In any case, much of my life was so mundane as to make for a tedious account. However, in order for you to follow my story, there are a number of important events from my time in that city that I must commit to paper so that you may better understand the twists and turns of Fortune's wheel that later came to pass.

I begin with an account of my first proper conversation with my master, which took place around five months after my arrival in Algiers. Until that point I had mainly been tasked by Pierre with running errands, while Pierre attended upon my master whenever he was at home. However, one evening in the midst of the bitter Algerian winter, Pierre walked into the vestibule where Joaquin and I whiled away the hours and addressed me in a formal tone: 'Tom, the master has requested your presence.'

My face must have been a portrait of astonishment at these words. The master had, until this date, barely acknowledged my existence in his household.

'Follow me,' said Pierre, and he turned on his heels and led me across the marble courtyard, up the stairs and into the living room. As I entered, I saw my master seated at his desk, beneath a lamp. Pierre announced my arrival in Turkish, a language that I could now understand and could speak increasingly well.

My master put down his papers, stood up and gave Pierre permission to leave. His dark brown eyes looked me up and down; I felt small under his steady gaze. For the first time, he spoke to me. He spoke in Turkish, taking time to choose his words and pronouncing them with clarity, as if to aid my understanding.

'So, Tom, Pierre tells me that you have learned your duties well.'

'Thank you, master,' I replied, my eyes trained to a patch of marble floor just ahead of his slippers.

'He says that you are already able to speak Turkish – not an easy language for anyone from your country to learn, I believe. You must be an intelligent young man.'

'Thank you, master.'

'And can you read and write?'

'Yes, master: in English, and some French, Latin and Greek, but not in Turkish.'

'Well, I shall ask Pierre to put that right. While you are in my household, you must learn to write Turkish and Arabic. They are proper, beautiful languages, not like the mongrel language of the merchants and sailors – *sabir* – that you'll hear in this city.'

'Yes, master.'

'And from now you shall come and attend to me in the evenings. Sometimes I will call for you, sometimes for Pierre, so be ready.'

'Yes, master.'

'Thank you; that will be all. Please tell Pierre to return.'

Thus concluded our first conversation. I was surprised both at the polite way that he addressed me and at my own nervousness. That evening, over supper, I recounted the conversation to Pierre, who digested the news with an expression of indifference.

'I can teach you what little I know of Turkish letters,' he said, 'but I know even less Arabic.' He shook his head from side to side. 'And the place to learn that is at school, where they will also teach you about the Koran, the holy book of Islam.'

As I lay awake that night, unable to sleep, I turned over and over in my mind the prospect of attending an Islamic school and succumbing to the religion of the infidel. I was deeply troubled, recalling my vicar's diatribe about the sin of apostasy, of abandoning my own religion, and fearing that my soul would be eternally damned. What little sleep I had that night was fitful and filled with torments.

Mercifully, I did not have long to wait before the dreaded prospect of the school turned into reality. The next morning, Pierre returned from his errands in the city and told me that he had enrolled me in a school a few streets away. It was, he said, a good school, under the patronage of one of the master's friends. The master had directed him there on the grounds that, as Pierre put it, 'Master Mussa teaches not only the words but the meanings also.'

I was to start the very next day. As this news sank in, the torments of the previous night began to stalk me, distracting me from my chores. The night brought scant relief. More than once I woke in a cold sweat from a nightmare of hell and fire.

The following morning, Pierre led me to the school. I was bleary-eyed and felt sick to the pit of my stomach. The school was situated in a busy side street not far from the Grand Market. I realised that I had passed it once or twice on my errands; its carved wooden façade had caught my eye but I had not realised what lay within.

The school consisted of a single room on the ground floor. It took my eyes some moments to adjust to the darkness of the interior. What little air there was had a damp edge and musty smell. Ahead of me, around two dozen boys, all younger than I, sat in rows upon grass mats. They turned and gazed up at Pierre and me with wide eyes. At the far end of the room, the teacher sat upon a wooden bench. He recognised Pierre and came over to greet us, welcoming us in Turkish. He instructed me to take a mat and to sit at the front of the class. Pierre gave me a wink and departed. 'I'll expect you back not long after midday,' he said, 'and don't think that you'll be excused from your work this afternoon: you won't be.'

I picked my way through the pupils to a spot that appeared to have been reserved for me. There I unrolled my mat and sat down in the manner I observed the other boys had done. They each had a slate that had been covered in white clay, upon which they inscribed their strange writing with a reed. The teacher brought a fresh slate and a reed. He knelt down on one knee beside me and inscribed some words in a flourish from right to left. As he wrote, he spoke to me in Turkish: 'I am writing some of the most important words from the Koran for you. They are in Arabic. You will hear them and see them over and over again. Today, you will understand little, but if you study with care then, *inshallah*, in time you will understand all.'

He read through some of those key words, pointing at each one in turn and pronouncing it for me. The words were both basic, everyday words and important religious words. My eyes struggled to make any sense of the script. 'Patience; it will come,' he said. 'And today you must understand this word.' His finger traced a line below the word which he pronounced in Arabic and then translated into Turkish. My limited knowledge of Turkish meant I was unable to interpret the word in English. Sensing my incomprehension, he explained that it was the word for a child who has no parents. 'Orphan' I said. He nodded his head and smiled. Then he clapped his hands to regain the attention of the other children, who had been fixated with me all the while and quite distracted from their own learning. He addressed them in Turkish. 'Yusuf, begin please. Recite *sura* number ninety-three.'

The child began to recite. When he had finished, the teacher was well pleased and asked the next boy to recite and then the next and the next. I listened. Occasionally the teacher would ask a boy to translate a word or phrase into Turkish, to ensure that he and the others had grasped its meaning. At these points, I was able to piece together some sense of the content, which seemed to describe a caring God who provided for his followers and expected them to provide for orphans, for those in need.

Once all the recitals were over, there followed some further discussion on the meaning of the sacred text, some of which I followed, but most of which I did not – as the language of the Koran, when translated into Turkish, was not the day-to-day Turkish language to which I had been accustomed. At the end of the lesson, the teacher asked the children to come over to the corner to wipe clean their slates. I joined the end of the queue. As they waited, the children laughed and chattered, occasionally glancing back in my direction. They began to file out of the room on to the street. As I took my turn to wipe the slate, the teacher spoke to me from his bench. 'We shall see you tomorrow, after morning prayers,' he said.

'Yes, I'll be here,' I replied.

As I walked home through the bustling little streets, I put myself in the place of the orphan from the *sura* and wondered if my God had not forsaken me, but was yet providing for me in His own mysterious way, according to His own unknowable design.

I returned to the master's house and resumed my daily chores. When the evening came, I sat with Joaquin in the vestibule and told him about my morning at the school. He winced as I described my attempts to decipher the Arabic text. *'Mas dificil,'* he said, shaking his head from side to side.

Pierre appeared at the door from the inner courtyard and told me that the master wished to speak to me again. I followed him up to the living room and stood just inside the door. The window was open and the curtains rippled in the cool evening air. As previously, the master rose from his desk and signalled for Pierre to leave. Then he invited me to take a seat on one of the cushions beside the low table. I felt embarrassed, knowing this to be a great privilege. He came and sat on a cushion facing me and addressed me in Turkish.

'So, Tom, you attended school today?'

'Yes, master,' I replied.

'How did you find it?'

'It was difficult but I learned something, master,'

'I suppose you learned about one of the *sura.'*

'Yes, master. We learned the *sura* about the morning light.'

'Ah yes,' he said with a smile, 'the *Ad-Duha,* the Glorious Morning Light. Do you know much about the Koran?'

'Only a little.'

'Well, Master Mussa will put that right in time. The Koran is a wonderful book that contains the revelations of God, the *sura,* spoken by the Angel Gabriel to the Prophet Mohammad, peace be upon him. The *sura* you have learned this morning was the second revelation, from the time when the Prophet Mohammad, peace be upon him, was living in Mecca.'

He stood up from his chair and walked over to a book case, from which he retrieved an old leather-bound book. He walked back over to me, holding the book with great care.

'This Tom, is the Koran, the divine word of God. Look after it well; this book was given to me when I was a child.'

'Thank you, master,' was all that I could say. I knew that I had again been greatly honoured. I could not guess what I had done to merit it.

He leafed through the book and placed the ribbon to mark a certain page. 'Here,' he said, passing me the book. 'This is the *sura* you were learning this morning. Let your eyes become used to the words while you remember the recitals from the other children.'

I surveyed the text. Though I could not read the words there was already something familiar about them, from the inscriptions I had seen in the schoolroom that morning.

'And so, tomorrow night you will tell me what you have learned about the next *sura*.'

'Yes master,' I said as I returned to my feet. My pulse quickened at the prospect of having to report back on my learning. I tiptoed from the room, cradling the book in both hands.

That night, after supper, I did not play cards with Joaquin and Pierre but instead sat on my straw bed in the flickering lamp-light with the book. I traced the inscriptions in its leather binding with my fingertips, before leafing through its pages. The writing was exquisite and the margins were decorated with intricate floral designs. I spent about an hour reading or rather surveying the *sura* I had learned that morning, until my thoughts began to swim and I was engulfed by sleep.

The next morning, and the morning of every school day after that for the next year and a half, found me waiting outside the schoolroom with the other boys after morning prayers until Master Mussa invited us in. Each day we learned a different *sura*. If the *suras* were short, we learned more than one; if they were long then we learned only those *ayahs* or verses from the *sura* that Master Mussa instructed us to. In this way, day by day, my knowledge of Arabic improved. After several months I was able to read fluently and some months later I was able to write in Arabic as well as most of the other boys in the class.

My understanding of the text came first from my teacher and second from my master, who summoned me several nights each week and seemed to take a genuine interest, even pleasure, in my learning. At first he would explain the meanings of the *suras* and the essential aspects of Islam. Later he demanded that I recite the *sura* to him in Arabic and he began to test me on detailed points of understanding and to engage in more complex theological discussion. This was how, over the following months, I became conversant not only in the sacred Arabic language of the Koran, but also in the tenets of Islam, the so-called Five Pillars; in the *hadith*, or holy sayings; and in the history of Islamic civilisation, which was of enduring interest to my master.

I should add that I treated this as academic learning, rather than spiritual learning. I was not asked to attend the Mosque for prayers and nor, aside from the curiosity of youth, did I have any desire to attend it or to participate in prayers. In truth, I remained troubled that I might already be committing the sin of apostasy. By day I put these concerns to one side; by night they haunted me, wracking my conscience.

During this time I became friends with many of the boys in my class, though they were by varying years younger than me. At first they remained curious about my foreignness, looking on me as some exotic oddity, and rather disdainful about my status as a *tutsaklar*, or prisoner of war, and my inability to read or recite the Arabic language. Over time, as I earned Master Mussa's favour and impressed my classmates with my recitals and ability to answer the teacher's questions, I became accepted and on increasingly friendly terms. These boys tended to be from the households of the richer citizens of Algiers, the sons of Ottoman officials or merchants. From the older boys, in the gossip before and after school, I learned about various happenings concerning important people and events in the city and so, in a piecemeal and round-about way, about the customs and politics of the city.

After a year and a half of this routine, by which time I was now sixteen years of age, I had become sufficiently fluent in my recitals of the Koran and sufficiently accomplished in my ability to read and write the sacred verses that my master decided that I should end my schooling.

My discussions with my master, which continued to take place on several evenings each week, had become deeper over time, and it was clear that I had risen in his esteem. In truth, this also meant that I had lost some of the early deference that I had shown him. I remained always courteous and respectful but I became confident when engaging him in discussion, even challenging him and questioning him on points of history, theology or philosophy, which he appeared to relish.

It was with some sadness that, after my last day at school, I bid farewell to my school friends and teacher and returned to work full time in my master's household. This state of affairs did not last long.

Chapter 8: Money

Some moments in life are crossroads: events occur or decisions are taken that reshape your destiny. I reached one of those crossroads at the end of my second year in Algiers. The turn of events that followed has often caused me to wonder at the mysterious workings of Providence, of fate or chance or Fortune, call it what you will. Given its importance in my story, I will endeavour to set out what happened as well as I can remember in the pages that follow.

It began one evening, not long after I had finished my schooling. I was instructed to attend to my master, who was entertaining guests.

Preparations for supper had kept the household busy all afternoon. Pierre, in one of his most fastidious moods, oversaw the cooking. Various dishes had been prepared with assiduous attention to detail: olives; dates; savoury rice; couscous; meatballs; hollowed-out onions filled with minced lamb and rice; and lamb wrapped in grape leaves. The main dish was a beef and onion stew, cooked for hours in a clay pot and spiced with pepper and cumin. The dishes were served on large, circular platters of patterned silver, known as *sini*. I helped to carry the platters into the living room, setting them upon the low, circular table around which the guests would sit on their silk cushions. My stomach groaned at the delicious smells, knowing that I would not be able to eat until much later and resisting the temptation to pinch a morsel or two.

While the meal was being laid out, the master and his three guests talked outside on the roof terrace overlooking the city and the bay. At the appointed time, Pierre went up to the terrace to announce that the meal was served and the four men came inside and sat down to eat. Pierre and I took our places at the door, ready to clear away the platters or to attend to any other need.

With nothing else to do I listened to the conversation, which proceeded in a lively, almost heated, Turkish. From their conversation I was able to identify two of the guests. One was called Youssuf, he was the *emin* or official who supervised weights and measures in the city. The other was called Mehmet, he was the *gümrük emin* – the Controller of Customs – and I was almost certain that he was the man in the purple cloak who had bought George and Catherine at the auction. I had seen these two men once or twice before, when they had visited my master's house. They were discussing both the state of the coinage in Algiers, particularly the silver coin known as the asper, and the work of the Treasurer of the Mint – one of the officials accountable to my master in his role as Grand Treasurer of the city. I did not know the other guest, a thin man with a sleek black moustache and flashing eyes.

'Day by day, the Pasha grows increasingly concerned about the weakness of the asper,' said the unknown guest. 'He says he will not tolerate it.'

'They say that the Genoese merchants are now demanding two hundred aspers for each ducat,' said Youssuf, his bushy eyebrows raised high above his beady eyes, signalling his outrage.

'I heard one Spanish captain demanding two hundred and fifty aspers for each of his ducats at the quayside this very afternoon! Said it was the going rate he'd get in the Grand Market!' Mehmet exclaimed.

'The infidel thief!' Youssuf shouted.

'Let's catch him and chop his hand off,' said Mehmet, 'make an example of him.'

'But why is it happening?' demanded the unknown guest.

My master sat stroking his beard in a repetitive movement. 'It is a mystery,' he said calmly, 'and one that we need to solve.'

'It will be a Genoese plot, backed by the Spaniards, you mark my words,' said Mehmet. Youssuf nodded his head in agreement.

'They're trying to impose a tax on our currency,' said Youssuf.

'People across the city have had enough,' added the unknown guest. 'They have seen the prices for pretty much everything they buy rising month after month.'

'Many prices in the market have doubled since this time last year,' added Youssuf, 'and the people don't like it.'

'They'll be rioting before we know it,' said the unknown guest.

'I'd send the corsair galleys after those Genoese merchants, to teach them a lesson,' Mehmet shouted, banging his fist on the table.

'Peace friends,' said my master. It may well turn out to be the case that this is some kind of plot or illicit tax organised by the foreign merchants.' Then he addressed the controller of weights and measures. 'But it is strange, is it not Youssuf, that this could happen when our coins have not been debased, not for several years at any rate. They haven't been mixed with some base metal or clipped, you are sure?'

'No. Not that I have found. I asked my men to melt down some newly minted aspers, and the silver content was just as it should be; just as the Sultan himself has decreed.' Youssuf produced an asper from somewhere and threw it to my master, who caught it. Youssuf laughed as he continued. 'You see, it's still just as big and as full of silver as it's been for years.'

'And that is the curious thing,' said my master, looking down at the coin in his palm, 'because I have not heard that the aspers in Istanbul have likewise become weaker of late; and our aspers should therefore be worth just the same as theirs. It seems to be a problem that is peculiar to us in this city.'

This reasoning elicited approving nods from the guests around the table.

'Like I said, an Italian plot against us,' said Mehmet.

'Whatever it is, we must get to the bottom of it,' said the third guest, 'because the Sultan will not stand for the same coins in different parts of the empire having different values. And the Pasha will not tolerate the humiliation of seeing his own coins weaken. It is an insult to our city.'

'Nor will he tolerate increasing discontent amongst the masses from ever rising prices,' added Youssuf.

'All that is understood,' said my master. 'I will summon the Treasurer of the Mint in the morning, to see if he can explain what has happened, whether there has been something amiss at the mint.'

'You'll be wasting your time with him,' said Mehmet. 'Youssuf has already told us that there's nothing wrong with the coins themselves.'

'That may well be right, but I will see what he has to say for himself,' said my master. 'And now, let us talk of happier things. Mehmet, I believe your eldest daughter is soon to be married?'

Following the prompt, Mehmet switched the course of the conversation over to the forthcoming wedding. It was evident that he was the type of man who enjoyed being the focus of attention. His elaborate descriptions of the nuptial arrangements accounted for most of the remainder of the discourse that evening: how the couple had been matched; the nobility of the groom's family, though surpassed by his own; the fine clothes and jewels that the bride and various other members of his family would be wearing; the details of the wedding festivities including the number of guests, the lavishness of the decorations and, of course, the exorbitant cost of it all. It was clear that this wedding would be a significant event in the city's social calendar, given the bride's noble lineage.

The conversation had moved on but my attention was arrested by the mystery around the coinage. My late father had often told me that I had a passion for puzzles, and a practical mind for solving them. I stood at the doorway, gazing across the room and out of the window into the twilight, turning the mystery over and over in my mind.

At one point in the evening, my master clapped his hands and summoned me over, not on this occasion to wait upon his guests but instead, and much to my surprise and embarrassment, to recite a *sura* from the Koran. He asked me to recite the *sura* of Noah, about which he and I had conversed only the previous evening. Blushing, I recited the verses in my best Arabic.

'You see my friends,' he said when I had finished, 'what a marvel is this boy, who but a year and a half ago spoke no Arabic. Master Mussa has taught him well.'

'Ah but he can only recite the words as sounds; he does not understand their meaning,' said Mehmet, looking at me disdainfully and reaching for an olive.

'That's right,' said Youssuf. 'They only learn recitals; they know nothing of the meaning of the words. He is but a pale infidel slave after all.'

My master smiled. 'As I say, Master Mussa has taught him well. If you do not believe it then ask him, ask the boy; test him on his understanding.'

'Tell me, boy,' said Mehmet, swallowing his olive and rising to the challenge, 'how did Noah escape from perishing with the unbelievers?'

'On his ark, sir,' I replied, 'when the flood came, he and his family and his animals were safe on his ark.' I saw a smile on the face of my master. Mehmet frowned. His unblinking eyes glared at me over his hooked nose.

'Yes, yes,' he said, 'so he has learned that one. Tell me, slave, do you know, let me see, the *sura* of the Great News?'

'Yes, sir,' I replied.

'Well go on then. Recite it,' said Mehmet.

I could picture the verses of the *sura* set out on the slate board at the front of my old schoolroom.

'In the name of Allah, Most Gracious, Most Merciful,' I began, again in Arabic.

Mehmet twisted his lip beneath his trimmed moustache. 'Get to the substance,' he said.

I continued my recital: 'What are they arguing about? About the Great News, about which they cannot agree.'

The two other guests expressed noises of approval and smiled.

Mehmet clapped his hands once and shouted, 'Enough! So you can recite that one too. But tell me this, slave, what is this Great News about which they cannot agree?'

I thought about this for a while. Mehmet looked around his guests with the glint of vindication in his eye and a sneer upon his lips. The others kept their eyes trained upon me, their breath bated.

'Sir,' I replied in Turkish, 'there is some debate over what the Great News is. Some say it concerns the status of the Emir Ali and his vice-regency; but most believe the Great News is about the resurrection.'

My master clapped his hands in delight. The other guests joined in the applause. My cheeks flushed again and I stood still. 'You see, Mehmet,' he said, 'Master Mussa has taught him well.'

Mehmet reached for another olive then switched his gaze out of the window.

At around nine o'clock the guests departed. Pierre and I cleared away the platters, saving the best scraps for ourselves, and rearranged the cushions while my master attended to a few of the reports that Joaquin had collected for him that evening. Before he retired for the night to his family's rooms, my master spoke to Pierre. 'Bring Ahmed, the *emin* of the mint, to me at the Treasury tomorrow, after midday prayers.'

Pierre and I finished tidying the room and Joaquin joined us to wash the kitchenware.

The mystery of the weakening coinage and rising prices preoccupied me during the late supper I ate with Joaquin and Pierre, throughout our card games – all of which I lost – and even as I read through a *sura* in the Koran before I went to sleep, as had become my habit. It was a puzzle that trapped a nerve in my curiosity. And the more I thought about it, the more I suspected that I knew something that – even if it did not explain the whole mystery – was a material factor within in its solution.

The next day proceeded as normal. I busied myself with my regular chores and when they were done I sat with Joaquin in the vestibule, awaiting further instructions. Pierre had gone out that morning on the master's bidding and had returned around noon; he had not spoken to us since then. His first words to me were late in the afternoon, to say that the master had requested that I attend on him that evening, which was by now customary. Then he dispatched me on an errand to buy some tallow for our lanterns. Perhaps my awareness of such matters had been heightened by the previous evening's discussion, but I remember being surprised at how expensive the tallow had become since my last errand there. It was during my return from the tallow-maker's shop that I at last arranged the logic in my mind so that it shone a dim light on the mystery of the rising prices.

It was with a feeling of excitement that I entered the living room that evening and waited at the door for my master's instruction. That excitement, which welled inside me and tingled right to my fingertips, did not diminish during the slow hour in which my master remained engrossed in the papers on his desk. Unusually for him, for he was a patient man, that night I heard him sigh in exasperation more than once. At length he put his papers down and walked over to the window, as if to gaze out into the dark sea beyond the twinkling lamps of the city.

I summoned the courage to speak. This was, indeed, a feat of bravery on my part, so accustomed had I become to only speaking to my master when spoken to, and so sensitive was the subject on which I wanted to speak. I could contain my thoughts no longer.

'Master,' I said. I had to repeat the word to catch his attention.

He turned round to face me, surprised perhaps, as if he had forgotten that I was there at all.

'Yes Tom.'

'Master, there is something that I, I must tell you... about the money.' My voice and my Turkish vocabulary both faltered.

'Go on.'

'I mean, I think I know why the aspers have weakened in value.'

I had now caught his attention and he walked over to where I stood, my back pressed against the door. He was only about four feet away, so that I could speak in a low voice, almost a whisper, and he would hear. His eyes were fixed on mine. I gulped hard.

'Well, when I was on my voyage here, to Algiers, on the ship of Murat Reis,' I struggled for breath, 'his crew captured a Spanish ship, the *Santillana*, on its way back from the Spanish Main.'

His gaze remained fixed on me.

'That ship was carrying a very large cargo of silver. Murat Reis brought it to the harbour here.'

At these words, I thought I could see in his eyes that his mind was already racing through the implications of this information, perhaps reaching the same conclusion as I had done.

'Master, I don't know what happened to that cargo. But perhaps it was offloaded here in Algiers.'

He thought about this for a few moments. 'It is possible, Tom, but I was not notified of it. And Mehmet, the *gümrük emin*, and his customs officials should have known about all cargos being landed.'

'Well perhaps I am wrong then, and forgive me master, but if this silver was landed and melted down and was then minted into new coins, it could explain why the aspers have lost their value without being debased.'

His eyes now looked on me with what seemed like surprise or confusion, before his expression hardened. I feared the worst, and though he was not a violent man I thought for a moment that he might strike me for my insolence.

'Yes,' he said at last, 'I follow your meaning. If there were suddenly many more coins in the city then the effect would be the same as if we had deliberately debased the currency. For it is well understood that when there is too much money chasing too few goods then the shopkeepers and merchants put their prices up as they run out of stock.'

'I believe that this happened in England, sir, in the recent past.'

'Tom,' he said, 'I have heard no other plausible explanation for this mystery and the situation is now grave indeed. Ahmed, the Treasurer of the Mint, shed no light on proceedings this morning. But what you are saying is potentially very serious. The ship could not have been unloaded of its silver cargo without the knowledge of Murat Reis, a distinguished person in this city. Nor should this have happened without Mehmet's knowledge; his men should have kept a close eye on any comings and goings from the Spanish ship, and should certainly have spotted a whole cargo of silver being offloaded. And nor should Ahmed be in the dark, if it was the foundry within his mint that was used to melt the silver down and turn it into new coins.' He stroked his beard. 'Your reasoning raises serious allegations against important men. You had best say nothing to anyone about this.'

'Yes master,' I replied. 'I have told no one.'

'Good, and thank you,' he said. 'You are an intelligent man, Tom. I will look through these papers again tomorrow in light of what you have told me. Now, that is all for this evening. Thank you.'

He returned to the window overlooking the sea. My heart still pounding, I went down to my room, where I found Pierre and Joaquin playing at cards, Pierre with his glass of cognac in one hand.

I sat down on my bed and placed my back and head against the wall, enjoying the cool sensation on my neck. I was pleased that I had plucked up the courage to share my thoughts with my master but I was unsure as to the consequences. My sleep that night was fitful.

The next evening, after supper, my master summoned me once more. When I arrived in the living room I again found him at his desk, reading his papers. He turned round to face me as I entered and beckoned me to approach.

'Tom, I have read through these accounts from the mint and I can see no evidence in support of your theory. However, I would now like you to look over them, to see what you can find.'

I edged closer, right up to the desk, struggling to come to terms with his words. He had elevated my muddled thoughts to the status of a 'theory', like something from his books of ancient philosophy.

'See here,' he said, pointing to neat columns of figures in Arabic numerals under various headings. The words and numbers appeared restless under the flickering light. 'These are the balances of gold and silver in the mint, at different dates in time, you see, right back to when your ship docked and for some time before.'

I nodded to show that I understood.

'And these, here, are the inflows and the outflows from the mint. You see, the silver comes in, measured in *dirhams*, and the new coins go out, measured in *aspers*.' He pointed to the relevant places on the pages and then stood to vacate his chair for me. 'My head is spinning with these numbers, so I'm going to retire for the evening, to be with my daughters. Take a seat at the desk and let me know tomorrow if you find anything of interest.'

When he had left the room, I sat down at the desk, my fingers tracing the patterns of mother of pearl inlaid in the wood, appreciating both the strangeness of the situation and the honour that he had bestowed upon me. I hoped that Pierre would not catch me here, in my master's chair, lest he think that I had taken great liberties at my master's expense.

I let my eyes familiarise themselves with the accounts presented before me. The words were Turkish – some took me a little while to decipher and some remained unintelligible, but I managed to gain a good sense of what the tables were showing. As my master had noted, I was able to see updates on a daily basis since the date of my arrival: inflows of silver and gold by value – some in bullion, some in old or foreign coinage; outflows of new silver and gold coin; and the remaining balance of silver and gold held in the mint. As my master had commented, there was no evidence of a large increase in the outflows of silver coin of late that would support my theory.

A breeze stirred through the open window, rustling the papers. I turned the pages over and looked back further in time: the outflows remained fairly regular and were similar to the more recent numbers. There was no evidence of a sudden inflow of silver consistent with the cargo of the *Santillana* having been landed, melted down and issued as new coins. I began to lose both heart and concentration.

My interrogation of the numbers was interrupted by the chorus of a score of *muezzins* across the city, calling the faithful for the night prayers. I continued to pore over the numbers until the candle that flickered in the lantern had burned right down. I could see no different interpretation from my master's: everything was in order. I concluded that either the accounts were right and my theory was wrong or the accounts were wrong, which would still allow for my theory to be correct. I blew the stub of the candle out and returned to my quarters. Pierre and Joaquin were already fast asleep.

In the morning, I made sure I was in the vestibule before my master departed on his daily business as I wanted to catch a word with him. I did not have to wait long; nor did I have to prompt the discussion as he spoke to me as soon as he had dispatched Joaquin on some errand.

'So Tom, did you find anything of interest?'

'No master. The accounts seemed in order. So either I am wrong or the accounts are wrong.'

'That was my interpretation too; but if the accounts are right, then the weakening of the currency remains inexplicable. I'm going to ask Youssuf and his men to pay the mint a visit today to check that the accounts stack up and to have a general look around the place to see if everything is in order. He'll report back directly to me.'

He swept out into the street and I closed the door behind him. Over the course of the morning, as I attended to my usual chores, I continued to mull over my theory, trying to reconcile it with the conflicting evidence from the accounts. I tried to think of anything more I could do to prove my theory one way or another, of whether I could substantiate any of my suppositions. The report of the controller of weights and measures would shed more light on the matter, but I wanted to be able to contribute something myself, if that were possible. My motivation was not only to please my master, but also because my pride was at stake.

It was while I was sweeping out the inner courtyard that I thought of one small thing that I could try. I resolved to pay Jacob and Silas a visit in the *bagnio* that evening. I knew that, during their period of captivity, they had mostly been working on repairing the mole: the massive breakwater that sheltered the city's harbour from the Mediterranean swell. It was a gruelling task that took a heavy toll on the men assigned to it. My reason for visiting them was that I thought they might have had the opportunity to see, during the daytime at least, the traffic to and from the *Santillana* before Murat Reis and his crew had departed. If the silver cargo had been brought ashore during daylight, then they should have noticed.

Late in the afternoon, I explained to Pierre that I had some business to do on behalf of the master and that I would need to go out for an hour or so. He looked surprised but did not question me further. I felt a pang of guilt at misleading him. I ran down the hill, in the knowledge that Jacob and Silas only had a couple of hours free after work each day, before the gates of the *bagnio* were locked at dusk.

The *bagnio* that was home to Jacob, Silas and a few hundred other slaves belonging to the state, was one of several dotted around the city. It was located at the southern end of Grand Market Street, close to the *Bab Azzoun*, the main gate leading out of the city to the south. The *bagnio* was a large, old rectangular building that jostled for space with its neighbours along the main thoroughfare. The heavy doors of its gatehouse were wide open and the guards uninterested as I strolled in.

Arcaded galleries on two stories faced each other across the *bagnio's* inner courtyard, linked on either side by high walls to complete the enclosure. The courtyard was a cauldron of humanity. At this time of day, the *bagnio* brimmed not only with slaves, who had finished their day's work, but also with motley ranks of men from all walks of life. These others had come to the *bagnio* to purchase some good or service, usually illicit, for within the confines of the *bagnio* were several makeshift shops and taverns. In return for a cut of the profits, the guards turned a blind eye to the enterprise of their inmates. There was even a hospital, of sorts, and a small chapel. In truth the *bagnios* were not, in my day at least, the hell-holes that encaptivated and terrorised the imaginations of all good Christian folk back home. Squalid and flea-ridden as they were, their incumbents fared no worse than convicts in many an English gaol.

I threaded my way through the crowd. The air in the courtyard was filled with a *mêlée* of languages – Italian, Spanish, French, Dutch and English – and with the stench of a hundred unwashed men. As I crossed the courtyard, I looked out for Jacob or Silas amid the throng. Not seeing them there I climbed the staircase in the far corner, proceeding to the upper arcade that gave access to their room. In the event, I saw Jacob, leaning on the balustrade overlooking the courtyard. He had a clay pipe in his hand and was watching the sunset, which was throwing golden light and the shadow of a minaret across the courtyard below. My approach disturbed his reverie.

'Well, if it's not young master Tom,' said Jacob as I approached. 'I see you're keeping well.'

'Yes, thank you Jacob,' I replied, 'it's good to see you again.'

'You mean it's good to see you still alive!' Silas interjected, emerging from the dark room that was home to the two of them and a dozen other men. 'Yes, we're still here, loving this place more with every day that passes.'

I blushed on account of my guilt at the relative good fortune of my position. I could never tell whether Silas had ever wholly forgiven me for the choice I had made aboard the *Sword*.

'Let him be, Silas,' said Jacob. 'What brings you here, Tom?'

I sat down on the balustrade beside Jacob, my back capturing the warmth of the sun.

'I have a question that I thought you might be able to help me answer,' I said.

'Go on,' said Jacob.

'Well, I've been thinking about the *Santillana* and her cargo.'

'All that silver, you mean?' asked Silas.

'That's right. Do you know what happened to it?' I asked. 'I mean, do you know whether it came ashore?'

'Well now,' said Jacob, taking a draw on his pipe, 'I don't so much as recall seeing any silver coming ashore.'

He paused in thought. Silas shook his head from side to side indicating that he could not help.

'But, what I can say,' Jacob went on, 'is that by the time the *Santillana* sailed away, she did seem to sit much higher in the water than when she had docked. Remarked as much to you, didn't I?' he looked at Silas.

'That you did, and I daresay you were right,' Silas replied, 'though it was a little hard to see because she was anchored some way down the shore.'

'So she was,' Jacob said nodding, 'along the bay, to the south.' He pointed in the direction of the Bab Azzoun, the top of which was just visible over the wall of the *bagnio*. 'They anchored her there on about the second day that we were sent to work on the mole. And, as I say, she lay much deeper in the water on that day than she did when she sailed away.'

'Didn't see much traffic going to and from her, mind you. Her crew had been sold off with the rest of us, so she was like a ghost ship,' said Silas.

A pause ensued and I realised that I had got about as much information in response to my question as they were able to give. I thanked them and was grateful that they did not ask about my interest in the matter, given my master's insistence that I keep it to myself.

'Have you had any news from home?' I asked, keen to change the subject of conversation.

'News of our ransom you mean?' asked Silas with a sneer.

'Frizell said he would write to petition His Majesty's government on our behalf,' said Jacob.

'But we ain't holding our breath,' added Silas.

'And what news of Adam and Will?' I asked.

'Well now,' said Jacob, 'Adam is still away on a corsair galley. To be honest, I doubt whether we'll see him again, poor lad. And as for Will, he's doing well, working as a butcher's lad these days: his first master sold him on at a fair profit, I believe. He drops in, like you do, from time to time.'

'As a youngster, he may not be as patient as we are for his ransom to arrive,' said Silas.

'You might, catch a word with him, if you're similarly inclined.' Jacob drew on his pipe and exhaled with a wink.

'You'll find him in the butchers' street,' added Silas, 'just follow the river of blood.'

'Thank you,' I said, 'I'll try to meet up with him some time soon.'

I took my leave and hurried up through the narrow, bustling streets. The cool promised by the dusk had enticed the inhabitants of Algiers out of their houses; the streets had come alive. When I returned to the master's house, Joaquin opened the door in haste and, with agitated hand gestures, told me that I was to proceed straight up to the master because he had asked for me some time ago.

Pierre cast me a frown as I entered the living room, before departing with a quiet cough, allowing me to take his place at the doorway. My master turned and beckoned me over to his desk. I felt like a schoolboy about to receive a reprimand from the schoolmaster. He rose to his feet to address me.

'I have news for you, Tom. Youssuf has done as I instructed and cross-checked the accounts of the mint against the inventory he found there.'

My eyes fixed on my master's; my breathing became shallow.

'On the face of it, everything seems to be in order,' he said.

My heart sank.

'The overall value of the gold and silver at the mint appears to be in keeping with the figure in the accounts.' He pointed at a number on the paper in front of him which had the current date upon it, as if to emphasize the point. 'And I trust Youssuf: he is a man of his word,' he added.

I stood there, no longer able to hold his gaze. I was annoyed at my pointless efforts and embarrassed that I had wasted the master's time and called into question the integrity of his associates. However, my master did not seem cross with me. I waited, longing to be given permission to leave, but it did not come. When I dared to raise my eyes up to gauge his expression, he was smiling at me – not a mocking smile but a kindly one.

'Let me tell you about another conversation that I had today,' he said, 'one that I think may be of interest to you. But come, let us first sit down upon the cushions.'

I followed him and sat down opposite him where he indicated, on one of the fine, silk cushions, as if I were one of his high-ranking guests.

'This afternoon, and not entirely by chance, I managed to catch a few words with Ali Biçnin. Do you know him?'

'Yes, I mean, I know of him.' In truth, everyone in the city knew of Ali Biçnin: the most extravagant renegade corsair captain then resident in Algiers.

'Well then, you will know that Ali Biçnin is currently funding the construction of the fine new mosque on Grand Market Street.'

I nodded. Everyone knew that Ali Biçnin was funding it: his benevolence had not been dispensed discreetly. Over the months that had passed since my arrival, I watched almost daily as its edifices took shape. There must have been hundreds of men working on its construction.

'I was asking him about the progress on his mosque. It's important that I take an interest as he seems to have half the workers in the city building it and the other half providing the supplies.'

'Yes, master.'

'Anyhow, in his usual modest way – incurable Venetian as he is – Ali Biçnin took pains to tell me just how much money he was spending on the mosque.'

It began to dawn on me why this conversation mattered.

'This was of course, exactly what I wanted to hear, and I took careful note to remember the numbers involved. I asked him how he was obtaining all the silver he needed to pay all his workers because, as you know, it is the silver asper that is the coin that wages are paid in. He laughed, and told me that each month of late, he had been taking around twenty thousand Venetian ducats to the mint and exchanging them for the equivalent sum in silver aspers – which he then had his men cart off to the mosque to pay his workers. And several carts they would have needed too. Suppose, as Ali Biçnin claimed, the mosque sets him back two hundred thousand ducats in total, then that would amount to 24 million aspers at the official rate of 120 to one. Enough to flood the whole city with silver coins, I should think.'

As I stood there, struggling to comprehend the sheer number of silver coins involved, he stroked his beard with his right hand. He seemed to be watching my expression, gauging my reaction.

'And that's the interesting thing,' he continued, 'particularly for your theory. When I looked again at the accounts of the mint, you can check them for yourself again in a moment if you like, I found no transactions registered that correspond to those that Ali Biçnin described. And while I wouldn't stake my reputation on his word alone – it's in his nature to exaggerate – I'm prepared to take him loosely at his word for now.'

'So neither the inflows of Ali Biçnin's gold were recorded, nor the corresponding outflows of silver?' I asked.

'That's right. And yet, you may be sure that the workers on the mosque have been paid, else they would have downed their tools long ago. They may be working for the glory of Allah, but they also need to put bread on their tables. They are all free men after all, not slave labour.'

'I see,' I said, though in truth my mind was stumbling forward trying to make sense of this new information.

'So here is my theory,' said my master, 'building upon yours.'

My heart leaped.

'The silver that was the cargo of the ship... the *Santillana*,' he struggled with the pronunciation, 'has indeed been secretly brought ashore and coined into aspers at the mint. And Ali Biçnin's golden ducats – well, they have been quietly pocketed by someone, or by several people, because they are not in the mint, which is where they ought to be. While the figures over there tell us that the overall value of the reserves in the mint is correct, there is too little gold and too much silver, given what should be there if Ali Biçnin's transactions took place.'

I ventured a response to ensure that I understood. 'So if the theory is wrong, and the *Santillana's* silver was not involved, the reserves should be awash with Ali Biçnin's gold and empty of silver.'

'Exactly, which is obviously not the case, just look at the figures over there, and that's why our theory still holds good. There's a little gold for sure, but not the tens of thousands of ducats that Ali Biçnin has paid in. Tom, the more I think about it, the more I think our theory holds water. What we lack is not logic but the evidence to prove it.'

I felt proud of the way he referred to it as *our* theory, even though he had developed it to a level of sophistication that was beyond my learning or experience. I decided that this was the right moment to reveal the news that I had learned from Jacob and Silas.

'Master, may I tell you what I have learned this evening.'

'Please do.'

'While you were at supper I was meeting with some acquaintances of mine in the *bagnio*. They were captured by Murat Reis around the same time as I was.'

'Go on.'

'They have often been working on the mole these last few months. I wanted to learn whether they could tell me anything more about the *Santillana* and her cargo.'

'And did they?'

'Yes, indirectly. They told me that over the course of several days while Murat Reis was still resident in the city, the *Santillana* sat higher in the water, as if she had been unloaded of her cargo.'

'And did they see the cargo coming ashore?'

'No they didn't. They said the ship was taken from the harbour and anchored some way along the shore of the bay, to the south of the city. They never saw any boats going to or from her, which would not be surprising as her crew had all been sold in the slave market with me.'

My master stroked, almost tugged at the end of his beard in silence. At length he spoke. 'So the theory is that the silver was brought ashore unseen, perhaps at night, outside the city. It was presumably hidden away somewhere and then secretly brought into the city, to the mint. And for each new load of silver received in the mint, whoever is behind this scheme simply took the equivalent amount of gold away from the mint for themselves, in the belief that, since the books of the mint still balanced, there would be no grounds for suspicion.'

I nodded in agreement.

My master got to his feet and walked over to the window to look down over the bay, as if looking out to where the *Santillana* had been anchored, though all was now obscured by darkness.

'Tom, you must keep this matter entirely between yourself and me. Tell no one else, do you understand?' He continued to face out of the window as he spoke these words.

'Yes, master.'

'I can tell you that Mehmet, the Controller of Customs, owns a farm, a summer villa with a stretch of shoreline, a little way down the coast to the south of the city. His good name must be preserved until there is evidence to substantiate our theory and to link him to the plot. As must Ahmed's – without whose knowledge as Treasurer of the Mint, none of our version of events could have unfolded.' He turned to face me. 'We need proof, Tom, and it is my duty to find it.'

'Of course, master.'

'It is said that Mehmet is the natural son of none other than the Sultan Murad III, Allah grant rest to his soul. I must proceed with the utmost care.'

'Mehmet's a prince?' I interjected.

'Mercifully not,' he replied with a wry smile. 'Mehmet was only a natural son, and it is said that Murad III, his father, had more than one hundred children. Nevertheless, it does make him the half uncle of the current sultan, Murad IV. And with the recent turmoil in the court following the murder of Osman II, Allah grant rest to his soul, it is difficult to know from out here whose star is rising and whose is falling. So I must act with great care, in case Mehmet has powerful connections. Making an accusation against him will be a serious matter indeed and could place us both in peril. And yet, if I do nothing then I fail in my duty and risk my reputation as our currency is undermined; which is why we need proof; hard evidence.'

A few minutes of silence ensued, my master continuing to gaze out into the darkness. I remained seated on my cushion, wondering how dangerous this game was in which I was now embroiled. At length I broke the silence. 'Master, am I right in thinking that it was Mehmet who purchased my two young friends, a boy and a girl, back on that day in the slave market.'

My master continued to face out of the window. 'Yes, you are right,' he said.

'If I could make contact with George – the boy – I could ask him discreetly whether he knew anything about the silver from the *Santillana*.'

I received no answer for a while. At length my master turned from the window to face me. 'Very well, I will send you on an errand to Mehmet's house tomorrow. You can try to make contact with the boy while you are there. But on no account must you reveal our suspicions to this boy.'

'Of course, master.'

'Now, I bid you goodnight Tom.'

I raised myself from the cushion and walked out of the room. Outside, from the upper gallery of the courtyard, I looked up and saw the sky awash with stars, the same constellations that I could look upon a world away on my island. My breast heaved with nervous excitement. I went down to my room and exchanged only a few words with Pierre and Joaquin before I went to bed. Once sleep had stilled my churning thoughts, I remember that I dreamt of my home on the island. I had returned there alone on a ship made of silver. I was back at the manor asking Mr Dillington where the money was to ransom me. He was telling me that he had received no letters from the consul. My mother and sister were both there too, crying.

Chapter 9: Evidence

I woke early, my tiredness overpowered by stomach-turning nervousness about what the day might hold in store. The morning was long, stretching out through a series of routine chores that provided no distraction for my thoughts. Every second, every minute was elongated so that the hours crawled forward, escalating my sense of anticipation. It was not until noon that Pierre tasked me with an errand: I was to go to the house of Mehmet, the Controller of Customs, with a letter from our master. It was not a house that I had visited before.

I walked down to the lower part of the city, to a quarter where the houses seemed more spacious. I followed Pierre's directions and located Mehmet's house. As I banged the fist-shaped knocker upon the studded wood of the door, my heart was racing at the prospect that George himself might answer. Instead the door was opened a sliver to reveal wary eyes set deep within a wizened face. The voice of an old man enquired as to my business. When I explained that I had a letter from my master, the *Hazinedar*, to the Controller of Customs he ushered me into the vestibule and then into another, larger ante-room. His wrinkled hand grabbed the letter. Without so much as a nod or grunt in acknowledgement, he pushed aside the heavy curtain that separated the ante-room from the inner courtyard of the house and scuttled away into the interior. The curtain swung back into place, embroidered artichokes dancing upon its folds.

Moments later I pinched a fold of the curtain between my thumb and forefinger and nudged it a couple of inches to one side, creating a small aperture through which I could view the courtyard. I had hoped to see George or Catherine at work there, but the courtyard was empty except for a gurgling fountain in the far corner. It was a large courtyard of the standard, arcaded design found throughout the city but the surrounding house extended upwards by an additional storey. Various doorways led off from the courtyard, some closed with curtains, others with wooden doors. There were grilles over the windows. I saw the old man disappear through one of the curtained doorways to my left, which I presumed led to a staircase to the upper floor where Mehmet would have his personal rooms.

A movement behind one of the grilled windows opposite me caught my eye. My heart began to pound so hard that I feared someone would hear it. I had but a moment to decide what to do next: whether to enter the courtyard to investigate further or whether to stay put in the safety of my vantage point behind the curtain. I was conscious that to stray into another man's home uninvited was a very serious matter in a society that placed such a high value on privacy; but if I did not go, I might never know whether George or Catherine were here. I made my decision.

I pushed the curtain a few more inches to the side and crept into the shadow of the arcade. With slippers silencing my footsteps, I darted around the courtyard until I approached the window on the far side through which I had seen the movement. I crouched down for a moment beneath the window, listening not daring to breathe. If I were caught in this position, I would be flogged or worse. From inside the room there came the chinking of crockery. Still crouching, I edged towards the adjacent doorway, which was covered by another curtain. With trembling fingers, I took hold of the heavy fabric and moved the curtain a fraction so that I could glimpse the interior. In the mottled light from the grilled window I made out the shape of a youth, taller than me, his back right in front of me. The youth, who was busy preparing a meal, was dressed in the plain, local style with a calf-length, seamless cloak. He had an iron ring around his right ankle and bare feet. He turned for a moment to one side to reach for a spoon and I made out the profile of his face. It was George. Quietly, unobserved, I slipped past the curtain and stood behind him.

'George,' I whispered. He jumped out of his skin, dropped a pot, which smashed on the floor and stood facing me, brandishing a wooden spoon and a ferocious stare.

'George, it's me, Tom.'

It took him some moments to make out my features, not helped by the fact that I stood with my back to the curtain, beyond the reach of the light from the window. It took him a little more time to make any sense of the situation. Then, of a sudden, he rushed at me and flung his arms around me in a firm embrace.

'What are you doing here, Tom? How–'

'Shhh. Not now,' I interrupted him. 'I only have a few seconds. Can you meet me to talk?'

George shook his head with a look of bewilderment.

'I'll come back this afternoon, during the afternoon prayers,' I said, 'and I'll hide myself away in the shadows outside your house. If you can get out, I'll see you there.'

I put my finger to my lips to curtail further conversation and left the room. Back in the courtyard, I could see the curtain covering the doorway of the ante-room opposite me and was tempted to bolt straight across the courtyard to reach it and the safety that lay beyond. As that temptation crossed my mind I saw, to my horror, a rippling in a curtain to my right. The old man who had taken the letter emerged, doubtless on his way back to the ante-room where he would expect to find me waiting. There was no way that I could run either around or across the courtyard without his seeing me. I was trapped inside. My thoughts raced as fast as my heartbeat. I stepped out into the courtyard and across to the fountain. I made a point of splashing the water over my face and drinking with a loud slurp.

The old man spun on his heel and looked at me, first with a look of confusion, then with one of unmistakeable anger. He hobbled towards me as fast as his frail legs would carry him and started to berate me. I offered profuse apologies, feigning a limited grasp of Turkish, but he lashed out an arm with surprising strength to give me a cuff on the ear. He cursed me in some local dialect as he pulled me by the arm back over to the ante-room. I made no attempt at resistance as he dragged me through the vestibule and pushed me out into the street, slamming the door behind me.

I returned in haste to my master's house. As Pierre let me in I explained to him that I had to return to Mehmet's house before afternoon prayers to wait for his response. Pierre frowned at me. Once more, I regretted lying to him, but had thought of no other way to excuse myself without revealing information that my master had told me to keep to myself. I ate a couple of filled dumplings, swept the courtyard and the roof terrace, and then headed back out, eager not to miss George should he succeed in slipping out of his master's house.

By the time I returned to Mehmet's street, the shade had begun to creep across the cobbles. I found myself a quiet corner where a side street branched off. From here I could keep watch over Mehmet's house, the shadows cloaking me. I rested my back against the cool wall and waited.

As the minutes passed, I watched the shade fill the street and scale the walls of the building opposite me. Lizards scuttled between the cobbles and up the walls in search of continued warmth. Every few minutes a decrepit old man would shuffle past, ancient fingers caressing *misbaha* beads in unending prayer; or a boy would pass by, sometimes with a donkey or mule in tow. I bought a cup of water from one young water-carrier with one of the copper coins that I carried in my purse. Occasionally a gaggle of women would sweep past, all shrouded in white. Sometimes the passer-by would be a tall African with a chain or a Jew in black garb. As I stood waiting at that street corner, I could feel the hot pulse of the city, its lifeblood coursing down one of its thousand veins.

As time passed I began to doubt whether George would manage to find a way out, indeed whether he ever managed to escape from his master's house. It occurred to me that I had never seen him about in the city. I reflected on whether I could have thought faster inside Mehmet's house and made some better arrangement or even extracted the information I needed from George there and then. Perhaps the old man had realised that George had been conversing with me and had locked him up to punish him.

From above me, somewhere beyond the neighbouring rooftops, I heard the local *muezzin* begin the call for afternoon prayers. Distracted for a moment by the sound, it was not until the door of Mehmet's house had banged shut that I noticed that someone had appeared on the street. Any hope that it might be George vanished as I saw the old man who had chastised me that morning now stooping and stumbling down the hill. I retreated further into the shadows of the side street, which proved to be one of the many dead ends that littered the labyrinthine city. I watched the old man pass by, praying that he would not look my way. I waited for a breathless minute before returning to my former position at the street corner.

119

A short while later, the studded door opened again and I watched a second figure emerge from the house. This time the door did not bang shut. George took one, wary step into the street, looking up and down but making no further advance. I took this as my cue and ventured out from the shadows and across the street. Once again, George embraced me.

'Quick,' he said, 'step inside.'

I did as he asked and he shut the door behind me.

'Old Hassan – the porter – will be at the mosque for half an hour, sometimes less,' he said, 'so we should have a bit of time, but not much.' His face looked white with nerves but his eyes were bright.

'If he returns,' I said, trying to sound reassuring, 'then I'll say that my master sent me back to collect a reply. You kindly let me in.'

'The master's family and his other servants are still inside,' he added, 'so we must keep our voices low.'

I nodded in agreement, and almost whispered, 'So how are you, George?'

Before answering he invited me to take a seat beside him on a low bench set along one side of the vestibule. 'I'm all right,' he said. 'Catherine is here too. She lives in the women's quarters, so I don't see her much. But she's also in good health.'

'That's good,' I replied. 'And are you treated well?'

'Could be worse,' George grumbled. 'My master provides a roof over our heads and enough food for us to live on, but I work hard for it.'

I nodded again, to show that I understood. 'It's good to see you, George.'

'How did you find me?' he asked.

'My master and yours are friends, or rather acquaintances. I recognised your master when he came round to dine with us the other night. I remembered him from the day of the auction, and my master confirmed that he was the one who bought you and Catherine. Anyway, my master sent me here on an errand, so I took my chance to see if I could find you; and it worked.'

I smiled and he smiled back. I was keen to enquire more about his life here but I was equally aware of the purpose of my visit and that time was short. I had to focus on extracting any relevant information that he could provide. I reasoned, perhaps trying to justify my actions to myself, that by helping to prove the case against his master I might be able to do something to assist George and Catherine. I knew that I was putting George, without his knowledge, in a precarious position.

'George, I need to ask you something, but can you keep this conversation a secret?'

'Of course,' he replied; his cheeks flushed a little.

'All right. Do you remember that Spanish ship, the one the corsairs captured on our way to Algiers?'

'The *Santillana*?' he replied. 'Of course, I was up in the crow's nest while we gave chase to her on the *Sword*.'

'Good. And do you remember what her cargo was?'

'Of course I do. It was silver, and lots of it.'

'That's right: a shipload of silver bullion. I wonder if they managed to offload it.'

'They surely did and I reckon I know where it ended up as well.'

My eyes must have lit up, encouraging him to continue.

'My master has a farm, not far from the city, along the shore. I accompany him there with the rest of the household when he's in residence. Only old Hassan stays here, to watch over the place.'

'Go on,' I said.

'Well, not long after I started working in my master's household, I was taken down to that farm. While I was out working in the fields I spotted the *Santillana* anchored a little way offshore.'

'Do you think she was anchored near the farm for a reason?'

'Yes. My master's farm has a jetty, mainly for loading grain and other crops. One evening, just as dusk was falling and I was finishing my work, I noticed a boat arriving at that jetty as if from the *Santillana*. I dallied long enough to watch it unload and then return to the ship. I know that a fair few boatloads passed between the *Santillana* and the jetty that night. I even heard some of the crew of the *Sword* talking as they unloaded the cargo from the boats. I couldn't understand the Dutch ones, but I recognised some of their voices.'

'Were they bringing silver ashore?'

'Yes. They took it into one of the barns on my master's farm. Then they went away.'

'And what happened after that?'

'Well, I don't think I was on the farm long enough to see all the comings and goings but in each of the remaining days that I was there, a wagon would arrive on the farm at around midday. The men from the wagon would load it up with boxes of silver from the barn. They took pains to make sure that the silver was hidden under a good layer of hay from one of the other barns. And they headed off back in the direction of the city.'

'And was your master involved?'

George paused, his eyes wary. 'Yes, I saw him. He had the barn opened for them and he watched them load the wagons. He would check that the silver in the wagons was all covered over with hay, and the men sure felt it if it was not hidden to his liking. He also made sure the barn was properly locked up afterwards. Like I say, I don't think I was there to see everything that went on. I spend most of my time here in this house. I don't really go out anywhere else.'

'Thank you, George. You've told me what I needed to know.'

He looked at me, as if lost in thought.

I felt I should say more. 'You know that if I can do anything to help you and Catherine then I will.'

George said nothing. It was the first time I had ever seen his eyes without their lustre.

'Now I must go,' I said, patting him on the arm, 'before we both get into trouble with Hassan. My ear is still ringing from where he boxed me earlier on.' He gave me a knowing nod.

I rose to my feet and George followed.

'Send my best wishes to Catherine,' I said. He nodded and opened the door for me.

I stepped out into the street, looking around to make sure that old Hassan was not hobbling back. The street was deserted and I scampered back up the hill to my master's house.

That night, my master again asked me to sit with him and share our news. I sat upon the same silk cushion as on the previous night. I knew that a letter had arrived from Mehmet in the early evening, though Pierre had taken it directly to my master.

'So, Tom, in a moment you must tell me whether you discovered anything from your friend in Mehmet's house. But first, I will tell you what Mehmet replied in his letter. In my letter to him I had said that we had found nothing suspicious in the mint and enquired as to whether he or any of his contacts could shed any new light on proceedings, as my suspicion remained that a large amount of silver had entered the city recently.'

He unrolled Mehmet's letter in his hands and read snatches of words. 'He says he is "regrettably none the wiser"; "none of his customs officials knows anything about it"; "wishes he could be more helpful".' He allowed the letter to roll itself back up and placed it at his side. Then he smiled at me with a glint in his eye. 'So does that tally with what you learned today?'

'No master, it doesn't.'

'I didn't think it would.'

'My friend, Mehmet's servant, told me that he had witnessed the cargo of silver from the *Santillana* being offloaded into a barn on Mehmet's farm. Mehmet had been there to supervise proceedings, as he also was when the cargo was transported into the city, concealed in hay wagons.'

'You are sure he said that Mehmet was there?'

'Yes, he said that his master personally ensured that the silver was well hidden in the wagons.'

'And you believe your friend.'

'Absolutely,' I said.

'How old is he?'

I had to stop and think for a moment. 'He is about fourteen years old.'

'And does he know whether any of the silver is still in the barn?'

'He didn't say.'

'Well, it's been around two years now, but if they were being careful about it, not rushing things, there remains a small chance there might still be some there. And it's our best chance of getting some hard evidence.

'How would we find out?' I asked.

'I would have the barn searched, by the *oçak*.'

The *oçak* were the Turkish janissaries – the men that Joaquin had taught me to make way for should I meet them in the street. They both fought for the city and upheld its laws.

'But first,' he went on, 'I must speak to the Pasha about this matter, particularly on account of the parentage of the chief suspect. If we were to make a false accusation against Mehmet then it could turn out very badly for us, Tom, very badly indeed. I will speak to the Pasha tomorrow. I now have sufficient cause to justify a search of Mehmet's farm.'

He stood up and walked over to his desk, rummaged among a pile of papers and then held one aloft. Though I could not read it from the other side of the room, I could make out that it was one of the reports provided from the mint.

'And here it is,' he said, waving the paper in his right hand. 'The numbers that show that there is too little gold in the mint and too much silver. Now that we can link the silver to Mehmet's barn, we have grounds for a search. And if we find any silver there then we have grounds for a trial.'

I lowered my eyes to the floor. From what I had seen, justice in the city was brutal and swift: adulterers were drowned; fraudsters were strangled; and even petty thieves had their right hands cut off and slung over their shoulders before being paraded through the streets. I had no wish to be involved in such justice being meted out on anyone. The thought of it made my stomach turn.

'Mehmet is not the only one who should face trial,' my master continued. 'Someone in the mint must also have been complicit. Ahmed, the Treasurer of the Mint, must either have known and been party to this arrangement or else he is wholly incompetent at his work.'

I nodded slowly in agreement, reluctant to cast the net further and bring more people to face justice on my account.

'Thank you, Tom,' he said, 'that will be all for tonight.'

I stood up, bowed my head and left the room.

The next morning, my master set off early, dressed in a particularly fine outfit with an embroidered vest, his best slippers and a large silk turban. I guessed he was on his way to the palace to speak with the Pasha.

The minutes again passed like hours that morning. I tried to immerse myself in my chores – sweeping the rooms, preparing dinner, watering the plants on the roof terrace – but I could not shift my thoughts from imagining what was unfolding in the palace and what was going to happen thereafter.

At about 11 o'clock there was a loud knock on the door, which Joaquin answered. He came to find me as I was at work on the terrace and told me that I was wanted immediately. When I reached the vestibule, a man was waiting for me, pacing around the small room. I could see straight away from his striking uniform that he was a member of the janissary, the dreaded *oçak*. His egg-shaped turban was so tall that he had to stoop to avoid the ceiling. He wore a smart red jacket with a broad sash around his waist in which he carried his *yataghan* sword and pistol. His blue pantaloons ballooned out above his boots. He looked me up and down dismissively, his bare chin thrust outwards beneath his trimmed moustache.

'Follow me,' he ordered.

I followed his long strides out of the house and for a short distance until we reached a building in the shadows of the Kasbah. I knew this to be the headquarters of the janissary. The place filled me with trepidation. At the front of the building I could see a group assembled. There were about a dozen men, most in the same uniform as the one who had escorted me here, and a similar number of horses being held by stablehands. As I approached, I was relieved to see my master amongst the throng. He saw my approach and beckoned me to join him, stepping out from the crowd.

'Tom, I want you to come with us. We are going to search the barn. Do you know how to ride?'

'Yes,' I said.

'Good. Here is your horse.' He turned and pointed to a fine, brown stallion and summoned the stablehand to lead him to me. Then he signalled to the captain of the janissaries that we were ready to depart. The janissaries and my master all mounted their steeds and I did likewise, clambering into a magnificent red saddle. 'We ride immediately,' he shouted over to me, 'so that there is no time for a warning to be given ahead of our arrival.'

This was the first of many occasions, from that day forward, on which I accompanied my master on his business. Long afterwards I reflected that he had no reason, no need to bring me with him on that day but he had a generous disposition. Few masters would have behaved in such a way towards a servant in their household, and for that I will be forever in his debt.

We rode in pairs, which was all that the street could accommodate, even though it was wide by the standards of the city. The noise of the hooves clashing against hard cobbles, coupled with the dazzling red and blue of the uniforms, must have created quite a spectacle. We drew the gaze of many an onlooker as we passed and sent many a child scuttling out of our path into the safety of the adjoining side streets and alleys.

We rode out of the city through an imposing gate in the southern wall known as the New Gate or *Babbaxidir* and across the stream that tumbled down beside the city wall. It was the first time that I had left the confines of the city since my disembarkation from the *Sword* two years before. It was a wonder to behold the greenery of the fields spreading out like a lush carpet before us, dotted with whitewashed farmsteads.

We rode in a tight formation towards the sea until we joined the main road running south from the city, skirting the wide bay. We passed camel trains and herds of sheep and cattle, all heading for the city. As we rode, my master brought his horse up beside mine so that he was able to talk to me. 'The Pasha said that Mehmet's mother has no influence in Istanbul. Indeed, that explains why Mehmet was sent all the way out here.'

'So the Pasha is not going to protect him?' I asked.

'No. *Inshallah* there will be a trial tomorrow.'

We had not ridden for more than a couple of miles before we left the main road and headed off down a small track leading towards the shore. Ahead of me I could see farm buildings arranged within an encircling wall. We rode up to the gate of the compound and dismounted. The horses were tethered: some to rings on the wall and some to trees. The leader of the *oçak* rapped on the gate. I wondered whether anyone would be inside if the household was resident in the city. At length an old man opened the gate. He was evidently stunned by the imposing men that towered before him and was brushed aside. The janissaries streamed into the farm compound and we followed. My master spoke to their leader and pointed in the direction of the three barns that surrounded the whitewashed farmhouse.

The janissaries divided themselves into three groups and marched off towards each of the barns. I followed one of the groups in the direction of the only barn that was locked – the others having an open doorway. My master was at my side. It took only a couple of kicks by one of the heftier janissaries to splinter the door, making its lock redundant. His comrades forced the door open. The old man flapped around us in a panic until one of the janissaries pinned him against the wall of the compound. The rest of our search party entered the barn. We were confronted by an untidy array of hay stacks. Various farm tools lined the wooden walls. The janissaries began to rummage through the hay with their hands and their feet in such a flurry of activity that the air inside the barn was soon thick with blades of dried grass and dust. My master and I watched over the proceedings.

The first of the haystacks proved to consist of nothing more than hay, as did the second and the third. I began to think that the silver, if it ever was here, was long gone. More haystacks were dismembered in the frantic search: nothing. I exchanged a quick glance with my master, whose face was etched with doubt or concern, an expression that I had rarely witnessed on him. One by one the haystacks were taken apart, right down to the floor. Nothing was found. The groups searching the other barns began to muster in the doorway of our barn. I overheard that they too had found nothing. All eyes seemed to be turning towards my master. With the searching over, the barn descended into silence, broken only by occasional mutterings amongst the *oçak*. The dust in the air began to settle on the floor. The heat inside the barn was intense.

As a distraction from the awkwardness of the situation, my right foot kicked around idly in the hay. Behind me, I could hear my master and the leader of the *oçak* conversing about what to do next. Meanwhile, the old man from the gate had been released to intrude on the scene. He was shouting and pulling the splintered door back and forth, as if for effect. The janissaries allowed him to continue, perhaps voicing their own disgruntlement at their wasted efforts.

As the splintered door swung back and forth, the bright afternoon sun flashed in repeatedly, illuminating the motes of hay dust in the hot air of the barn. Amid the flashes, my eye caught the sudden glint of something half buried in the hay and the dirt on the floor. I cleared the hay away from it with my foot, and there it was: a gleaming, silver coin.

'Master,' I called, twisting round. He looked over in my direction, cutting his conversation short. 'Master, look,' I said again, like a young boy showing his father a curious shell that he has found upon the shore.

He walked forward calmly. All eyes in the barn followed him. I pointed the curled-up tip of my right slipper at the small, shiny object in the hay below me.

He stooped down and picked it up, holding it up so that it glinted in the unbroken sunshine; even the old man had ceased his tantrum. I could see it was not a local coin. My master examined it. The captain of the *oçak* came to inspect it too. Once he had seen it he moved over in my direction, causing me to wonder at his next move. Then he too began to kick around in the hay near my feet. Moments later he had found what he was looking for, another coin and then another. The other janissaries joined in. In total five coins were found – hardly a treasure trove but sufficient to suggest that a hoard of silver had once been concealed in the barn. My master brought the first coin, the one I had found, over to me to inspect. I now saw that it was foreign in its design. I could only presume that it had come from one of those strange lands in the Americas where the Spaniards hold sway.

I exchanged glances with my master.

'Proof,' he said, 'hard proof.'

The janissaries spent another half an hour or so kicking around amongst the hay in that barn. They also went back to search the other barns in more detail. They found only a couple more coins for all their sweltering efforts, and only in the same barn where the first coins had been found. But they were sufficient. Mehmet would have some explaining to do.

There is not much that I need report about our return to the city, though I relished it: the easterly breeze blowing in from the sea, ruffling my hair; the spiky cactuses lining the roadside and the aloes with their strange, fleshy leaves; goldfinches singing in the trees and darting among the vines; the rolling hills beyond the fields; and the approaching city, on which the late afternoon sun now fell, softening the glaring white of its buildings with a tint of gold. Above all I enjoyed the knowledge that our mission had been a success and that my master was content. A couple of the janissaries walked back to the city with the old man from the farm, as my master had requested that they take him into their custody, in case he were needed as a witness during the forthcoming trial.

Back inside the city, our cavalcade returned to the janissaries' quarters. As my master was engrossed in conversation with the *oçak* captain, I left my horse with a stablehand and walked back alone to our house, a swing in my step. The janissaries retained custody of six of the coins; my master retained the first one – the one that my right foot had found, guided perhaps by the unseen hand of Fortune.

That night, after we had eaten in our separate quarters, my master again asked me to come up to his living room to discuss matters. I sat down upon my usual cushion; my master remained standing, his back to the window.

'Tomorrow, there will be a trial,' he said. 'Both Mehmet and Ahmed will be brought before the *kadi*,' which is their word for a judge. 'You must be there, Tom. I will call you as a witness.'

I said nothing but nodded.

'I intend to call your friend too – the one from Mehmet's household.'

I knew he was referring to George and I winced, which did not go unnoticed. The last thing I wanted was to bring George into conflict with his master. His life was doubtless hard enough without that.

'Is that necessary, master?'

He seemed to sense my concern and to reflect on the matter.

'Perhaps it is not, though we may yet need to state that we could bring forth a witness to testify that the silver from the ship was offloaded into Mehmet's barn with his full knowledge. It may not come to that, though, if they confess when confronted with the facts.'

'Will they confess?' I asked.

'They would be fools not to, once they hear the strength of the case against them. They would be better to admit that they brought in the silver but to seek to excuse their actions on some pretext or other.'

'Will that work for them?'

'We must wait and see,' he said. He produced the strange silver coin from the silk purse that he kept in his scarf. 'They have a lot to explain; a lot to excuse.'

We spoke some more about the proceedings of the day. He was keen to know how I had liked my horse and my excursion into the countryside. I told him that I had loved them, that they reminded me of the life and freedom I had enjoyed at home. It was a statement that seemed to move him and, for the first time, he enquired some more about my former life, back on the island. He questioned and I answered for about another half an hour until I had given him a detailed picture of my life back home. Then he bade me good night and I returned to my room on the ground floor. Joaquin and Pierre were engrossed in a game of cards and I watched them and chatted about nothing in particular for a while. Then I went to my bed and fell soundly asleep, my body aching from the exertions of the day.

Chapter 10: Justice

The sun had not long risen when my master left the house the next morning. I was up and waiting to catch a word with him in the vestibule before he departed. He had selected a fine outfit for the occasion: a blue caftan with a white embroidered trim, beneath a velvet cloak. A large turban added gravity to his appearance. He told me to expect a summons later in the day. Islamic justice was swift, so there was every chance that the trial would be over before dusk. As far as I was concerned the verdict could not come soon enough; I just wanted it all to be over. My nerves felt like they had already been strained to breaking point.

It was early in the afternoon when a messenger arrived at the house to escort me to the courtroom. The court was already in session. There were around two dozen people in total, including clerks and messengers, all sat cross-legged upon the multitude of carpets that littered the floor. The *kadi*, or judge, sat apart on a cushion against the far wall and everyone else sat facing him in a rough crescent. He was an old man, clothed in a plain brown caftan and modest turban. His wrinkled face was illuminated by his white beard and eyebrows. My entry into the room brought about a pause in proceedings as the *kadi* glanced up and noted my arrival. Two dozen pairs of eyes surveyed me, triggering a fresh wave of palpitations. I spotted my master in the front row and he inclined his head as he caught my eye.

I sat down on one of the cushions at the back and to the left of the courtroom and tuned into the conversation, which was in Turkish. A scribe was writing down the key points at a table beside the wall to my left. My master, sitting cross-legged in his blue caftan, was setting out the case against Mehmet, the Controller of Customs, and Ahmed, the Treasurer of the Mint. The two accused men were also sitting in the front row, but on the other side of the *kadi* from my master. Mehmet looked bored and seemed more interested in the decorations of the ceiling than my master's words; Ahmed, in contrast, sat with his head cocked as if straining to follow each of my master's points.

'This court should be aware,' my master explained, 'that in the year before last, Murat Reis, in command of his ship, the *Saif al-Din*, captured a large Spanish vessel named the *Santillana del Mar* and brought her here to Algiers, laden with a very large cargo of silver from the Americas. And to bear witness to these facts, I ask my servant, who was present on board the *Saif al-Din* at the time, to confirm that they are true.' He looked over his shoulder towards me.

All eyes in the court turned again to me. The scribe raised his head and asked my name, which I gave to him. Then I swallowed hard and said, in my best Turkish, 'Yes, the facts as they have just been set out are correct.'

As I finished, Mehmet tutted in disgust and exclaimed: 'Well, of course he would say that, he's no more than an ignorant, dishonest slave boy, who will say anything his master bids him. Surely your case doesn't rest on the word of this infidel slave?'

I felt blood rush to my cheeks, gripped by a mixture of shame and anger.

'Come now Mehmet,' my master responded calmly, 'at the very least you know that he is an educated young man.'

At this point, from over to my right, another voice cut in – it was Youssuf, who was the official responsible for the enforcement of weights and measures. 'I can vouch for that. He can recite the Koran and explain its finer points, as you know full well.' His point was addressed to Mehmet. It prompted an outbreak of whispering amongst the onlookers in the room.

'Thank you,' said the *kadi*, 'please proceed, Ibrahim.'

My master continued to outline our theory, explaining how he believed that a massive quantity of illicit silver had recently been minted in the city. This, he argued, had led both to the weakening of the currency, which had brought shame upon our city, and to the recent price rises, which had caused consternation and hardship amongst the people.

When he had finished setting out the case, the *kadi* asked Mehmet to respond. Mehmet's voice crackled with anger as he spoke. 'Well, *Hazinedar*, you have concocted a clever theory, a theory that could exonerate you from your mismanagement of the city's finances and your responsibility for the spiralling prices and shameful weakening in our currency. But it is a theory that is wholly without foundation, wholly without evidence. I have done nothing wrong. I have no case to answer here. This whole case is a scandal, and my good name has been slandered.'

The Treasurer of the Mint nodded in whole-hearted agreement, his heavy turban swaying back and forth as he did so.

Having waited for Mehmet to finish saying his piece, my master stood up and walked the few paces over the carpeted floor to the *kadi*. With a theatrical gesture he brought forth the strange, silver coin I had found in Mehmet's barn and held it aloft, so that it glinted in the light streaming through the windows, before presenting it to the *kadi*.

'This, he said, is evidence that a quantity of silver from the Americas was stored in Mehmet's farm, a little to the south of the city.'

Over to my right, I saw Mehmet's eyes bulge for a moment, before he regained his composure and his expression returned to one of indifference. The *kadi* inspected the coin in his palm with interest, squinting as if to interpret some of the curious inscriptions. As my master returned to take his seat upon his cushion he posed a question to Mehmet. 'Your farm has its own jetty, does it not, for loading and offloading cargos?'

Mehmet snapped back: 'Yes, of course it does, but it is purely for agricultural goods, that is not against the law, is it *Hazinedar*? And this coin that you say you found, how can this court know whether you really found it on my farm? All that they know is that you claim to have found it there. I simply don't believe you and why should anyone else?'

My master smiled and nodded his head. 'Then if you do not believe me, perhaps you and the court will believe the captain of the *oçak*?'

Right on cue, the captain of the janissaries, dressed once again in his splendid uniform, rose to his feet. As he stood I saw that his fists were clenched. Slowly, in full view of those assembled, he unclenched his fingers. On each of his palms was a small pile of silver coins, which he revealed as if this were the culmination of some magic trick. As he walked or rather processed towards the

133

kadi, balancing the coins on his open palms, those seated in front of him made way, so that he could pass unhindered. He handed the coins to the *kadi* and then turned and addressed the rest of the court. 'My men found these coins on Mehmet's farm yesterday. Perhaps the court will believe *me*.' Then he returned to his seat.

A hush descended upon the court, which my master punctured. 'As I was saying, a quantity of silver was stored at your farm. How do you account for it?' He again aimed his question at Mehmet.

Mehmet rolled his eyes. 'I know nothing of this silver. I have done nothing wrong.'

'Perhaps then, I will need to call your servant, Suleiman, as a witness. He looks after your farm and we have him in our custody.'

Mehmet sat in stubborn silence, his arms folded on his lap. Ahmed looked increasingly uncomfortable.

My master continued. 'But perhaps that will not be necessary and my friend the Controller of Customs will come to remember about the silver in his barn in due course, it was some time ago after all.'

Again, Mehmet offered no reply.

'So, you contrived, with the assistance of the *emin* of the mint here, to smuggle the silver into the city, hidden in hay wagons from your farm. It is curious though, that there is no record of its arrival – but then you are responsible for such things, as the official in charge of customs, are you not, Mehmet?'

'If there had been such a cargo, then doubtless it would have been recorded. Since there is no record, it is evidence that this cargo of silver is pure fantasy, nothing more than a handful of strange coins.'

'If only that were so,' my master continued. He turned to the Treasurer of the Mint. 'And you, Ahmed, it was your job to take this smuggled silver and melt it down, no questions asked. How much was your cut?'

Any blood left in Ahmed's face now drained out. 'The accounts of the mint are all in order,' he said in a loud voice that was clearly intended to convey confidence but was instead undone by its lack of conviction. He produced a roll of paper and waved it around in the direction of the *kadi* so that one of the clerks came and collected it from him and passed it to the judge. The *kadi* unrolled the paper and squinted at what I presumed was a set of accounts for the mint.

'And what do these figures purport to show?' he asked Ahmed.

'They show that the accounts are all in order, that the value of the coins and bullion in the mint is just as it should be.'

The *kadi* let out an exasperated sigh, clearly finding the document as impenetrable as I had done at first. He put the paper down on the floor so that it curled up upon itself once more.

'Well,' he said, 'it should be straightforward to prove that one way or another. What is your case, *Hazinedar?*'

'My case is that though the value of bullion and coin in the mint is indeed correct—'

Mehmet interjected a peal of exaggerated laughter that sent a shiver to the end of my spine.

My master continued unfazed. 'The accounts are nevertheless by no means in order. They show too much silver and too little gold.'

'Oh, I presume you have evidence of that too?' replied Mehmet.

I observed that Ahmed's eyes had grown as wide as an owl's as he waited on my master's next words.

'Ahmed, please tell me how much gold there is in the mint today,' my master asked calmly.

'As shown in the accounts,' Ahmed motioned towards the roll of paper in front of the *kadi*, 'there is around five thousand ducats' worth of gold in the mint.'

'Five thousand ducats, that is a reasonable sum,' my master said. Then he turned to the *kadi*, 'I would like to call another witness.'

The judge nodded his assent.

'Now I could at this point call upon any of a number of workers in the mint who might support my version of events, but lest their testimony be questionable, I will instead call upon the evidence of an independent witness, Ali Biçnin.'

A collective gasp of surprise was shared around the people who had come to watch the proceedings in the court. I turned over my shoulder and watched the great corsair stand up at the rear of the room. As he stood, he smoothed down his velvet cloak, which flowed over his magnificent crimson caftan.

'Ali Biçnin, could you tell the court how much gold you have been exchanging in the mint in recent months please?' my master asked.

The old corsair smiled a wide smile. His eyes twinkled beneath his huge red turban, which sprouted a flamboyant array of ostrich feathers. '*Hazinedar,*' he replied in his unmistakeable Italian accent, 'as you know, of late I have been regularly bringing ten thousand gold ducats to the mint each month, exchanging them for the silver aspers with which I pay for those working to the glory of Allah on my humble mosque.' This revelation of the scale of his expenditure elicited further gasps from the some of the onlookers in the court.

'Thank you, Ali,' said my master, signalling that he had heard enough. The corsair sat down ceremoniously and my master turned back to face the *kadi*. 'So, ten thousand ducats brought to the mint each and every month over this last year and more; but where has all this gold gone, because as the Treasurer of the Mint has told us there are only five thousand ducats in total in the mint? It has simply disappeared.'

He paused, either for dramatic effect or to let the audience catch up, before continuing to set out his case.

'And, just as miraculously, every month for these past two years, Ali Biçnin's men have been paid, paid in millions of newly minted aspers, that have flooded the city with silver and undermined our currency. Minted out of what? Perhaps they were minted out of thin air or out of "a fantasy"? Or perhaps the truth is that they were minted out of a silver cargo, brought here by Murat Reis, without paying any customs duty and smuggled to the mint by these two men,' he pointed at Mehmet and Ahmed. 'I allege that they have pocketed Ali Biçnin's gold and in doing so made a handsome profit over whatever they paid Murat Reis for his cargo of silver.'

Mehmet sat smirking, his head held high. Ahmed sat ashen faced, shaking his head from side to side; it looked to me to be in bewilderment rather than in denial.

The *kadi* looked at them. 'Well, Mehmet, what do you say in response to Ibrahim's allegation?'

'I say what I have said all along, that I have done nothing wrong. As Ibrahim himself concedes, the value of the bullion and coin in the mint is just as it should be.'

'And what do you say for yourself?' the *kadi* now addressed Ahmed.

There was a long pause before Ahmed replied. 'My response is the same as Mehmet's, the accounts are in order.'

The *kadi* raised his thin, white eyebrows to affect a look of incredulity. He maintained his gaze on Ahmed. There followed a prolonged silence in the courtroom. All eyes remained fixed on the Treasurer of the Mint. My heart throbbed in my breast. In the end Ahmed capitulated.

'As I said,' Ahmed faltered, 'we did nothing wrong. All the gold was converted into silver at the official exchange rate. It was all in order. The mint lost nothing.'

Mehmet flashed Ahmed a murderous look. The latter lowered his eyes to the floor. His head and shoulders seemed to sag under the oppressive weight of his turban.

My master waited a few more seconds before intervening to remove the pressure on Ahmed. 'But the people have suffered from the rising prices. They are angry Ahmed. And the reputation of the city has also suffered from the weakness in its coinage. It was your responsibility to ensure this did not happen.' He paused again for a moment before concluding in a final address to the *kadi*. 'What has occurred here, as I have set out, and as Ahmed has now admitted, has been a most serious act of dishonesty, of fraud no less, which has given rise to the serious repercussions for the city that we all know about, indeed that we have all paid for, out of our own pockets.'

Silence descended again upon the court. The *kadi* rose to his feet. 'That concludes this session of the court,' he said. I would like to speak privately to the Controller of Customs and the Treasurer of the Mint. I will also consult with the imam concerning any precedents that we may draw from scripture. The court will reconvene immediately after dusk prayers.'

Everyone rose to their feet and the tension that had gripped the courtroom for the past half hour evaporated into fervent chattering. My master told me that I could leave and I did not hesitate for one second. I walked home alone, my mind revisiting the proceedings as they had unfolded and wondering what would happen next. As I walked and wondered I bit each of my fingernails down to the quick, before I realised what I had done. On reflection, I thought my master had done enough to prove his case. I knew also that he had great faith in the fairness of Islamic justice. However, I also knew that the case was complex, and the defendants, or at least Mehmet, had powerful friends and relatives. I dreaded the repercussions should the verdict not go in my master's favour and Mehmet walked free.

When I arrived back at the house, Pierre set me to work white-washing one of the exterior walls. I was grateful for the task, as I needed to do something to keep busy and to divert my thoughts. When, after an hour, and with the assistance of a long ladder, I had finished one wall, I volunteered to do another. I painted and painted, climbing up and down the ladder, until my arms and legs ached beyond reckoning, until my hands and clothes were splashed with lime, until the walls of the house sparkled in the evening sunlight. The sunset brought neither pleasure nor relief; the longer the delay in my master's return, the more I feared that the verdict had gone against us.

The night had fallen and dusk prayers had long concluded by the time my master returned. I had given up waiting for him in the vestibule and had retired to my bed to rest my weary limbs and to seek some distraction or solace in the verses of the Koran. In truth I read little as the text seemed to swirl in the flickering light and I found myself reading the same lines over and over again.

Joaquin came from the vestibule to tell me that the master had returned and wished to see me. I leapt out of bed and took the stairs to the first floor two at a time. When I entered breathless into the living room, I found my master sitting on his usual cushion, a bowl of dates laid upon the low table in front of him. He invited me to sit and to help myself to the dates. I looked for some clue as to the outturn of the trial in his expression but it was inscrutable.

'Tom, the *kadi* has delivered his verdict. Please, help yourself.' He gestured to the dates again and took one himself. I had little option but to do likewise.

'After the court session had concluded this afternoon,' he continued at last, 'the *kadi* spoke separately with the two accused men. The *kadi* is wise; he is a shrewd judge of character. As he explained to us once the court had reconvened, he first spoke with Ahmed. When he was alone with the *kadi* and was confronted with the evidence against him, Ahmed confessed to his role. Please, have another date. Would you like some water?'

I took another date but declined the water. My master continued his account of the proceedings.

'It was Ahmed who committed the fraud, by falsifying the accounts of the mint. He deliberately omitted to record either the inflows of silver bullion from Mehmet's farm or the inflows of gold bullion from Ali Biçnin. And as we suspected, though it was never recorded, the silver bullion from the *Santillana* was melted down and minted into new coins, which Ali Biçnin took away with him to pay his workers. Meanwhile, Mehmet took away Ali Biçnin's gold.

'Now the best that can be said of this sorry tale, and the *kadi* made note of this, was that the gold and silver were exchanged at the proper, official rate, so there was no theft in that sense, which is why the overall value of bullion and coin in the mint remains correct. But, as the *kadi* made clear, that did not excuse the failure of Ahmed to undertake his duty and record these transactions.'

'And Ahmed confessed to all of this?'

'Yes, to all of that and more; more than even we had conjectured. Ahmed told the *kadi* that, for his part in the scheme, Mehmet had paid him three hundred ducats. And so, you may wonder how Mehmet benefited from this enterprise.'

'Yes – it's hard to see how he profited at all, because the gold he took from the mint was only of the same worth as the silver he paid into it, at the official rate anyway.'

'That's right. In principle, Mehmet could have sold the gold he took from the mint in the market and made himself a handsome profit, because it would have fetched a much better price in silver in the market than the official price he paid Ahmed for it. But it seems he did not do that, maybe because there would have been witnesses.'

'So how did he make a profit then?'

'Well, as Ahmed explained to the *kadi*, Mehmet paid Murat Reis for his silver cargo partly in gold, which Murat would have used to pay off his crew's share of the spoils, but mostly Mehmet paid him with letters of credit that he held from the Jewish moneylenders in the city.'

'And those letters of credit can be used like money in every port,' I added.

'Yes, that's right. Now, in total, both the gold and the letters of credit that Mehmet paid to Murat were worth a good deal less than the value of the silver that was landed. That amounted to some seven hundred boxes, each containing around two hundred marks of silver, plus sundry other coins like the ones we found in the barn. What made this deal worthwhile for Murat Reis was circumventing the customs by landing his cargo at Mehmet's farm, so that the state did not take its share of the silver. That made

Murat more than willing to sell his silver at a very favourable price for Mehmet, well below the official price. So, everyone was happy.'

'And the difference between the low price Mehmet paid for the silver and the official price at which he sold it to the mint was how he made his profit,' I said.

'Exactly. We don't know how much profit he made, because we don't know the price at which Mehmet and Murat Reis struck their deal – and Mehmet certainly wasn't about to tell all – but it probably earned him several bars of gold bullion: a small fortune in other words.'

'So Mehmet did not confess then?'

'Not in so many words, no. Having extracted what seemed likely enough to have been the truth from Ahmed, the *kadi* discharged him into the custody of the janissaries and next summoned Mehmet for a discussion, which again the judge later recounted to those assembled in the court.'

He paused to eat another date before continuing. 'So the *kadi* confronted Mehmet not only with the evidence that had been presented against him in the court but also with Ahmed's confession, which had revealed the details of their scheme. Mehmet, however, stuck to his line that he had done nothing wrong.'

My master saw me raise my eyebrows and smiled.

'Mehmet said he had struck a fair deal with Murat Reis and had exchanged the silver for gold at the mint at the official rate. He claimed to have had every intention of paying the customs duty that was due on the silver out of his own pocket, but had not yet had the chance. He could not for the life of him understand why Ahmed had not recorded all these transactions in the mint, but that was not Mehmet's responsibility. Likewise, when the *kadi* asked him why he had hidden the silver in hay wagons and smuggled it into the city, Mehmet had replied that he was only taking reasonable precautions to avoid being robbed!'

I shook my head from side to side in disbelief at Mehmet's gall.

'And that's not all,' my master continued, his eyes shining. 'When he was challenged about the payment of three hundred ducats to Ahmed, Mehmet feigned ignorance and then outrage, claiming that if Ahmed had such a quantity of gold in his possession then it must surely have come either from embezzlement or from defrauding Mehmet himself of some of the gold he was due in exchange for the silver bullion he had brought to the mint. Can you believe it? He was so bold as to make out that he was the victim in all of this!'

At this point, my master's account of the proceedings was interrupted by his hearty laughter, such as I had never heard from him before. 'Mehmet the victim!' he repeated. 'Can you imagine?'

When he had composed himself he continued. 'Now, while we can never look inside a man's heart and discern his true thoughts and intentions, the *kadi* explained to the court that, because well over a year had passed since the silver was first taken to the mint, it was reasonable to doubt whether Mehmet would ever have got round to paying the share that was due to the customs. Thus there was good reason to believe that Mehmet had committed an act of fraud but there was no absolute proof.'

'So he got away with it?' I asked, almost dumbfounded.

'Not exactly, but I will come to the punishments in a moment, after I have told you about the *kadi's* verdicts. As for Ahmed, the *kadi* judged that he was guilty of dishonesty for failing to record the transactions in the mint in accordance with his duty and for enriching himself, as he had confessed, by three hundred ducats in the process. Moreover, having consulted with the imam, the *kadi* wisely reasoned that because Ahmed's actions had, in effect, taken from the mouths of every labourer in the city, whose wages now bought less food for themselves and their families, he was guilty of nothing less than theft, and theft on a scale that is almost impossible to imagine.'

As I heard this, I remember chewing on the inside of my cheek, my fingernails having already been dispensed with, and reaching uninvited for another date, to avoid coming to terms with the punishment that I suspected would be served on Ahmed.

'As for Mehmet,' my master continued, 'the *kadi* found him likewise guilty of dishonesty, but not of theft. That caused some murmuring of dissent in the courtroom. The *kadi* justified his decision on the grounds that Mehmet had not confessed and there was no absolute proof that he had intended to steal. Moreover, he reminded us of the warnings in the Koran that serious punishments, or *hadd*, should be applied sparingly, but that all men will account for their sins in the end before Allah.'

141

My master caught me shaking my head once more in incredulity. He smiled. 'You must learn to trust, Tom, in the divine wisdom of scripture.'

'Yes, master,' I replied. My mind had already raced on to wondering how a free Mehmet might exact his revenge on us.

'You must remember also that for a man such as Mehmet, to be found guilty of dishonesty is a very grave matter. As the *kadi* pronounced his verdicts to the court, both Mehmet and Ahmed sat very still and solemn. For Ahmed, the punishment for dishonesty was to receive one hundred strokes with the *bastinado*.'

I could not help but recall the sight of men receiving this punishment in the square outside the Pasha's palace, often surrounded by a large crowd of onlookers. The convicted men were upended and beaten with sticks either on the soles of their feet or across their buttocks, after which vinegar was poured on their wounds.

'In addition,' my master continued, 'for the crime of theft, the *kadi* sentenced Ahmed to the punishment prescribed by the Sharia, which, as you know, is amputation of the right hand.'

I did know this only too well. And in this city, the thieves who received this punishment were paraded around the main streets whilst sat backwards on a donkey, with their severed hand dangling from a string over their shoulders.

'As for Mehmet, he was sentenced to the same punishment for dishonesty as Ahmed: one hundred strokes of the *bastinado*. And he will be required to pay to the customs their rightful share of the silver cargo, which will likely account for all the profit and more that he had made from this scheme.' He paused, as if awaiting my reaction.

'His punishment does not seem just compared to Ahmed's,' I ventured.

'Well, what you must understand is that for a man of noble birth, such as Mehmet, the public humiliation of the *bastinado* will be acute, more painful than the physical pain of the strokes. And what is more, his reputation and indeed his career in this city are both now lost, for the Pasha will never let him serve as an official here again. So his punishment is, in effect, banishment. Believe me, Tom, when I say that if you had been there in the court, and had heard the *kadi's* words, and had looked into both Mehmet's and

Ahmed's eyes, you would have seen that both men had received a just sentence.'

I digested the news about Mehmet's banishment and my thoughts turned to George and Catherine and what their master's banishment would mean for them.

Before I had resolved that issue in my mind, my master continued. 'And that is not quite the end of the matter. For the *kadi* also judged that, although there was no conclusive proof and he had not been present to defend himself, it was very likely that Murat Reis had conspired to avoid paying the customs that were due on his prize when he landed at Algiers. As such he too now has a stain of dishonesty placed upon him that will make it very difficult for him to do business here in Algiers ever again.'

So it was that this affair concluded. I did not go to watch justice being served upon the two villains but I know that many people in the city did, especially when word got round that these two were responsible for the price increases that had impoverished so many.

Chapter 11: Escape

My master once told me that life is like a river: though it may seem settled in its course, sometimes the smallest thing, perhaps a stone falling into a distant, upstream pool, can divert its flow in a new and unexpected direction.

In the days that followed the trial my life began to settle into its new course. No more was I the humble house servant who swept the courtyard, whitewashed the walls and watered the plants. Instead, my master took me into his confidence in his official affairs. At first he tasked me with ensuring that the finances of various institutions for which he was responsible were in order. He allocated me a small room on the ground floor of the house in which to work. He furnished it with a desk and chair, a fine woven carpet, two chests engraved with Koranic verses, and an ornate wooden bookcase on which I kept various ledgers.

In the evenings, after my master had eaten with his daughters and I with Pierre and Joaquin, he would often invite me into his living room. We would sit as we had done in those evenings before the trial, on our respective cushions with the low table between us, and we would discuss all manner of things. He would tell me about the latest intrigues in the Pasha's court, about the news carried on the latest merchantman from Istanbul, and small details about the lives and accomplishments of his children, two girls named Aisha and Havah, whom he held in great affection. Most evenings we would also talk about the *sura* and the *hadith* – the Koranic verses and the sayings – and also about the life of the Prophet, peace be upon him. He would often ask me to recite from the Koran, which seemed to give him great pleasure. He even encouraged me to address him by his first name, Ibrahim, but I never became comfortable with that.

Soon I began to accompany him in his daily business around Algiers. Through this experience I came to discover a great deal more about the inner workings of the city – just as a clock-maker's apprentice learns about the hidden, intricate mechanisms that constantly move and interact beneath the clock face, whereas everyone else sees only the hands of the clock in motion. I learned about the comings and goings of the various merchantmen and their diverse cargos, about the great public works that enriched the fabric of the city, about the goods that were exported and imported, and about the finances of government and affairs of state.

In this way, though I retained the iron ring just above my right ankle and still slept on my straw mattress, I became my master's trusted assistant and confidant. In time, he began to assign me responsibility for advising on some of the most important financial affairs of the city, so that my name came to be known by no less a person than the Pasha himself. In truth, I already had some popular renown as the 'slave boy' who had helped to put an end to the rising prices in the city and to bring the perpetrators to justice. My master had been generous enough to allow me to share in the recognition for these achievements.

Life was good for my master too. In reward for his services to the city, the Pasha granted him control of the customs, the role that had been forfeited by Mehmet, so he added the title of *gümrük emin* or Controller of Customs to that of *Hazinedar* or Grand Treasurer. This made him busier, and more in need of my assistance, than ever.

It was upon my advice that one of his first acts in his expanded role was to take the gold that Mehmet had finally paid to the customs and exchange it for silver at the mint, now under the control of a new and reputable *emin* or treasurer, freshly arrived from Istanbul. The gold in the mint was then used to buy back a large quantity of silver coins from the people of the city, in much the same way as old coins were recalled and exchanged for new ones whenever there was a change of Sultan. Only this time we did not mint fresh coins embossed with the image of the new Sultan, we simply took silver coins in and paid out an equivalent value in gold. This helped to restore the value of the silver coinage somewhat, though prices did not fall as much as we and the people would have hoped. For this act, my master received due recognition from the Pasha, both for having saved the reputation of the city and for having relieved the suffering of the people. In those heady days, both he and I – his famous 'slave boy' – were greeted in the warmest terms wherever we went in the city.

I look back on these times as some of the happiest of my life. The city had become a place of promise and of hope; my faraway island but a distant memory, a place for dreams and heartfelt memories. I had my friends in Pierre and Joaquin, in Jacob and Silas, in Will and George – who had been sold with his sister to a new master following Mehmet's departure for Istanbul – and in the boys from the school who were growing into young men, and of course in Ibrahim, who became, if truth be told, a father figure to me. I was gainfully employed in work that well suited my particular abilities. My master afforded me a modest allowance with which I purchased a few clothes and books.

In short, though I retained my iron ring, I reckoned that I had more freedom than many a free man, and certainly a more interesting and fulfilling life than I would be leading back in England. The same could not, alas, be said for George and Will, nor for Jacob and Silas. For the two younger men, though they both now had decent, tolerable masters, life in the city continued as a mundane grind. They had not been able to fashion a new life for themselves that in any way satisfied their youthful expectations or dissipated the longing for their faraway homes. And it was not in George's nature ever to forgive the people who had brought him here, who had attacked his parents and had stolen his sister. I believe he held the city collectively responsible for those deeds. For Jacob and Silas, though the hankering for home and for escape from their servitude remained, it did not burn with the roaring fire that impassioned George and Will.

I recount the strength of George and Will's feelings as a way of justifying one of my most conspicuous and risky actions from my time in Algiers. It needs justification for it involved a gross betrayal of trust on my part. It took place in the fifth year of my captivity. It happened like this.

In the course of my work supporting my master in his additional role as Controller of Customs, I found myself one day in the customs house that stands beside the harbour. I was inspecting some transactions to ensure that the appropriate share of the value of the cargo involved had been apportioned to the city. As I was known by all who worked there to be the assistant of the

Controller of Customs and Grand Treasurer, I had the freedom to come and go within the building as I pleased.

On that particular day, I chanced to overhear a heated conversation involving an English merchant captain, Consul Frizell and one of the customs officials. The conversation was happening in three ways: the merchant and consul were conversing in English; the consul was then doing his utmost to interpret into *sabir*, the lingua franca of the merchants, so as to be understood by the customs official; and Frizell was also struggling to interpret the official's increasingly irate words back into English for the benefit of the captain. As I listened in, the customs official, brandishing a piece of paper in his right hand, was alleging that the captain had paid too little duty on his incoming cargo. He was demanding a payment in compensation that sounded like an excessive amount.

I walked over to them and called out to the customs man in brusque Turkish. 'What is the matter here? May I see the paper?'

He passed it over to me. I soon spotted what had attracted his attention. The cargo had been valued at 30,000 ducats, but the "3", written in Arabic numerals, could easily have been mistaken for a "2". In the event, the standard customs duty of 3 per cent had only been paid on the sum of 20,000 ducats. The customs man had noticed this but was not just demanding the extra 300 ducats now due; he was surcharging this with a fine of a further 200 ducats. Consul Frizell was struggling to explain.

I switched into English, which caught the merchant captain by surprise. He looked me up and down, taking in my foreign attire and iron ankle ring.

'There has been a mistake over the amount of customs due. You have paid duty of 600 ducats on a cargo valued at 20,000 ducats, but see here,' I showed him the paper, 'the actual value of the cargo was 30,000 ducats, so you are due to pay a further 300 ducats, added to which this man is fining you 200 ducats for attempted under-payment.'

'The thieving Turk,' said the captain. 'What happens if I choose not to pay?'

'I'm afraid he's liable to call in the janissaries to enforce it.'

'And if I make ship and weigh anchor immediately?'

'Then you're likely to receive a parting volley from the guns in the fortress over there.'

The red-faced captain exchanged glances with the consul, and then surveyed the customs man, as if weighing up his options. The customs man stared back.

'I could see if I can quash the fine,' I volunteered, 'but you would still have to pay the additional duty.'

'That's the best result we can possibly hope for,' Frizell said, underlined by an emphatic nodding of his head.

The captain continued to weigh up his options, but eventually concurred. 'If you could try to do that,' he said to me, 'I'd be indebted to you.'

I turned to the customs officer and spoke to him in Turkish, giving my words an official tone that *sabir* would not have conveyed. 'There has clearly been a mistake. The captain has paid what was asked of him, but the confusion over what was due,' I pointed to the paper that I still held, 'was the fault of the customs men involved, not of the captain. As such no surcharge is payable.'

The customs man protested, doubtless because he would have taken a cut of this fine for himself, but he knew the weight that was attached to my view and that he could not gainsay me. After remonstrating for a minute or two he conceded, snatching the paper back and ordering the captain and consul to follow him in order to settle.

I nodded at the captain. 'You must only pay the extra customs duty that you owe: 300 ducats. Then you will be free to depart.'

I looked on from a distance as the captain settled the amount due. On his way out of the building he let Frizell walk ahead and stopped to speak to me in a hushed tone.

'Thank you. As I said, I am indebted to you and I am a man of my word. The consul mentioned that your petitions for a ransom were never answered. Perhaps I can help.'

He cast a glance down to my ankle ring. I understood his meaning. Here was a ship heading back to England, and an offer of transport upon her, a chance to escape.

The captain's offer set my mind racing. It suddenly made real a dilemma that I had only ever contemplated in the abstract when, like every foreign slave in the city, I had imagined far-fetched ways of escaping my servitude and finding a way home. In my mind, these normally involved a nocturnal escape bid in a stolen boat or else swimming out to sea, seeking to intercept a departing merchantman. And now, right here in the broad light of day, I was being presented with that opportunity. I knew, of course, that the punishment for attempting to escape would be severe for both me and, if judged complicit, the captain as well. But that was not of major concern to me at that moment. Instead I weighed up what my heart told me to do, to seize this opportunity to return home to my family, against what my head told me to do, to hold on to this new life that I had fashioned for myself. Mercifully, I did not have time to agonise over my dilemma; I had to make a snap decision.

I decided that there were others who needed this chance to escape more than I did. My rapid thoughts fixed on George and Will: Silas and Jacob would be out working I knew not where; Catherine might not be reachable, and even if she were, might not be inclined to accept the offer.

'Captain,' I answered, 'there are others who need your help more than I. If you would extend the same courtesy to another two young Englishmen, who are sorely in need of safe transport home, then I would consider that you had more than repaid any debt you feel that you owe me.'

The captain looked at me with a knotted brow, as if puzzled by my response. The consul, overhearing something of our conversation with concern etched upon his face, gave a small cough, which prompted the captain to respond.

'Two men, you say, when my offer was for one place. Very well. I see that you know how to drive a hard bargain and I respect that in a man. My ship will weigh anchor in an hour. I will send a boat to the quayside to wait for your two friends; it must leave the quayside in three quarters of an hour. The boatman will wear a green felt hat, so that your friends will recognise him.'

'Thank you,' I said. I did not dally to see the pair depart nor to reconsider my decision but left the building and headed into the city. I sprinted towards the butcher's shop where Will worked, which was on one of the narrow streets that led up from the harbour towards the Grand Market. It was less than five minutes away at the pace I was moving. I did not give myself time to think up some clever excuse, but instead crashed headlong into the shop, not even bothering to step around the blood on the floor. Struggling for breath, I asked the butcher if I could speak to Will.

The butcher knew me both from my previous visits and on account of my part in the silver affair. He motioned me into a room at the back, where I found Will at work, preparing a sheep's carcass so that its blood would drain out in the manner required by Islam.

'Hello, Tom,' he said, wiping his blade upon his apron. 'What brings you here at this time?' Then he noticed the colour in my cheeks and my lack of breath and his expression changed to one of concern.

'Will,' I said, in English of course, so that we would not be understood by the butcher, 'there is a ship leaving for England in around half an hour, with a boat at the quayside waiting to take you and George aboard. The captain has offered to take you home.'

For a moment, the news did not seem to register with Will. 'But how will I explain where I'm going to Karim?' Karim was his master, the butcher.

'You don't need to explain anything,' I said, annoyed at this unnecessary delay. 'Just go, and leave any explaining to me.'

Will put down his knife, and took off his apron.

'Just leave, you mean, just like that?' he asked, evidently in a state of shock.

'Yes,' I replied, grabbing him by the arm and leading him out through the butcher's shop.

'Hey!' Karim cried. 'Where do you think you're going?'

'Sorry,' I called back in Turkish as we left. 'One of our friends is gravely ill and has asked to see Will before he dies.'

It wasn't the best excuse, but it was all that I could think of, and we did not hang around to see whether the butcher believed it. Instead I pulled Will down the street at pace.

'Now go,' I said, 'the boatman will be at the quay and will have a green felt hat. Find a cloak or something to cover up your ankle ring. I'm off to give word to George.'

I had to shout those last words as Will had taken to his heels and was heading off down the street whereas I had come to a halt.

'I will Tom, I will,' he cried back, and then he was gone as the street joined with another and he passed out of sight.

The shortest route to George's new house required an about turn that would take me back up the street and past Karim's shop. That felt too risky. Instead, to avoid an encounter with the butcher, I slipped into one of the adjoining alleys and then found a parallel street leading back up into the city. My mind was already gripped by visions of the janissaries that the butcher would be speaking to, asking them to track down his wayward slave and myself to boot. I did not even begin to think about how I would explain my actions when the authorities caught up with me. That would have to wait.

Focussing on weaving my way through the crowded streets at breakneck speed helped me put such thoughts to one side. I barely even noticed the stitch that needled in my abdomen. I reckoned I had only ten minutes to find George, if he were to stand a chance of making it to the boat in time. I threaded my way north along Grand Market Street, dodging market stalls and donkeys and water carriers and livestock. I passed the square in front of the Pasha's palace and took a left turn on the corner where Ali Biçnin's mosque, now complete, basked in splendour. I ran so fast for so long that I felt like I was going to be sick at any moment. Sweat trickled down my forehead and stung my eyes. Clouds of dust trailed from my slippers.

I darted up a narrow alley until I reached the short cul-de-sac where George's new master's house was located. I rapped upon the door and waited. I rapped again, harder. I was about to turn away dejected when the door opened a fraction and a frowning, middle-aged man peered out. I glimpsed enough of his face to see the disdain in his eyes.

'Is George in?' I asked, almost bent double as I gasped for breath. The man's frown deepened. 'George, the servant boy, he lives here,' I added.

'The master and his household are staying in their villa in the countryside,' the man replied. He began to close the door but I jammed my foot in.

'Where is the villa?'

He glanced down at my foot then fixed a furious stare upon me.

'Please. Where is the villa?' I repeated, keeping my foot steadfast.

'It's in the hills, a few miles away.'

'And when will they return?'

He kicked my foot clear of the door and slammed it in my face. I could hear his footsteps receding inside.

In despair I shouted in English, 'George, are you in there?'

I waited, there was no reply.

'George, answer me if you're in there,' I shouted again.

There was no response other than that of a large sparrow that started to sing on the rooftop above. Otherwise all was quiet, save for the constant murmur of the crowds in the Grand Market below. I had no reason to doubt that the doorkeeper was telling the truth: George was miles away in his master's country villa, well beyond my reach in the minutes now left before the boat was due to depart. Catherine would doubtless be there too.

I paced around in the cul-de-sac, trying to resolve what my next move should be. There was still a space going spare on a ship bound for England and I now seemed certain to be in a lot of trouble if I stayed, when Karim caught up with me as he surely would. Then, as suddenly as a lizard darts for cover, I decided what I must do.

I turned on my heels and retraced my steps down the hill. I cut across Grand Market Street, continuing straight down towards the harbour. I was running full pelt again and I stumbled several times on account of both the gradient and of the uneven stones that paved the street. I pushed past men carrying their goods up the hill from the warehouses to the market. I almost knocked over a man carrying a basket of vegetables, who cursed me and might well have beaten me too had I not departed in haste.

A minute later I passed through the marine gate and on to the quayside. There I slowed right down to a walking pace so as to avoid attracting attention, though my shortness of breath and redness of face were hardly inconspicuous. I did not dare look down but I imagined my ankle ring gleaming in the sunshine. I stood at the water's edge and scanned along the crowded mole jutting out into the water and then along the bustling quay beneath the city wall. I concluded that I must be too late. I could see the English ship ready to set sail in the harbour but could see no green-hatted man waiting at the quayside, nor Will for that matter. My dejection was complete.

Then I heard someone call my name. It was Will's voice and it came from a little boat that lurked in the shadows right beneath me. It was moored so close to the quay that it had evaded my sight. Opposite Will in the boat and staring up at me was the green-hatted mariner, fear etched in his eyes. He was poised to push off with his oar.

The boat was moored by a rope tied to a rusty iron ring at my feet. I knelt down on one knee and whispered down to them.

'George isn't coming with you, Will. I couldn't reach him in time. He's away at his master's country villa. I tried.'

'Well, come on then, what are you waiting for?' asked Will.

I knelt there in silence.

'Come on, Tom, there's no one going to stop us now. This is our chance. You said there's room for two.'

'Get a move on, if you're coming,' hissed the anxious boatman, casting his wary eyes to and fro along the quayside. He shook the rope that led up to the ring beside me and I untied the knot, my trembling fingers prolonging the simple task.

'No, it's not my time to leave,' I said.

'What do you mean? Have you gone mad?' asked Will.

'No. I don't think so.' I felt tears well in my eyes and my voice faltered. 'I must stay. Send word to my mother and sister that I'm all right, and not to worry about me. Promise me that.'

If I had thought for a moment longer about my family back home then I would have leapt into the boat. They were what made my decision so difficult. But at least Will would get word to them that I was safe. It was for that reason that I had run so hard to catch him before the boat departed. In the boat down below Will exchanged looks with the green-hatted boatman, who uttered some words beyond my earshot.

'Promise me, Will.'

The boatman pushed the boat away from the wall.

'Yes, I will, Tom. I promise.'

The boatman rowed away, working his oars in haste.

'Good luck, Will,' I mouthed, tears now rolling down my cheeks. I turned away, lowered my gaze to avoid attention, and walked back through the gate to be swallowed up once more by the great, unfeeling city.

I made my way up the hill with heavy limbs and heavier heart, wondering what I had done, or rather what I had chosen not to do. I berated myself for the opportunity – the fulfilment of forgotten dreams – that I had let slip by. My legs ached from the exertion of my rapid circuit of the city. I took a rest beside a fountain in a small square in the shadows of a side street. I washed my face in its water then sat on a shaded step, cornered by cool, ivy-clad walls.

I sat and I thought and I concluded that I would have to tell my master what I had done. I had little option. Will's master Karim knew who I was and who I worked for. When Will did not return he would know that I was complicit and would seek reparation. I wondered what the punishment was for assisting a slave to escape. I put my head in my hands and sat on that step for a long while.

I spoke not a word of the matter to Pierre or Joaquin on my return but instead went and sat in my little room. I surrounded myself with my ledgers and pretended to work. In reality, I did nothing but sit and reflect on what had passed and what might now come to pass, all the while dreading the sound of my master's return.

The hours passed and the scant light from the courtyard faded away, leaving me in a gloomy half-light. I heard the call for afternoon prayers and then the call for evening prayers. I lit a candle and sought some solace in the Koran that my master had bestowed on me. He had put his faith in me and always treated me with generosity and kindness. I had betrayed his trust and abused my position. I deserved whatever was to befall me.

A starless night had fallen by the time I heard the front door close and the slippered footsteps of my master in the courtyard. I hesitated before stepping out to confront him. I had rehearsed my words of confession a hundred times that afternoon but now they deserted me.

'Master,' I said, unable to meet his eyes.

'Yes Tom?'

'I need to tell you something.'

'Go on.'

'I have let you down and deserve my punishment.'

'I think you had better come upstairs,' he said, leading the way into his living room which Pierre had prepared with his usual eye for detail. 'Please, sit down,' he said, gesturing me as usual towards a cushion.

'Thank you, but I'd rather stand,' I said. He remained on his feet too.

'Well now, Tom, tell me what you have done, and let me be the judge of your actions.'

I swallowed hard. 'Master, I helped one of my friends to escape on a ship back to England.'

'Why did you do that?'

'An English sea-captain, whom I met in the customs house, offered me passage back home. Without thinking, I offered my place to a friend.'

Ibrahim paused to reflect on this. 'And why did you do that?'

'Because I knew he so desperately wanted to go home.'

He nodded. 'Actually, what I wanted to know was why you gave your own place away, why you did not go yourself?'

I stood for some moments, watching a pair of moths circle a lamp. I lowered my eyes before I replied.

'Master, I have a good life here. You have shown me great kindness. I could not just desert you.'

I looked up from the floor and saw that he smiled.

'And yet you were stolen away from your home like your friend; there would be some justice if you stole yourself away back home again.'

I stood there in silence, not knowing what to think or say.

'Tom, you have more than repaid any debt that you feel you owe me. I would have been saddened, certainly, by your departure, but I would have understood. That you decided to stay and gave your place to another only underlines the quality of person you have become.'

'I am sorry master. I fear that I have brought shame on your household. My friend Will – the one who escaped – his master knows that I belong to you. When Will does not return then his master will come looking for me, as he knows that I was complicit in Will's escape.'

'Then your fame is your undoing,' said my master with a chuckle. 'Tom, tell me the name of your friend's master and where I can find him. I will see to it that he is compensated fully for his loss and causes neither you nor me any further trouble.'

I looked up into his eyes, my own beginning to moisten once more. 'I do not deserve that, master.'

'That is for me to decide. Believe me, it will be but a small price to pay for the services you have rendered to me and that you will provide for me in the future. Now go and get some sleep. I can imagine that you've had quite enough of today.'

'Thank you, master,' was all I could reply.

I left the room and went down into the courtyard and then into my bed, giving only a silent nod to Pierre and Joaquin as I passed. I fell into a deep sleep and dreamed of a ship sailing away over the dark waters to England.

Chapter 12: Deliverance

After the drama of Will's escape, my life settled back into its former rhythm. Never again, I vowed, would I test the forbearance of my master. Will's master, Karim, was quietly paid off and we never spoke of the matter again.

I found fulfilment in my work and, as the seasons passed, even my heart seemed destined for happiness. My master told me of his desire to see me matched with his younger daughter, Aisha. He had always spoken of both Aisha and her sister, Havah, in the fondest terms. Since Havah had now married and left the household, his mind had focussed on securing Aisha's future. I was honoured that he had thought to join her with me.

I had only ever seen Aisha in her all-concealing dress, and then but rarely. I had never seen her face nor spoken a word to her, though I had sometimes heard her speak. She had a gentle voice, a soft echo of her father's. And I felt like I knew her already, given all that my master had told me about her. I suspected that she also knew a considerable amount about me from the same source.

Pierre said he thought my marriage to Aisha was now a certainty. 'Remember poor Joaquin and me when you have your own house and family,' he said and winked at me.

'Don't worry. I won't be too hard on you,' I replied.

He raised his hand as if to cuff me round the ear before his face creased into a smile.

Though I was filled with the apprehensions that I assume would visit any prospective groom in a similar situation, I was not averse to such an eventuality. I looked forward to the end of my servitude and my establishment within my master's family, which would come with marriage to his daughter.

As is often the way in life, however, accepted certainties are rolled aside by capricious Fortune, to whom we are all enslaved. So it was with me when this happy period, so full of promise, came to a sudden, shattering end and I found myself adrift once more in unknown waters.

It was on one evening in what I later ascertained to be the month of June, 1628 – almost six years after I had first been taken – that my master returned home from a meeting with none other than the Pasha himself. My master bore fateful news.

A merchantman, freshly arrived from Istanbul, had brought correspondence from the Sultan's court, the Sublime Porte. One of the Sultan's edicts was a summons for my master, to return to Istanbul without delay in order to take up a new position, the nature of which had not been disclosed. My master's speculation ran in two directions: either this was an accolade and he was about to receive one of the highest official positions in the empire in reward for his work in this far-flung outpost; or Mehmet, the disgraced former Controller of Customs, had worked his influence within the Sultan's court to exact his revenge, in which case my master's return would mark the end of his career and possibly worse. Either way, he was not keen to return to Istanbul, not least as he and his children were settled in Algiers, and he would have to leave at least one of them behind because Havah now had her own family in the city.

Having considered his options, my master decided to take the next ship bound for Istanbul, which would leave in just two days' time. He chose to leave Aisha behind, in the care of her sister, but I was to accompany him on his travels.

'You will marvel at the wonders of Istanbul,' he told me, 'it is a city like no other.'

Not for the first time he described to me the pinnacled glory of the Blue Mosque, the ancient dome of the Aya Sofya, the beautiful courtyards of the New Palace and the labyrinthine Grand Bazaar with its thousand shops. His words were uplifting but there was sorrow in his eyes.

'I can think of no better man than you to have at my side when I return to Istanbul,' he said, 'whatever way the Sultan's favour is to fall.'

That thought filled me with both excitement and dread: I would accompany my master either in his new, high office or to the depths of Mehmet's revenge, for Mehmet would not have forgotten my part in his downfall. Our fates were entwined.

Our imminent departure afforded me little time to dwell upon these prospects. There was much to be done in terms of making arrangements for my master's household while he was away. It was soon apparent that he expected years to pass before he returned to Algiers, if he was ever to return at all. This meant that his most important possessions were to be packed into chests and conveyed with him on the voyage, while the rest of the household – people and objects – had to be found new homes and masters.

Pierre, alone, was to remain at the house until his master could provide further instruction from Istanbul. Joaquin was to be sold on to a new master. Pierre was to arrange that and since my master had many acquaintances, some of whom would be in need of a new manservant, Joaquin would be spared the ordeal of the slave market. Nor would he run the risk of becoming a public slave forced to labour on the wave-battered mole, on the scorched roads or, worst of all, chained to an oar on the galleys. He was grateful for that, even if he was apprehensive about what his new master and household would have in store for him. I knew though that Pierre would see him right.

I had many tasks assigned to me, mostly involving preparations for the voyage and tying up loose ends of my master's official interests. My master later told me that the Pasha's face had turned pale when Ibrahim had told him that he was leaving at once for the Sublime Porte. Powerless to prevent it, the Pasha was evidently concerned about having to transfer my master's many powers and responsibilities into new, inexperienced hands.

In addition to these chores, I also had my own affairs to conclude. In truth, it took me but a few minutes to pack my possessions into a chest. I had a modest collection of clothes and a few books, including the precious Koran that my master had entrusted to me, but beyond that I had only the pack of cards that Jack had given me and a small amount of money. Pierre offered me a small bottle of his best cognac, but I declined, which he seemed most relieved about.

Undertaking my valedictory tasks took me to various places around the city and gave me the opportunity to bid farewell to the many friends I had made from both work and school. I called in at the house where George was now a manservant. Fortune had been kinder to both himself and Catherine since they had left Mehmet's household. Their new master – a merchant – was much more reasonable than Mehmet had been and was often away at sea.

George had never shown any contentment with his lot in Algiers, but he tolerated it with dignity. He was blossoming into a fine young man: stocky and powerful as I remembered his father had been; stronger than me, despite my greater years.

'Do you think we shall ever meet again Tom?' he asked me.

I shrugged my shoulders and smiled. 'Yes, I think we shall if it is God's will.'

I saw the old smouldering look in his eyes, but he hugged me and told me to take care. As I left him, it was not the only time that I shed tears that day.

I visited the *bagnio* to say goodbye to Jacob and Silas on the evening before our departure. Silas was as cynical as ever but they both wished me well, particularly when they understood the uncertainty of the fate that awaited me in Istanbul. They each embraced me, clasping me with the grip of sinews strengthened through years of toil.

'You watch your back in that place, master Tom,' Silas warned me, before listing the perils of the 'heathen capital'.

Jacob tutted. 'I'll wager that you end up back in England before I do, one way or another,' he said. 'Make sure there's a pitcher of ale waiting for me on my return.'

'And me,' added Silas.

'I will,' I said. It was with moist eyes that I left them, casting a final glance back over my shoulder to see them leaning side by side on the balustrade overlooking the courtyard of the *bagnio*, wisps of smoke from their clay pipes ascending into the warm evening air.

It was early on the morning of our departure, not long after dawn prayers, that Havah and servants from her household came to the house to collect Aisha and her possessions. I have a vivid memory of the scene as the two women walked away arm in arm down the street. My master waved them off with dignity from the door of his house but then retreated into the vestibule in unstaunched grief.

He had given his younger daughter a parting gift, which he had asked me to buy for her from the gold *souk*. It was a delicate necklace with an emerald set in a central pendant; I had spent an age choosing it. I wondered if she wore it as she walked away that morning, the woman to whom I had never spoken, had never even seen without her veil, yet to whom I was in some way now pledged. It was a strange feeling, watching Aisha disappear from view, wondering whether she would ever be my wife or whether my life as I knew it was slipping away.

My master retreated to the roof terrace alone. I suspected it was to compose himself and also to catch a final glimpse of his daughters as they made their way through the city streets below.

An hour later, we were ready to depart. Pierre gave us a formal nod from the doorway and we headed down the street towards the harbour. We were just the two of us, the master and I, walking side by side at a measured pace. Pierre had overseen the loading of our possessions on to the ship on the previous afternoon.

We passed through the marine gate on to the quayside. Sunshine washed over us and plunged deep into the clear water. Ahead of us, bobbing in the lee of the mole, sat our ship, the *Yunus* – in our language, the *Dolphin* – a three-masted, square-rigged merchant vessel, lying low in the water under her full cargo. She was due to set sail at noon.

The ship was a magnet of activity, attracting a flotilla of small boats from the quayside. We hired one and were duly rowed out across the harbour. I relished the smell of the sea and let the fingers of my right hand dip into the water, leaving a sparkling wake. Never once, in all my time in Algiers, had I satisfied my desire to immerse myself in those inviting waters; nor would I have a chance to now.

We paid off the boatman and climbed up the ladder to the main deck, where my master was greeted by the captain, a young man, not much older than myself, dressed in sleek robes and a jewelled turban. The captain signalled to one of the officers to come and show my master to his cabin. I followed them down to the lower deck.

The cabin was a small room at the stern of the ship, with just enough room for a short bed, a chest, a narrow table, a chair and a stool. Above the bed was a shelf, which I noticed had some of my master's books already arrayed upon it: Pierre's handiwork, no doubt. A small window looked out of the stern, its lattice of panes refracting sunbeams around the cabin.

Having shown my master to his cabin, the officer motioned towards a cramped space just outside the room, where I saw my chest had been set down. This was to be my living quarters; I had a new hammock rolled up in the chest that I would hang up at night. That brought back memories of the dead man's hammock I had gratefully inherited after the capture of the *Santillana*.

I returned to the upper deck to watch the last of the provisions being loaded. All of the cargo had already been stowed down in the hold. A few people, who were not planning to sail, were clambering down to the boats that would convey them back to the quayside.

Above us, the sun had reached the high point of its daily passage across the sky. There were no clouds and the midday heat was tempered only by the breeze that circled lazily around the harbour. I looked up at the city stacked above me, its whitewashed houses almost dazzling in the noon light.

My master came up to join me, placing his hands upon the ship's rail. His eyes scoured the harbour and found what he was looking for. A little way along the mole I could see a pair of women who were waving towards the ship. Despite their all-concealing clothing, he recognised them as his daughters and waved back vigorously. One of the women, who must have been Havah, held up a small baby – his grandson. My master's smile must have been visible over on the mole; he carried on waving and mouthing silent words of farewell.

Overhead the mariners were at work on the shrouds and the ratlines. The sails were unfurled, flapping in the breeze as they fell. The bosun supervised the many hands required to work the tackles hoisting the ship's two tenders aboard and into their cradles on the maindeck. The anchor was drawn in and the *Dolphin* set sail.

Over to my left I saw our escort ship, a corsair galley named the *al Wahid* – the *Peerless*. The galley would provide protection for our passage across the Mediterranean, which the Ottomans call the White Sea. I heard the cries of the coxswain, the crack of his whip and the groans of the slaves as the great oars of the galley began to sweep through the water in unison. Her lateen sails would be unfurled once she was clear of the harbour.

I was glad to see her alongside us. The *Dolphin* was not heavily armed – she carried just four guns on the lower deck and a bow chaser – most of her space was devoted to cargo. I noticed that she also carried a few janissaries – I had seen them slouching together down on the main deck, though whether they were simply travelling back to Istanbul or whether they were a defensive unit for the vessel, I did not know.

We sailed south east, around the great bay of Algiers, passing the spot where the *Santillana* had unloaded her silver contraband at Mehmet's farm. I saw the old farm buildings huddled together beyond the jetty and wondered whether the old man still kept watch there on behalf of his absent master, or whether the farm had been sold on since Mehmet's inglorious departure.

Beyond the bay we continued on an easterly course, the Barbary coast slipping past at a brisk pace. The breeze that had been light in the harbour had now stiffened so that we darted through the waves. The ship deserved her name.

I went below deck to my master's cabin. He sat at his desk poring over a chart of the White Sea. 'Istanbul,' he said with a sigh then a smile, pointing his right forefinger down on to the far corner of the chart. He had opened the small window behind him and the breeze stole in, toying with the edges of the chart.

'With a wind like this behind us, we should be there in little more than a week,' he said before launching into a story from his youth, which he had spent in Istanbul. As he spoke his eyes often looked up towards the timbers of the low ceiling as if he was half remembering, half dreaming.

The crew of the *Dolphin* were much more rigorous in maintaining the prayer schedule at sea than their counterparts aboard the *Sword* had been. The midday prayers had preceded our departure and almost all of the crew joined in the afternoon prayers. Having sought permission from my master, I whiled away the time following the afternoon prayers on the quarterdeck. I took up one of his books and sat with my back to the bulwark at the stern. We had by now lost sight of land and were out in the open sea.

As the sun set the wind began to shift about, causing the sails overhead to flap. I put down my book as the captain appeared on the quarterdeck, issuing orders to trim the sails. The rays of the lowering sun caught the emerald in his turban reminding me, with a sudden sense of loss, of Aisha. The bosun relayed the captain's orders around the ship and a swarm of mariners scurried up the rigging. The *Dolphin* began to roll in the swell. Foam from the surging waves sprayed over the bulwark, dousing my hair and clothes. I stood up, noticing that the wind had become warmer. It was now blowing from the south east.

My master joined me on the quarterdeck. His face had grown pale from the rolling of the ship and he gripped the rail above the bulwark so tight that his knuckles turned white.

'The wind has changed,' I said.

He nodded. 'Yes, now it blows from the great desert.'

'It feels like a storm is coming.'

He nodded again.

Above my head, the sails were now being furled and fastened to the yard arms. The foresail and mizzen sail were reefed. I did not envy the crew as they balanced precariously and wrestled with the ropes and canvas. By some miracle, despite the lurching of the ship, none of them fell. The *Dolphin* heaved to, ready for the storm.

'I am loath to return to my cabin in these conditions,' said my master, 'but I fear it is the best and safest place for me. I never was much of a sailor.' He smiled but there was apprehension in his eyes.

I followed him down and he invited me take the chair from under his table while he sat down on the bed. The pitch and roll of the ship seemed amplified in the cramped confines of his cabin. He closed his eyes and began to count his *misbaha* prayer beads with the fingers of his right hand, his lips twitching in silent prayer. I leant against the table to steady myself. Around us the timbers creaked and groaned.

The storm lasted for hours. There was no dusk prayer nor night prayer. Those fortunate enough not to be out wrestling with the rigging, were either swinging in their hammocks or crouched in corners, talking in low voices. Our supper that night was a kind of biscuit, distributed by a young lad. The freshness of the provisions at least meant that there would be no weevils. I thought of the poor slaves in our escort galley, the *al Wahid*, chained to their benches with nothing to shelter them as they were lashed by the waves and by the whip. I shivered as it crossed my mind that Adam might have the misfortune to be amongst them, if he yet lived.

As the night wore on I sat with my master, who had no inclination to attempt to sleep in these conditions. He had extinguished the lamp, lest it crash down and set the timbers alight, and had closed the window; the lack of air made conditions worse. We passed the time in the darkness talking. He told me more stories from his youth, but his words were often interrupted by a sudden lurch of the ship; there was no delight in his voice now.

I must have nodded off to sleep in that seething darkness, as I awoke at the table with my head upon my forearms. The pitching and rolling had subsided. A faint light was creeping in from the window as dawn stalked the waters. On the bed, my master still sat fingering his prayer beads. I don't know whether he slept for even a minute that night. His face was deathly pale against the dark planks of wood behind his head.

'I'm sorry,' I murmured, 'I did not mean to sleep.'

'You were fortunate,' he said. 'The storm has not long passed.'

'Do you need anything, master?' I asked. I was keen to escape from the confines of the cabin and to inhale some fresh air.

'No, thank you.' He smiled.

'I think I'll go up on deck to check the state of the ship,' I said.

'Of course,' he replied.

I headed up on to the quarterdeck. The sun was breaking through clouds over calm water on the eastern horizon. The call to prayer rang out and the crew began to assemble on the main deck, ready to prostrate themselves. I figured that many would be thanking Allah for their deliverance from the storm. My master was among them.

I looked to starboard, where I expected to see the *al Wahid* shadowing us at her usual distance. Instead there was nothing but open sea. I walked across to the port side and again saw nothing but empty waters. We were alone.

After the dawn prayers, the captain ordered that the ship's sails be unfurled, ready to continue on our voyage. I saw my master walk over to the captain and engage him in conversation. When they had finished, and the captain had returned to his cabin, I crossed over the deck to where my master was standing.

'We have lost our escort,' I said.

'Yes, the captain told me. He said that he thinks we were blown a fair distance off course during the storm. We will continue on an easterly heading and hope that we rejoin the *al Wahid* shortly.'

I noticed an unusual weakness in his voice, which might have been from tiredness or from his fragile condition. His eyes were bloodshot.

'You must be tired, master,' I said.

164

'Certainly, but tired as I am I can see more sense than that foolhardy, young captain. We should be sailing due south now. The storm will have blown us too far north, to the west of Sardinia.'

I nodded to placate him, having no personal opinion on the matter.

'These are dangerous waters, Tom,' he said, shaking his head. 'We are but weakly armed.'

He returned below deck; I hoped he was returning to his cabin to seek some sleep. After a few moments I followed him down. I propped myself up with my back against my chest and closed my eyes. I heard snoring inside his cabin.

I was awoken some time later by shouts from above. The shouts were distant and I guessed they were coming from the crow's nest up on the main mast. I cocked my head to one side and listened, straining to hear the words above the lapping of the sea and the gentle creaking of the timbers.

Word began to filter down through the ship that another ship had been spotted. Down at the far end of the lower deck I could see the group of janissaries begin to stir. They made their way up on to the main deck and I followed them. We all stood alongside the port rail, looking at a small fleck on the horizon, straining our eyes in the bright morning sunshine. We were looking to see whether she was the *al Wahid* coming to rejoin us.

As the minutes passed it became clear that she was not our escort. The shape of the vessel, which had grown to about half an inch in size, indicated that she was a three-masted, square-rigged vessel like our own. Beside me at the rail, men fidgeted and talked and watched. I thought about waking my master but concluded that if he were sleeping then it was for the best that I left him down there in peace.

We waited and watched. The captain and a couple of his officers had spyglasses trained on the other vessel. He gave occasional orders to trim the sails. The wind was now gusting from the north east, sometimes catching our sails, sometimes easing, leaving our sails listless.

I waited, straining my ears for scraps of information from the crow's nest or from those with spyglasses. Some of the janissaries returned below deck. I decided it was time to wake my master. I went below and knocked on the door of his cabin. After a few seconds he told me to enter.

'Master,' I said, 'a ship has been sighted, but she is not the *al-Wahid*.'

'Do you know what kind of ship she is?' he asked.

'No, only that she is a large sailing ship.'

He edged out of bed, still in his clothes from the previous day, and knelt down at his chest, from which he extracted his own spyglass. 'Then let us go and inspect her in more detail,' he said.

We returned to the port rail on the quarterdeck and he surveyed the ship through his spyglass.

'It is as I feared,' he said. 'The sails of the ship carry the cross of St John. We are in Allah's hands now.'

'Has she seen us?' I asked, guessing the answer.

'Oh yes. Be assured of that. She will be bearing down on us in all haste.'

We stood there, on the quarterdeck, for around a quarter of an hour. My master lent me his spyglass and I was able to make out the red crosses emblazoned upon the ship's sails. I could see that, though large, she was more slender than a cargo ship.

On the decks around us and on the rigging overhead, the crew now went about their tasks in haste. The captain ordered that the ship be turned to a south-easterly heading, which was closer to the direction in which I gathered our escort had last been seen during the storm. Our best hope lay in finding her and returning to her protection, though my master said that he doubted whether even the presence of the *Al Wahid* would deter our pursuers. He seemed to have no hope that we could out-run them.

We returned below deck and into a maelstrom of activity. The two guns on each side of the ship were being hauled into place, but there was none of the professionalism of the gun teams aboard the *Sword*. The gun carriages were tangling with the possessions of the crew which were being strewn across the deck. The men laboured and tempers flared. I stayed well out of their way.

Over at the bow of the lower deck, as if on an island of calm in a sea of confusion, the company of janissaries were preparing for battle. Some were priming their muskets and pistols. Others were examining their blades.

We picked our way along the deck to my master's cabin and he asked me to sit on the chair at his small table. He opened the chest and retrieved a pair of wheel-lock pistols which he laid with great care upon the bed. Then he removed a short sword, encased in its scabbard, which he again laid upon the bed.

'I prayed to Allah that I would never have to use these again,' he said – as much to himself as to me.

'Must you fight, master?'

'Not only is it our sacred duty to fight these soldiers of the infidel,' he said, his eyes now fixed on his sword as he unsheathed its blade, 'in truth, it makes little difference. If they capture me then they will either kill me or enslave me – so that I might die another day, chained to an oar or in the rat-infested pits of the *bagnio* in Malta.'

I shuddered. How cruel fate would be if I were to meet my end at the sword of a Christian or in a slave pit in some remote outpost of Christendom.

'You might be ransomed,' I said.

'I'd rather it did not have to come to that,' he replied. 'God willing, we will fend off the infidel, and I will play my part.'

His words had a hollow ring, as if he did not himself believe them.

'Now leave me, please, as I shall change my clothes.'

I stepped outside and closed the door to his cabin. I knelt down to gather my things together. My little corner of the deck was out of the way of the gun crews so my few possessions lay undisturbed. I pushed them into a recess and concealed them with my folded hammock, as if to protect them from the carnage that now seemed inevitable. My fingers trembled. As I knelt, I pleaded to God to spare us all from bloodshed and to allow us to continue our voyage in peace. I dredged up long-forgotten prayers from my childhood to fill those dreadful minutes.

My prayers exhausted, I considered how I should act if the two ships were to join in battle. It was clear in my mind that the crew of the ship that was bearing down upon us were the enemy. But I knew that they were Christian men, in some sense like me. Should I fight them, alongside my master? I certainly felt loyal enough to him to follow him into battle, even against fellow Christians. And yet I had no weapons, save for my trembling fists.

Further minutes passed; it had now taken much longer than I had expected for my master to change his attire. I wondered whether he too was praying or struggling to put on some ageing piece of armour. I waited for the call to assist him, but it did not come. By now the gun crews were ready. The janissaries began to file up onto the main deck.

The door of my master's cabin opened at last. He stepped through the doorway, stooping so that his fine turban could pass beneath the frame. He now wore a white, sleeveless vest and white pantaloons. Around his waist was a red silken sash, in which he had thrust his two pistols and his naked sword. I stood to face him, to do his bidding.

'Step inside,' he said. His tone was grave.

He followed me back into the cabin. I turned to face him. In that cramped space our faces were only inches apart. I could feel his breath upon me, his eyes boring into mine.

'Tom, whatever happens, I want you to stay here and wait for my return.'

I was about to protest, but the words failed me.

'If I do not return, then I want you to ensure that this reaches Havah and Aisha.'

He passed me a letter, which he had evidently written during the last few minutes.

'Yes, master.' I took the letter in my hand.

'And this letter is for you,' he said, passing me another freshly written parchment. 'It ensures your freedom in the event of my death.'

I cast my eyes down. The lettering, normally so neat, was untidy in places, perhaps from where the ship had rolled or his fingers had trembled. I looked and saw that his hands were not shaking: he was his usual, calm self.

'Thank you, master.'

'Leave my cabin only if the ship is going down or the infidel drag you out.'

I nodded.

'May God preserve you, Tom,' he said, as he left the room, closing the door behind him.

I sat down on the bed, a letter in each hand, and I closed my eyes.

From the other side of the door and above me on the main deck came the noise of battle preparations. And yet here I was in a small haven of peace and solitude. I sat there, reading through the letter that would secure my freedom, if my master fell. I prayed to God to keep him safe.

From a distance, away to our port side, I heard the sound of cannon fire. I figured that our pursuers were closing in on us. I looked through the small window of the cabin but there was nothing in my field of vision but calm open sea. I wondered if, by some miracle, we had spotted our escort, who might at this moment be rushing to protect us. The suspense – the not knowing – was unbearable. My haven was a prison; my solitude a torment.

Moments later, two loud explosions reverberated through the timbers as our own guns returned fire. Sulphurous smoke seeped beneath the cabin door. I hunched myself up on the bed, next to the window, clutching the letters in each hand. There I waited and prayed.

My prayers were interrupted by a volley of cannon fire from the other ship, followed immediately by the splintering crash of metal upon wood. That infernal noise was echoed in the screams of injured men above. I reasoned that we had taken a hit to our rigging, perhaps to a mast, but I imagined a gaping hole below the waterline that would send us down to our doom.

I felt our ship turn. For a moment my thoughts returned to the hope of rescue; perhaps our escort had been sighted after all and we were now on a new course to meet her. But such hopes were short-lived for I concluded that the sudden turn was more likely an unintended consequence of the damage we had sustained.

I glanced out of the window. I could now see the ship that was pursuing us, a short distance astern on our port side. I could see her gleaming, golden figurehead jutting towards us. Behind it men were massing, their armour glinting in the sunlight, their muskets levelled towards us. I retreated into the corner of the cabin away from the window. I sat down on the floor, brought my knees up to my chest and closed my eyes.

The sound of small-arms fire erupted, as volleys were exchanged back and forth across the narrowing stretch of water that separated us from our fate. The screaming followed.

I sat hunched up in the corner, desperate to escape from the isolation of the cabin, but torn by the disloyalty that leaving the cabin would entail. Was I to disobey what could be my master's last request of me? He had entrusted me, after all, with his final letter to his daughters. I had abused his trust once before and had sworn never to do so again.

In the end, I could bear it no longer. I decided that I must take a look at what was happening up on the maindeck and then return to the cabin. I would be quick, lest my master should return and catch me away from my post. I tucked the two letters into my breeches, opened the cabin door and peered along the deck. The sulphurous gun smoke lingered but the lower deck was deserted. The gun crews had all gone up on to the main deck to join in the coming battle.

I picked my way through the mess that littered the deck and headed for the hatchway closest to the bow, which I figured would be furthest away from the encroaching onslaught. Above my head, on the creaking timbers of the main deck, I heard the running of many feet and a thud as if a man had fallen. I heard shouts and screams and gunshots.

I placed my hands upon the rungs of the ladder and climbed towards the open hatchway. At that moment, the *Dolphin* lurched forward as the pursuing ship rammed into our stern. I gripped the rungs and just avoided falling.

Through the hatchway above there came, for the first time, the screech of metal upon metal. Hand to hand combat had begun amid the continuing exchange of fire. The cacophony of shouting and screaming reached a new intensity.

I was shaking with fear as I inched my head upwards so that my eyes were just above the level of the deck. Before me was a depiction of living hell. I could see that our main mast had taken a direct hit and had splintered, bringing a fair amount of the rigging down. That provided the tattered foreground to the vision of madness unfolding beyond.

Most of the crew of the *Dolphin* were amassed within the cramped confines of the quarterdeck. A group from the other ship had surged into their midst. I could see the scarlet tunics of the janissaries in the thick of the action; there was no room for them to swing their scimitars. Daggers were thrusting and pistols firing at point blank range. Men were tumbling or being thrown overboard. I saw marksmen up in the rigging of both ships, firing down on their adversaries and sometimes taking a shot themselves, which sent them plunging headlong into the sea or on to the deck. I looked everywhere for my master.

I ducked down for a few moments to compose myself. I could no longer see what was happening but I could hear it. The horror was unrelenting. When I dared to raise my head again, I saw that the men of the *Dolphin* were being pushed further back towards me. Some already had their backs to the broken main mast. They were now fewer in number and they were outnumbered by the men that were streaming on to our ship. I looked up into the *Dolphin's* shredded rigging and saw a lone mariner in the crow's nest. His comrades had fallen. On the deck only a couple of janissaries remained, carrying on the fight to the bitter end.

I could still see no trace of my master and the retreating crew began to obstruct my view as they were pushed back along the maindeck towards me. A few yards over to my right, a barrel stood against the bulwark. I figured that it would offer me a better vantage point than my current position. But it would involve exposing myself to our attackers for a few seconds before I could take shelter behind the barrel. I confess that I hesitated there upon the ladder but in the end I resolved that if I wanted to find out what had become of my master then I had to do it.

I pulled myself up behind the desperate line of mariners who were still struggling to fend off the incursion. Keeping my head down, I darted for the barrel. From in front of me, there came a loud explosion and a rattling noise like gravel being thrown against a door. I felt a sharp pain in my left arm, above the elbow, as I hurled myself down on to the deck behind the barrel. Beside me two of the men from the *Dolphin* reeled backwards, one clutching his face and screaming, the other clutching his neck and gurgling. He fell on to the deck not two yards from where I crouched; his body writhed in agony but he was unable to scream.

Mustering what little remained of my courage, I peeped over the top of the barrel and surveyed the battle from my new vantage point. I cannot faithfully describe the carnage that confronted me: it terrified me to the depths of my soul. And yet my plan had worked. Ahead of me and to my left, up on the poop deck, I caught sight of my master. He was still fighting. I saw his sword arcing and glinting, saw his white vest spattered with blood. Men were falling right in front of me but my eyes were now fixed upon him.

'Surely,' I muttered, 'surely someone will surrender and stop this.'

I saw my master dispatch an adversary who slumped upon the rail of the ship. I saw him ready himself to take on another. And then I saw him laid low by a shot from above; the tell-tale flash and wisp of smoke came from up in the rigging of the enemy ship. I saw his distant assailant punch a jubilant fist into the air and begin to reload his pistol.

The last mariner in the crow's nest of the *Dolphin* had taken a bullet in the temple. The last of the janissaries had fallen too. The remaining crew of the *Dolphin* were a spent force. Their battle cries had been silenced and they began to cry for mercy. The final skirmishes were ending. The shooting ceased. The enemy had taken the quarterdeck and were looking down upon the vanquished crew assembled on the maindeck. A veil of acrid smoke hung over the deck, smothering the screams of the wounded.

As I could no longer see much from my hiding place because of the men arrayed before me I had to decide what to do next. I knew my orders, to stay put in the cabin. And I could see the hatchway just a few yards to my left, open and inviting: I could have been back down in the cabin within seconds. But my master might yet be alive and in need of my help. I stayed put, concealed behind the barrel.

The crew of the *Dolphin* began to throw down their weapons and to retreat further from their conquerors. I could see despair and fear in their eyes; could hear it in their voices, in the terse words they exchanged as they awaited their fate.

Up on the quarterdeck, a man clad in full armour advanced through the serried ranks of our assailants who made way for him. He stopped at the top of the steps leading down to the maindeck and began to give orders and to point here and there. His men responded, many filing down on to the main deck to shepherd what was left of the *Dolphin's* crew along towards the bow.

The remainder of his men began the sinister task of finishing off the wounded and disposing of the dead. They moved here and there, searching the bodies before dumping them over the side of the ship. They were working around the decks, working towards the spot where my master lay.

In that moment, I knew what I must do. I emerged from my cover and darted across the deck, picking my way through the dispirited survivors and leaping over bodies. As the fighting had ceased and I posed no danger in my unarmed state, no one seemed to pay me much attention. I pushed past members of the enemy crew on the quarterdeck with no thought to my own safety and climbed the steps up to the poop deck.

Bodies littered the timbers. It took a few seconds for me to spot where my master had fallen. I rushed to his side before the enemy crew reached him. He was alive: wounded but conscious. A sense of relief rushed over me and almost overwhelmed me; I had to brush tears from my eyes. I pushed his weapons away from his body to show that he posed no threat and lifted him so that he was propped up against the bulwark. I could see that he had a single, gaping wound in his chest. His breathing was laboured.

'Master,' I said, 'can you walk?'

'Tom,' he whispered, 'you should not have come.'

'Come on,' I said, 'I've got to get you down to the rest of the crew. The fighting is over.'

At that moment a blow to the back of my head sent me reeling across the deck. I turned, dazed, and saw a thick-set man in leather armour standing over me, pointing a bloodied sword down towards the maindeck. His eyes were wild and he was screaming at me in a foreign tongue.

Behind him, one of his comrades began to search my master while another picked up his pistols and tucked them into his belt. I took a hard kick from my assailant's boot to my left thigh and another earful of shouting, which clearly meant that I should rejoin the rest of my crew.

But I could not move. Instead I watched, transfixed in horror, as his two comrades stooped to haul up my master, grasping him at each armpit. It became clear that they were about to dispose of him too: to cast him over the side as if he were already dead. I staggered to my feet as if to return to the maindeck but then veered back towards my master.

'Mercy!' I shouted. *'Ayez pitié!'* I probably shouted in Turkish and Arabic too, such was my desperation.

My assailant grabbed me around the neck and pulled me down on to the deck, half throttling me. His comrades continued to hoist my master upwards. I took another kick to my ribs as I lay spread-eagle on the deck, then another to my wounded left arm, which caused such a surge of pain that I almost fainted, but I carried on shouting for mercy for my master.

Over to my right, across the poop deck, I saw another man approaching, sword in hand. I saw the glint of his armour, beneath a white tabard embroidered with a red cross. He wore a helmet, its open visor revealing intense, grey eyes. I hoped against hope that this man had come to intercede, to halt this needless barbarity.

'Show mercy. *Donnez merci*,' I shouted again, gesturing frantically towards my master.

The armoured man looked me up and down with curiosity then transferred his gaze to my master, inspecting his wound. He pointed his sword at me and gave an order to my assailant in French. 'Bring him to my cabin; alive.'

Then he pointed his sword towards my master and instructed the other men again in French: 'Get rid of him.' Then he turned and walked away.

'Wait! *Attendez!*' I cried but to no avail. The two men hoisted my master up and threw him overboard. He went without protest, without a cry, his eyes lifted upwards. I heard the fateful splash below.

Then the murderous pair came and pulled me up by my armpits while their companion, who had been so liberal with his boot, went off to molest some other poor soul. For a dreadful moment I feared that they had not heard their instructions and were about to cast me overboard to my own watery grave. Instead, they dragged me backwards in a daze across the deck and over to a boarding plank that had been erected between the two ships. In truth I must have fainted along the way, whether from the pain or from the horror, as I do not remember the whole of that ordeal. They hauled me over from the *Dolphin* on to their ship, across the main deck and then up to the quarterdeck, dropping me in a heap outside a cabin door. There they left me.

Chapter 13: Edward

I do not know for how long I was slumped outside the cabin; I drifted in and out of a dismal consciousness. I can remember waking at one point to find that a cord had been tied tightly around the top of my left arm, above my wound, and I noticed that my sleeve below was drenched in blood. My back was propped up against the wooden planks of the cabin. A throbbing pain emanated from my left arm; my ribs were bruised.

Around me, as I came round, activity continued apace. Ahead I could see the forsaken *Dolphin*, parts of her rigging in tatters, still clamped with grappling hooks to this ship that had ruined her. There was much coming and going between the two ships, as booty and weapons and captives were brought aboard and stowed below deck.

As I sat there, I thought little of my own predicament and much of my master's fate. Over and over, my mind recreated the moment he was cast overboard, still living, still breathing. His life had been snuffed out like some half-burned candle; all that he had still to give to the world now lost forever. And I was the bearer of his final words to his beloved daughters. My heart stopped as I checked for the two letters he had given me – one for his daughters and one for my freedom. I felt them tucked away in my breeches. I wept.

It was while I was slumped outside the cabin that the man who had sent me there, the man who had sent my master to his watery grave, approached. I was alerted by his heavy footsteps upon the deck. He still carried his sword in his right hand but was now without his helmet, revealing a close crop of greying hair. His face was red from his exertions, beading sweat.

He cocked his head as he looked down at me, as if appraising me. I lowered my eyes and braced myself, fearful that he was going to kick me as he passed into his cabin. Instead he reached down and checked the tight cord around my arm, and he spoke to me.

'So what are you then, English, French?' Those gruff words in heavily accented English almost took the wind out of me with surprise.

'English,' I whispered.

'Well, well, an English slave bound for Constantinople. And one who seeks to spare the infidel from their fast road to hell. Come on then, who are you?'

I felt too weak, too miserable to protest or to answer. I wiped the tears from my eyes when I thought he wasn't looking.

'Speak to me lad,' he said. 'Your fate might depend on what you tell me now.' As he spoke, he removed his tabard and unfastened the leather straps of his breastplate.

'My name is Thomas Cheke,' I said, 'servant to Ibrahim Ali, Grand Treasurer of Algiers.'

'The one I had thrown overboard?' he asked, his back turned to me so that he didn't see me nod. 'Wouldn't have lasted more than a couple of days with that kind of wound anyway. He was handy with his sword, mind. Took at least three of our men with him.'

I tried to place his accent but failed. He spoke English as if it were his mother tongue but his accent was a strange mixture. As I sat there, the world began to spin: the deck, the rigging, the sea, the sky.

He pulled off his thick woollen shirt, which was drenched with sweat, revealing a stocky torso, his skin red and scarred and blotchy. He entered the cabin and continued to question me from within. 'And how did you come to be in the service of such a distinguished official?'

'He bought me, a few years ago,' I murmured. I began to feel faint again.

'Come on lad, has the cat got your tongue?' he said, emerging back at the cabin door, now dressed in a black outfit that looked like a monk's habit. A small white, eight-pointed cross was embroidered on his breast.

I would have said more but words failed me. The dizziness intensified and I passed out.

When I woke, I was no longer on the deck but lying in a small bed inside a cabin. The smell of wood and ointment and sweat filled the stuffy air. It was dark outside and the cabin was illuminated by a single lantern creaking overhead.

176

A damp flannel lay across my forehead; it slipped off as I struggled to raise my head. My blood-soaked clothes had been removed, as had the cord around my left arm, though I could still see the mark where it had bitten into my flesh. My wound was now wrapped in a bandage. My bedding was saturated with sweat.

The man in the black habit was hunched over a table, reading something. It seemed to me that he sighed in frustration. His face now looked tanned rather than red and several old, white scars decorated his leathery skin. He noticed that I had woken.

'Ah, I was thinking it was about time that you returned to the land of the living.'

There was a hint of warmth in his voice. I said nothing and looked away.

'Come now, Thomas. I'm not going to harm you; indeed, I should change that dressing of yours.'

He stood up rather stiffly, came over to the bed and unwrapped the bandage from my arm with gentle fingers. A signet ring glinted on his right hand. He inspected the wound and I cast my eyes down upon it for the first time. I was surprised at how bad it looked; it had not felt like much more than a graze at first.

'You were lucky,' he said, as he poured out some ointment from a jar and rubbed it upon the wound, making me wince. 'The grapeshot from those swivel guns can be deadly. If it doesn't kill you outright, the wounds can become septic and that can be the end of you.' He tore a strip of bandage from a roll. 'Still I'm happy to say that that won't be happening here, not to a strapping lad like you, though I don't doubt that your fever will last for a while yet.'

He finished wrapping the new bandage around my wound and picked up the flannel that had slipped from my forehead, dunking it in a pail of water beside the bed.

'Here, put this back on your forehead,' he said, handing the flannel back to me.

I obeyed in silence.

He sat down on the bed beside me and brought a cup of water to my lips. 'Drink this. It will restore your humours and ease your fever.'

I drank, glad to feel the water moistening my parched mouth.

'There, that will do you a power of good. You know, Thomas, you're a free man again now. You have the rest of your life to look forward to.'

He spoke as if he meant well, but if he sought to rouse my spirits, he failed. I lay my head back on the bed. The man shrugged his shoulders, got up and returned to whatever he was reading upon the table. My body shivered, even as it dripped with sweat. I shut my eyes and re-opened the dark thoughts circling in my mind.

When I next woke it was light outside. I was alone in the cabin but a hammock had been strung up next to the table. I sat up, waves of pain surging through my body, and exerted all my remaining strength to reach the cup of water beside my bed. I drank it all and lay back exhausted. I slipped in and out of fitful sleep.

At length the man returned. He opened the cabin door and, seeing me awake, bade me a hearty 'Good morning, Thomas.'

I laboured to sit upright. He walked over and took a look at my bandage.

'That looks much better,' he said and replenished the cup from the pail of water, holding it out to me. I drank it and felt a flicker of gratitude before reminding myself that I owed him none.

'Good. We'll soon have you skipping across the deck,' he said with a smile. 'Are you well enough yet to tell me how you came to be a slave?'

Though half of me wanted to recoil and maintain a silent protest, the other half thought that I should show some recognition for his efforts, lest I antagonise him. With a strong sense of betrayal, I deigned to answer him.

'I was taken from my home one night by a corsair captain by the name of Murat Reis.'

'That old scoundrel!' he exclaimed. 'Now there's a dose of ill fortune. Mark my words, we'll catch up with him again one day, and then he'll rue the day he ever took up company with the infidel.'

I was intrigued that he knew of the old corsair, and that made it a little easier for me to tell him more.

'I'm from the Isle of Wight. He landed with a party of men and took me, a couple of other children and some gunpowder, then sold us in Algiers along with a prize ship he captured on the way.'

'The Isle of Wight, eh? That's to the south of England is it not?'

When I heard him refer to 'England', I suddenly put at least one place to his accent. He was Scottish. I had heard merchants from his country speaking once or twice when I had visited London as a boy. But his accent also had a foreign lilt, which reminded me of someone, I couldn't think who.

'That was a bold move,' he continued, 'even for old Murat, to strike so close to His Majesty's fleet. And taken on land, you say. Aye, I've heard tale of that, down in Cornwall and in Ireland too. We spend all our time hunting down the corsair scum that floats upon the Mediterranean. Maybe we should go hunting a little further afield sometimes. Here—'

He offered me his right hand and gripped mine.

'Pleased to meet you, Thomas Cheke. I can tell that you are a gentleman.'

'Perhaps I was once sir; not anymore.'

'Well, one of the first things we'll do is get that ankle collar removed. It saved your life back there, you know? Had I not seen it, then God forgive me, I would have run you through for all your whinging.'

I feigned a smile but was unnerved by the power this man held over me. 'Please sir,' I said, 'who are you?'

'Ah,' he laughed, a deep laugh from the depths of his lungs, 'forgive my poor manners. I am Brother Edward.' He must have noticed my confused reaction and smiled, patting me on the leg. 'Welcome aboard *La Gloriosa,* a ship of the Order of St John.'

The Order of St John: I remembered how my master both respected and feared them.

'Where are we heading for?' I asked.

'We are bound for Malta which, with a fair wind behind us, is but two or three days' sail to the south east, and I should be glad of some civilised company during the voyage. That hammock's for you, by the way. You got one night in my bed, but now that you're back to your senses, I'll be having it back.'

'Thank you,' I said, and my gratitude was real.

'Did you have any possessions aboard the infidel ship that you want carried over?'

'Just a small chest,' I replied.

'Well let's hope we can still find it, now that our crew have ransacked everything. Do you think you're well enough to walk over to the other ship?'

'I'll try,' I said, still shivering.

'Here, I found a clean tunic and a pair of breeches for you,' he said, handing me a bundle of clothes. 'Put these on while I go and tell the captain that we'll be heading across to the *Dolphin* for a few minutes – he's keen to separate the ships and to make sail.'

I put the clothes on, which turned out to be a slow and agonising process. Then I staggered out of bed. Edward met me at the cabin door and gave me his arm to help me balance.

The sun was high in a clear blue sky. I saw that the *Dolphin* had been brought alongside the *Gloriosa*. The crew had clearly been busy repairing her main mast and damaged rigging. There was a constant to-ing and fro-ing between the ships with various lengths of wood, rope and other materials being carried over the gang planks that crossed from one main deck to the other.

We crossed over to the *Dolphin* and went below deck. As Edward had suspected, the victorious crew had already taken almost everything of any worth. I led him towards the stern and stopped outside my master's cabin. By a stroke of good fortune, my folded hammock lay undisturbed in the corner in which I had left it. I picked it up along with the chest that it concealed. I glanced into the cabin, which had already been ransacked. I could not bring myself to search through my master's remaining possessions for anything of value that might be saved. I nodded to Edward and we returned to the *Gloriosa*.

Up on the poop deck, the captain of the *Gloriosa* appeared to have been waiting for our return. I noticed that he also wore the black habit of the Order of St John. He gave an order and his crew began to dismantle the gang planks and unfasten the grappling hooks. Edward and I paused for a few minutes on the quarterdeck, watching the well drilled activities of the *Gloriosa's* crew, now divided between the two ships, until the *Dolphin* inched away. The sails were unfurled on both ships and trimmed to make the most of the light winds. Over my head, the main sails billowed, puffing out their great red crosses.

We returned to Edward's cabin and I placed my chest down beneath the hammock, taking a quick look to ensure that its contents were intact.

'Get some more sleep,' he said. 'The fresh air will have done you good but your body needs rest. I'll go and see about getting you something to eat'

'Thank you,' I said. I was grateful both to be alone once more and for the prospect of food. Though I had been bed-ridden in the cabin for the Lord alone knows how many hours, this was the first time that I surveyed it in detail. The cabin was larger than my master's had been. There was a chest in one corner and a bookshelf above the bed. I inspected its contents and found well-thumbed pamphlets of works by Marlowe and Shakespeare, a Bible and another thick tome with *Don Quixote* inscribed in golden letters on its spine.

I slumped into my hammock, swinging to and fro with the roll of the ship. Before long I had fallen asleep. It was not the restful slumber that Edward had prescribed but rather a restless sleep during which the terrible scenes of the battle were re-enacted. I was a paralysed spectator, powerless to intervene.

It was dark when I was woken with a shake. For a moment, I knew neither where I was nor what had befallen me. Then a spark illuminated a lantern that was hung from the ceiling, revealing Edward's solid frame.

'Come,' he said, shaking me again. 'It's time we got some food inside you.'

I stumbled from the hammock. Edward steadied me and passed me a pewter bowl and spoon, and a tankard. My stomach yearned for food. I followed Edward out of the cabin, across the quarterdeck and down a set of stairs. I noticed that the crew aboard the ship made way for him as he passed, many giving me a curious stare. Down on the cramped lower deck, which was lit by a procession of lanterns, we were given a portion of gruel and a measure of frothy ale. I followed Edward to a table; the men already seated there shuffled along the benches to make room. The food and drink revived my spirits somewhat. It had been years since I had tasted alcohol and I felt its effects almost at once.

'I can see you had a good rest,' he said, 'it's put some colour back into your cheeks.'

'Yes, thank you,' I lied. I finished my ale and my thoughts began to swim around my head.

'So how does it feel, Thomas, to be a free man again?'

'Please,' I replied, 'call me Tom. I'm just getting used to it, freedom I mean. I had become used to my position.'

He nodded, as if he understood. Around us, in the rocking lantern light, some fiddles started up and men were singing shanties in their strange tongue. The air was filled with the pleasant smoke of dozens of clay pipes.

'Is it the language of Malta that they speak?' I asked.

'Aye, it is. Never could understand head nor tail of it myself, though I've lived there a few years.'

'You speak to them in French?'

'Aye, this ship is on its way back from France. Most of the crew speak a little.'

'And if I'm not mistaken, you speak English with a French accent?' I had realised that his accent reminded me of Pierre.

'So help me God,' he replied with a laugh. 'Aye, I've spent many a long year in France. Too long for comfort.'

'But you are a Scot, are you not?'

'You have me down to the letter, my young friend. I was born and raised in France, but my parents were Scottish.'

'And you became a monk?' I said, the alcohol making me bold as well as curious.

'Not exactly,' he replied, smiling as he withdrew a clay pipe from a pouch that hung from his belt and began to stuff it with tobacco. I noticed that he carried two pistols in his belt for good measure. It took him several attempts to light his pipe.

'All the men make way for you.' I added. 'It is not how we treat the monks at home.'

'Indeed. The monasteries have fallen into a sorry state on our fair isle.' He lit his pipe, inhaled and looked at me through clear, grey eyes. 'Thanks to fortune, good or ill, I was pledged to the Order of St John when I was but a babe in arms. Now I am a knight of the Order. And in this part of the world, men still make way for us.'

'I can see why. I never did see a monk who was handy with a sword before and carried pistols in his belt.'

He laughed and I surprised myself by laughing too.

'So how is it that you came to be born and bred in France?'

'Ah, therein lies a tale. I may tell it to you some day. Suffice it to say that my father ran into a few difficulties back in Scotland, difficulties that I'm happy to say are now behind us.' He laughed again and I joined in too, though I knew not why, intoxicated as much by the atmosphere as by the ale.

He banged the table with his empty tankard and shouted to one of the men further along the deck to bring us some more ale. Two more tankards duly arrived, their froth spilling over the table. No one cared.

I sipped my ale as Edward savoured his pipe and exchanged the odd word in French with a number of the men, who I guessed were the ship's officers. My mind began to whirl. I tried to make sense of all that had passed. Here I was, free once more, yet what value is freedom without the means to enjoy it? I realised that I was utterly dependent on this man, Edward: the man who had had my master killed. Without Edward I was but a lone, penniless lad, unfit to work and adrift upon a ship of strangers. I drank more for sorrow than for mirth that night. And though I laughed sometimes, my heart was not warmed.

I do not know the hour at which Edward hoisted me up from the bench and helped me to stagger back to his cabin before spilling me into the hammock. A drunken sleep ensued, pitching and rolling between wakefulness and confused dreams.

Edward woke me as he returned to the cabin the next morning. He ushered fresh sea air in with him. As he entered, he folded a piece of paper and slipped it inside his habit, frustration etched on his face. Through the cabin door I could see that the sun was already high; it hurt my eyes. Edward threw me a piece of hard, unleavened bread from a plate on the table.

'You missed breakfast,' he said.

My head still swam, my arm throbbed and my ribs ached. He watched me gnaw at the bread. When I had finished he said: 'Right, let's remove that ankle ring of yours.'

I followed him across the deck to where a carpenter was busy working with his mates amid a morass of wood and rope and tools. Edward told the carpenter to prise my ankle ring off. The thick-set, sun-burnt man inspected it then went away to look for the right tools. When he returned he asked me to lie back upon the deck with my right heel resting upon a stool. He positioned a narrow length of iron against the point of the rivet that fastened the ring together. Taking a firm hold of the ring in his left hand, he began to hammer the rivet out. With every blow of the hammer I flinched, until I shut my eyes and watched no more. But the carpenter was deft at his work and the rivet soon fell out and rolled away across the deck. After that the ankle ring fell open, revealing a soft, white band of skin beneath. He handed me the ring, wiped his brow on his apron and returned to his work.

Edward offered me a hand up. 'That could come in handy for someone else,' he said, eying the ankle ring with a glint in his eye.

'No it won't,' I replied. I walked over to the starboard rail, unaccustomed to the lightness of my right leg, and threw the ankle ring far out into the sea. It disappeared beneath the waves with a pleasing splash.

Edward watched me with his hands on his hips and nodded with a smile. He returned to his cabin, while I took a wash from a bucket of sea-water upon the deck and changed into some fresh clothes that I had brought in my chest. The clothes Edward had given me were damp from the sweat brought on by my fever, which had now abated.

I savoured the sky and the sea for a few moments then rejoined Edward in his cabin. The window was open, allowing sunlight and fresh air to stream in. He was hunched over the table peering down at some paper, perhaps the same piece as before. He pointed to a stool in the far corner of the cabin, under the window, and invited me to come and join him at the table. As I passed I glanced down and saw that the paper contained an array of symbols. When I brought the stool over to the table he folded up the paper and inserted it into a pocket in his habit.

'So Tom, what will you do now that you're a free man?'

'Oh, I don't know,' I replied. 'I guess I'll have to find a ship to take me back to England. Do you think I'll find one in Malta?'

'Och aye. Ships from most of the major ports call in at Malta. You'll find one bound for England before long. I reckon that'll be safer than heading for some Mediterranean port and trying to make your own way up through France.'

'But you came by ship from France?'

'Aye, I did. But I wasn't travelling from England. I've been living in Paris for a while. In truth, I've not been in England for a couple of years, nor Scotland for that matter – not since my brother died.' His eyes dipped for a moment before he continued. 'Now tell me, how was it that a gentleman like yourself came to spend so long in captivity. Could you not arrange a ransom?'

'No, but in the first few months I tried several times. The English consul in Algiers said he would send my letters back to England, but my father is dead and my family is no longer wealthy, so I appealed to the benevolence of one of the local gentlemen for help.'

184

'To no avail?'

'No. I suspect my letters never reached him, for I never received a reply, not even from my mother. I asked the gentleman, Mr Dillington, to pass my letters on to her but I never received so much as a word in reply. And after a year or so, I guess I gave up hope of a ransom. I had enough to occupy my thoughts in Algiers.'

'So you have heard no news of home in all these six years?' He let out a low whistle.

'No, nothing; I don't even know if my mother and sister are still alive.'

'Well, I fancy their fortunes were better served in England than if they had been taken with you to that hell-hole of Algiers. They had a lucky escape. I've heard of that old dog Murat Reis and other corsairs like him taking whole villages into captivity: men, women, children, even babies.'

'In truth I have never understood why he didn't take my mother and sister too. Instead he tied them up and left them there, and that was the last I saw of them. He just took me.'

'That's odd, I agree, very odd. Still, Fortune smiled on them that night, for the Turks show no respect for the dignity of Christian women. They treat them like cattle; sell them to the highest bidder.'

'So it was with me and the other captives.'

'And did you never think to escape?'

'Oh yes, I dreamed of it every night for a year and more; invented intricate plans for how I would smuggle myself aboard a parting ship and gain my freedom.'

'But nothing ever came of it?'

'No, as one year ran into another, I got used to life there and, in truth, I lost my fervour to escape. Once I even had the chance to escape, on an English merchantman, but I gave my place away to a friend.'

Edward put his pipe down and looked at me with wide eyes. 'There's few folk who would have committed so noble an act as that, Tom: to give up your own freedom for that of another man.'

I looked down at the table and made no reply. I had no intention of revealing the truth that I could have escaped too, but had chosen to stay, to continue my promising life in Algiers. I felt embarrassed, fraudulent even, but Edward seemed to misinterpret my reaction for one of modesty.

'Well, thank God and His Providence, that I was able to rescue such a fine and honourable young man as yourself, Tom, and to restore you to your freedom.'

'Thank you,' I said, still avoiding his gaze. My thoughts lurched back and forth with the ship, veering between happiness and guilt, gratitude and anger. Here I was, befriended by a good man who had restored my freedom and nursed me back to health, yet inwardly I grieved for the loss of my master and for the end of the life that I had worked so hard to create for myself in Algiers. As I contemplated my future I realised that I faced the prospect of a life of penury, should I ever make it back to England. My years in captivity meant that I had missed out on the chance to learn an honest profession and I had no other means to fall back on now that my family was impoverished.

Edward picked up his pipe again, lighting it at the third attempt. After a few minutes of contented smoking, he restarted the conversation.

'Though it will pain me to lose your good company so soon after our paths have crossed, I will see to it when we reach Malta that you are boarded safely upon a fast ship back to England.'

'Thank you,' I said, still pondering my predicament and wondering whether a fast ship back to England would turn out to be a blessing or a curse.

'It's a shame, Tom, as I have enjoyed our brief acquaintance. There are only a few left in the Order now with whom I can converse in my native tongue. The English *Langue* – that's the English-speaking faction within the Order – is all but extinct; our domains in England, Scotland, Wales and Ireland are all confiscated. So I have to make my way in the French *Langue*, though in truth I'd sooner keep company with the rats in the hold than with some of my French brethren.' He laughed and put down his pipe.

'So you still consider yourself a Scot, rather than a Frenchman?'

Edward's face feigned injury. 'How can you even ask me such a question?' He smiled. 'Aye, once a Scot, always a Scot, wherever you are in the world; though in some ways my welcome is warmer in France these days than in Scotland.'

'Why, is your family still in difficulties?'

'No, far from it. My father – God rest his soul – was reconciled with the young King James. But, in my case, to be a 'Papist', to be a 'recusant' as they say, wins you few friends in Scotland. You'll have seen the same in England.'

I nodded, knowing that it was true, particularly on my island.

He continued: 'in the past there were members of my family that stayed true to the Roman church, but these days the grip of Protestantism is strong. The legacy of John Knox runs deep in Scotland. And so I have become something of a curiosity at best, and more likely an embarrassment: the rarely mentioned, conveniently forgotten 'Uncle Edward' who lives abroad and fights the Turks.' All trace of mirth disappeared from his eyes. 'Well I can tell you, Tom, the infidel couldn't give a damn whether a man's a Protestant or a Catholic: he'll enslave him or run him through either way, and take his wife and children to boot.' He banged the table with his right fist. 'The powers of Christendom would do well to keep an eye on the danger lurking on their borders, rather than embroil themselves in futile wars that pit Christian against Christian.'

I felt guilty about raising a subject that clearly troubled him and sought to change the conversation by asking him about the Order. It proved to be an investment with a handsome return. For the remainder of that morning, indeed right up until the watch-bell chimed to signal that it was time for the midday meal, Edward regaled me with tales of the Order of St John from its glorious past. He told me of its heroic defence and then retreat from Rhodes and about the Great Siege of Malta. He promised to introduce me to some ancient veterans of the Siege when we berthed in Malta, if they were yet living. He described in great detail the building of the wonderful new city of Valletta, which I would soon behold. He recreated the decisive battle of Lepanto, when the forces of Christendom had finally rallied against the Ottoman threat and had shifted the balance of power in the Mediterranean. I listened enthralled.

We ate dinner with the crew below deck and then returned to the cabin. All through the meal and well into the afternoon, Edward spoke of his time in the Order and of the 'corso' – by which he meant his voyages on the Order's ships as they hunted down infidel ships all around the Mediterranean: scouring the North African coast; weaving through the Greek islands; and, best of all, destroying the corsairs. He had spent five seasons at sea, interspersed with periods of service on Malta, including in the

Order's famous hospital, where he had learned the science of medicine. He was more circumspect about his activities in more recent years, saying only that he often spent spells abroad in the service of the Order.

In return, I told him about Algiers. He was particularly keen to learn about its defences, its arsenal, its corsair fleet and aspects of its administration. I found myself eager to please him and was able to tell him much that was new to him. He listened, sucking on his pipe, inhaling both the smoke and the information I recounted. I drew on all the knowledge that I had acquired from my work. I was candid about the details of the city, but guarded about disclosing my feelings for the place and its people, particularly for my master and his family. I said nothing of my ambitions, of the happiness and satisfaction that I had attained there, even in my servitude.

Edward seemed well pleased with what I told him. I felt no loyalty to the city, particularly now my master was gone, and hence felt no guilt at revealing its secrets. 'Truly Tom,' he said at one point, 'it was God's Providence that delivered you into my company, so that you could become an instrument of His work.'

I felt glad to be working my way into Edward's esteem. Indeed, it seemed a prudent course of action, given the vulnerability of my current situation and the uncertainty over my future.

When evening came we again made our way down below to take supper alongside the crew. On the way, Edward introduced me to the captain of the *Gloriosa*, whose cabin occupied the remainder of the space beneath the poop deck, alongside Edward's.

The captain, whom Edward introduced as *Fra'* or Brother Guillaume, was a tall, slim man in his forties. He was of few words, which were all in French, and was taking his meal alone in his cabin, ensconced with his books and charts. He did not invite us to join him.

'Tom has already given me some important intelligence about the defences of Algiers that will be of great benefit to the Order,' Edward informed the captain in French.

The captain nodded in acknowledgement and gave me a thin smile. I struggled to follow the rest of his conversation with Edward but the captain appeared to bemoan the fact that the capture of the *Dolphin* followed by the necessary repairs to her rigging had set us back so much. Even now, he said, we were limping along only as fast as the *Dolphin's* patched-up rigging would permit. Edward's words remained polite but his eyes betrayed impatience and we soon left *Fra* Guillaume to his books and charts.

On the way down below deck, Edward muttered in my ear. '*Fra* Guillaume is as full of the joys of life as you were during the worst of your fever. He's always like that. But I'll not complain as he knows how to handle his ship. And that matters more than good company when you're out at sea.'

We took our serving of gruel and our places at one of the communal tables on the lower deck. Edward ordered us a tankard of ale each, followed by another. We ate and drank, replenishing my body and my spirits. I was keen to learn more about Edward's upbringing in France and, emboldened by the alcohol, ventured to start up a conversation along that line. 'You said you were brought up in France.'

'Aye, I did. My father and mother were in exile in Paris when I was born.' He spotted my raised eyebrows. 'It was a troubled time then in Scotland. My father was the Earl of Arran and a supporter of Queen Mary, but the country was under the control of the Regent Morton, acting in the name of the Queen's son, the boy King James. Certain matters came to a head and my father and his wife and brother had to leave. They settled in Paris and so I came to be born there.'

'But you said that matters have since been put right?'

'Indeed I did. Your memory serves you well. I would have thought the ale had turned last night into a haze after the way you staggered back to the cabin.'

I blushed and he continued: 'A few years later, my father and some friends were reconciled, one might say, with the young King James.' He gave me a wink that I did not understand. 'My father was restored to his former titles and estates and received the King's favour as a loyal supporter of the King's mother. Indeed, my father was even elevated to become the Marquess of Hamilton'

'And did you all return to Scotland then?'

'No, not quite all of us; my fate had already been set upon a different course.' Edward opened his tobacco pouch, extracted his pipe and began to fill it. 'At the time when my father had been stripped of his titles, the future for my family looked bleak. Yet we still had some money and I was of noble birth, so it seemed at that time a good idea to my father to pledge my life to the Order of St John.' He lit his pipe and inhaled a few times. 'The Archbishop of Glasgow, who was for a long time the ambassador of the Scottish court in Paris and a dear friend of my parents, helped to arrange for the *passaggio* which pledged me to the Order. And, well, the world moved on: certain events came to pass in Scotland, the politics changed but I was already committed to the Order, and so here I am.' He sucked on his pipe. 'Here I am,' he repeated in a low voice.

'Could you ever leave?'

'Leave? The Order you mean?' He laughed and pointed to the eight-pointed star on the breast of his habit. 'You see this star? I guess it's like that ankle ring of yours, except it stays with me even when I take my habit off and no carpenter can prise it from me. And anyway, who am I to question God's will?' He laughed again and I was glad to see his spirits revived.

After supper we returned to Edward's cabin. I climbed into the hammock while he sat at the table under the lantern, his eyes fixed on the peculiar sheet of paper that I had glimpsed earlier and that he had retrieved from somewhere in his habit. I again stole a glance or two at it over his shoulder. There were no words at all upon it, but rather rows of symbols. I scrunched up my eyes and peered harder. I could just about make out what the symbols were. They looked like the suits of playing cards: hearts; clubs; diamonds and spades. I wondered whether they comprised some kind of game or puzzle to while away the hours during a long voyage. Edward sighed as he looked at them. At length he left the table and knelt down at a chest, rummaging around in some papers that he stored there. He retrieved a small, blank sheet of paper, some ink and a pen and returned to his seat at the table.

I kept a furtive eye upon him from my hammock. Over his shoulder I could see that he was copying the symbols on to the new sheet. I said nothing and left him to his task while I wondered what these symbols might represent. When he had finished, he took his pipe once more from his pouch, filled it and lit it. Then he reclined as far as his wooden chair would permit and sat staring at the two sheets of paper, placed side by side. He punctuated his pipe-smoking with occasional muttering, sighs and shakes of his head.

With the rocking of my hammock and the satisfied feeling in my belly, I fell into a deep, restoring sleep.

Chapter 14: The Cipher

Edward was sitting at the table when I woke. He had propped up a small mirror and was attempting to shave: a hazardous task given the pitch and roll of the ship. When he caught my eye in the mirror he explained that he would sooner trust his own hand than one of the Maltese barber-surgeons'. He finished with more than one cut to his cheek for his efforts and offered me a turn with the blade. I declined: in those days, my beard grew slow and fair so there was not much to show from the few days that I had been at sea.

We breakfasted below deck, during which Edward asked me more about how I had spent my time in Algiers. Though I had come to trust him, despite the horrific circumstances of our first encounter, there were episodes from my life in Algiers that I thought best to keep to myself, such as my Islamic schooling and knowledge of the Koran. I thought it safer to talk about my administrative work for my master; Edward was intrigued by the detailed workings of the city. He insisted that, when we returned to his cabin, he would make a note of the key information, lest he forget it. He also said that he had some friends in Malta who would be very interested in learning what I could tell them about Algiers, or as he called it, 'the nest of vipers'. I found myself willing to oblige him, mindful perhaps of how my prospects had become dependent upon his continued favour, but also because I had begun to warm to him.

In particular, I remember that I told him about how I had helped my master to solve the mystery of the silver coins. Edward was fascinated by the matter and impressed by my contribution to its resolution. His broad chest heaved with laughter when he learned that the son of a Sultan had been sent back to Constantinople with his tail between his legs, his backside sore from a public beating. He also delighted in the knowledge that Murat Reis was now *persona non grata* in Algiers. He praised me for my cleverness. 'I tell you Tom,' he said with a broad smile, 'the Lord works in inscrutable ways. I am sure that it was by His will that you were taken to that hell-hole, so as to help to bring about its downfall. And it was doubtless by His divine plan that you were delivered to us.'

I nodded but only with a polite smile. I confess that I had long ago given up on God's Providence delivering me from servitude. Indeed, by the end of my time in Algiers, I had come to terms with my life there. Still, Edward had put ideas such as fate and Providence back into my mind and I turned them around there from time to time.

Back in the cabin Edward, as good as his word, sat me down at the stool on the opposite side of the table and found some paper, ink and a pen. He asked me to recount particular details of the city that had interested him most: the lay-out of its defences; the number of ships in the corsair fleet; the names and characteristics of its high officials and my opinion on their capabilities. He was thorough in his questioning and note-taking. When he concluded, which was just before midday, he set his pen down with a sigh, folded the papers and stored them in his chest. As he did so he muttered, as much to himself as to me: 'At least this will be something to keep them happy since I can't crack that damned cipher.'

'Is that what you were reading yesterday, a cipher?' I asked, my curiosity getting the better of me.

He nodded with a grunt. 'Little escapes you, does it Tom? Well, it would be generous to say that I was reading it. Looking at it, aye. But in truth I can make neither head nor tail of it. I'd show it to you but...' He shrugged his shoulders and seemed to weigh up his options. 'Well, I suppose there's not much chance that you're in Richelieu's employ; not even he would be that devious.'

The watch-bell chimed for midday.

'Right, let's go down to lunch,' he said.

Disappointed that my curiosity had not been sated and fearful that the opportunity had now passed, I followed him downstairs. We ate our meal with few words exchanged. He smoked his pipe, engulfed in his thoughts. After lunch he suggested that we stretch our legs a bit, and led the way up to the poop deck. I followed him to the stern, where the pennant of the Order of St John – the white, eight-pointed cross on a red field – thrashed like a tail behind the ship. He stood, looking out over our wake, watching the *Dolphin* labouring a short distance behind. The breeze ruffled the folds of his habit. After some moments he spoke to me over his shoulder, still gazing out to sea. I strained to make out his words above the flapping of the pennant and the clanking of the rigging.

'As you've guessed, the paper you saw contains a cipher. It was given to me in Paris by a friend of the Order. The problem is that I can't for the life of me decipher it, though perhaps sharper minds than mine will be able to back on Malta.'

'Did your friend give you any sense of what the cipher might relate to?'

'No. He had but a moment to pass it into my hands and told me to convey it to the Grand Master of the Order in Malta. He was due to meet with me the following morning to tell me more, but he failed to appear. I took that as my cue to leave Paris in haste. I suspect it relates to plans that Richelieu has formed.'

'Who is Richelieu?'

'Of course, forgive me Tom. Almost every Englishman would know the name – since England and France are at war once more - but not an Englishman who has been in captivity abroad these past few years. Richelieu is a Cardinal, and is the Chief Minister of King Louis VIII of France. In practice, he runs the nation's affairs.'

'He sounds like a formidable priest,' I said.

'Aye, he's that all right. With all of the powers of Europe at each other's throats, and France in the midst of it, I'm guessing that the cipher may relate to one of Richelieu's secret designs, but I'm damned if I know what. All I know is that a friend of the Order, at great personal risk, thought that the Grand Master needed to be aware of its contents.'

'May I see it?'

'Well, I've been thinking about that.' He turned to face me, his expression was grave. 'As you know, I am a firm believer in God's Providence and I reckon that it is His will that I should entrust you with a copy of the cipher, lest something should happen to me. But you must swear to me that, unless I tell you otherwise, you will pass the cipher to no one, nor reveal that you have any knowledge of it at all, save to the Grand Master himself.'

'I understand.'

'Swear it.'

'Yes, I give you my oath.'

'Good. Then first I must tell you that whatever befell the man who gave me the cipher, I fear that the same fate may soon visit me. If Richelieu's henchmen find out whom he passed the cipher to, as I suspect they will, then they will come looking for it, they will come looking for me.' He cast a wary look over his shoulder.

'Could they be here on this ship?' I asked.

'I don't think so, though I prefer to take no chances.' He placed his hands upon the butts of his pistols that hung from his belt. 'This is a ship of the Order and I am the only passenger aboard. To my knowledge, we took on no new crew at Marseilles. I confess though that the possibility that Richelieu's agents are aboard is another reason why I have been glad of your company these past couple of nights.'

'I hope I can be of some use, should the need arise,' I said.

'I'm sure you will be. There will be other ships sailing from France to Malta,' he added. 'That will increase the danger. So it makes sense for you to have a copy of the cipher. It will profit our enemies little to retrieve one copy of it so long as one of us retains the other. They will not know that a copy has been made and that you possess it. But if they catch you with me, then they may suspect you have knowledge of it, in which case your life will be in danger too. Whatever happens, I will have failed the Order if the cipher is lost before its meaning is revealed to the Grand Master.'

I nodded in agreement.

'Come,' he said, 'I will give you the copy I made.'

He led me back down to the cabin and closed the door behind us. He lit the lantern that hung from the ceiling, the natural light in the cabin being scant, even in the early afternoon. He gestured to me to take the stool while he removed the two sheets of paper from the lining of his habit. He unfolded them and laid them flat on the table: one in front of his chair, the other for me to inspect. I still have my copy to this day; it is creased and worn around the edges but its symbols remain as clear as they were when I first laid eyes on them. This is what I beheld:

My eyes followed the rows of symbols downwards, recognising them as the four suits from a pack a playing cards. I noted the different length of the rows, the different sequences, the varying gaps dividing the groups of symbols.

'You see,' said Edward with another grunt, 'why this has foxed me. It has driven me to distraction these past few days, and cost me plenty of sleep at night. I wake at ungodly hours to see those cursed, inscrutable symbols parading before my eyes. In truth, I have come to wonder if my old friend was simply mistaken, and all this paper shows is some instructions for a game of cards.'

'The different suits must signify something, they must relate to numbers,' I said, half talking to myself.

'That was my thinking too,' said Edward, 'and the numbers must in turn relate to letters. Believe me, I've tried everything I can think of. But there are only four symbols: the four card suits.'

'Yes, and amongst those, one – the spade – appears hardly at all. I've never seen anything like it,' I said.

'What could the damned things mean?' he asked. He filled his pipe with tobacco then sat back and smoked it, fixing his eyes on me as I pondered the symbols. It may have looked to him as if I were giving the cipher intelligent consideration but in truth any avenue that popped into my mind to explore soon revealed itself to be a cul-de-sac.

We sat there, at each side of the table, for around half an hour until our musing was interrupted by a commotion out on deck.

'Quick,' said Edward, folding his paper away inside his habit. I did likewise folding the paper and placing it into an interior pocket in my jacket, alongside the letters that my master had given me. Edward extinguished the lantern and we proceeded out on to the quarterdeck.

Many of the crew were already gathered along the starboard rail and we joined them. I found myself a spot from which I could see out across a wide expanse of sea. I wondered whether we had sighted land but instead my focus was drawn by the pointing fingers of the crew to a ship on the horizon. Edward had seen it too and went to retrieve his spyglass from the cabin. I followed him up on to the poop deck which was less crowded. The captain and a number of his officers were also there, their spyglasses fixed upon the distant ship. I noticed that one of them carried my master's spyglass, its Arabic inscriptions out of place in Christian hands. After a few moments Edward had seen enough and passed me his spyglass.

'What do you make of her?' he asked.

I saw the familiar shape of a corsair galley, with her distinctive lateen rig, and concluded that she was the escort ship from which the *Dolphin* had been fatefully separated.

'I believe that she is a galley known as the *al Wahid*, which was to have been our escort on our voyage to Constantinople. We lost each other during the storm – before you found us.'

'Is she heavily armed?' Edward asked.

'I'm not sure – I was never aboard her; but she is a corsair ship that was to protect us, so she must be something to be reckoned with.'

'Captain,' Edward called. *Fra* Guillaume approached. 'Tom tells me that she is most likely a corsair galley, the escort for the ship we've captured.' The captain nodded in acknowledgement, then walked over to his officers and began to issue instructions.

Moments later the bosun was down on the quarterdeck ordering the crew to make ready for battle. Some climbed up the shrouds and on to the ratlines; some trimmed the sails. Others went below to prepare the guns. Above me I could see signal flags being raised to communicate instructions to the crew aboard the *Dolphin*.

My stomach turned at the thought of another battle. I felt my legs weaken and grasped the rail to steady myself. If the prospect of an exchange of cannon fire was not fearful enough, the thought of a boarding party of janissaries or corsairs running amok aboard the ship made my spirits ebb away. I had no ankle ring to save me now.

'Will we give chase?' I asked.

'No, I don't think so,' Edward replied, 'though it looks like we will pretend to for a while, as a show of strength. The captain is not one for a gamble. We have a good prize already and he will be keen to deliver her safely to Malta. Taking on a corsair ship would be risky, particularly with the crew of the *Gloriosa* now divided between our two ships.'

'I'm glad,' I said.

'There is another question though,' Edward continued, 'which is whether the corsairs will be brazen enough to attack us.'

'Do you think they will?' I asked.

'I suspect your guess is as good as mine,' he replied peering through his spyglass again as he spoke. 'Their captain's nose will be out of joint at losing a ship under his protection. I should think he will have some explaining to do, particularly as he never fired so much as a shot in her defence.'

'Yes, that's true. The Pasha will certainly be displeased.'

'Still, it would be a confident corsair indeed that took on a ship of the Order, particularly so close to Malta. In the old days, Dragut Reis might have been brave enough or mad enough to try it, but there are few fashioned from his mould these days, thanks be to God.'

We watched on together for some minutes more: Edward through his spyglass; I with my naked eye. The sun was high in the clear sky above. The sea between the *Gloriosa* and the galley was a deep blue, the odd white crest of a wave breaking here and there. I imagined the corsair crew, watching our two ships from afar, calculating whether the wind conditions would give them the advantage, contemplating their next move. Below deck I could hear the cannon being hauled into position.

'Look,' said Edward, handing me his spyglass, I think she's turning away. I raised the spyglass to my eye and trained it upon the corsair galley. Around me a cheer rose up from the crew as they observed what I now saw. The galley, which had been running in a north easterly direction as if to intercept us, began to change course towards a southerly bearing. In a few moments more I could only see her stern as she sailed away.

Edward put a strong arm around my shoulders. 'Och, what a shame! They didn't have the stomach for it,' he said, a deep laugh rising up from his belly. I did not admit that I had not had the stomach for it either.

The captain passed another set of instructions to the bosun and then the order was given to desist from our battle preparations. The mariners began to trim the sails once more and new signal flags were hoisted to share the good news with their crewmates on the *Dolphin*.

'Come,' said Edward, his arm still around my shoulders. 'We have work to do down below.'

We returned to the cabin and set ourselves up as before: sitting on opposite sides of the table, the sheets unfolded and laid out in front of us. A pen and inkpot and spare sheets of paper lay alongside. Edward sat with his pipe, I with both elbows upon the table, my chin resting in my hands as I surveyed the rows of symbols.

'If this is a cipher,' I said at length, 'then you are right: the symbols must relate in some way first to numbers and then to letters. Yet there are only four types of symbol, and one of them is barely used. So each symbol must be able to translate into more than one letter.'

'Indeed,' Edward replied, 'but I am at a loss to know how. Clearly, it is possible for the symbols to combine. I have already translated them into Roman numerals, such that one suit represents an 'I', one a 'V' and one an 'X'.'

As he spoke he picked up the pen, dipped it in the inkpot and then began to set out numbers alongside letters on one of the spare sheets of paper.

'In such a way,' he continued, 'one can readily combine the symbols to form any number from one to 26 that would translate into letters of the alphabet – I being A, II being B, III being C and so on. But the results from using Roman numerals have proved meaningless, no matter in which order I translated the numbers into letters, for example if twenty-six signifies A, and one signifies Z; or if the series begins with A at fourteen, then B is fifteen and so on. I have tried it every way I can think of, backwards and forwards, but to no avail.'

I took up the pen and experimented for a few minutes, only confirming what Edward had just told me. He sucked on his pipe all the while. In the end I gave up, pushing the pen aside in frustration.

Edward smiled, his eyes seemed to twinkle. 'Are you familiar with the works of Francis Bacon?' he asked.

'Not really. I've heard of him, I think, but in truth I was no great scholar, even before I was taken away to captivity.'

'Well, I have an interest in his works because we use ciphers sometimes to convey secret communications within the Order. Some years ago, Francis Bacon set out a very clever method of translating letters into a cipher. This method consisted of just two letters – such as A and B. So, for example, A could be written as AAAAA, B could be written as AAAAB, C could be written as AAABA, D as AAABB, and so on.' Edward set all this out in writing as he spoke.

'So with just two letters, or two symbols, he could create the whole alphabet,' I exclaimed.

'Exactly. And in fact, Bacon's cipher was devilishly clever because he could create a false message in the way that I have just set out for you, and also create an even more secret, true message by slightly varying the way he presented the letters, in a way that a

trained eye could easily identify. So if he wrote an A like this—'
Edward wrote a letter 'A' down on the paper, 'then it was really an
A, but if he wrote it down like this—' Edward wrote down a
slightly different letter 'A', 'then someone familiar with the code
could immediately see that it was really intended as a B and could
decipher the true meaning accordingly. Confused?' he laughed.

'I think I follow,' I said. 'Could it help us with this cipher?'

'I have not yet found a way to make it work. It could be though
that the French are using some variant of Bacon's cipher. They
have doubtless intercepted a few English ciphers of this kind. It's
straightforward to swap Bacon's letters for symbols like card suits.
For the last few days I've been experimenting around that, but
again to no avail.'

We returned to silence, both pondering the symbols set out
before us. I took up the pen and began my own experiments.

'So Bacon's method uses two letters or symbols to signify letters
of the alphabet,' I said.

Edward nodded in confirmation.

'But in this cipher there are four symbols,' I continued. 'Would
it not be possible to undertake a similar approach to Bacon, but
using more than two letters or symbols? Using three symbols or
letters like this, say.' I set out the following letters:

A is AAA
B is AAB
C is AAC
D is ABA
E is ABB
F is ABC
G is ACA

'—and so on. That could easily be translated into symbols—'

A is ♠♠♠
B is ♠♠♣
C is ♠♠♥
D is ♠♣♠

'—and so on,' I finished, laying down the pen on the table
between us.

200

Edward frowned at my working on the paper and exhaled a lungful of pipe smoke. At length he said, 'So there you have used three different symbols or letters, and can once again create the whole alphabet.'

He picked up the pen and completed the series, right through to the letter Z.

'I'm using 26 letters in the alphabet,' he said, 'because that is how the French write it these days. And look, you don't need to use so many symbols to create the alphabet. This is much more sparing than Bacon's method. Each letter can be created with fewer symbols.' He looked at the series as if in amazement at what he had just set down on paper. 'Ingenious,' he exclaimed.

I picked up the pen again. 'And now let's try this,' I said, reworking the alphabet, this time using all four card-suit symbols so that:

A is ♠♠♠
B is ♠♠♣
C is ♠♣♥
D is ♠♠♦
E is ♠♣♣

I completed the series and we both looked upon it for a minute in admiration.

Edward picked up the actual cipher once more and shook his head. 'But in the French cipher, as you've already spotted, they only use three of the symbols routinely; one hardly features at all. And sometimes they only use one symbol or two symbols in a row.'

We both sat there, perplexed, trying to think it all through.

'All right,' I said at length, 'so we stick with three symbols to make the letters of the alphabet. The fourth symbol means something else.'

'Such as what?'

'Such as a number, maybe. Or perhaps it tells you not to translate the symbols from numbers into letters but to keep them as numbers.'

For the rest of that evening I focussed my thoughts on unlocking the secrets of the cipher until numbers and symbols danced before my eyes. I could not tell you what we ate in the meal that evening, nor the ungodly hour when the flame in the lantern surrendered and we took to our beds defeated. Our minds exhausted, we had made no further progress. The cipher, if indeed it was a cipher, remained impenetrable, tantalising and tormenting us from beyond our mental reach. Our spirits had plummeted from their elation earlier in the day. All night long, whether dreaming or awake, I turned the cipher over and over in my mind, infected with the same cryptic disease that held Edward in its grip.

The following morning, I was surprised to find myself awake before Edward. I lay rocking in my hammock to the sound of his snoring and the creaking rhythm of the ship. My half-closed eyes roamed around the dingy cabin, picking out objects in the half-light: the shelf above Edward's bed with his collection of books and the jar of ointment he had used to tend to my wounded arm; his sword and pistols, stowed within easy reach on the floor beside his bed; a set of rosary beads, suspended from one corner of the bookshelf and swinging with a faint rattle.

Those rosary beads must have kindled something in my memory. As I lay there, I recalled the men of Algiers, fingering their *misbaha* prayer beads, and the poor men without a *misbaha*, counting the prayers of the *tasbih* on their fingers in the way Jack had taught me long ago upon the *Sword*. How clever it was, I thought, that they could count all the way to ninety-nine on just one hand.

I thought again of Francis Bacon's peculiar way of counting, which only used two numerals but could count to any number by combining those numerals. I clenched the fingers of my left hand into a fist then opened them again, one by one. In doing so, I realised that Bacon's method could be replicated on one hand, using the position of the fingers: extended or clenched; up or down. And I figured that the way the men of Algiers counted to ninety-nine on one hand was similar to Bacon's method, only instead of using two finger positions, they used three: finger down, finger half up, finger fully extended.

My heart leapt inside me. Those finger positions were just like numerals. That's how they could count all the way up to ninety-nine with only five fingers. The thumb half up, all other fingers down, signified our number one. The thumb fully extended, all other fingers down, signified our number two. I began to count out the numbers on my hand to check. I counted my way up, one by one, combining different finger positions. The forefinger and thumb both extended signified eight. The middle finger half up but all other fingers down was nine; middle finger half up and thumb half up was ten. I made some mistakes and had to go back and start again, but I soon reached the combination of the thumb, forefinger and middle finger all fully extended, which signified twenty-six. As I lay there, looking at the two extended fingers and thumb of my left hand, the importance of this finding began to reverberate around my mind. The combination of three fingers and three different finger positions was sufficient to cover all twenty-six letters of the alphabet.

My heart was now pounding fast. I was wide awake. I reasoned that if the cipher used the symbol for each card suit instead of a finger position – say heart for finger down, club for finger half up, and diamond for finger fully extended – then just three suit symbols in combination, like three fingers, could generate any number between one and twenty-six and, in turn, any letter of the alphabet.

No longer able to contain my excitement within the hammock, I swung myself out and sat down at the table in the half-light, squinting at the paper that I unfolded before me. The more I stared at the symbols, the more I thought it might just work. Once I felt confident that I had arranged my thoughts straight in my mind, I retrieved a scrap of paper, pen and inkpot from Edward's chest, which despite my best efforts closed with a thud, causing him to stir a little. I retook my seat at the table and, with a trembling hand, began to translate the combinations of symbols into numbers. It was a slow and error-prone process at first, but the more I worked at it, the faster and surer my translation became.

My frenzied scribbling made Edward sit upright in his bed. I made a hurried and breathless attempt at an explanation, which only left him looking bewildered as well as bleary-eyed. So I showed him how to count up to twenty-six using just my thumb and two fingers, explaining that the combination of three fingers in three positions was like arranging up to three suit symbols in any combination, just like in the cipher.

Edward laughed when he saw me do this, inducing a bout of raucous coughing. When I reached twenty-six he clapped as if I had just performed some marvellous conjuring trick rather than some simple counting method that almost anyone in Algiers could have replicated. I laughed too and repeated the trick, now saying 'heart' when I had all fingers down, 'club' when I had my thumb half raised, and 'diamond' when I had my thumb fully raised. I continued, tentatively at first but growing in confidence, right up until I had three fingers raised, for which I said 'diamond, diamond, diamond.'

Again Edward laughed. He shook his head as if in disbelief as he clambered out of bed to observe the workings on my paper. His eyes traced the blotched rows of numbers and symbols, taking it all in. Meanwhile I lit the lantern, to give us more light by which to work.

'I think I follow your method Tom, and it's certainly a work of genius, but what about this rare fourth symbol, the spade?' he asked.

I had already thought about that. 'Maybe, when there is one of the spade symbols, which only appears at the first point on a row – look – then we must interpret that row of symbols as a number rather than a letter. If there is no spade, then the corresponding number should be translated first into one of our numbers and then into a letter of the alphabet.'

As I concluded, Edward sat down at the table, grabbed a fresh piece of paper and the pen and dipped it in the inkpot. 'Let's try it then, he said.' To begin with he wrote out the whole alphabet using just three numbers:

A is 1
B is 2
C is 10
D is 11
E is 12
F is 20
right through to: Z is 222.

'All right,' he continued, 'so let's begin with the following:
♥ is 0
♣ is 1
♦ is 2
and ♠ tells us when it is a number that follows.'

'And because the spade is a special symbol,' I added, 'it could also indicate which suit is associated with which number, if only we knew the ordering of the suits. It's like the key to the cipher.' We applied the symbols to the numbers that made up the alphabet:

A is ♣
B is ♦
C is ♣♥
D is ♣♣
E is ♣♦
F is ♦♥
Right through to Z is ♦♦♦.

We looked across at the original cipher, to see if we could now make any sense of it. Frustratingly, though it translated into an array of letters, it made no sense. Edward scrunched up the paper and threw it over to the far corner of the cabin. He immediately reached for another.

'So let's try it like this instead,' he said:

♣ is 0
♦ is 1
♥ is 2
and ♠ is again the special symbol to identify a number.'

Hurriedly we looked back at the original cipher and again began to match the symbols against the numbers and hence letters. Edward wrote the corresponding letters down:

'D – B – U – C – K – I – N – G – H – A – M'

Then there was a gap between the rows, and then the next row began with a spade: the number symbol.

'So that makes 23,' said Edward, checking against our schedule of symbols and numbers. 'And then: A – O – U – T.'

There followed a larger gap before the next set of rows of symbols began. Edward sat back with a look of immense satisfaction.

'What do you think it means?' I asked.

'I couldn't say exactly, but it would appear to involve the Duke of Buckingham and the twenty-third day of August. Perhaps the next rows will tell us.'

He set about translating the symbols into numbers and then letters in just the same way. He was in such haste that he erred a couple of times, but I pointed out the mistakes and he corrected them. It took him just a couple of minutes to complete the set of rows. The full translation of the cipher was now revealed. I set it out clearly below; with all the blotching and Edward's corrections, the original was much less neat.

Original symbols	Cipher numbers	Standard numbers	Letters
♦♦	11	4	D
♥	2	2	B
♥♦♣	210	21	U
♦♣	10	3	C
♦♣♥	102	11	K
♦♣♣	100	9	I
♦♦♥	112	14	N
♥♦	21	7	G
♥♥	22	8	H
♦	1	1	A
♦♦♦	111	13	M
♠♥♦♥	212	23	23
♦	1	1	A
♦♥♣	120	15	O
♥♦♣	210	21	U
♥♣♥	202	20	T
♦♦	11	4	D
♦♦♦	111	13	M
♦	1	1	A
♦♦♥	112	14	N
♥♣♥	202	20	T
♥♦♣	210	21	U
♦	1	1	A
♠♦♥♣	120	15	15
♦	1	1	A
♦♥♣	120	15	O
♥♦♣	210	21	U
♥♣♥	202	20	T

Edward sat back again, reading the second set of deciphered letters aloud:

'D – M – A – N – T – U – A 15 – A – O – U – T'

I looked at him, wide-eyed, for an explanation.

'Well now,' he said, 'it looks like this one concerns the Duke of Mantua, and the fifteenth of August, the feast of the Assumption.'

'Two people, two dates – what can they mean?' I asked again.

'Indeed, that is the question,' Edward replied, still surveying our work and beaming with satisfaction. 'I have an idea – and I don't think the dates are their birthdays – but this is something that we can discuss with the Grand Master when we arrive in Malta. For now, I know it's a little early in the morning but this deserves a celebration.'

He walked over to his chest and retrieved a bottle of brandy and two small crystal glasses. He carefully poured out the brandy and set the glasses down upon the table. Then he gathered up the papers, including the ones discarded on the floor.

'Let's keep hold of the papers with the original cipher on,' he said, 'but I propose that we now destroy all our workings, so that only we know that we have cracked the cipher.' He pointed to his temple. 'It's in here now,' he said, 'safest place for it.'

I nodded in agreement as Edward opened the casing of the lantern. He lifted the first paper up by the corner and lit it with the naked flame. When the flames spread and the paper became too hot to hold on to, he discarded it through the window at the stern. I watched the burning embers float away in the breeze as he set the next paper alight.

When the ritual burning was complete, we each hid a copy of the original cipher in the lining of our clothes. With the pleasant smell of burning paper lingering in the cabin, we sat down once more to enjoy the brandy.

'To your health, Tom,' he said, raising his glass, 'and God's Providence.'

The rest of that day passed without incident. The ships made good progress, aided by fair weather and a brisk westerly wind. The crew were in buoyant mood, knowing that they were closing in on their destination and their share of the prize. Edward and I spoke no more of the cipher but instead returned to tales of the Order and memories of home. Edward was still in high spirits when we went below deck for dinner. But he kept his thoughts to himself and a smile upon his face, rather than engage in conversation with the crew.

That night, as darkness engulfed us, I remember standing on the poop deck, leaning on the rail; Edward smoking his pipe and gazing across the open water while I surveyed the stars in a cloudless sky. The evening air was mild, the sea around us black as coal.

Towards midnight there came word from the crow's nest that land had been sighted. In the early hours of the morning we sailed into a channel between two dark strips of land. Edward told me that Malta lay to the south of us and her smaller islands – Comino and Gozo – lay to the north. We anchored for what remained of the night in a sheltered cove.

Chapter 15: Malta

The *Gloriosa* had already weighed anchor by the time I woke. Edward was packing his collection of books and other possessions into his chest. He bade me a cheerful 'Good morning'.

I stretched my limbs, swung myself down from the hammock and ventured out through the open door on to the quarterdeck. The coast of the island was slipping by on our starboard, the rising sun stealing into craggy coves and sweeping across golden sands. The smell of sun-baked earth laced the air.

We took a quick breakfast, of the usual gruel. There was a happy mood amongst the crew. Below deck personal possessions and hammocks were being stowed away and the ship was being made ready for disembarkation.

It took me only a minute to pack my few belongings into my small chest. Thereafter, there was nothing more for me to do but stand at the starboard rail and survey the passing coast-line across the narrow strip of sparkling sea.

Edward stayed in the cabin, writing at his desk. He joined me at the rail after a while, the folds of his black habit rippling in the stiff breeze. 'You'll like Malta,' he said.

'I'm just looking forward to being back on dry land,' I replied.

'Well, you're sure to find that, and much more. I've been away a few months. It will be interesting to see what's changed. Some new palace or church will be under construction, I'll wager.'

'Sounds like a lively place,' I said. 'Do you keep a house there?'

'No, not as such, though I would say that Malta is my home now, more than any other place on earth.'

'Where do you live when you're on the island then?'

'I usually stay in one of the inns of the Order – we call them *auberges* – each one belonging to one of the Order's *langues*.'

I must have looked bewildered, so Edward continued his explanation.

'The Order is divided up into several *langues*, roughly according to the native language of its members. Each of the *langues* has its own *auberge* in Malta. Since there is no longer an English *langue*, for my sins I take refuge with the scoundrels in the French *auberge*.'

'What happened to the English *langue*?'

'It withered away after the Reformation, when the Order's estates were confiscated. The old English *auberge* still stands in Birgu – that's the old city of the Order, just across the Grand Harbour from the new city. You'll still find the odd Englishman, Scotsman or Irishman lingering in one of the foreign *auberges*, but we are a dying breed.'

'So will we stay in the French *auberge*?' I asked, still unsure what would befall me once we landed.

'Not this time,' he replied with a laugh. 'I think it would be wise if we kept a low profile, at least until I've discharged our intelligence to the Grand Master. The fewer French knights that know I'm back in town, the better.'

'Where will we stay then?'

'Well, the ship will berth in the creek of Birgu, and we could do worse than seek lodgings there. It will be easy to disappear there for a while.'

'That's the old city, you said?'

'Aye, or rather one of the old cities. It was the home of the Order for quite a few years after we left Rhodes. It's very different from the new city – Valletta – as you shall see soon enough. The cities lie around the Grand Harbour, just beyond the end of this headland.' He pointed a few miles down the coast.

Around us, the sails were being trimmed and the decks were being scrubbed with a newfound intensity. I looked behind to see the *Dolphin* skipping through the waves in our wake. A banner of the Order of St John was being hoisted on her main mast.

As we neared the end of the headland, the coast receded to reveal the mouth of a large inlet. The land on the far side of the inlet jutted out to a point, upon which crouched a mighty fortress, golden in the morning sunlight. A towering curtain of walls extended behind the fortress.

As we continued our approach, I perceived that the fortified stretch of land was either a narrow island or a peninsula, for the coastline broke again beyond it, allowing the sea to intrude in another inlet. The land between the two inlets rose up like the upturned hull of a ship. Buildings of honey-coloured stone peered out above encircling walls. Waves crashed upon the rocks at the foot of the walls, erupting in fountains of white spray.

Edward spotted the direction of my gaze. 'That's the new city – Valletta; it's amazing to think that, barely fifty years ago, all of that was nothing but a barren headland. Now look at it. And this is Fort St Elmo,' he pointed at the fortress at the tip of the headland. I felt our vulnerability to its guns, which seemed to have us within their sights.

'The Turks took it during the Great Siege, but only after they had all but reduced it to rubble. Now it stands proud once more.' He took in a large breath of air through his nose, as if inhaling the spirit of the place.

We rounded Fort St Elmo and entered the inlet beyond it. This opened out to become the Grand Harbour. Another stretch of massive walls flanked the city, which now lay on our starboard. On our port side, several fingers of land thrust out into the harbour as if reaching towards the new city.

As we sailed into the harbour, the wind eased and the waters calmed. We were heading towards one of the out-stretched fingers of land, which seemed to have an even larger fortress at its tip than Fort St Elmo and was also protected by a sea wall. Edward said that this was Birgu, and that its fearsome guardian was Fort St Angelo. We rounded the tip, right under the cannons of the fortress and entered one of the creeks that lay between the fingers of land.

The creek was filled with boats and ships of almost every description. I marvelled at the skill of the crew for steering us in without collision. Quays lined both sides of the creek. Above them the land rose up, supporting a mass of buildings which jostled for space. Along the bustling quaysides, people stopped to watch our arrival.

The crew dropped anchor and furled the sails. Edward and I remained at the starboard rail outside his cabin, watching the flurry of activity. At one point, the captain came over and took Edward to one side. They exchanged a few words which, in all the commotion upon the deck, were out of my earshot. When Edward rejoined me he told me that they had been discussing his share of the prize money from the capture of the *Dolphin*.

We took our place in one of the first boats heading ashore, leaving our belongings to follow. We clambered up on to the quay on the Birgu side of the creek. As I enjoyed the unfamiliar feeling of solid ground beneath my toes, I saw Edward look around, as if trying to pick someone out amid the crowd. Then I saw his hands brush over the butts of his pistols, which I knew were concealed in the folds of his habit. Only his rapier was visible at his side.

We crossed the quay and took one of the narrow lanes that scaled the hill from the creek. Edward walked at a brisk pace and was soon perspiring with the effort. There seemed to be purpose in his haste. At the top of the hill we reached a square that was half shaded by a large church. Edward cast his eye around the square and darted off towards one of the narrow streets that led away from the opposite side. The street twisted around a blind corner. We followed it for fifty yards or so before Edward stopped outside a small inn.

'We'll try in here,' he said, looking up and down the street.

He pushed open the door to reveal the dark interior of a dining room. Its wooden fittings were like the inside of a ship. An old man rose from a chair in a far corner to greet us. He bowed to Edward as much as his age-stiffened joints would permit and offered me a slight nod.

'We need a room for a few nights,' Edward said in French.

'Of course sir, come this way,' the old man replied. His French had a strong, lyrical accent.

We followed his laborious steps up two flights of stairs to the second floor. He showed us to a small room overlooking the street. Modest as the room was, I was overcome at the sight of two proper beds, and the prospect of sleeping in one.

'Is this to your liking, sir?' the old man asked.

'Yes it will do,' Edward replied. 'I will have our belongings delivered here from our ship.'

'May I ask what ship you have come from sir?'

'That is not your concern,' Edward replied.

'Of course, sir. May I at least ask your name?

'I am *Fra* Benoit.'

'At your service, sir.' The old man made a painful attempt at another bow and began to retreat through the door.

'Oh and send for a messenger,' Edward called after him.

'At once, sir.' The door closed and I heard the innkeeper's slow descent of the staircase.

'Benoit?' I whispered.

Edward laughed then lowered his voice. 'Of course not, but it would be best not to shout the name of Edward Hamilton from the rooftops. We can't be too careful.'

'Are we in hiding?'

'Aye, you might say that. Did you spot the French brig, the *Belle Dame*, that was moored up in the creek? I last saw her in the harbour in Marseilles, as I departed on the *Gloriosa*. She has overtaken us.'

He stepped over to the window and gazed up and down the street. 'Remember,' he said, still peering out of the window, 'tell no one about the cipher. Your life may depend on it.'

A minute later we heard footsteps running up the stair. Edward turned around, fumbling in a pocket inside his habit. He extracted a sealed envelope.

There was a knock on the door. At Edward's command a young man entered. His hair was a thick mass of black curls and he had keen brown eyes and a swarthy complexion. He was out of breath. Edward passed him the envelope and a coin. 'Deliver this at once to the Magisterial Palace for the attention of the Grand Master.'

'At once, sir.' The youth bowed and left the room.

Edward turned to the window and surveyed the street below. Something in the street captured his interest. He spoke to me over his shoulder. 'I wrote a note this morning requesting a meeting with the Grand Master tomorrow. I sent him your intelligence on Algiers as well. We shall see what he has to say about the cipher but first I have a few affairs to attend to, if you wouldn't mind accompanying me?'

'Of course,' I replied, for I had formed no other plans and reasoned that my prospects were best served for now by staying close to Edward.

At length, Edward pulled his gaze away from the window and we left the room. On the way out of the inn, Edward instructed the innkeeper to keep safe any messages addressed to him. We retraced our steps back to the main square, where Edward bought some fresh, leavened bread from a stall, which we shared as a late dinner. We drank some water from the fountain and then headed back down the steep lane to the quayside.

Edward found one of the boatmen from the *Gloriosa* waiting at the water's edge. He slipped him a silver coin from his purse, instructing him to deliver our chests to the inn, to the room of *Fra* Benoit. The man looked confused for a second before nodding with a knowing look and clambering into his boat to return to the ship.

We threaded our way along the bustling quayside, heading toward the fortress that loomed at the end of the town. I heard a dozen languages and saw as many different styles of dress. What was most striking for me was the visibility of the women. I had become so accustomed to women covering their faces in veils and their bodies in all-concealing *haiks* that the renewed appearance of women's faces – their eyes, their smiles, their frowns – made me want to stop and stare. Edward afforded me no time for that.

The quayside came to an end almost at the ramparts of Fort St Angelo, which was separated from Birgu by a deep channel that had been cut through the rock. Edward hired a boatman to take us across the harbour to the new city. As we walked down the steps to the waiting boat, Edward threw another anxious glance back along the quayside. We took our seats at the stern of the boat.

'Where are we going?' I asked, as the boatman rowed us out into the Grand Harbour.

'I am in need of some new clothes,' Edward replied. He looked me up and down with one of his bushy eyebrows raised. 'By the look of it, I'd say you are too.'

I flushed with embarrassment and then we both laughed.

It was a hot July afternoon. The sun bore down upon us, reflecting off the sea with redoubled intensity. I scooped the irresistible water in my hand and poured it over my hair; it trickled down my nape and forehead, stinging my eyes.

Edward looked back over the stern and spoke to the boatman in French. 'That ship there,' he said, pointing back into the creek at the *Belle Dame*, 'when did she arrive?'

The boatman screwed up his eyes and followed Edward's finger into the *mêlée* of boats and ships. 'The French ship?' he asked as he pulled on the oars.

Edward nodded.

'I think yesterday, sir.'

Edward gave me a quick glance. 'We must be on our guard,' he said.

We moored at a quayside below the towering wall of the new city and Edward paid the boatman. Then we climbed a steep road that wound its way up to a gate in the sandstone wall. As we approached the gate, Edward nodded a greeting to a knight of the Order. The knight was overseeing the soldiers who guarded the gate and inspected the snaking procession of carts entering the city. He wore a scarlet tabard over his breastplate, a white cross embroidered upon it. He reminded me of the image of Edward from our first encounter, which was carved into my memory. The knight stood just inside the gate, evading the full glare of the sun. His helmet glinted as he returned Edward's greeting, nodding his head forward just enough to catch the sunshine.

Beyond the gate, the street continued upwards into the city in merciful shade. We left it by way of a flight of stone steps that led up to a long narrow street flanked by tall buildings. We rested in the shade for a few moments while Edward regained his breath and mopped his brow. As we sat there, an intrepid kitten came and brushed its black fur against my calf before slinking back into the shadows.

Looking left and right, my eyes could follow the length of the street, which was as straight as a ruler. On my left it ended at the foot of a high wall, defending some stronghold within the city. On my right the street seemed to disappear into the deep blue of the sea, and from that direction a cool breeze was being inhaled into the city.

We continued upwards along a street consisting of a long flight of broad steps. Houses and shops lined each side with colourful doors that split in two, so that the top half could open while the bottom remained shut. Every door had an ornate knocker, sometimes in the design of a creature from the land or from the deep, and often in the form of a clenched fist, such a familiar sight in Algiers. As we pressed on, my weary legs were relieved to feel the gradient of the street becoming less severe. Paving replaced the steps as the street began to level.

Our street crossed another, running in parallel to those lower down the hill but wider and busier. Most of the buildings opening on to this street were shops, though people evidently lived above them as open balconies were coloured by drying clothes. At this junction Edward turned right and we walked into the cooling sea-breeze until he halted outside a small clothes shop. He took a long look back up the street in the direction we had come from then stepped inside the shop.

The shopkeeper – a small, slim man with dark hair and an olive complexion – recognised Edward, and greeted him in lyrical French.

'Fra Edward, it is good to see you again. I trust you are well.'

'Yes, thank you, Paulo. This is my friend Tom.'

Paulo offered a courteous, broken-toothed smile in my direction, flashing his eyes up and down me, then returned his attention to Edward.

'I need a new hat, and a new cloak,' said Edward.

'Yes, of course,' replied the shopkeeper. He unravelled a measuring tape from a pocket and took Edward's measurements before scuttling off into a corner.

I cast my eye around the cramped shop. Most of the clothes consisted of various black vestments of the Order. They seemed to intensify the darkness of the interior. The shopkeeper returned with a black cloak, the eight-pointed star of the Order embroidered upon it, and a pair of black hats. He draped the cloak around Edward's shoulders, having to reach up on tip toes. Then he passed both the hats to Edward and produced a looking-glass for Edward to inspect himself in, making clever use of the minimal light that seeped in from outside.

Edward peered into the mirror as he tried one hat and then the other. Both were of a simple design with a narrow brim and a soft crown. Having chosen one, the shopkeeper congratulated Edward on his choice but then gave his clothes a disdainful glance. Edward caught his eye and his meaning; his own head tilted down so that he could take stock of his attire.

'Do you think my clothes are in need of a change?' Edward asked.

'Well, of course, you look very fine in them, but then—' Paulo fingered the collar of Edward's doublet, 'this collar would be considered a little large these days, I mean, by the most refined members of the Order.'

Edward sighed. 'Very well, do you have something in the latest fashion?'

The briefest of smiles played upon the shopkeeper's lips. He bowed his head and scurried away, before returning with a black doublet – sporting a narrower collar - and matching breeches. Edward handed me his weapons and retreated into a back room to try the clothes on. When he returned, the shopkeeper wrapped the cloak over Edward's new attire. 'Magnificent,' he said.

By the time he had finished, Edward had also purchased two pairs of garters and three pairs of stockings. Both men looked well satisfied. Edward paid for his new apparel on his 'account at the *auberge*' and asked Paulo to deliver his old clothes to our room at the inn in Birgu under the name of *Fra* Benoit. He fastened his belt around his waist, his rapier hanging sheathed at his left side. Then he stowed his pistols away into the belt, one at each hip, and paraded out of the shop.

I could not help but smile as he passed. 'Very fine,' I said.

'Good,' he replied, peering up and down the street. 'Then let us now find something to suit you.'

'Oh no,' I said, 'I have no money to speak of.'

'Tom,' he laughed, 'I am indebted to you for your assistance aboard the ship. Now let me repay some of that debt by replacing that infidel attire of yours. It would not be seemly to appear like that in the presence of the Grand Master, Antoine de Paule.'

Shocked at the prospect of meeting the Grand Master of the Order of St John, I followed Edward into another clothes shop further along the same street. There the obsequious shopkeeper furnished me with a green felt doublet, a matching pair of knee-length breeches and a pair of hose. Before we left the street I had also acquired a new pair of boots and a fine leather sword belt. As we proceeded, I put on each new item of clothing, so that in the end I was wearing a splendid new outfit. I did not send my old clothes back to our room at the inn, though I carefully retrieved the papers from the pocket of my old tunic and concealed them inside my new doublet. My only regret was in bidding farewell to my slippers, which were the height of comfort but were not at all to Edward's taste. The final purchase of the day was a small cake of soap, which Edward procured from one of the cluster of market stalls squatting along the street.

The sun was sinking by the time we had finished, tinting a curtain of clouds in rosy hues. We took a different route back towards the Grand Harbour. As we went, I heard a church bell

218

strike up somewhere in the heart of the city. It was the first peal of church bells that I had heard since I had been taken from Mottistone. That sound, so strange yet so familiar, brought a tide of memories flooding back into my mind. Another bell started up close at hand, then another and another until the whole sky pulsated with the chorus of chimes.

'The bells are ringing the *Angelus*,' said Edward, reading the wonder in my eyes.

Our street ended at a road that skirted the top of the city wall. From there I could look down across the Grand Harbour to the promontories that pointed towards us. Upon the finger of land that was Birgu, the stones of the buildings were soaking up the evening sunlight. It was like looking down from the lofty cliff-tops back home. The breeze from the open sea sent waves scurrying across the harbour, crashing them on to the fortified fingertips.

Mingling with the sea air I smelt the scent of exotic plants, heavy with pollen, and the cooking from a thousand kitchens. It was as if I was waking from a dream, or lapsing into one. I felt so alive; and life was good again. We sauntered along in our finery, following the street down through the gate in the city wall and back to the quayside, where boats were waiting to take us back across the harbour.

That evening we ate in the small, wooden dining room in our inn. A lantern hung from the central beam overhead. The innkeeper served us a stew with unsalted meat and some freshly cooked bread. Edward ordered a flagon of red wine. At another table an old man with barely a tooth to his name slurped at his stew. Having served our meal, the innkeeper retreated to the same chair in the corner upon which we had found him earlier, swatting the flies that dared to pester him.

After our meal, Edward reclined on his chair, his cheeks red, his pipe lit and his dusty boots propped up on a stool. I sat savouring the fullness in my stomach and the chance to rest.

Our reverie was interrupted by the patter of rapid footsteps approaching in the street. They stopped outside the door of the inn. Edward put down his pipe and sat bolt upright so that the stool beneath his feet toppled on to the stone floor. The door was thrown open, ushering in a waft of evening air that swung the lantern above us, making shadows twist around the room. Young, dark eyes flashed around the dining room until they alighted upon

Edward. With relief, I recognised the same, curly-haired lad who had taken Edward's message earlier. He walked over to our table and, with a breathless bow, passed a sealed letter into Edward's outstretched hand.

Edward nodded in gratitude, handed over another coin and the messenger turned on his heel and departed. For a moment, Edward's fingers traced the wax of the seal. His eyes swept the room, from the toothless man to the innkeeper, then back to the letter. Then he broke the seal and opened the letter, scrunching his eyes up to make out the words in the shifting lantern-light.

'It is from the secretary of the Grand Master,' he said.

After a minute's reading, he placed the letter into a pocket in the lining of his new doublet.

'We have an appointment tomorrow morning, at ten o'clock,' he said. Then he picked up his pipe again, which was still smouldering, and returned to his thoughts.

After supper, despite our aching limbs, Edward was keen to take a stroll. The intense heat of the day had dissipated into a warm summer's evening. He led me up along tight, meandering streets that teemed with life. The men and women of the old city had spilled out of their homes to engage their neighbours in animated conversation. Children darted amongst the shadows with playful shouts.

We arrived at a small square, right up in the corner of the city, lined on two sides by the city wall. I followed Edward up on to the ramparts and put my hands on the parapet, which was still warm. It was a fine vantage point, from which I could see not just the rooftops and towers of Birgu but also the creek on the other side of the city – 'Kalkara Creek', Edward called it – and the next finger of land beyond.

'This part of the city is called 'the breach' because this is where the Turks managed to break through the walls, until they were forced back.' He chuckled to himself. 'They say that even old Jean de Vallette, the Grand Master at the time, who must have been eighty if he was a day, was fighting the Turks hand to hand in the streets until they retreated in disarray.'

My mind conjured up images of wizened, half-starved knights battling against legions of janissaries. Truly it seemed miraculous that the Turks had not prevailed and that the knights of the Order had lived to see another day.

'I saw earlier, when we were buying your new doublet, that you carry more papers, besides the copy of the cipher,' said Edward, still gazing out into the night.

'Yes. I carry a letter from my late master to his daughters, which I promised to convey to them. I also have a letter that was to secure my freedom, should I have ended up in Constantinople without him.'

'Well, you won't be needing that anymore,' he turned to me with a warm smile. 'Tomorrow, we'll see if we can find a way to have the other letter conveyed to his daughters. Are they in Algiers?'

'Yes,' I replied, letting out an involuntary sigh. 'Are there communications between Malta and Algiers?'

'There's always a way,' he said, 'or rather, money always finds a way, which reminds me, we must also see about obtaining my share of the prize. I'd like to share that with you Tom, in return for your help in revealing the meaning of the cipher.'

'There's no need,' I said, taken aback, though my thoughts were sent spinning by the prospect of having some money to put to my name. 'It is enough that I have my freedom and the prospect of a fast ship back to England, if you'd be so kind as to arrange my passage.'

'No, I'd like to share it, Tom. I am not a poor man. The Lord alone knows how much money I have made during my voyages with the Order; there have been a lot of prizes. And, as you can see, my tastes are not all that expensive.' He brushed some dust off his new cloak as he spoke. 'So I am not desperately in need of riches – indeed, whatever I have left when my time is up will go to the Order anyway. So it would be as well for you to take a share.'

'Thank you,' I said. 'Do you think the value of the prize will amount to much?'

'Oh, she was a fair ship, that one you were on, well laden. And my share – as one of the only two Knights on board – may be quite valuable.'

A thought flashed in my mind. 'Do you think it would be enough for a ransom?'

He laughed. 'I guessed that you might say that.'

'For my friends: the children who were captured with me?'

'It could be. It all depends on how much their masters ask for them.'

'Then please let's try.'

'All right. I know someone who might be able to help and who should be able to get that letter delivered to Algiers. Let's see if we can find him after our audience with the Grand Master tomorrow. Now come, it's late and we could do with some rest.'

We headed back to the inn. Not even the blisters on my heels could detract from the lightness of my step. Inside, the innkeeper lit a candle for us, to light our way up the staircase.

Our belongings had been brought up to our room from the *Gloriosa*. I walked over to my bed and perched upon it, feeling the material of the blanket with my fingertips. It may have been nothing special as beds go, but to me it felt like the most luxurious bed in the world. I pulled off my new boots and laid my new doublet and breeches across the end of the bed. Then I rolled back the blanket and slid in, allowing my spine to unfurl as I rested the weight of my head upon the pillow.

At a small table against the wall, by the dancing candle-light, Edward sat working once more upon the translation of the cipher, ready to present it to the Grand Master in the morning. I heard the busy scratching of his pen as he set out neat rows of symbols, numbers and letters on the paper. After a few minutes, he stood up, folded the paper and hid it in the lining of his new doublet. He hung up his new clothes in the tall wardrobe that loomed in the darkest corner of the room. He placed his pistols and rapier beneath his bed. Then he picked up the chair from beside the table, tilted it and wedged its back beneath the handle of the bedroom door, making it difficult for anyone to force entry. Satisfied that it was wedged tight, he blew out the candle.

Chapter 16: Grand Master

Edward threw the shutters wide open. They clattered against the stonework, dispatching an echo along the street. Morning swept in.

During our brisk breakfast of bread and cured meat in the dining room, Edward asked the innkeeper for a bucket of water to take up to our room. The old man hobbled off somewhere in the interior and returned some minutes later, struggling under the weight of a sloshing bucket. Edward showed no inclination to assist him, so I offered to carry it up to our room.

When Edward rejoined me he stripped to the waist and put his whole head inside the bucket, so that the water flowed over the brim and between the floorboards. He emerged with rivulets cascading down his shivering torso and lathered himself with soap before rinsing by means of another immersion. He set his small mirror, razor blade and a cup of soapy water upon the table and sat down to shave. He all but instructed me to give myself a wash too. The water in the bucket felt ice cold. I emerged invigorated. Edward appraised me as he peered into his shaving mirror: 'There now, you've a healthy colour in your cheeks at last!' he said.

Once washed and dressed, both in our splendid new outfits, Edward closed the shutters with care, leaving a narrow opening that afforded us sufficient light to gather our possessions. At the foot of the stairs, we found the innkeeper ensconced in his usual seat. Edward instructed him to allow no one into our room and received a grumbling acknowledgement. Before he stepped out into the street, Edward inched his head out of the doorway and glanced to the left then the right, signalling for me to keep back. Then he strode out from the inn and I followed him in a rapid descent through the streets of Birgu to the quayside, struggling to keep pace on account of both the haste in his step and the blisters on my heels.

The breeze upon the Grand Harbour had eased to a whisper. Edward hired a boatman to convey us across the glassy water to Valletta. On reaching the other side of the Grand Harbour, I scurried along behind Edward's swirling cloak as he strutted up the steep road towards the gate in the city wall. Basking lizards scuttled out of our path and into hiding.

We entered the city as its many bells sounded the half hour. With no pause for breath we scaled the familiar steps that led up like a rib to the spine of the peninsula upon which the city was built. We crossed the street of clothes shops we had visited the day before and continued upwards. As the land levelled, the street opened out into a fine *piazza*, flanked on one side by a twin-towered church, after which we turned right into another long, straight thoroughfare, stretching right down to the sea. This street was crowded with people and lined with imposing edifices, interspersed with grand squares. Edward's pace was unrelenting. His head twitched from left to right; the occasional nod signifying a face he recognised in the crowd.

The street opened into another broad *piazza*, an entire side of which was occupied by a large but finely proportioned building. Its stonework gleamed in the bright morning light. Edward stopped at last.

'The Magisterial Palace,' he said, his eyes still surveying the people passing by.

He approached the entrance to the palace and a young man stepped forward. He wore armour and was cloaked in the insignia of the Order. His hand rested on the hilt of his sword.

'We have an appointment with the Grand Master at ten o'clock.' Edward spoke in French and in a commanding tone.

The young knight nodded and replied in French. '*Fra* Edward Hamilton, come this way.' He paused and gave me a quick glance up and down.

'He is with me,' said Edward.

The young knight turned on his heel and we followed him into the building. An arcaded inner courtyard opened out before us but, before we reached it, the knight veered off up a flight of stairs on the left, leading us through a doorway and on to a wide staircase of low, marble steps that spiralled upwards in an oval to the upper level of the palace.

The staircase opened at the corner of a corridor above another interior courtyard. The knight led us down the corridor, which was the most magnificent and the most colourful that I had ever seen. Its floor was patterned marble; its walls were adorned with tapestries and murals; its ceiling was decorated with exquisite paintings and delicate plasterwork. We stopped at another corner of the corridor, where the knight gestured into a doorway in front of us.

'The Grand Master will receive you shortly. Until he is ready, please wait in here. And please leave your weapon with me until you have finished your audience.'

The knight took custody of Edward's rapier. His eyebrows arched when Edward also produced his pistols, which had been concealed in his habit. 'You may collect these when you leave,' he said.

I followed Edward into the room, which was large and lavish and occupied by a score of men in pristine attire, loitering in pairs and small groups. The whispers of their discourse drifted up to the high ceiling above. Edward nodded in greeting to one or two of the men but kept us apart. We sat down on cushioned chairs alongside one of the walls. As we waited, Edward's right boot tapped a silent rhythm on the sumptuous carpet. My eyes flittered around the room, taking in the ornate carving of the ceiling and the detailed friezes that lined the top of each wall, showing knights from the Order in dramatic scenes, often pitted against turbaned enemies.

Each of the interior walls of the room had a door. Occasionally, one of these doors would open and men would be ushered in or would slip out, eyed by all within the room. After around a quarter of an hour, a door in the wall to our left opened to reveal a short man in the black habit of the Order. He scanned the room as if searching for his prey. His eyes settled on Edward, who met them with an expectant gaze. The man approached us with a noticeable swagger. As a hush settled upon the room and ears craned in our direction, he spoke in measured French: '*Fra* Edward Hamilton, His Serene Highness will receive you now.'

Without waiting for a response, the man turned and walked back towards the door through which he had appeared. We followed, Edward smoothing down his cloak with his palms. Eyes around the room followed the three of us until we walked through the door and the short man closed it behind us.

We stepped into a large drawing room, occupying one corner of the palace. The walls were decorated in a striking red material, their colour matched by the curtains and carpet. At the far end of the room, an old man sat in a throne, exuding power. Grand Master Antoine de Paule was dressed in the black of the Order, with the white, eight-pointed star emblazoned at the centre of his doublet. He had a neat silvery moustache and beard; his short hair was brushed back from his forehead. He watched our approach with shrewd, unblinking eyes. The short man announced our arrival.

'Your Serene Highness, *Fra* Edward Hamilton.'

Edward advanced, bowed low then knelt down on one knee before the old man and kissed a ring on his outstretched hand, before returning to his feet.

'Your Serene Highness, may I present to you Master Thomas Cheke,' Edward said in French; my name jarred alongside his foreign words. I stepped forward until I was a pace behind Edward's left shoulder and bowed low. I felt sick to the pit of my stomach at the prospect of having to speak French to such an important man. I had become accustomed to hearing the language spoken aboard the *Gloriosa* and here in Malta, but I had not yet had to speak it myself. Edward came to my rescue.

'Thomas is involved in the matters that I am about to relay to you, Eminence. He is also the source of the intelligence on the current situation in Algiers that I conveyed to your office yesterday.'

The old man nodded ever so slightly in acknowledgement, more with a movement of his eyes than a tilting of his head. 'Be seated,' he said, in a quiet voice of unquestioned authority.

He gestured with his right hand that we should take two seats that were set at a right angle before him so that we would have to turn sideways to look at him. Edward took the seat closest to him and I took the other. The secretary, for that is who the short man was, sat down at a table behind the Grand Master and took up a quill.

'Now, Edward, tell me what you learned in France,' said the Grand Master.

'As you know, Eminence, my business in France was to discover information of use to the Order and to further our interests at the court.'

The Grand Master gave another slight nod in affirmation.

'Well, the court of King Louis is consumed by the insurrection of the Protestant Huguenots and by war with England.'

The Grand Master listened; his gaunt face betrayed no reaction.

'The Huguenots are holed up at La Rochelle on the west coast, where Richelieu's army has them besieged. The English have tried in vain to raise the siege and it is doubtful that the city will hold out much longer.'

'We will not grieve for them,' said the Grand Master.

'Indeed not, Eminence. But the English forces, under the Duke of Buckingham are known to be preparing for one final effort to raise the siege.'

'Will they succeed?'

'Buckingham's reputation depends upon it, given his past failures. He will throw everything into one last push.'

'If La Rochelle is saved,' said the Grand Master, frowning, 'and the Huguenots are able to keep the French army occupied at home in the months ahead, then a long shadow will fall over those nations of Europe that are still loyal to the True Faith. King Louis's armies are needed to support the Catholic cause on the battlefields of Germany.'

'Indeed, Grand Master,' replied Edward, a little breathless. 'And that is where the intelligence that we have acquired comes in.'

He cast me a quick wink, out of sight of both the Grand Master and his secretary. Then he produced the paper with the cipher upon it from the pocket of his doublet, rose and passed it to the Grand Master. The old man's eyes widened by a sliver as he scanned the rows of symbols.

'I trust that you have deciphered this?'

'Yes, Grand Master, with the help of Thomas.'

'We are indebted to you then.' The Grand Master shot a glance in my direction. I blushed. The secretary put down his quill and strained to see the paper.

'The cipher uses an ingenious way of counting. It does not use numerals from one to ten but instead uses a system of counting in which there are only three numerals. This enables any number to be expressed with just three symbols, or rather three of the suits of cards as you can see before you.'

'Indeed. Go on,' said the Grand Master.

Edward now produced the second piece of paper that he had worked up at the inn, this time with the meaning of the cipher revealed. He again handed it to the Grand Master.

'As you can see, the cipher spells out a message, or rather two messages.'

The Grand Master read silently from the paper. Edward recited the hidden meaning from memory: 'D Buckingham 23rd August; D Mantua 15th August.'

The Grand Master's eyes were still fixed on the second piece of paper. 'You have done well, very well, in securing this intelligence.' He lifted his eyes to Edward. 'And do you have an interpretation for this message?'

'Yes, Eminence, I believe I do. When I was passed this cipher by an acquaintance in Paris, a friend of the Order, I was told that it related to secret orders issued by Richelieu.'

'Go on.'

'I believe it refers to two planned assassinations: it shows the victims and the dates on which the plans are to be executed. I suspect that more general instructions must already have been issued to Richelieu's agents, so all that was left was to confirm the precise dates, doubtless to fit with some broader plans concerning troop movements and logistics.'

'And who gave you this cipher?' asked the Grand Master.

Edward glanced at the secretary before responding, causing the Grand Master to cock an eyebrow.

'Eminence, it was Henri Pelloquin.'

'Henri Pelloquin – yes – that stands to reason. A true friend of the Order. I knew his uncle well: he was the Grand Prior of France in his time. And I have heard that Henri paid dearly for his kindness.'

I saw surprise flash across Edward's face. 'I do not know, but I fear the worst. He passed me the cipher at the sign of peace during Mass in the Cathedral of *Notre Dame*. Apart from telling me that it related to Richelieu's plans, Henri only had time to tell me to meet him in the church of St Jean de Latran after Mass the next morning. When he did not appear the next day, I took that as my cue to leave Paris.'

'That was a wise decision. I have learned that Henri is dead. The news was carried on a ship that arrived from Marseilles two days ago.'

'I fear that ship carried more than just news,' said Edward, his voice low.

'Yes, you would do well to be on your guard. Still, we must ensure that Henri did not give his life in vain. Can you tell us anything about the motive of these assassinations?'

'A little, Eminence, but only my own speculation. The reason for killing Buckingham is clearer. Richelieu despises him because Buckingham double crossed the Cardinal and everyone in the French court knows it. Buckingham promised to help Richelieu oust the Protestants from La Rochelle, only to switch sides and come to their aid.'

'Well, as it is written in scripture,' said the Grand Master, a thin smile on his pale lips, 'whatever one sows, that will he also reap. Buckingham's double-dealing is just the kind of thing I'd expect from Richelieu himself.' His smile broadened a little. 'Small wonder he was piqued.'

'Quite so, Eminence. The Cardinal may also have calculated that removing Buckingham would reduce or remove the threat of the English forces, as La Rochelle has now become a personal cause for Buckingham, whereas others in England might leave the Huguenots to fend for themselves. They have caused more than enough cost and trouble already.'

The Grand Master nodded. 'And Mantua?'

'That, I concede, I know less about. I can only reason that perhaps the Duke of Mantua, or at least his removal, is also of some strategic importance to Richelieu.'

'Indeed.' The Grand Master set the papers down upon his lap and smoothed his beard with his right hand.

The room fell into silence, save only for the scrawl of the secretary at his desk. I cast my eye around the friezes lining each wall. Edward sat stock-still.

The Grand Master broke the silence. 'The reason for disposing of Buckingham is self-evident. The motive for removing Charles Gonzaga, the Duke of Mantua, is less clear. As I recall he is also the Duke of Nevers, in France, so it may be that this is some local affair for Richelieu.'

'Doubtless the Cardinal seeks to effect some purpose through his removal, Eminence. Perhaps he considers that the Duke's heir will be more malleable to his influence,' said Edward.

'Perhaps,' said the Grand Master, who paused in thought for a few more moments, his eyes staring straight ahead, before continuing. 'We must now decide upon how to make best use of this intelligence.'

A new voice entered the conversation from behind the Grand Master's throne. It was the secretary, lifting his head from his scribing. 'I presume, Eminence, that it is in our interest to see the plot against Buckingham succeed – as you so wisely said - in the cause of the True Faith.'

'Perhaps, perhaps,' replied the Grand Master. He folded the papers and hid them in his doublet. Then he rose slowly from his chair, as if weighed down either by his cloak and vestments or by the burden of age and high office. He strolled over to one of the windows from which he gazed down into the square at the front of the palace. He now spoke with his back to us.

'Do you know the family of the Duke of Buckingham, *Fra* Edward?'

'Yes, Eminence. My late brother, the Marquess of Hamilton, knew the Duke well. They were at the court together, in London. Buckingham is from the Villiers family,' Edward replied.

'Indeed he is, and I was sorry to learn of the untimely death of your brother. You do not need me to remind you that it was a Grand Master from that same family of Villiers who led our Order through one of our darkest hours, from the evacuation of Rhodes to our establishment here in Malta. We owe a great debt of gratitude to his family.'

'In truth, Grand Master, I had not linked the two men, but I suppose that they may have been distant relations.'

The Grand Master continued as if he had not heard Edward's intervention. 'Moreover, Buckingham, or let me call him Villiers, has proven himself to be a Catholic sympathiser in a court dominated by Protestants.'

'That is true,' said Edward.

'Well then, I say it stands to reason that, while he has the ear of King James, he has the potential to be a very useful ally for the Order and someone who merits our protection.'

I saw the secretary raise his eyes and glance at the Grand Master before interjecting once more into the deliberation. 'Eminence, ought we not to recall the difference it could make to the Catholic cause across Europe if Buckingham's removal brought about the downfall of La Rochelle?'

The Grand Master, who continued to gaze out of the window, sighed. 'Sometimes *Fra* André we must put our duty to the Order above all else.'

'Of course, Grand Master,' said the secretary, though he sounded far from convinced.

'As for Gonzaga,' the Grand Master continued, 'that old fool still fancies himself as the King of Constantinople, or whatever mad title he invented for himself. That makes him a sworn enemy of the Turks and a generous benefactor for our cause.'

'Perhaps Richelieu would like to make an offering of his head to the Sultan; it wouldn't be the first time that France and the Turks have allied themselves together,' said Edward.

'Perhaps, perhaps... For all these reasons we need Gonzaga and God's Work needs him alive and well,' said the Grand Master.

Again the secretary glanced up at the Grand Master before continuing to scribe the record of the discussion. As if he had felt his secretary's eyes upon his back, the Grand Master turned to his left and spoke directly to him.

'*Fra* André, you must destroy what you have just written. The subject of our conversation, and what I am about to add to it, must have no record, for we dare not antagonise the French *langue*.'

'Of course, Eminence,' the secretary replied.

The Grand Master turned back to the window. The secretary's face betrayed confusion, anger even, as he made a point of ripping up the parchment he had just written upon.

'*Fra* Edward, we need to act upon this intelligence. It is God's Providence that it has come into our hands.'

'Yes, Eminence, I agree.'

The Grand Master now turned and walked back across the room to his throne.

'The timings of these assassination plots, for that is what they must be, are such that you must first warn the Duke of Mantua and then proceed without delay to England to warn Villiers.'

Edward paused, his brow knitted. 'Eminence, I am happy and honoured of course to obey you, but I wonder whether it would be more prudent to dispatch myself to one of these places and another knight to the other.'

The Grand Master's face again displayed no reaction. 'I understand your reasoning; but no one in the Order outside of this room must ever know of this course of action. That is why it must be you, and you alone, who undertakes this mission, unless you plan to be escorted by your young companion?' His eyes twitched towards me.

'As you wish, Eminence,' Edward replied with a bow of the head.

'Now, if you would excuse me gentlemen, I thank you on behalf of the Order for your efforts. Should you succeed in your endeavour then I am quite sure that, when the Day of Judgement comes, you will receive your just reward.'

The secretary took his cue, stood up and walked towards the door to show us from the room. We both bowed low to the Grand Master, seated once more upon his throne, and headed for the door.

'One more thing, *Fra* Edward.' The Grand Master's voice came from behind us. All three of us stopped and turned to face him. 'Be on your guard; for there are those who would sooner have you dead than have your message given to their enemies.'

Edward tilted his head forward in acknowledgement. The secretary opened the door and whispered in Edward's ear as he passed. It sounded like he wished him 'good luck' but I saw no cheer in his face.

The door closed. Eyes around the room lifted towards us in expectation. Conversations paused. Edward marched straight out of the room and swept along the corridor by which we had come, his cloak billowing, his boots ringing on the marble floor. I struggled to keep pace.

Instead of taking the broad spiral staircase down to the ground floor, Edward turned left, following the corridor around another side of the inner courtyard. He grumbled in English as he went. 'Mantua then England – he speaks of them as if they were mere villages on the other side of Malta that we could reach in a short ride!'

The corridor culminated in a flight of steps leading up to a closed door. A guard stood outside it.

'I'd like to see the Grand Armourer,' said Edward.

The guard banged his fist twice upon the door. We waited in silence for a minute until we heard bolts being drawn back. The door was hauled open with a groan of its timbers.

On the other side of the door was a stout, ageing knight in the familiar black habit. He greeted Edward in lilting French, clasping both of his hands. 'Fra Edward,' he exclaimed, 'I have not seen you in years!'

'Fra Basilio, it's been too long,' replied Edward, returning the warmth of the greeting.

We stepped into the midst of a long hall that stretched away to either side. Along its entire length, the high walls were lined with thousands of weapons: swords, muskets, halberds, pistols and maces. Down the centre of the hall, slender colonnades supported bristling fans of pikes and spears. At each end of the hall, an array of artillery pieces was displayed. Collections of armour were interspersed among the weapons; full suits of armour stood guard at intervals.

'And what can I do for you today?' said the old knight, 'I see you are unarmed. That's not like the Edward I remember of old.'

'Ha, no it's not! I had to entrust my weapons to the guard who escorted us in. But it is not for me that I have come today. Rather it is for my companion here. Fra Basilio, I present to you Master Thomas Cheke.'

The old man peered around Edward in order to size me up.

'We're about to embark on an errand, and Tom is short of a rapier,' Edward added.

'I see, I see. Well, Tom, I'm pleased to meet you. You have definitely come to the right place for a rapier. Can I tempt you with anything else? A breastplate, pistols, a musket perhaps?' He gestured in different directions as he spoke.

'No, thank you,' Edward replied, with a hearty laugh, 'we will be travelling light.'

'Oh, I see, well I'm sure I can accommodate that. Follow me, gentlemen.' There was a twinkle in his eyes.

He hobbled down the room, the joints in his legs clearly causing him pain. We followed him until he stopped at an array of rapiers. He traced his forefinger over a couple of the hilts and then stopped, tapping one.

'Why don't you try this one?' he said.

He lifted the rapier down and handed it to me. The rapier felt light compared to the ones I had wielded as a boy. At the end of the blade a decorated basket above the hilt protected my hand.

'Well, go on then,' urged Edward in English. 'Give it a try.'

I blushed and stepped away into some space so that I was able to slash and thrust unencumbered as the veterans watched me. The rapier hummed through the air, slicing through my embarrassment.

'What do you think?' asked Edward.

'I like it,' I replied.

'Like it!' replied Edward in exasperation. 'You may like it, but could it save your life? Could you kill a man with it?'

I let the blade come to rest upon my left palm, feeling the cool metal against my skin. I nodded, trying to conceal my inner voice that was telling me that I couldn't kill anyone.

'Excellent, excellent,' replied the old knight. 'Well then, let me find you a scabbard for it.'

He worked his way painfully down the hall and came back a few moments later with a scabbard. 'This should do it,' he said.

I fastened the scabbard to my belt and then placed the rapier inside it so that it hung at my side. In combination with my splendid green outfit, I must have looked very fine indeed. For the first time in my life I felt like a man.

'Good, good. And now, are you sure I can't tempt you with a little something else?'

'*Fra* Basilio, you are too kind. Really, we are now armed well enough for our purposes,' replied Edward.

'Wait,' *Fra* Basilio held up his wrinkled right hand, 'I know exactly what this young man needs.'

He hobbled down the hall in the opposite direction. I saw him browsing along the rows of weapons, as if searching for a book in a library. He reached to pick something up and headed back towards us. It was not until he was within a few paces of us that I could see what it was that he held: it was a minute pistol, barely larger than his hand.

'Well now, what do you think of this?' he asked with a triumphant smile.

The time had now come for me to venture to speak in French and I felt confident enough to do so. 'Does it really fire?' I asked, as the pistol looked like an intricate toy.

'Of course it fires,' the armourer replied with a frown. 'Now, let me see if I can find you some rounds for it.' He rummaged around in a few boxes until he found what he was looking for. 'Yes, these are the ones. See, you can easily slip it into a pocket, like this.'

He demonstrated with his own doublet.

'All right, he'll take it,' said Edward. For a moment I thought he might have been jealous, but then I figured that he would always prefer his pair of substantial pistols; he was not one for subtlety.

'Thank you,' I said, accepting the pistol. Following the armourer's masterful lesson in salesmanship, I was wondering how much Edward was going to have to pay for my new weapons, but he seemed to have no intention of paying anything. He clasped *Fra* Basilio's hand between his two large palms and shook it. 'Until the next time,' he said.

'Until the next time,' the armourer replied. 'I still remember the first time, on our *corso* aboard the San Paulo.' He looked at me. 'Ask him to tell you about that someday; it was quite an adventure.'

'I will,' I said in French, suspecting that Edward already had. 'Thank you, *Fra* Basilio.'

'Nothing, nothing. My pleasure.'

He opened the stiff door and we left with a nod to the guard, descending the flight of stairs to the main corridor.

'Do we not have to pay for the weapons then?' I asked.

'Goodness, no,' Edward laughed. 'They are the weapons of the Order, and we need them in the service of the Order. As you saw, the Order is not likely to run short any time soon.'

At the end of the corridor, we turned left and descended the broad oval staircase. Edward sought out the knight who had taken custody of his weapons. He was reunited with his sword and pistols. We both left the palace with a spring in our step, continuing along the main street that stretched down the hill towards the sea.

'Did that go according to plan?' I asked.

'In part,' Edward replied in a low voice. 'The Grand Master was as grateful as he could be in relation to such a delicate matter. Indeed, he all but promised me a reward if we succeed in our mission. I presume that means some high office in the Order: a nice priory or commandery somewhere or other; or perhaps a senior position here in Malta.'

'That sounds promising,' I said.

'Aye, but we've got one hell of a journey to get through first. And there's no guarantee of course that we will succeed. Particularly not if we've got Richelieu's agents on our tail.'

'That's why we paid a visit to the armoury, isn't it?'

'Aye.'

We walked along in silence for a minute or so, before Edward stopped and turned to me.

'You know, you don't have to come with me,' he said. 'I'm fine to do this on my own. There's sure to be a ship bound for England either in the harbour right now or within a few days that would take you home.'

'I know,' I said. 'But the Grand Master suggested that I should join you.'

'Aye, so he did; but you're not part of the Order. This isn't your problem to resolve. Hell, you've been through quite enough during all those years of slavery. You've got a mother and sister waiting for you back in England. It would be no dishonour at all to head for home now while you've got the chance.'

'What, when I've just been equipped with a fancy rapier and a tiny pistol?' I said smiling.

'They are yours to keep whatever you decide,' said Edward. 'They suit you.'

'What – are you saying I suit a tiny pistol?'

We both laughed. At that moment I felt sure that my prospects would be better served by sticking with Edward and seeing this mission through than heading back alone to an uncertain future in England. I also suspected that he could use my help rather more than he was prepared to admit.

'Well,' I said, 'I've already encountered some strange twists of fate, but I've come through them all right so far. Someone seems to be looking out for me.' I raised my eyes to the sky. 'So I reckon I might as well see where this particular path takes me: Mantua, by the sound of it. At any rate, I seem destined to end up back in England by August if we are to meet with Buckingham.'

'You're a good man, Tom,' said Edward, putting a firm hand upon my shoulder. 'I'm glad I didn't run you through when we first met.' He laughed heartily then lowered his voice to a whisper: 'Best not to mention either Mantua or Buckingham out loud – you never know who might be listening. And I've got no intention of going to Mantua, so you can put that thought out of your mind. But enough of this dallying, we've got things we need to do.'

Chapter 17: The Ransom

We set off again along the long, straight street that ran down the spine of the city to the sea.

'Where are we heading?' I asked.

'Right now, or later?'

'Now would do for a start.'

'We're heading to a merchant I know – a convert.'

'A convert?'

'A Jew turned Christian, or in this case more likely it was his father or his grandfather who converted, though whether they really did convert in this case is debatable. Still, I'm not the man to be testing his catechism – I'll leave that to the Inquisitor.'

'Why do you need to see him?' I asked.

'Because Simeon Azzopardi has contacts all around the Mediterranean. If anyone can get a payment through to Algiers then, by hook or by crook, he can.'

'You mean a ransom?' I asked.

'Of course that's what I mean. Didn't I say that I'd see whether we could get your young friends out of that hell hole?'

'Thank you,' were the only words that I could think of in reply but they did nothing to reflect the depth of my gratitude.

We walked along in silence for a minute or two. My thoughts lingered on the possibility of liberating George and Catherine from their servitude and returning them to their home. I imagined their mother, if she were still living, the tears in her eyes as she was reunited with her long lost children. I wanted to be there when that happened.

I imagined what it would be like to be reunited with my own mother and sister after all this time. In my heart I believed that they were still alive and well, but I could not know for sure.

Perhaps they had not been discovered in time; perhaps Murat Reis and his men had murdered them after I had been taken; or perhaps the plague had visited my village during my long absence and taken many a soul. The fact that I had never received a reply to my letters to Mr Dillington had sometimes given me cause to fear the worst, but I had no wish to dwell on such dark thoughts now. George and Catherine were going to be ransomed.

We had almost reached the end of the street. The great fortress at the tip of the peninsula, Fort St Elmo, lay ahead of us with nothing but open sea beyond. Just before we reached the fort, Edward took a right turn into a side street lined by a cramped and motley collection of buildings. He stopped outside a heavy front door and rapped its brass knocker, which was shaped as a lion's head. The door opened a few inches to reveal the face of a girl in a white linen headdress. There was a flicker of recognition in her eyes when she saw Edward.

'Is your master in?' Edward enquired in French.

The girl replied in broken French. 'No, he is not here at the moment. Maybe you can come back in an hour or so.' She closed the door.

Edward shrugged his shoulders. 'Simeon must have company. He likes to keep his business dealings private.'

We sauntered down the street to a stretch of wall beside Fort St Elmo. On the other side of the wall, the headland tumbled in a rocky descent into foaming waves. The full heat of the day beat down upon us.

Edward encouraged me to practise with my new rapier. I went through a rusty repertoire of cuts and thrusts and parries. Edward propped himself up against the wall so that he was in the shade and watched me. Sometimes he laughed. Sometimes he made suggestions to improve my swordsmanship. Sometimes he closed his eyes in rest.

I exhausted myself with my practice. Hot and parched I took a drink from a fountain across the street and doused my hair and neck in its cool water.

After a stifling hour had elapsed, we returned to the convert's house. This time the girl was happy to usher us inside. She led us along a cool, dark corridor to an interior room. The room was stocked high with papers and ledgers. Sitting at a table amongst them was an old man. He was peering at a set of accounts through spectacles that teetered on the bridge of his nose. Scant daylight ventured into the cluttered room and a candle burned upon the table.

The old man's eyes took a few moments to refocus upon our faces. 'Fra Edward,' he said, standing up behind his table. He extended his right hand, wrinkled and white, which Edward shook.

'Please take a seat,' he said in French, gesturing to both of us to take the chairs facing him across the table. 'How can I be of service to you?'

'Simeon, may I present to you Master Thomas Cheke, who has until recently been a resident of Algiers.'

'Pleased to meet you,' said Simeon, peering at me, his fingertips playing with the wisps of his white beard. 'I take it that your stay in Algiers was not wholly of your own choice, Master Cheke?'

'Not wholly,' I replied in the best French I could muster.

'By God's Grace, Thomas was able to escape from his servitude and came into my company,' said Edward.

'Edward, when you say by "God's Grace" are you referring to your sword, by any chance?' Simeon asked with the flicker of a smile.

'Simeon, you know me of old,' Edward replied.

'Indeed, and God's Grace has provided amply for you in the past.'

'And you have doubtless taken your fair share of it.'

'I am sure God's Grace knows no limit, so there is much to share. But Edward, tell me, are you on your travels again? Do you need me to arrange some credit for you with one of my correspondents?'

'Not on this occasion, no,' replied Edward. 'We need your help to arrange a ransom for some of Thomas's acquaintances who are still detained in Algiers.'

Simeon tutted and lifted down a ledger from a pile on a shelf behind him. I noticed that there was no dust on this ledger, suggesting that it was well used.

'Well now, Algiers is not the easiest of places to do business with, not least because of the activities of your fellow knights,' said Simeon, making a new entry in the ledger.

'I daresay,' said Edward, 'but if there is anyone in Malta who can arrange such a transaction, then my money is on you.'

'Except, of course, you are not allowed to gamble,' replied Simeon. I thought I spotted him wink at Edward through his spectacles.

'I wouldn't dream of it,' replied Edward, a smile creasing his lips.

'Can you give me the details of the people whom you wish to be ransomed?' Simeon directed his question at me so I again had to recall my limited French and attempt an answer.

'They are a brother and sister called George and Catherine Leigh. They are from England. And they must be about eighteen and fifteen years old.'

Simeon wrote down the details and I aided him with the spelling. Without raising his eyes from the ledger, he asked me in a quiet voice, 'And would you say that they would fetch a good price at auction?'

I thought for a moment. 'Hard to say,' I replied. 'George is a strong young man. I've not seen Catherine for years.'

'Is she – how can I put it – involved with one of the men of Algiers?'

'Not as far as I'm aware. She is in the same household as her brother, though she has always been confined to the women's quarters.'

'I see. And for how long have they been in Algiers?'

'Six years.'

'That's good,' Simeon replied, 'after that length of time, their owner is unlikely to be expecting a ransom, so he won't have set his expectations too high. Do you happen to know who their master is?'

'Yes. They are in the household of Dawood Yilmaz, an official of the city. My master encouraged him to take ownership of my two friends when they finished with their previous owner.'

'Your master, indeed?' Simeon raised a white eyebrow.

'My former master. He died.'

There was an awkward pause of a few seconds while Simeon finished entering details in the ledger. 'Well then,' he said, 'may I propose that you lodge the sum of two hundred ducats with me.'

My eyes must have opened like saucers.

'One hundred for each of them,' Simeon continued, 'though I expect the woman to sell for considerably more than the man if she is attractive. Of course, I will instruct my correspondent in Algiers

241

to make an opening offer of a fraction of that amount and to barter according to the response.'

'And what will your cut be?' asked Edward.

'One tenth of the full two hundred ducats, which will cover the interests of my correspondent too,' said Simeon in an emotionless tone.

'But only if the captives are freed,' said Edward.

'If either or both of them are freed, yes,' replied Simeon. He appeared well versed in this type of business.

'Agreed,' said Edward.

Simeon took a small sheet of parchment and penned an instruction for Edward's account to pay him two hundred Venetian ducats. He read the words out as he wrote them. Edward checked the details and signed. Then Simeon folded over the parchment and melted the end of a stick of brown sealing wax over his candle so that it dripped to form a seal over the fold. Edward imprinted his signet ring in the hot wax.

'Speaking of Venetian ducats,' Edward continued, 'I don't suppose you know when the next ship leaves for Venice.'

'They leave every other day or thereabouts. There is a ship, the *Santa Maria Formosa*, that leaves on the tide in the morning. She's rigged as a *polacca*, so she's fast. As it happens, I have a fair amount invested in her cargo,' said Simeon.

'And where is she berthed?' asked Edward.

'In Birgu Creek,' Simeon replied.

'Do you know the name of her captain?'

'Zen, I believe; Zuan'Antonio Zen.'

'Thank you,' said Edward, rising to his feet. 'Oh, and one more thing – I almost forgot. Tom, can you pass me that letter to your late master's daughters?'

I fumbled in the lining of my new doublet, retrieved the letter and passed it to him. 'The name of his eldest daughter and her address in Algiers are written here, in Arabic,' I explained.

Edward surveyed the Arabic script for a few moments then handed the letter over to Simeon. 'If you would be so kind as to ask your correspondents to see that this letter is delivered to its intended recipients in Algiers, I should be very grateful.'

'Of course,' Simeon replied. 'Consider it done.'

'As ever, a pleasure doing business with you, Simeon.'

The old man hobbled out from behind his table, edging between his piles of paper and stooping forward as if his back pained him. 'Sarah will show you out. Good day to you gentlemen.'

He shook both of us by the hand, smiling with all the teeth he had left.

We emerged blinking into the afternoon sunshine. Edward screwed up his eyes to peer up and down the street, visually probing doorways and the shaded entrances to narrow alleys.

'Thank you,' I said as we set off along the street in the direction of the Grand Harbour.

'My pleasure,' Edward replied. 'Like I said, what I don't spend when I'm alive will just end up in the coffers of the Order.'

The street skirted around a massive building on our right. 'This is the famous infirmary of our Order,' said Edward, throwing the building a glance as we passed. 'If you're ever taken ill, this is the place to come. We don't practise half the nonsense you'll find back in England. And you'll even dine from a silver platter here.'

'It won't be the easiest place to get to in a hurry, once I'm back in England,' I replied and laughed.

'Aye, that's true. The King of Spain didn't gift us these islands for the convenience of their location, apart from the convenience of fighting the Turks of course.'

We joined the street that ran alongside the parapet of the city wall, the Grand Harbour sparkling far below. A flotilla of boats and ships bobbed upon the tamed waves and a cooling breeze drifted over the water, carrying the scent of exotic plants and the cries of circling seagulls. We had the street almost to ourselves.

'Do you trust him?' I asked.

'Who? Old Simeon?'

I nodded. I remembered how the English Counsel in Algiers had failed to secure a ransom on our behalf. I had long wondered whether in truth he had ever forwarded on my letters to Mr Dillington, or whether he had simply pocketed any money that Mr Dillington had sent to free us. He had always reassured me with his earnest eyes that he had sent the letters but to no avail. In the end I no longer believed him: surely Mr Dillington would have paid the ransom, or replied at the very least, or my mother or sister would have written back to me.

'Well, I'd say that I trust Simeon as much as I trust any man. He's not let me down before and, in his business, he is only as good as his reputation.'

'So you think he'll really try to ransom my friends?'

'Aye, I do.' Edward replied. 'Mind you, in the world I live in, you never put your whole trust in anyone, save the Lord himself.'

'I take it you mean the Lord in heaven rather than the Grand Master?' I was only half joking.

'Above all, never put your whole trust in anyone in high office. Always watch your back when you're dealing with men like that.'

'Do you trust the Grand Master?' I asked.

'In relation to the matter in hand, you mean?'

'Yes.'

'Well, I'm sure he's capable of entertaining ulterior motives but I believe he was sincere in wanting us to avert what may otherwise come to pass.'

'You don't worry that he might himself be an ally of Richelieu?'

Edward laughed then lowered his voice almost to a whisper and glanced around to make sure there was no one close enough to overhear our conversation. 'The Order needs the income from our French estates, that's certainly true. If they went the way of those in the English *langue* then we'd be in a wee spot of bother. But there won't be much love lost between the Grand Master and Richelieu, if that's what you're worried about. After all, Antoine de Paule is from Provence, and though that country was swallowed up by the Kingdom of France more than a century ago, the rivalry between the *langues* of France and Provence is as fierce as ever.'

I too lowered my voice. 'I'm glad to hear that, especially after what happened to your friend.'

'Aye, Henri was a good man and a good friend. We must fulfil our mission so that his life was not lost in vain.'

'Do you think that Richelieu's agents are here in Malta?' I asked.

'I don't know. The news of Henri's death arrived in Malta before we did. So it would be quite possible for Richelieu's agents to be here too, if they had picked up my scent. God only knows what information they extracted from poor old Henri before he died, but it was common knowledge in Paris that he was connected to the Order, and it wouldn't have taken them long to realise that I was in town at the time. Someone might have reported seeing us together in the cathedral when he passed me the cipher.'

'But they don't know that we've cracked the cipher,' I said.

'Not unless they've been informed.'

'I thought you said you trusted the Grand Master.'

'I do.'

'Then how could Richelieu's agents know that we've cracked the cipher?'

Edward's eyes again swept the street to ensure that there was no one close by who could overhear his answer.

'Because I have my doubts about *Fra* André.'

'The Grand Master's secretary?'

'Aye – he isn't from the French *langue* either, he's from the Auvergne, but I'm not sure where his loyalties lie.'

'But they could lie with France?'

'It's more than possible. And he knows where we're staying in Birgu, assuming that lad who took my message told him yesterday, and he thinks he knows where we're heading to when we leave Malta.'

'You mean he thinks we're heading to Mantua?'

'Aye, that's right.'

'But I take it that we'll be sailing to Venice instead?'

'We will be, if we can find the ship, the *Santa Maria Formosa*, that Simeon mentioned.'

'Why Venice?'

'The Duke of Mantua has an ambassador there. He's quite famous – infamous I should say – for his antics. He will be able to send a message to the Duke. Our time is short, and doing it this way will be quicker than sailing up to Genoa or some other port on the west coast of Italy and making our way inland to Mantua. Besides, the Duke may not be in Mantua; he could be in one of his other domains. The ambassador will know. The date in the cipher is not till the fifteenth of August so there will be time to reach him with a warning, wherever he is. Warning Buckingham in time will be more of a problem, though in Venice we should be able to find a ship bound for England.'

'How will we find the Mantuan ambassador?'

'The Order has a priory in Venice; the prior is an old friend of mine. I'm sure he'll be able to help.'

'And meanwhile, any agents that the secretary puts on our tail will be hunting for us on the way to Mantua.'

'Exactly – so not a word more on Venice, understand?'

I nodded. The street was becoming busier and we halted our conversation. I could see that we were heading back towards the marine gate in the city wall. On our right, another large building loomed. I recognised its particular stench.

'This is the *bagnio*,' said Edward, his tone cheerful. 'It's where we keep all the infidel scum when they're not chained to the oars in the galleys.'

I didn't share in Edward's humour on this occasion. Instead I wondered whether any of the unfortunate souls who had survived from the *Dolphin* were now resident within those walls – their dreams of the palaces and mosques of Istanbul crushed in the stinking slave-house of Malta.

We pressed on. The street became crowded as traffic – people, carts and animals of every description – formed a disorderly procession to and from the quayside below. All had to squeeze through the marine gate, and we squeezed through with them.

Down on the quayside we found a boat to take us back across the harbour to Birgu.

'Are we going to find the ship that Simeon mentioned?' I asked, when we were midway across the harbour.

'Yes, but first I have an account to settle with the captain of the *Gloriosa*, *Fra* Guillaume. You can find the ship, the *Santa Maria Formosa*, while I'm gone. Simeon said that she's a *polacca*, so look out for a ship that has a lateen sail on her foremast as well as her mizzen.'

Both the *Dolphin* and the *Gloriosa* were still anchored in Birgu creek. The *Dolphin* sat higher in the water now that her cargo had been offloaded. Edward had the boatman drop me off at the quayside.

'Meet me back here in half an hour,' he said, as the boatman pushed away from the quayside with his oar, 'and keep your wits about you.'

I watched the boat slip away in the direction of the *Gloriosa*, then set about my task to locate the Venetian ship that Simeon had told us about. There were around a score of ships at anchor in the cramped creek. A hundred small boats plied their trade on the congested waters. They shuttled back and forth from both the Birgu side of the creek and from the city of Senglea, on the opposite side, which rose from the gentle waves of the harbour in a dense thicket of buildings, a towering church crowning its summit.

I walked along the quayside feeling suddenly alone in a foreign country. Edward had been more-or-less at my side since the moment I had met him. Being without him now felt liberating and frightening at the same time. My senses were primed. Danger seemed to lurk in every shadow and around every corner. I found myself scanning everything and everyone around me, much as Edward had done – looking for hiding places, sizing up people, alert for any sudden movements. I wished that my new green clothes were not quite so conspicuous.

About half way along the creek I spotted a ship that looked promising. A pennant bearing the winged lion of Venice fluttered from her main mast; lateen sails were furled on her fore and mizzen masts. The heat of the day made the air ripple, causing shapes to shimmer and blur, but when I screwed up my eyes, I could make out the painted wooden figurehead of the Virgin Mary at her bow. I concluded that she must be the *Santa Maria Formosa*.

My task accomplished, I considered how best to pass the time until Edward's return. My attention was drawn to the food stalls that lined the quay, wafting their aromas across the creek and stirring the appetites of a thousand hungry sailors. I would have bought some bread but I had not a single penny, or whatever currency they used in Malta, to my name. Instead I walked back to the spot where I had disembarked and sat down on the quayside so that my legs dangled down, the toes of my new boots skimming the water, my stomach rumbling with hunger.

In the sweltering sunshine, I was grateful for the rest. As I waited for the boat from the *Gloriosa* to ferry Edward back across the creek, I watched slender fishes dart like quicksilver among the shafts of sunlight illuminating the shallows. I began to feel drowsy and longed for the comforts of my bed in the inn.

A few minutes later I saw the ship's boat with Edward aboard push off on its way to the quayside. The steady stroke of the oars was hypnotic. The boatman navigated his way through the flotsam of the harbour and brought his boat to rest against the tarred rope lining the quay.

Edward's face bore a broad smile. 'As I suspected,' he said, climbing up the ladder to the quay, 'the *Dolphin* and her cargo turned out to be quite a prize. My share should keep me clothed and fed for a good while yet, and cover a few ransoms besides. *Fra* Guillaume was in as good a humour as I've ever known.'

'That's good,' I said, standing up on my creaking legs.

'Well, now, did you find our ship?' asked Edward.

'Yes, I believe so. She's anchored about halfway up the creek.' I pointed her out through the forest of shimmering masts.

'Excellent, then we'll board her in a wee while to arrange our passage; but first let's get something to eat. I'd say we've earned it.'

Edward led the way up a steep, narrow side street to a small square with hunched up buildings crowding its sides. On the far side, a bustling tavern spilled life into the square.

The innkeeper welcomed us and showed us to a table at the back of the cramped dining room. The stuffy air inside was heavy with pipe smoke and the boisterous tales of two dozen mariners. We ate a hearty lamb stew with ample fresh bread, washed down with a strong red wine.

As Edward filled his pipe after the meal I sensed he was listening in to the conversation of two men at the neighbouring table. His head was inclined so that his right ear was tilted in their direction and he had an unusual look of concentration about him. The innkeeper brought the pair at the next table a fresh bottle of wine. I heard him refer to one of the men as *Capitano* Zen'.

Edward reached out and gave the man sitting nearest to him a gentle tap on the shoulder. The man turned around in surprise.

'Are you Captain Zen?' Edward asked in French.

The man nodded again, his dark eyes surveying us.

Edward leaned in so that his head was close to the man's.

'Is your ship the *Santa Maria Formosa*?'

The captain nodded again. His companion craned his neck forward to listen in.

'I believe you are due to set sail tomorrow,' said Edward.

'Yes, in the morning; to Venice,' Captain Zen replied, his accent strong and lyrical.

'Then it is good fortune indeed that we should meet you here now. It has saved us a visit to your ship. My companion and I are looking for passage to Venice. Would you happen to have a cabin for us? We will pay you for your kindness, of course.'

The captain glanced at his companion before replying.

'Yes, signor, there is a cabin. It's yours for forty ducats.'

'Call it thirty-five ducats and we have a deal,' Edward replied.

Captain Zen agreed, extending his hand to confirm the arrangement. His sharp features betrayed his surprise that the haggling had concluded so quickly. 'I will have a boat waiting for you at nine in the morning at the quayside, near the fountain,' he said. 'For what name shall the boatman ask?'

'*Fra* Jerome,' replied Edward, without hesitation.

'Very good, I will see you in the morning.'

Edward returned to filling his pipe and Captain Zen resumed the conversation with his companion. In a corner of the room a man took up a fiddle and began to play.

We stayed for some time after Captain Zen and his companion had departed. Edward savoured his wine and puffed on his pipe. He seemed more relaxed than he had been all day, though he kept an eye on the entrance to the tavern, monitoring all who came and went.

The innkeeper furnished us with plates of bread, olives and goat's cheese. The fiddler played from one tune to the next.

All told we consumed two whole bottles of wine – Edward drank by far the greater share. He swayed on his feet as we left the inn, steadying himself with a heavy hand upon my shoulder, blaming the uneven stonework and thanking me several times for my company.

Evening had crept into the small square outside the tavern. Edward stopped to buy some tobacco from a pedlar who sat beside the fountain in the centre of the square. He offered to buy me a pipe but I declined. I liked the smell of tobacco – when it was fresh at least - but had never taken to the taste.

We ambled through the sinuous streets of Birgu, crossed the central square and meandered back towards our inn, both of us looking forward to our beds and one more night's sleep on *terra firma* before we endured a further week of nights under sail.

It was the time in the evening when the residents of Birgu come out into the streets, which rang with their chatter. Bare-foot children chased each other down alleyways; sleek cats followed suit.

It had been the perfect day and I enjoyed reliving it as we walked. I had met with no less a person than the Grand Master of the Order of St John. I had acquired a fine sword and a pistol to complete the transformation of my appearance from a slave to an adventurous young gentleman. Thanks to Edward's generosity, I had arranged a ransom for George and Catherine. And my belly was warm from a hearty meal and copious wine. Though my footsteps were heavy my heart was light as I was lost in these pleasant thoughts.

When we were only a few paces short of the inn, Edward came to an abrupt halt, his gaze fixed upwards towards our room.

'Look,' he said.

I looked but saw nothing out of the ordinary and figured that the wine had stirred his imagination.

'Look!' he said again, 'up at the window of our room.'

'What am I looking for?' I asked, still seeing nothing of interest.

'Look at the shutters,' he said, 'they are open.'

I thought about this for a moment; then I remembered how he had carefully positioned the shutters before departing.

'The innkeeper has opened them, or the wind has caught them,' I said. 'There was a fair breeze up today. You can still feel it now.'

Edward paused to consider this; he looked down at his cloak, which rippled in the breeze that swirled along the street. He shrugged his shoulders and we staggered the few remaining paces to the entrance of the inn. I opened the door for him and we stumbled inside. The room was dark; the lantern unlit. The innkeeper had vacated his usual spot in the corner.

'Something's not right,' Edward whispered in my ear, short of breath. He clutched at my sleeve to prevent me from advancing further. 'Come on, let's go.'

I closed the door again and we stepped back into the street. In that instant, Edward seemed to have sobered up. He grabbed my right arm above the elbow and pulled me a short way along the street and into an alley. We then followed the alley in a loop around a block of buildings until we arrived back on the same street, a little further away from the inn but still with its entrance in sight. There we waited, concealed in the shadows, watching.

Moments later the door of the inn opened and a man stepped into the street. He wore a dark outfit with a cloak around his shoulders. He looked up the street towards the alley that we had just entered. Another man stepped out of the inn; he rested his left hand upon the hilt of his rapier as he scoured the street. The first man gestured in the direction of the alley into which we had hurried a minute before; then the pair ran down the street in our direction.

My heart began to race, its throbbing accentuated by the alcohol coursing through my veins. As they approached I could make out their features clearly: both lean and tall, both dark-eyed with trim moustaches and beards. One's hair was slightly darker than the other's; he moved with a limp though that did not seem to hinder him.

Barely had the two men disappeared into the alley when Edward pulled me into the street again. Now we ran, away from the inn, twisting from one street to the next as if through a labyrinth, pushing people aside if they stood in our way. Every few paces we glanced backwards to see if our pursuers were on our heels.

Higher into the town we ran until we reached the defensive wall that separated Birgu from the rest of the island. At this point Edward took a right turn and we raced down the cobbled streets. Up in the church towers above us the bells began to ring, deep chimes echoing down the narrow streets; the clatter of our footsteps rose to meet them. Down we ran until we arrived back on the quayside, at the neck of the creek. Sweat poured from my brow. I wiped it with the back of a quivering hand.

We accosted an unsuspecting boatman, who was mooring up. Edward all but pushed him back into his boat. 'Row us over to that ship,' he commanded, pointing into the centre of the creek where the *Santa Maria Formosa* lay at anchor. 'But take the opposite side of the creek; approach the ship from Senglea.'

The boatman seemed about to protest, but either the look in Edward's eye or a glimpse of his pistols as he sat down in the boat was enough to persuade him to take up his oars and row in earnest.

I sat beside Edward, regaining my breath. We were both scanning the bustling quayside, now obscured by the dusk, for the two men. As our boat crossed to the other side of the harbour, the people on the quayside became a seething, indistinguishable mass.

'So now we know,' said Edward, reverting to English, 'Richelieu's men are on to us and there are at least two of them.'

'Somebody must have put them on our tail,' I said.

'*Fra* André,' said Edward, spitting into the dark water, 'I knew he was not to be trusted.'

'Well, let's hope he told them that we're heading for Mantua,' I whispered.

'They'll keep looking till they find us. They probably think that we've gone to seek refuge elsewhere, in one of the *auberges* perhaps.'

'They may expect us to return for our possessions in the inn,' I said.

'Quite so. I fear we must leave without them. If I can press upon Captain Zen the need to set sail without delay in the morning, then we should be on the open sea before they pick up our scent again,' said Edward.

'Let's hope so,' I replied.

'In any event, we must remain vigilant.'

As we approached the side of the ship the boatman called up to the watch on deck and asked them to lower a ladder. Before we climbed aboard, Edward rewarded the boatman for his pains but he pushed off cursing into the darkness.

When we clambered over the rail on to the deck a curious Captain Zen was there to greet us. His eyes took in our reddened faces and dishevelled clothes.

'*Fra* Jerome,' he said with a slight bow, 'you are earlier than expected. Welcome aboard the *Formosa*.'

'We were keen to sample your hospitality,' Edward replied.

The captain asked one of his officers to show us down to our cabin. It was situated at the stern on the lower deck. Our unexpected arrival attracted a fair amount of attention from the crew as we passed along the crowded deck.

The cabin was similar to my master's cabin on the *Dolphin,* though it was located on the port side. I sensed it had only just been vacated. There was a short bed, a table and a chair. Edward asked the officer to bring him a pencil and some paper and he sloped off along the deck to find some. By pushing the furniture into the corner I was able to make enough room to string up a hammock, if I could get hold of one.

The officer returned with the paper and pencil and Edward sat down at the table to write a short letter, speaking the words in French as he wrote them. He was asking Simeon to wait a couple of days and then to reclaim our possessions from the inn and take them into his safekeeping. He signed off the letter '*Fra* Jerome, *Santa Maria*'. Using some wax from a candle in the lantern he folded the letter and sealed it with his signet ring.

When he had finished we returned to the quarterdeck. Edward arranged with the captain for one of his men to deliver the letter to Simeon's house, and gave him the directions. The captain gave his man strict instructions to return at once and warned him not to be diverted by the temptations of the port, unless he wanted to be left behind when we set sail.

Once the mariner had climbed down into a boat and set off for the quayside, Captain Zen looked at Edward with a wry smile. 'I am surprised, *Fra* Jerome, that you are quite so eager to join us, though we are of course honoured to have the pleasure of your company for an extra night.'

'As you said yourself, captain, we did not want to be left behind,' Edward replied. I suspected that the captain saw the glint in his eye. 'We would appreciate it if you did not extend your hospitality to any other unexpected guests.'

'Other guests, *Fra* Jerome?'

'Particularly French ones.'

'I can assure you, gentlemen, that while you are guests upon my ship, you shall enjoy the protection of my crew.'

'Thank you captain,' said Edward. 'We are travelling light and my companion, Thomas, has need of a hammock.'

'Of course, I will have one brought to your cabin.'

We took our leave and returned to the cabin. I could have slumped down on the floor right then and slept upon the rigid timbers of the deck. My body was heavy from the exertion of the day, weighed further down by the volume of food and drink we had consumed that evening, and leaden from our breakneck sprint through the streets of Birgu.

Edward was nervous. He paced up and down as much as the cramped confines of the cabin would permit.

'One of us must keep watch at all times,' he said. 'We are like sitting ducks here. They know we are bound for Italy and, lo, here we are on a Venetian ship that's ready to set sail.'

'I don't mind staying up in here for a while,' I said. It was a lie: in truth I was so tired that I could have wept.

'No, at least one of us must be out on deck. I want to know whether anyone comes aboard tonight.'

We both headed back up to the poop deck and found a spot from which we could take in a broad sweep of Birgu's quayside and keep an eye on any boats approaching the *Formosa*. This was no easy task. Several boats crept across the harbour and deposited errant members of the crew on the ship's ladder. They slunk over the rail but most were accosted by the bosun before they made it to the safety of the lower deck. Since the bosun recognised them, we assumed they were no danger to us.

We were both happier out on deck than confined down below. Edward sucked on his pipe, its smoke spiralling upwards into the warm air. We compared notes on the descriptions of the two men who had emerged from the inn. After about an hour I alerted Edward to the return of the mariner who had taken his letter to Simeon. Edward intercepted him as he clambered aboard and offered him a couple of coins for his efforts. The mariner grasped the coins but, perhaps out of deference, seemed unwilling to look Edward in the eye. He slipped away down a hatch to the lower deck.

The night inched by. Rather than sleep in the cabin, in the end we decided to spend the night out on deck, taking it in turns to sleep. Mercifully, Edward let me sleep first. When he woke me for my watch he warned me with a painful grasp of my arm not to fall asleep. I did not, though how I achieved that feat to this day I know not.

Morning came and the rising sun stirred up a gentle breeze. My neck and limbs were stiff from the hardness of the deck and the chill of the early hours. To maintain our constant watch, we took breakfast in turns below deck, receiving a bowl of gruel each. Edward exhorted me to remain vigilant and I kept a close watch over the quayside and the waters around us. No boats approached the *Formosa* that morning.

At around nine o'clock the order was given to weigh anchor. With great skill, the crew navigated our departure from the creek, joining a small fleet of fishing boats and ships riding upon the tide. As we crossed the Grand Harbour, the morning sun ignited the imperious new city of Valletta on our port side and the indomitable old town of Birgu on our starboard.

We were soon under full sail and out on the open sea, the winged lion of St Mark streaming from the main mast. My heart was as light as the breeze. I felt as free as the seagulls that formed our winged escort high above.

Chapter 18: Venice

The *Santa Maria Formosa* was a sleek but heavily armed trading vessel. Her cosmopolitan crew were drawn from all around the Mediterranean, drawn to the melting pot of Venice and into her merchant navy. They sailed her with more skill and dedication than the crews of the *Sword* or the *Dolphin*, in my reckoning, equalled only by the crew of the *Gloriosa*. And they were driven neither by the *jihad* of the Barbary corsairs nor by the crusade of the Order of St John but by the pursuit of profit. Time gained was money earned; time lost was money forgone.

We passed the southern tip of Sicily by dusk on the first day and pressed on. The next day we sailed up the eastern flank of Sicily. Edward was my guide to the land unfurling along the horizon. We passed places that every youth in England has heard of in exotic tales but few have seen with their own eyes: Syracuse, Catania and Mount Etna brooding above.

We sailed on, through day and night, passing the toe of Italy then rounding her heel and heading northwest into the Adriatic. During these days, Edward and I kept ourselves aloof from the crew, just as the gulls following overhead were careful to maintain their distance, swooping down on rare forays to fill their bellies on scraps from the galley.

We mingled with the crew only for breakfast and dinner. Captain Zen always invited us to his table for supper. He delighted in exchanging sailors' tales with Edward and engaging in grittier subjects such as the politics of war, not least the turmoil that was now sweeping across Europe. I contributed when the conversation turned to matters concerning the Ottoman Empire. Captain Zen took much amusement from my description of Ali Biçnin, whom Zen said he had once known as Picenino, an adventurous but

255

penniless young merchant in Venice. Zen could not understand why Ali Biçnin had ploughed such a fortune into the construction of a mosque. On that he and Edward were of one mind.

They spoke of a golden era, when the ships of Venice and the Order had joined forces to defeat the Turks at the great battle of Lepanto. But I gathered that relations had soured of late between Malta and Venice. Captain Zen complained about Venetian ships having their cargos confiscated by the Order, for which Edward made no apology. 'If you trade with the devil then your cargos deserve to be forfeited,' was Edward's view on the matter. For Zuan'Antonio Zen, by contrast, money was the creed to which all nations adhered. Acts motivated by religion were his heresy.

Outside of these discussions with the captain, I remained almost always in Edward's company. Not only was he my guide to the places that we passed, he breathed life into those places through the stories he told. In particular, he built up a longing on my part to see Venice – *La Serenissima* – the city that rises from water. 'You'll be amazed by her riches,' he assured me. 'They say some Venetian merchants are richer than dukes, princes and even kings.'

The waters of the Adriatic were busy with boats and ships of varying types – from simple, single-masted fishing boats to galleasses and galleons. The captain seemed unconcerned about the risk of Barbary pirates. 'Thanks to our friends in Malta, and our own warships, I do not think we will be troubled by corsairs,' he said, 'and if all else fails, then we can look after ourselves.'

Edward agreed. He ventured that the local Uskok pirates sailing from the coast of Dalmatia posed a greater risk, though even they had been quelled for the best part of a decade and would be foolhardy to try their luck with a ship such as this. Edward had already inspected the *Formosa's* guns and was satisfied.

I remember these days as long and restful. When the heat of the day was at its most intense, I retreated to my hammock and slept, lulled by the creaking timbers and distant cries of the pursuing gulls. During the evenings, after supper, Edward and I would sit out under the stars, he with his pipe, talking about people and places, present and past. He loved to recount the exploits of the heroes of the Order, which he described with the art of a master storyteller, his colourful words betraying his love of reading. He pined for the books he had left in the inn at Birgu and promised to

256

make amends in Venice. When the chill of the night air began to bite we would return below deck, I to my hammock and Edward to his bed.

We dropped anchor just once at the port of Ancona, arriving before noon and staying overnight. This was one stop too many for Edward, who was keen to proceed in all haste to Venice. He was counting down the days to the dates contained in the cipher. He knew that we had few, if any, days to spare if we were to make it from Venice to England in time. Edward made his impatience known to Captain Zen, but there was business to be done, and the captain would not be moved.

'This was not mentioned when we agreed our passage, Captain,' Edward remonstrated.

'You did not ask, *Fra* Jerome. If you had, I would have told you,' Zen replied.

The *Formosa* was offloading a cargo of cotton and other African goods and took on board a cargo of silks and spices. The captain explained that the warehouses of Ancona were full of exotic goods brought on ships from the Levant and beyond, for onward shipment via the overland routes into Europe. The canny captain reckoned that the prices for silk and most spices would be higher in Venice and that he would therefore be able to make a handsome margin from the final leg of this voyage.

We set sail again in the morning, but not before Edward had considered alternative means of transport to complete our journey, and not before Captain Zen had been urged in the most forthright terms to weigh anchor. The last of the sacks of spices were not loaded until mid-morning and the sun was high in the sky by the time we departed Ancona.

We continued our voyage north, the land rolling past on our port side. Increasing numbers of vessels navigated the waters around us. Just as on land all roads are said to lead to Rome, so it seemed that all the sea lanes now led to Venice.

As dusk fell, the wind eased to a gentle breeze and the sea was becalmed. This was in sharp contrast to Edward's temper, which had not recovered from our unexpected stop-over in Ancona. 'We'd be there by now if we had pressed on,' he muttered, 'rather than drifting idly, like some lame duck. The men should be at the oars.' He took up a position on the poop deck, surveying the darkening horizon for signs of trouble and berating our lack of progress as he willed the ship onwards.

It was late afternoon on the following day that the *Formosa* completed the final leg of her voyage. Edward and I were watching from the poop deck as she passed through a channel between two narrow strips of land that shielded the lagoon of Venice from the encroaching Adriatic. Although the sky overhead was clear and the water of the lagoon a translucent blue, storm clouds threatened to roll in from the mountains ranging across the northern horizon.

We passed a succession of mudflats and small islands, most of which were given over to cultivation, before the great city began to unfurl her splendour. A thicket of buildings rose up from the lagoon, sprouting dozens of domes and pinnacles. I had never encountered such a concentrated mass of humanity. A score of ships lay at anchor in the harbour that stretched out before us, both warships and merchantmen, and hundreds of smaller boats littered the water.

We dropped anchor in the harbour, overlooked on each side by lofty, pointed bell towers. Edward said that the one on our starboard was the *campanile* or bell tower of St Mark and that the harbour, or basin, was named in his honour too.

Captain Zen did us the final courtesy of allowing us to leave upon the first boat, which was lowered over the side. He wished us good fortune on our adventure as he bade us farewell. The two boatmen from the *Formosa* rowed with the zest of sailors returning home. They chatted to each other over the rattle of the oars in the rowlocks and the lapping of the waters.

The harbour was awash with life. There were rowing boats like ours but also long, slender black boats with a central cabin, which appeared to be punted along by standing boatmen. These were the famous *gondolas* and *gondoliers* that Edward had described during our voyage north; he assured me that they were rowing, not punting. The evening air resounded with lyrical shouts as the *gondoliers* called to each other from boat to boat.

Edward asked the boatmen to set us ashore at the *Molo:* a stretch of quayside close to the *campanile* of St Mark, whose brickwork tower now soared above us, culminating in a pyramid spire. It was the tallest building I had ever seen, save perhaps for the spire of St Paul's in London.

The quayside opened out into a grand square, at the entrance to which two great columns stood like proud and rigid sentinels, guarding the interior of the city. We did not pass between them; instead Edward turned right and proceeded along the crowded quay. We threaded a path through the arcade of a magnificent building. Its design reminded me of the great cathedrals of England but also of the mosques of Algiers, a thought that I shared with Edward as we pushed our way along.

'This is the palace of the Doge, the elected ruler of Venice,' he explained, 'and it looks this way because this city lies at the crossroads between our world and the Orient. Like Janus, Venice looks both ways, with two faces: all too willing to be at peace with the Sultan for my liking.'

I imagined a whole city of people like Captain Zen, all focused on the quest for profit.

'Where are we heading?' I asked.

'To the Priory of the Order,' replied Edward, who knew the way, or at least made out that he did.

At the end of the Doge's palace the quay was interrupted by a canal leading into the interior of the city. This was crossed by an arched bridge just high enough to allow gondolas to pass beneath. A short distance along the canal the water was spanned at a higher level by an enclosed bridge, connecting the palace to a building on the other side of the canal. I stopped for a moment to watch a gondola disappear into the gloom beneath.

Edward pointed at the higher bridge linking the buildings. 'Look at the bars on the windows. They say they lead condemned men across that bridge to their doom.'

'Then I hope we don't get into any trouble,' I replied.

We continued along the bustling quayside, lined with grand edifices on the landward side and with gaily coloured mooring poles on the seaward. We crossed several further bridges spanning canals before Edward took a left turn into the city and we entered a maze of narrow streets and alleys, of bridges and small squares. I was amazed that he could remember the way, and in truth he hesitated on occasion, though he assured me that he'd 'been here before, many a time.' I half believed him.

At length we turned into a short, dead-end street with a stable block on the left and a church on the right. It ended in a grand doorway. 'Here we are,' he said in triumph.

He knocked on the door, which was opened by a servant whose tunic sported the eight-pointed star of the Order. He recognised Edward as a knight of the Order and ushered us inside.

'Is the prior in residence?' Edward asked in French.

'Yes, sir. Who shall I say seeks his company?'

'I am *Fra* Edward. He will know who I am.'

'Yes sir, please, wait in here.'

He showed us into a large room, lit by several lanterns and opening on to a cloister. Though there were comfortable seats Edward stood in anticipation.

'So you know the prior?' I asked.

'Och aye. We know each other of old, from the *corso*. Until a couple of years ago, Nicolò Cavaretta was Admiral of the Fleet.'

I gazed out into the dusk-filled cloister, watching members of the household scurrying about their duties.

'*Fra* Edward,' came a hearty shout from the doorway. 'How are you my friend?' The language was French but the lilting accent was unmistakeably Italian. I turned to see a silver haired man with a leathery complexion embracing Edward with both arms.

'I am very well, Prior,' said Edward, 'and I can see that you are keeping well too.' Edward cast an admiring eye around the room.

'Ah, it is but a modest abode compared to some I have known,' replied the prior with a mischievous smile, 'and it makes a pleasant change from Valletta.'

'I always thought you would retire back to Sicily,' said Edward.

'Well, God willing, there is still time, still time. But come, let us sit.'

He gestured to the chairs and sat down in one himself.

'And who is your companion?' He threw me a charming smile.

'Nicolò, may I present to you my trusted friend, Master Thomas Cheke of England.'

'Ah, an Englishman, so just like you, eh Edward?'

'Oh yes; we are as hard to tell apart as a Sicilian is from a Venetian,' Edward replied.

'Then I know that your wit has not deserted you, Edward, even if your body is looking a little the worse for wear. But come, you look hungry and thirsty, so please sit and we will bring you some refreshments. Iseppo—' the servant appeared in the doorway, '— please bring these gentlemen our best food and wine.'

'You are too kind, Nicolò,' said Edward.

'As we say: my house is your house. But this is an unexpected pleasure, I thought you were in Paris these days, no?'

'Indeed, I have been in Paris for a while, but I have just arrived from Malta this very hour.'

'And what brings you here?'

'We are here on the express instruction of the Grand Master himself, with a private and urgent communication for the ambassador of Mantua, to convey in all haste to the Duke of Mantua.'

'I see,' said the prior. He paused, clearly angling for more information. Edward did not bite. 'Is that old fool still fancying himself as the King of Constantinople?'

Edward smiled in tacit acknowledgement.

'Well, so long as he regards us as allies in his cause and is prepared to put his hand into his pockets then who am I too dispute his claim?'

'Indeed,' said Edward.

'Well, while you are in Venice, you must lodge here with us. When you have taken some refreshment, I will ask Iseppo to show you to your rooms.'

'Thank you, Nicolò, you were always the kindest host, but I regret that our stay here in Venice will be short. We must pass on our message as soon as we can and then find ourselves a ship bound for England – Tom, is keen to see his home again.'

'Of course, just let me know if we can be of assistance.'

'I would be indebted to you, Nicolò, if someone from your household could show us to the house of the Mantuan ambassador.'

'Yes, with pleasure. I will ask one of our brothers to escort you. Iseppo, can you ask Marco to join us.'

The servant departed, returning after a few moments with a platter of bread and olives and cold meats. He made a return trip for a bottle of wine and glasses.

As we helped ourselves to the food, and Edward and the prior engaged in discussion of Maltese politics, a young man of around my own age entered the room. He was of a powerful build, a fair complexion and had a pleasant countenance. He was dressed in plain black attire and he bowed as he caught the prior's attention.

'Ah, Marco. I have an errand to ask of you before supper.'

'I am at your service, Prior.' He spoke in rather hesitant French, of about the same standard as mine.

'Very good, Marco.' Nicolò continued in a stage whisper to Edward: 'Marco here is from one of the finest families in Venice but still needs to practise his French. Perhaps you can help him.'

'I'd be delighted to,' Edward replied.

'Marco, please take these gentlemen to the house of the Mantuan ambassador, do you know it?'

'Yes Prior, it is near the *Rio dei Mendicanti*.'

'Quite so. As you are in a hurry, I think it would be best to proceed there on foot, if you gentlemen don't mind?'

'Whichever way is quickest will suit us, thank you,' said Edward.

'Very well, lead them there directly, Marco. And let's have you back here for a hearty supper this evening, when we can relive some old times.' The prior beamed at the prospect.

'I look forward to it,' said Edward, rising to his feet.

I followed him and the young knight out of the room. As we passed through the vestibule, the young man reached inside a wardrobe and pulled out a cloak, with the bold white star of the Order embroidered upon its front. He wrapped it over his shoulders and fastened it with evident pride.

We stepped out into the street. It had started to rain, a heavy rain fresh from the mountains that extinguished the heat of the city and released the scent of summer from its stones. Edward drew his new cloak tight around him.

The rain did nothing to dampen Marco's spirits. As he walked he told us in his broken French that he was soon to depart for Malta to take up the *corso*, to carry the fight to the infidel, the sparkle in his eyes conveying his excitement at the prospect. He led us back into the warren of dark streets, twisting around blind corners and darting down narrow alleys. We passed shops and drinking-dens, warehouses, workshops, and candle-lit palaces with arched windows of clear glass. The rain was turning the unpaved streets into mud and making the paving slippery. This gave me a queasy feeling when we crossed bridges with no parapet to save us from tumbling into the black waters below.

By now the rain had almost cleared the streets. The few hardy souls who remained hurried on their way. We reached a large square, dominated by the hulking mass of a church. 'It is the *basilica* of *San Zanipolo* – that's what we call it – St John and St Paul,' Marco explained as he caught the direction of my gaze.

As we crossed the square, Marco pointed to another magnificent building ahead of us, its imperious facade luminescent in the darkness. 'And this is the *Scuola Grande di San Marco:* it is the most important *scuola* in Venice – my father is a member, along with many great adventurers.'

While the *scuola* faced on to the square, its flank ran alongside the canal that we were about to cross. 'It is the *Rio dei Mendicanti*,' Marco informed us, 'when we cross this bridge we leave the *sestiere* of Castello and enter the *sestiere* of Cannaregio.'

'*Sestiere?*' I asked.

'Yes,' replied Marco, 'the city is divided into six parts or *sestiere*; we are leaving one and entering another. The good news is that we are almost at the house of the Mantuan ambassador.'

This news was indeed welcome as the cold rain had by now seeped beneath my doublet and was trickling down my neck. We crossed the bridge and continued for a few yards past a tavern and a row of shops, most of which had closed for the night. We took a right turn at a crossroads and arrived at a large building with windows framed by gothic arches and with a coat of arms sculpted over the front door.

'This is the house of the ambassador,' said Marco, banging one of the two brass knockers that each took the shape of a ring held in a lion's mouth. 'He is famous in Venice for his love of the arts and of women.'

'So I've heard,' Edward muttered.

After a few moments, during which we stood huddled and dripping at the doorstep, a servant opened the door. He was tall and oily, his skin as greasy as his hair. He eyed our soaking, mud-spattered attire with marked disapproval.

'We have come to speak with the ambassador of Mantua,' said Edward in French.

The servant permitted us to enter with unconcealed reluctance. I looked around. The ground floor of the building seemed to be given over to business – it was packed with goods like a warehouse. Ahead of us, a marble staircase led up to more comfortable looking accommodation, befitting an ambassador.

'And whom do I have the honour of addressing at this inclement hour?' asked the servant.

'My name is Sir Edward Hamilton, of the Order of St John. I have urgent business with your master, the ambassador.'

'So has half of Venice it seems these days.'

Edward was evidently not impressed with the tone of the answer. 'Well, man, is he here then or not?'

'I will just go to check.'

The servant disappeared up the staircase for a couple of minutes then returned.

'I'm afraid that His Excellency is indisposed at this moment.'

'So, when will we be able to speak to him?' snapped Edward.

'I should think he will be able to receive guests in around an hour or so. You are most welcome to return again then. You said your business is urgent, didn't you? It cannot wait till morning?'

'No it can't,' said Edward, casting an impatient glance up the staircase. I guessed he was considering whether to ignore the servant and force his way upstairs to hunt down the elusive ambassador. In the event, he seemed to think better of it. 'Very well, we will return in an hour,' he said.

None of us was impressed by the lack of hospitality, particularly as the rain had in no way abated as we filed back out into the mud-filled street.

'Come on. I'll be damned if I'm waiting out in the rain for some jumped-up Lothario to finish his business. Let's get ourselves a drink. Marco, lead the way.'

Marco led us back to the crossroads and then to the small tavern situated just before the bridge crossing back to the square of *San Zanipolo*. It consisted of a single room, lit by a lone lantern overhead and a roaring fire in the hearth. It was sheltering a cluster of local boatmen, recognisable by their red hats and knee length breeches. They looked up and noted our arrival then returned to their conversation.

Edward ordered us mugs of *vin brulé*, a warm red wine that he said would put the colour back into our cheeks. We sat on stools beside the fire warming ourselves and drying our clothes, which began to steam. Marco was pleasant company. He was delighted by the opportunity to converse with a veteran of the Order and seemed keener to listen to Edward than to practise speaking French himself. Edward was only too happy to oblige and filled the time with tales of the *corso*.

After a warm and pleasant hour of Edward's tales, we prepared to brave the elements and stepped back out into the street. The rain outside was as intense as ever. Large raindrops bounced off the paving stones. We retraced our steps back to the dark side street of the ambassador's residence. Edward rapped the door knocker. Marco and I huddled behind him at the doorway.

From behind us there came a shout, '*Fra* Edward'.

We all turned around. My eyes were dazzled by a bright flash from the darkness that was accompanied by a loud bang. The flash came from a small, low alleyway that opened beneath one of the houses on the opposite side of the street. On my right, Marco was thrown back against the wall of the ambassador's house, the back of his head colliding against the masonry.

A few yards further down the street, I could just make out another figure. To my horror, I saw that he had a pistol levelled at me. I held my breath, braced for the impact, but the pistol was failing to discharge.

The man who had fired the shot that felled Marco now stepped forward out of the alleyway his sword drawn. He beckoned to his accomplice who pocketed his pistol and unsheathed his rapier. I watched him advance towards us with a pronounced limp. All this happened within a matter of seconds, but time seemed to have slowed almost to a stop.

There was another explosion, this time from my left where Edward stood holding a smoking pistol. The man who had fired the first shot tumbled backwards into the thick mud of the street. His limping accomplice pressed on towards us, swinging his blade. Edward cursed his other pistol, which failed to fire. He threw it hard into the face of the limping man who was almost upon us. The butt of the pistol glanced off the man's forehead. His dark eyes looked stunned for a moment and his advance was slowed just enough for Edward to unsheathe his rapier. Then their two swords clashed with the screech of metal tearing against metal.

There followed a dark, ugly, confusing brawl; not elegant exchanges but ruthless lunges and desperate parries from both men, their boots slipping in the mud. Edward managed to gash his opponent on the thigh of his good leg. The man's scream seemed to bring me to my senses. I had to help Edward. I reached into the lining of my doublet and retrieved my small pistol but Edward was in effect shielding his opponent from me.

A rapid succession of blows forced Edward on to the back foot. He was grunting and panting with the exertion. The man with the limp was a skilled swordsman and he pressed Edward some steps back up the street, towards the spot where the first assailant had fallen. I had thought the man dead but I now watched in horror as a hand reached up out of the mud and grabbed Edward around the right ankle. The blows continued to rain down on Edward who was struggling to parry them. With his right foot caught, Edward moved his left foot back to regain his balance. Instead he tripped over the man who had grabbed him. Aided by the slippery mud, Edward toppled backwards, rendering himself all but defenceless.

The limping man now raised his rapier to finish the job. In that moment I realised that I now had a clear shot. I aimed for the man's torso, praying that my pistol, so small and now so wet, would fire. It was the only thing that could save Edward now. I squeezed the trigger. To my surprise there was a flash and an explosion. The violent kick-back affected my aim. The man dropped like lead.

Trembling, I drew my rapier and advanced the few steps towards the tangled mess of bodies now lying in the filthy mud. Edward was levering himself up with one arm by pushing down on the head of the first assailant, while kicking off the body of the second, which had fallen across his legs.

As he raised himself to his feet, Edward glanced at me and muttered. 'About time you joined in the fun. Still, firing right into a man's head like that, that's how to get yourself a reputation. Now, are you going to finish this one off too?'

I looked from the blade of my rapier to the man squirming in the mud, more a bedraggled pile of clothes than a recognisable body. I neither moved nor spoke.

'Come on,' said Edward, 'if he dies then we just slip away into the night; but if he lives then he'll have the local militia hot on our heels, you mark my words.'

I still held back, unable to commit such a terrible act outside the heat of battle.

'He's as good as dead anyway,' Edward hissed, 'but if by chance he should live a few hours you can be sure he'll try to pass on his orders and seek to orchestrate his vengeance upon us. I know this kind of man, he is unrelenting. He didn't think twice about shooting Marco without warning, and he wouldn't have hesitated to slit your throat either.'

I stood there, still and silent. Around us I glimpsed covert faces, attracted by the commotion, glancing from darkened windows and peeking from doorways, their eyes upon us. I could hear their whispering.

Edward let out an exasperated sigh. 'So conscience makes cowards of us all,' he muttered as he walked over and kicked the contorted heap of a man so that he lay with his face upwards. I recognised him as the other man who had pursued us in Birgu. Calmly, clinically, Edward drove the point of his rapier into the man's chest, into his heart. There was a dull cracking sound followed by spasms in the man's body for a moment or two and then stillness. Edward wiped his blade on the man's sodden clothes, sheathed it, reclaimed the pistol he had thrown from the mud and then walked over to where Marco lay in a crumpled heap beside the ambassador's doorway. Edward felt for a pulse in Marco's neck, but we could both see that he was lifeless.

'Dear Lord, how do I explain this to the prior?' Edward muttered. 'He was just a boy.'

Edward knelt over him, made the sign of the cross and uttered a few words of simple prayer. Then he unfastened Marco's cloak and managed to pull it from underneath him. I thought he was going to place it over him, to protect his broken body from the rain and the eyes of onlookers, but instead he bundled it up and handed it to me. 'Keep hold of that for now, we'll dispose of it later.'

Edward banged on the door of the ambassador's house. The door was unbolted and opened a sliver; the eyes of the oily servant peered out into the gloom. Edward kicked at the base of the door with his boot and slammed his weight into it so that it sprang open knocking the servant backwards into the hall.

'Your master had better have been on important business as, thanks to his delay, three men now lie dead right outside his house.'

The servant gaped at us. Edward was now as intimidating as he was dishevelled. His cloak and clothes were both drenched and covered in mud. Open wounds leaked blood from his brow and right cheek.

I closed and bolted the door behind us.

'Ambassador!' Edward yelled up the stairs. 'Ambassador!'

After a few moments, a gaunt man appeared at the head of the stairs. A long, green cloak swirled around his patterned stockings as he descended the staircase. His perfume mingled with the stench of mud and filth that we had brought into his house.

The servant began to apologise for allowing us to enter but the ambassador's eyes flashed him a look that cast him back into silence.

'Who the devil are you?' he asked in French, looking us up and down with utter disdain. 'And what do you want with me at this ungodly hour? I do hope that racket outside was none of your making, that you haven't brought shame upon my household.'

I could see Edward's face flush in rage. 'Ambassador, I am Sir Edward Hamilton, a knight of the Order of St John. Please excuse our appearance. Had you welcomed us but an hour earlier you would have found us in much better condition.'

'Then I regret that I did not, sir. Still, what do you want with me?'

'Ambassador, we may only have a few moments. Listen to what I have to say.' Edward spoke the words through gritted teeth.

The ambassador pulled a face, but it was a look of resignation that indicated that he had no choice but to hear Edward out. Outside the door behind me I could hear raised voices.

'We have been sent here by the Grand Master of the Order to give you an urgent message that you in turn must convey to your master, the Duke.'

The ambassador glared at his servant, indicating that he should leave us. Edward continued. 'A couple of weeks ago, we gained possession of a cipher in Paris. When it was deciphered it revealed a French plot to assassinate the Duke of Mantua.'

'I am sorry to say gentlemen, that rumours of such plots are commonplace. It is a reflection of the times we live in.' He sighed as if losing interest.

Edward stepped forward so that his face was up close against the ambassador's. 'But there was more specific intelligence. The assassination is due to take place on the fifteenth of August, and is part of a wider plan that we believe emanates from Cardinal Richelieu.'

The ambassador's eyes widened. 'On the fifteenth of August, you say. And Richelieu likely behind it. That gives me a little more to go on, gentleman, and I do appreciate your efforts,' he glanced again at our clothes. 'But it is difficult for me to gauge whether this threat is in earnest.'

At this point, Edward's temper boiled over. He grabbed the ambassador, clutching a fistful of his ruff in his right hand and pointed back towards the front door with his left. 'Three men lie dead at your doorstep. Two of them would have gone to any lengths to stop this message getting through to you. Is that earnest enough for you?'

The ambassador's expression now turned from one of sneering disdain to one of outright horror. 'At my door? That's what all that noise was in the street? My God!'

'If you had received us when we first knocked on your door then I daresay this might have been avoided. Or perhaps you would have preferred it if Richelieu's men had come in and shot you too?' Edward was still seething.

Behind my back there was a sharp knock on the front door. This brought the servant scuttling back towards the door but again a withering look from his master stopped him and made him retreat a few steps.

'My God,' the ambassador repeated in panic, 'you have brought the Lords of the Night to my house.'

'Remember the date,' said Edward, 'the fifteenth of August, that's when Richelieu's assassin will come. Pass this warning on to the Duke. I will assume upon your honour that you will do that.'

There was a faint nod of agreement, but the pale-faced ambassador now seemed pre-occupied with developments outside his front door.

'Is there a back door?' Edward directed his question at the servant as much as the ambassador.

'Only the water door onto the canal,' the servant replied.

'Then have you a boat?'

There was another, more frantic knock on the door behind my back and more shouting.

'Yes, yes, take it,' the ambassador replied. 'But how can I explain this? People will have seen you come into my house!'

'Tell them that we were coarse drunken villains and that we barged our way into your house and stole your boat to escape. If you tell them that the Order of St John was involved then it could play very badly for you and for Mantua, if Richelieu comes to think that the Order and Mantua were conspiring against him. Much better to deny everything,' said Edward.

We left the ambassador dumbfounded in the vestibule as loud knocks pummelled his front door. The servant led us in haste through to the water door from which steps disappeared down into the dark water of the canal. A boat was moored up alongside the steps, one of the gondolas that we had seen earlier. Edward stepped in gingerly, the boat rocking under his weight. He grabbed the oar that stood wedged beside the door.

'Don't just stand there; untie us and get into that cabin,' he barked at me. Still clutching Marco's cloak, I untied the rope that was looped around the mooring pole and stooped down into the cabin.

Edward used the oar to lever us out into the canal, upon which there was an eerie calm. The black, lapping water around us was spotted with the rain. Edward steered us towards and under the bridge we had crossed earlier, between the square of *San Zanipolo* and the tavern we had sheltered in just minutes before. I looked out of the window of the cabin to see the canal disappearing into the darkness ahead, a long procession of moored boats on each side.

Voices started shouting behind us, perhaps coming from the water door of the ambassador's house or from a neighbouring alley that led to the canal.

'To hell with this,' said Edward. 'I'd feel safer on land.' He brought our cruise to an abrupt halt on the opposite side of the canal, almost losing the oar in the process.

'Moor us alongside there,' he said, pointing at some stairs leading up from the water into the square. I did as he instructed and we jumped out and clambered up into the square. We broke into a run.

'Can you remember the way?' I asked.

'Not exactly. Throw that cloak on there.' He pointed to a pile of rubbish at the entrance to a courtyard that we were passing.

We ran past the full length of the church beyond which the square funnelled into a long, broad street. Edward glanced over his shoulder: there was no one else at all in the expanse of the square, no one on our tail, just the interminable rain. He slowed to a walking pace.

'What was the matter with the cloak?' I asked.

'That cloak was probably the only thing that linked poor Marco directly with the Order,' Edward replied, labouring for breath and clearing his throat with a series of coughs. 'Now we've removed it, there are three unknown men lying dead in a street as a result of some unknown feud, with hopefully nothing to link them back to either France or the Order, presuming the ambassador keeps his mouth shut.'

'Do you think he will?' I asked.

'He will if he knows what's good for him.'

After we had continued along the street for a couple of minutes we spotted a side street leading away to our right that we both thought we remembered from earlier. There followed a twisting and turning succession of streets and bridges – some lit and paved, others dark and mud-filled.

After about quarter of an hour and a couple of wrong turnings that forced us to retrace our steps, we arrived back at the entrance to the priory. Edward knocked on the door, casting one last look over his shoulder, but no one seemed to have followed us. The door was opened by the same servant, Iseppo, as before, who was taken aback by the state of our appearance.

'We must speak with the prior,' said Edward.

Iseppo ushered us into the room in which the prior had received us earlier that evening.

'Please, wait here, I will find him for you.'

We sat and waited. A fire now crackled and spat in the hearth, its flames filling the room with shifting amber light that made shadows dance upon the walls.

After a minute or two, the prior strolled in, both palms placed upon his belly. 'Gentlemen,' he beamed, 'you missed a fine supper.' We stood up and the prior's eyes saw from our bedraggled state and our expressions that all was not well.

'Please, be seated,' he said, taking a chair himself. 'Where is Marco?'

'Nicolò, I am afraid I have bad news, terrible news.'

'Then tell me, Edward.' The prior's expression was impassive.

Edward seemed to struggle to find the right words. 'When we were outside the ambassador's house, we were attacked. I am so very sorry. Marco is dead.'

'Attacked? Edward, there is much that you are not telling me. Three armed men don't get attacked in Venice for no reason.'

Edward paused. A log split in the fire. When at last he spoke, it was in a low voice. 'As you know, we were sent by the Grand Master to Venice to pass on a message to the ambassador. What I did not realise was that there were already men here in Venice who knew of our mission and were determined to stop us.'

'So what was that message? What was Marco killed for?'

'I'm afraid I cannot say.' Edward's face looked as if he were torn. The Grand Master had instructed us to tell no one in the Order about our mission. I guessed that Edward's vow of obedience to the Order now weighed heavily on his conscience.

'What, you cannot tell me, old friend? Be reasonable, I have to send word to Marco's family saying that their boy is lost. And you can't even tell me what he died for.'

'Nicolò, I am not free to tell you. You may tell his family that Marco died valiantly, fighting for the Order.'

'In a street brawl in Venice, I don't think so.'

'I am truly sorry, Nicolò. They opened fire on us from behind our backs. I did not know they were here.'

'Well, Edward, you should learn to be more careful, for they clearly knew that you were here.'

'Yes they did, thanks to that traitor Fra André, I'll wager.'

The prior frowned for a moment. 'The Grand Master's secretary you mean?'

'No less. Apart from Tom and the Grand Master himself, he was the only person who knew of our mission.'

'Then it seems he has friends in low places as well as high places,' said the prior. His tone was bitter. 'It is a terrible state of affairs but it seems your mission is such that some within the Order itself would seek to undermine it. I can understand better now why you wish to keep it to yourself.'

'It is not out of choice, Nicolò, it is out of duty. You know I would trust you with my life.'

The prior nodded. 'Questions will be asked, of course.'

'I know. The ambassador seemed on edge about the prospect of some 'Lords of the Night' coming to pay him a visit.'

'He has good reason to fear them. It is their job to ask questions, and they have effective ways to get the answers they are looking for. I'm afraid even our doors will not keep them out, should they come looking for you with their henchmen. They have licence to go anywhere, to question anyone.'

'Well, let's hope they don't trace us back here then,' said Edward.

'Indeed, or not till you are long gone. If they do come then I will make sure that you are warned and are able to slip away. We have a large garden beyond the cloister, which provides ample opportunity for escape, should the need arise.'

'Thank you Nicolò.'

'And now, I see that you are exhausted and wet through. I shall have a bath prepared for each of you and then you should get some rest. I shall have some clean clothes laid out in your rooms.'

This time I added my heartfelt thanks to those of Edward. My damp clothes were clamped to my skin, my whole body sagged with weariness and I trembled with the cold.

The prior stood up. 'In the morning, Edward, you can tell me your plans. But now, you'll forgive me, I must write to Marco's father to inform him of this terrible news.'

'Of course,' we both replied.

The prior left the room and exchanged a few words with Iseppo. The servant ushered us upstairs. We were each given a small room, more like a cell than a bedroom, with a bed, simple furniture and a crucifix upon the wall. Iseppo also showed us where we would take our baths and said he would return with a clean outfit for each of us.

Edward was lost in his thoughts for the remainder of the night. I heard him muttering maledictions on Captain Zen for his unexpected stopover in Ancona, on the Mantuan ambassador for his 'indisposition', and of course on *Fra* André for his treachery.

After we had bathed, Edward cleaned his weapons and reloaded his pistols, shaking his head at the one that had failed to discharge. I cleaned and reloaded my own pistol too. I figured that it was best to leave talk of our next moves until the morning, when our minds would be rested. However, that night brought only fitful sleep, despite the comforts of the bed, the warmth of the bath and the weariness of my body. My thoughts turned the horrific events in that dark, mud-filled street over and over.

Chapter 19: Homeward

We ate our breakfast in the priory's refectory, overlooking the garden. Early morning sunshine streamed through the open windows. I was wearing the fresh clothes that had been laid out for me: a doublet, gathered breeches and hose – all in mercifully inconspicuous shades of brown. I also had a cloak and a small hat up in my room. Edward's outfit was a touch grander, finished off with a modest ruff and sash garters.

The prior set his plate down on our table and sat down beside me and opposite Edward. His eyes looked heavy, as if he was short of sleep. On his plate was the same simple but welcome meal that we had been given: bread, cheese and cured ham.

'So, have you made some plans?' the prior enquired in a way that hinted that we ought to have done.

'We plan to leave for England at the earliest opportunity,' Edward replied.

'I think that is wise,' said the prior in a low voice. 'Talk of the events of last night is already rife in the markets this morning; soon the whole city will know.'

Edward's eyes widened. 'Is there talk of any suspects?' he asked.

'Not that I have yet heard, but the Lords of the Night will be very thorough in their investigations. It won't take them long to identify Marco. Watch out for them, you will know them by their turquoise hats and by the witless henchmen that follow them.'

The thought sent a shiver down my spine. It would be a bitter twist of fate to have lost one set of pursuers only to have gained another.

'Do you plan to travel by sea?' the prior continued.

'Yes,' Edward replied, 'though in truth I feel sick at the prospect. I've spent precious little time on dry land these past few weeks but I fear that the overland routes across Europe are too dangerous at this time.'

'I agree,' said the prior, 'these are troubled times.'

'How can we find ourselves a ship bound for England?' Edward enquired.

'Well, let me see, you could try at a *taverna* known as the *Leon Roso* at the Rialto, near the fishmarket. I believe it is a regular haunt of English merchants and mariners. The current dangers of travel by land and our good work in suppressing the infidel pirates at sea seem to have attracted many more English merchantmen to the city of late.'

'That is good news for us,' I said, between mouthfuls.

'If you want to go to the *Leon Roso* then you are welcome to take my gondola. I will have my boatman take you to the Rialto. It is only a short walk from there.'

Out of politeness we initially declined the offer, but the prior was keen that we accept. His insistence, coupled with the prospect of by-passing unwanted attention, persuaded us.

'When you have found yourselves a ship, you can send for your clothes and I will have them delivered to your cabin.'

'Thank you,' we both replied.

'Do you have sufficient money to keep you going, Edward? It is no problem to draw on your account in Valletta.'

'Yes, thank you. I still have sufficient, all in Venetian ducats, which reminds me that I should exchange some for English coins if I get the chance.'

For the rest of the breakfast, Edward and the prior exchanged small talk. This ebbed and flowed between shared memories and enquiries about fellow members of the Order. *Whatever happened to him? Where is he now? Goodness, is he still alive?* I was happy to listen to their conversation as I savoured my cheese and ham. It was good to see the two old knights talking once more as friends despite the events of the night before.

Before we took our leave of the prior, Edward once again offered his most sincere apology and condolences for what had happened to Marco. The prior informed us that he had already dispatched a letter to the young knight's family. I sensed that he was a man well versed in untimely death, but this one had hurt him. 'He was only a boy,' he said and looked away into the garden.

We donned our cloaks and hats and walked out into a glorious summer morning. The overnight rain had cleansed the city, bringing a freshness to the air. We left the priory and walked around the corner to a broad quay where the scent of the sea, lying tamed in the canal before us, mingled with the smell of the sun on the rain-soaked pavement. The prior's gilded gondola was waiting for us there. An immaculate gondolier, the star of the Order upon his shirt, helped us aboard. Edward and I sat side by side in the cabin and watched the turquoise water begin to drift by.

The gondolier, who spoke only in the local Venetian dialect, made only one attempt at conversation, to confirm we were heading to the Rialto. He then left us in peace while he called out songful greetings to people he knew on both land and water.

We glided beneath low, single-arch bridges and past a succession of tall houses, whose walls emerged from the water of the canal. The houses were painted in bright hues: yellow, pink, beige and green. Their straight lines were softened by colourful awnings, shading the windows and rippling in the breeze. Their red slate roofs sprouted funnel-shaped chimneys and lofty, sun-soaked terraces.

From my window in the cabin, I kept a close watch on the houses, the alleys running between them, the quays and the bridges. I scoured them all for the men in turquoise hats, whom the prior had warned us of and whom the ambassador clearly dreaded.

At the end of our canal we reached a marine crossroads. A long canal ran east to west while ours continued on to the north, lined with buildings until it reached the open lagoon, with the glimpse of islands in the distance. Our gondolier turned left, heading west towards the centre of the city.

This canal was wider, a major thoroughfare. It was brimming with gondolas: many like ours with cabins decorated in varying degrees of splendour; and many of a simpler design, without a cabin, which tended to carry goods rather than people. I watched goods of every description passing by: fruit and vegetables, sacks of foodstuff – which might have been flour, grain or spices; round cheeses; cured meats; candles; barrels; crates; and materials of every sort – silk, wool, linen – and in every colour. There were rowing boats too, less agile than the gondolas in these cramped waters and weighed down with cargo.

We passed more fine houses and warehouses, all with water doors opening on to the canal. In between them ran streets and alleys, some that crossed overhead in bridges and others that ended abruptly at the water's edge.

This major canal was joined at intervals by others, branching left and right, some perpendicular to our own and others at acute angles that followed the ancient channels of the lagoon, twisting through the islands and mudflats that spawned the city. Every alley, every canal was a potential source of danger. Edward was watching them too. We exchanged few words.

I recognised a canal on our right: it was the one that ran between the ambassador's house and the square of San Zanipolo. How different it now looked in the sunshine, with the shimmering waters reflecting upon the tinted walls of the houses. It was now a vivid scene. The square was crowded with market stalls and with boats unloading their wares at the steps upon which we had disembarked last night. I wondered whether the ambassador's gondola was still moored amongst them.

And then the scene was gone, and we were back between the rows of houses and warehouses. Sometimes we were jostled in the water, as gondolas competed for space. The cries of our gondolier now had a less cordial tone.

The canal ended in an imposing edifice at which we turned first left then right, our gondolier manoeuvring with skill and audacity through the oncoming traffic. At one point I shut my eyes expecting an imminent collision. Instead, when I opened them, I beheld a glorious sight: a majestic river stretching out to our left and our right, for we joined it at the apex of a graceful curve.

'It is the Grand Canal,' said Edward, watching me crane my head out of the window. 'There is no finer street in all the world.'

'Grand' was an understatement. To my right, as far as my eyes could see, the canal was lined with sumptuous palaces. Their magnificent facades overlooked the glistening waters, which were churned by the wake of a hundred boats. In addition to the smaller gondolas, such as ours, there were bigger gondolas, some with large cabins to seat several people and some serving as ferries for standing passengers. There were single and double-masted fishing boats, barges and rowing boats. They vied for space on the water and at the quaysides, their boatmen loading, unloading, bargaining, gossiping or just lazing in the sunshine.

To my left, framed by Edward's window, I could see a mighty bridge of white stone adorned with arcades and balustrades, arching over the whole, broad sweep of the canal in a single span. I noticed that Edward was surveying it too. 'Let's hope it lasts longer than the last bridge,' he muttered.

Our gondolier picked his way across the breadth of the canal, in the shadow of the bridge, and then rowed alongside a quay lined by a long arcade. The arcade provided an abundance of shadows in which to lurk, to watch unseen. My pulse quickened. I knew that we were about to leave the prior's gondola and that danger thronged around us. My gaze flitted from one passer-by to another, looking for any sign that they might be in the employ of the Lords of the Night.

Our gondolier drew up alongside an array of boats moored up at a quayside. He tied our gondola to another, which he then used as a stepping stone to hop ashore. We followed, the boats rocking precariously underfoot.

'*El Leon Roso?*' Edward enquired, referring to the tavern we were seeking.

The gondolier seemed to understand and gesticulated in the direction of a bell tower, its belfry visible above the red-tiled rooftops. Edward rewarded him with a coin from his purse and the gondolier ambled away with a spring in his step.

The quayside bordered a square that was crammed with market stalls under a patchwork canopy of awnings. The surrounding buildings must have kept the stalls in shade for most of the morning but the sun had now risen above the roofs so that the striped awnings afforded the only protection. We picked our way through raucous fishmongers hawking their fare, some of which still flipped and slithered upon the stalls.

Beyond the fishmarket, we proceeded along a bustling street and through an arcade to a busy little square. At one end of the square was a church bedecked with a large clock; at the other end was a curious statue of a crouching man who was bent low under the weight of the platform he was bearing.

We entered a building that Edward explained was a bank. Here he was able to exchange some of his Venetian ducats for English coins. The money-changer he spoke to was able to speak French and Edward was able to extract some further directions for the *Leon Roso*: we were to turn left at the junction beneath the bell tower of St John the Almsgiver and we would find the tavern a short way along that street. These instructions proved accurate. As we turned the corner beneath the bell tower we saw the sign of a red lion hanging from a building about half way down the street.

The tavern consisted of a single, low room, so low in fact that the crown of my hat skimmed the beams supporting the floor above. The room was crowded, dingy and full of pipe smoke. I imagined that this was exactly to Edward's taste.

Clusters of men stood or sat on stools around upright barrels that served as tables. Some were fashionable merchants; others were shabby seafarers. Their talk was all in English.

Edward sat himself down on a stool beside a barrel in a corner of the room and I did likewise. He extracted his tobacco pouch and began to fill his pipe. A burly, bow-legged man approached, wearing a stained apron and a wary look.

'What can I get you gentlemen?' he asked.

'A tankard of your best ale for each of us,' said Edward, lighting up his pipe.

The innkeeper returned after a few moments and placed two frothing tankards down upon the barrel.

Edward handed him a coin. 'Get one for yourself,' he added.

'Very kind of you, sir,' replied the innkeeper.

He was about to leave us when Edward said, 'We need to find passage aboard a ship to England.'

'You've come to the right place then, sir,' replied the innkeeper. 'Where you heading to?'

'We're joining up with the Duke of Buckingham's army,' said Edward.

'Well, you'll need passage to Portsmouth, or thereabouts, for I hear he's gathering his army there.' Without warning, the innkeeper turned to face the rest of the room and bellowed: 'Any ships sailing for Portsmouth?'

We both winced. All eyes in the tavern were now upon us.

There was a stir among one of the standing groups, then a stout man with a bald pate and protruding belly approached us. He was middle-aged and well groomed. The innkeeper left us to our business.

'I have a ship sailing for Portsmouth in the morning. But who is asking?' said the stout man.

'I'm Edward Hamilton and this is my friend Thomas Cheke. We are seeking passage to Portsmouth.'

'How much are you offering?' asked the man, sizing us up.

Edward puffed on his pipe as if contemplating a price. 'That depends on the accommodation.'

'I'd rent you my own cabin if you named the right price,' said the man with a laugh.

'A simple cabin will suffice,' said Edward, 'so long as your ship is seaworthy.'

'Well, I can offer you both. The *Pride of Rye* is one of the fastest merchant ships on the high seas and well armed too. So what's your offer?'

'We'll pay you six pounds sterling, once you have delivered us safely to our destination.'

'Make that ten pounds, half paid up front and you have yourselves a cabin.'

'Eight pounds, half up front,' said Edward, extending his hand to suggest that they had reached a deal and holding the man's gaze.

The man frowned for a moment and then clasped Edward's hand with a smile.

'And so now you know who we are, what is your name, sir?' asked Edward.

The man blushed. 'My apologies gentlemen; I am Linus Lapthorn, part-owner of the *Pride of Rye*. A pleasure to meet you, I'm sure.' He ran his hand through what remained of his hair. 'I would advise you both to be on board by this evening, as we set sail in the morning just as soon as we have ourselves a pilot and clearance from customs.'

'Of course,' replied Edward. 'I take it that your ship is moored in the basin.'

'That's right, just off the island of San Giorgio Maggiore, or Big George, as I call it. You'll easily spot her. So, gentlemen, I look forward to your company on our voyage, but please excuse me as I have certain business still to conclude.'

'As do we,' said Edward.

Lapthorn gave us a slight nod and then returned to his previous company at the other end of the room.

'Well now,' Edward said, turning to me, 'I think it's time for a spot of early dinner.'

We dined upon spit-roasted pork and fresh bread, washed down with another tankard of beer, all served by the bow-legged innkeeper who rolled back and forth amongst the various tables.

'And so,' said Edward, lighting up another pipe when his meal was finished, 'first I must send word to the prior to consign our belongings to the *Pride of Rye* and then I need to buy a few provisions for the voyage. We should try to keep a low profile to avoid unwanted attention.'

'I agree,' I said, 'though every man in this tavern now knows where we're heading and upon which ship.'

Edward shrugged. 'Well, there's no helping that now. We must stay vigilant.'

The innkeeper was able to furnish us with a reliable errand boy who took a short note from Edward back to the priory. We settled our bill and stepped out blinking into the sunshine. My squinting eyes swept the street in both directions but saw no danger.

Edward had a mental list of things he wanted to buy and assured me that there was no better place to browse for merchandise in all the world. Narrow streets branched away in every direction crammed with shops of every description. It was a vibrant mercantile labyrinth and we plunged straight in.

In Edward's reckoning, so long as we kept moving we would be hard to track should anyone be on our tail. While Edward kept his eyes peeled for a particular street or a certain shop, I maintained a look-out for turquoise hats. I did not know the type of headdress that I was looking out for, but I imagined that the Lords of the Night wore wide-brimmed hats with a tall crown, at least by day. As often happens when one has conceived of a specific danger, I sometimes thought that I caught sight of something turquoise, before it disappeared around a blind corner or vanished into a darkened alley. On several occasions I felt sure that that we were being watched from some shaded window or doorway, which made the hairs on my nape stand on end.

Edward's first acquisition was a spyglass, to replace the one he had left in our room at the inn in Birgu. 'I won't set sail without one,' he insisted. The glassmakers of Venice had stolen the art of making spyglasses from the manufacturers in the Low Countries and had perfected it. Edward was delighted with his purchase, which had a sleek brass casing and, according to the shopkeeper, promised 'the highest levels of magnification known to man'.

Next we turned to the booksellers, which in Venice – Edward explained – are much less controlled by the whims of the authorities than they are in England or France. In one bookshop he purchased two weighty works in Latin by one Hugo Grotius: *On the Law of War and Peace* and *On the Truth of the Christian Religion*.

'You'll not find a sounder mind when it comes to reasoned argument than Grotius,' Edward assured me. He said that I could read the book on Christian religion before him, adding with a wink: 'It might help you to straighten your thoughts on matters of faith.' The books were wrapped in cloth to form a heavy parcel that I was given to carry.

Edward was pleasantly surprised – and I was relieved – to find a work in English in the next bookshop we visited. It was a new quarto edition of one of Mr Shakespeare's plays: *Othello – the Moor of Venice*. 'How appropriate,' Edward said as he added it to his bundle of acquisitions.

Finally, we visited a sumptuous tailor's shop, where Edward purchased the latest doublet, breeches, hose and hat in the Venetian style. He offered to fit me out in similar attire but I assured him that – between my current outfit and the one that had been cleaned back at the priory – I was well provided for. I did, however, ask him to buy me a new hammock, to replace the one which I had left behind in Birgu. He was only too glad to comply and managed to barter two for the price that the seller had initially offered for one, saying that he'd keep the second in reserve lest his bed upon the *Pride* turned out to be lice infested. We each took a rolled-up hammock under one arm and continued on our way.

We crossed the gleaming white Rialto bridge – a magnet for hawkers, sightseers and courtesans – and meandered through the city in what Edward hoped was the general direction of St Mark's. We passed through squares, large and small, paved and unpaved, with their wells and market stalls. Each square or *campo* was a receptacle of life, filled with the sounds of playing children and baying livestock. Husbands and wives were busy about their various labours while old women gossiped and old men idled.

We crossed a succession of hump-backed bridges linking one island to the next. Our route took us along grand streets and twisting alleys. We rounded blind corners, found shade in covered alleyways and passed churches, bell towers, palaces and theatres. Best of all, we walked beside the canals. Often their waters churned under the endless procession of boats, but sometimes they were so still that they mirrored the magnificent buildings above. In such tranquil places it was hard to remember that these canals remained the veins of the sea, so perfect was the marriage of land and water.

At times, Edward and I found ourselves alone in some forgotten backstreet, the kind of place where robbers might strike and no one would notice let alone come to your aid. At other times we were like flotsam washed along in a seething tide of humanity, coursing through the arterial streets of the city. More than once my heart jumped as I thought I spotted a turquoise hat or headscarf approaching, only to lose sight of it again in the throng.

I saw men from every corner of the world: Moors, Christians, Jews; men from the Orient, from Persia and India, from Barbary and from the tropical lands beyond the great desert of Africa; men from the New World, from the far north and from Russia. The women, if not so diverse in origin, were more so in costume. A hundred languages and dialects mixed and melted into a sonorous clamour that reverberated through the city.

Such were my impressions of Venice as we entered the *Piazza San Marco*. The confines of the streets suddenly gave way to a great, paved expanse, flanked on either side by long, tiered arcades, and culminating in the magnificent, triple-domed *basilica* of St Mark. Without seeing it with my own eyes, such a place would not have been conceivable within the limits of my imagination. Here was I, Thomas Cheke, a penniless former slave taken from a sleepy village on a small island; here was I, in the famous *Piazza* of the Doges, the finest square in all of Christendom, in a city that was the marvel of the world.

As we strolled across the square, as leisurely as our various acquisitions and aching arms would permit, Edward spied or rather smelled an alluring coffee shop. For me the aroma brought back memories of the coffee shops of Algiers. Edward suggested that we stop for a cup. He told me to savour it as a final indulgence before our return to the privations of life at sea. I was only too happy to acquiesce.

The coffee shop was located in the long arcade that flanked the northern side of the square, competing for custom with *tavernas* and *osterias*. We took our cups and sat on a wooden bench in the arcade. This was a good vantage point from which to survey the *Piazza* but was itself inconspicuous, lying in the shadow of an arch.

The coffee soon exerted its desired effect, quickening my heartbeat and sharpening my senses.

We picked up our belongings and walked across the *Piazza* towards the *basilica*. Edward planned to pass some time inside the great church, taking advantage of its shaded interior both to keep cool and to hide. We entered through one of the large doorways, framed by a succession of sculpted arches, above which four bronze horses stood frozen, mid canter.

Inside the *basilica*, the late afternoon sunshine filtered through circular windows beneath the domes, transforming the interior into an elliptical patchwork of light and shadow. In the light, golden mosaics sparkled; in the shadows, clouds of incense lingered like lost souls. We stayed for about an hour, sometimes knelt in prayer, at other times processing around in the stream of sightseers and pilgrims, awed by the innumerable icons and invaluable riches.

By the time we left the *basilica*, the shadows had lengthened across the patterned flagstones of the *Piazza*. Evening encroached. We turned into the short adjoining square, which Edward called the *Piazzetta*. On our right loomed the great *campanile* of St Mark. At its foot a building resembling a classical temple extended in a procession of white arches towards the stretch of quayside known as the *Molo*. On our left, adjoining the *basilica*, was the palace of the Doge. Its bright façade ran in a long, double arcade down to the *Molo* and almost into the lagoon itself. Ahead of us, at the end of the *Piazzetta*, were the massive, stone columns that I had seen upon our arrival the previous day, forming a portal for the city. A winged lion prowled on top of one; the other supported the figure of a soldier, standing upon a vanquished creature, a dragon perhaps.

Beyond the columns, St Mark's basin opened out before us in a beautiful expanse of calm water, littered with boats and ships and glistening in the first hues of sunset. I saw no sign of the *Santa Maria Formosa* and presumed that she had already departed: time is money, after all. Linus Lapthorn had indicated that the *Pride of Rye* lay off the island of San Giorgio Maggiore, which Edward pointed out on the far side of the basin. Its bell tower was the shorter counterpart of St Mark's *campanile* that I had seen on our arrival. Amongst the flotilla of vessels that covered the water in that direction, an English merchant ship was visible; the flag of the

Union hung from her mainmast, the flag of St George from her foremast.

We hired a gondola from the *Molo* and cruised across the basin, watching the city slip away behind us into fading embers of light. The air was still warm and I trailed my arm through the open window of the cabin so that my fingertips glided through the water. As I looked back, part of me wished to stay longer, to discover more of Venice's secrets; but another part of me shuddered at the thought of poor Marco. And I imagined the Lords of the Night gathering in the *Piazza* of St Mark at dusk, piecing together the intelligence about their wanted men and issuing forth with their gangs of henchmen to scour the city. When I thought of them I was only too glad to see the looming hull of the *Pride of Rye*.

The *Pride* turned out to be a large trading vessel with three tall masts and a more rounded shape than any of the ships I had sailed on before. A reassuring row of gun ports lined her side.

We drew up alongside and Edward slipped the gondolier a coin before we hauled ourselves and our possessions up a ladder and on to the main deck. We were greeted by an officer who led us to the captain's cabin beneath the poop deck. Through the open door, we saw the captain, hunched over a table and scrutinising a *portolan* chart, which showed illustrations of various ports and landmarks that we were due to pass on the voyage. He had close-cropped, greying hair and wore plain, black clothes. As we approached, obstructing what little light was filtering through the door, he looked up with a frown before laying a pair of compasses down upon the chart and standing to greet us.

'I presume you are the two passengers,' he said. There was little warmth in his tone or demeanour. 'Mr Lapthorn mentioned you'd be joining us. We have already taken your chest aboard and down to your cabin.'

'Thank you. I am Sir Edward Hamilton and this is my colleague Master Thomas Cheke.'

I nodded politely in the captain's direction.

'And you are welcome aboard, I am sure. I am Richard Ratsey, the captain.' He seemed reluctant to offer his hand but Edward shook it nonetheless and I followed suit. 'I will ask one of the crew to show you to your cabin. It is rather plain but I trust it will suit your purposes. We are unaccustomed to conveying passengers.'

'As long as you convey us safely and quickly to England then I am sure it will meet our needs,' Edward replied.

The captain stepped out on to the main deck and asked one of the ship's hands to take us to the port cabin on the lower deck. The lad, who looked a few years younger than me, led us down through the aft hatchway to the dingy lower deck. In the gloom I could make out a row of four cannons on each side, interspersed with the hammocks and chests of the crew as well as victuals and various kinds of nautical supplies. At the far end of the deck, up in the bows, the cooks were busy in the galley preparing a meal, their red faces illuminated by the fire in the oven. A pleasant smell of baking bread and stewing meat wafted back along the deck.

There were two hatchways leading down into the hold through which lantern light emanated upwards. I could hear men busy down below and glanced down through the hatch to see neat rows of stacked barrels and bulging sacks.

As promised by Captain Ratsey, our cabin was simple, with one side curving inwards following the shape of the hull. There was room for my hammock only if we pushed the table right back against the window in the stern and placed Edward's chest beneath it. There was no room for a second hammock, even if the bed had been lice-infested, which to Edward's good fortune and relief it was not. The lad brought us a taper to light the lantern.

We placed our belongings on the short bed and Edward sat down to check the contents of the chest. He was relieved to see his clothes washed and neatly folded. My green outfit was there too. In addition, the kind prior had included two bottles of wine, a round cheese and a cured leg of ham. 'Good old Nicolò,' said Edward with a smile as he strung the ham up from the ceiling.

The ship's bell rang for the evening meal and another lad appeared at our door. 'Good sirs, Mr Lapthorn would be pleased to have your company for supper this evening.'

'And we should be pleased to join him,' said Edward.

The lad led us back along the lower deck, where the crew were assembling with their bowls and cups in a file leading up the galley. We climbed back up to the main deck. The sun had set but the sky was still the rich blue of a fine summer's evening. Lapthorn had the other cabin under the poop deck, beside the captain's. He greeted us at the door.

Lapthorn's cabin, which was set up in reverse to the captain's, was much more spacious than ours. The furniture was well made and the shelves were lined with books and ornaments that gave the cabin a homely feel. The stern window was open, allowing the evening breeze to stir the curtains. The table had been laid for four, set with bowls of glossy pewter, crystal glasses and silver cutlery. Lapthorn invited us to take the two chairs opposite him.

'The captain will join us shortly,' he assured us, 'he is just finishing his preparations for tomorrow. I trust you find your cabin sufficient?'

'Yes, thank you,' said Edward. His tone intimated that he would have much preferred Lapthorn's own cabin instead.

'Good, then let me welcome you properly aboard with a drink.' He poured us each a glass of red wine from a bottle in the centre of the table, and poured a further one for the captain.

'Let us drink to a fair wind and clement weather on our voyage.'

'And Godspeed,' said Edward. We lifted our glasses, glinting in the swaying lantern light, and chinked them together. I savoured the taste of the wine as I listened to the sounds drifting in through the window from the busy waters below.

One of the cooks arrived, knocking on the cabin door with his foot and carrying a pot of stew and a fresh loaf of bread which he deposited in the centre of the table. He ladled a portion into each of our bowls, chunks of lamb with fresh vegetables in a thick stock, and then departed with his best effort at a bow.

'I told the crew that we had distinguished guests joining us for the voyage,' said Lapthorn with a smile.

Either the smell of the food or the end of his preparations brought the captain into the cabin with a quiet apology. He took his seat beside Lapthorn.

'So, Richard, are we ready to set sail?' asked Lapthorn in a jovial tone.

'We are all but ready,' replied the captain. 'We are fully laden and I've asked the purser to make sure the cargo is securely stowed down below.'

'And the paperwork?' enquired Lapthorn, sipping at his glass.

'We can expect the customs officials to give us permission to sail in the morning. I have arranged for a pilot to escort us out from the lagoon into the open sea.' The captain's tone was grave.

He turned his eyes and his attention down to his bowl of steaming stew.

'Excellent, first rate,' replied Lapthorn, ripping a crust off the loaf.

'How long until we reach Portsmouth?' asked Edward.

'With a fair wind behind us, I believe we can make it in a fortnight. With an ill wind, perhaps double that.'

'Then let us pray for a good wind,' said Edward.

'Have you been in Venice long?' enquired Lapthorn.

'No, not long,' replied Edward. 'We were passing through on our way back to England.'

'And what has brought you so far from home?' asked Lapthorn.

'I am a Knight of the Order of St John,' replied Edward, 'a resident of Malta.'

The captain's grey eyes flashed up from his bowl for a fleeting moment.

'I see,' replied Lapthorn.

'And my companion here, Tom, is returning home to England after enduring a spell of captivity at the merciless hands of the Turks.'

'Indeed,' replied Lapthorn. Both his and the captain's eyes fixed upon me; I must have blushed – it was not how I would have described the last few years of my life.

'And where were you held captive?' Lapthorn enquired.

'In Algiers,' I replied.

Lapthorn shook his head with a sigh. 'How frightful.'

'I rescued him from a ship bound for Constantinople,' said Edward. 'We captured or killed the entire crew and I was a whisker away from dispatching young Tom to a watery grave before he revealed himself as a God-fearing Englishman.'

'And how did you come to be in captivity, Tom?' asked Lapthorn.

'I was captured by Barbary corsairs when I was fourteen, taken from my home on the Isle of Wight.'

'I see; how terrible,' said Lapthorn, looking genuinely appalled.

The captain flashed me another look, his eyes boring into me for a second or two before his attention returned to his meal.

There followed a lull in the conversation as we made short work of the stew before Edward resumed. 'And what type of trade are you in?' he asked Lapthorn.

'Oh, anything really, anything that makes a handsome return. We're carrying all sorts down below: spices by the sack load; every kind of glassen ware; fine damask silks and enough wine to soak an army.'

'And this is your ship?' I asked.

I saw captain's forehead crease in a frown.

'It's half mine,' replied Lapthorn, 'and half my brother's. Though Richard here is of course the master when we're at sea.'

'Do you always travel with the ship?' I asked again.

'No, not by any means, but I wanted to come to Venice to see for myself what we might buy cheaply here that is selling for a good price back home. Wine, for instance, is in short supply back in England, given the present hostilities with France, but there is plenty of cheap wine on the market here and plenty of demand for it in Portsmouth. It's not bad, is it?' he added, patting the bottle.

Edward and I nodded to show our appreciation.

'I trust your voyage has been worthwhile?' said Edward.

'Oh yes,' replied Lapthorn. 'My only regret is that I could have filled a score of ships, each one generating a very handsome profit, such are the opportunities for trade in this city. Still, our outward cargo fetched a very good price.' He reduced his voice to a mock whisper. 'They simply can't get their hands on enough tobacco here and there will always be a healthy market for our wool. Best in the world, you know.'

The mention of tobacco must have prompted Edward to extract his pouch and to start filling his pipe.

'Wait a moment,' said Lapthorn, standing and walking over to a chest beside his bed. From it he removed a large pouch which he brought to the table. 'Try this,' he said, beaming. 'It's the finest tobacco in all Virginia. I brought a whole shipful of it over to England. I had to keep a good measure back for my own use; couldn't bring myself to sell it all.'

Edward helped himself, delight glinting in his eyes. Lapthorn offered it to me too but I declined. Clearly the captain was not one for pipe smoking either. He wrinkled his nose in disdain.

Edward and the merchant puffed away on their pipes. I sipped at my wine, noticing that the captain had barely touched a drop of his.

'I heard you were enquiring in the Red Lion as to the whereabouts of the Duke of Buckingham,' said Lapthorn.

'Aye, that's right,' said Edward.

'What's your business with him?' asked the captain, with unconcealed disapproval.

'Tom here plans to enlist in the Duke's army, to fight the French.' Edward looked at me brazenly, encouraging me to confirm his lie.

'That's right,' I added.

'Captain Ratsey sailed in the Duke's fleet a couple of years back, when we routed those Huguenots.'

The captain flashed Lapthorn a look of pure anger. 'We may have won that particular encounter, but it was not at all clear to me that we were fighting on the right side.'

'Quite so, quite so,' continued Lapthorn, who seemed to be either oblivious or immune to the captain's sensibilities. 'I could never understand that particular alliance with the French either. Of course, the tide has since turned and now we find ourselves on the side of the Huguenots and against our erstwhile allies, Cardinal Richelieu and the French king. What a fickle, complicated world we live in.'

'Some men are more vain and fickle than others,' Ratsey observed. 'They play with armies as if they were mere chess pieces, won and lost for their personal glory and enrichment.'

'And Buckingham is now preparing an English force for a new campaign against the French?' asked Edward.

The captain rolled his eyes and snorted to indicate his disgust, leaving Lapthorn to provide the answer. 'That's his plan, but his efforts to date have been nothing short of a national scandal.'

'How so?' I asked.

'Not wishing to dampen your spirits young master,' replied Lapthorn, 'but the Duke's attempt to lay siege to *Saint Martin de Ré* last year, ended in abject failure.'

'Eighty ships and six thousand men to his name and still he couldn't lay a successful siege,' added Ratsey. 'Many a good man was lost in those days thanks to Buckingham's self-conceit and ineptitude.'

'But the Duke plans to return, to finish off what he started?' I feigned enthusiasm.

'Indeed he does, young master,' replied Lapthorn. 'The fleet is being assembled as we speak, and he is gathering an army to set sail for La Rochelle, to raise the siege on that long-suffering city. I am sure they could well use the services of a strapping young fellow such as your good self.'

'This one has already proved himself in some tight situations,' said Edward, nodding at me with a glint in his eye.

This prompted Lapthorn, who seemed to have spent much more time on land than at sea, to enquire for the full story of how Edward had released me from captivity. He was delighted to hear Edward's tale. 'Goodness' and 'Heavens' he would exclaim at each new stage of the battle between the *Gloriosa* and the *Dolphin*. The captain listened but did not join in the conversation.

When Edward's tale had concluded with his triumphal return to Malta – but with no mention of the cipher, of course – Captain Ratsey took the opportunity to excuse himself. 'Forgive me, gentlemen, I need to make the final preparations ahead or our departure tomorrow.'

'Of course,' we all replied, standing as he took his leave.

After the door had closed behind the captain, Lapthorn sat down and poured out another glass of wine for each of us. 'Richard's a dour soul,' he half whispered. 'You'll never find a captain anywhere on the high seas who is more diligent or assiduous in his work, but he's a man of few words and, how shall I put it, puritan taste.'

We resumed our conversation. Lapthorn told of his journey to Virginia and back, which stoked my imagination. He and his brother jointly owned another ship, the *Gilded Swan*, which plied its trade on the Atlantic. They owned warehouses in Portsmouth, in London and in Jamestown, Virginia and had agreements to share warehousing in Antwerp and Venice. They transported cargos across these vast distances and by his account to great profit.

When the bottle was empty and Edward and Lapthorn had each finished their second pipe, the conversation reached a natural conclusion. Edward and I thanked Lapthorn for his hospitality and retired to our cabin. Edward stretched himself out as far as his short bed would permit and I climbed into my hammock.

'No wonder Richelieu wants Buckingham dead,' said Edward in a low voice, as he blew out the candle in the lantern.

'Because he fears that this time, the English forces will prevail?' I whispered.

'Perhaps,' came Edward's reply out of the darkness. 'For it seems that Buckingham now regards rescuing La Rochelle as essential to preserve what little remains of his reputation. He will throw everything at this venture, where a wiser head would cut his losses.'

'So if the Duke is removed then the English threat might recede.'

'Exactly, leaving Richelieu free to finish off the Huguenots and then focus his attention on pressing matters elsewhere in Europe.'

'In places like Mantua, you mean?' I asked, my weary mind struggling to keep pace.

'No, not in Mantua, in Germany; I reckon that Richelieu believes that Mantua can be brought to heel without the use of force, once the present Duke is removed. The cardinal's long arm is felt on many other fronts in the current wars across Europe and, in my view, the future of Christendom will be decided on the battlefields of Germany.'

'I see,' I said and yawned.

'But that's not all,' hissed Edward. 'Remember this is personal. Buckingham had a pact with Richelieu and the Duke reneged on it. I'll wager it's because of that, more than anything else, that the Cardinal wants vengeance.'

'Badly enough to have him assassinated?'

'Without doubt.'

We exchanged no more words that night. The waters of the lagoon were calm and my hammock comfortable. I was soon induced by the gentle rocking of the ship into a deep and restful sleep.

The next morning, Edward and I were taking breakfast at a rough, communal table on the lower deck when a boatload of customs officials clambered aboard. They came from the *Dogana*, a low building that occupied the tip of land at the end of the Grand Canal, from where they could keep watch on the comings and goings in St Mark's Basin.

The officials, who were armed and intimidating, climbed down into the hold with Captain Ratsey and the purser and inspected the cargo. I could hear their voices rising up through the hatchway a few yards from my seat. Their work completed down below, the captain re-emerged on the lower deck, followed one-by-one by the officials. They stood waiting around the hatchway for the whole group to reassemble.

As they were waiting, I overheard one of the officials asking Ratsey whether he had taken any passengers on board. Both parties had resorted to speaking in broken French as the only common language. 'We're looking for two men,' I heard the official say, 'one old, one young.'

Suspecting Ratsey of being scrupulous to a fault, I felt sure that he was going to identify us. I shot an alarmed glance at Edward, whose hearing was not as sharp as mine, but he was engrossed in his new pamphlet of *Othello*. I dared not make a sound nor kick him under the table for fear of drawing attention to ourselves.

Captain Ratsey cast his eyes along the deck with a frown. He could not have failed to notice us at the table just yards away from him. I sat paralysed, my heart palpitating, my mouth suddenly dry.

'Two men, you say,' Ratsey replied.

The customs official nodded.

All eyes were now on the captain but he shook his head. 'We are a cargo ship, not a passenger ferry,' he said. They took him at his word.

The purser was the last man up from the hold. He closed the grille over the hatchway and the whole group continued up on to the main deck.

I remained stock-still, listening, fearful lest another member of the crew might yet give us away. From the snatches of conversation I could hear, I gathered that the customs officials were taking their levies from Lapthorn. I prayed that they would not question him too given his garrulous disposition. After a few minutes, during which I apprised Edward of our narrow escape and of our debt to Ratsey, I heard the officials take their leave and then climb down the ladder to a waiting boat below. Edward continued to Act Three of *Othello*.

We weighed anchor and set sail with a stiff northerly breeze filling our sails, the serene city gliding away behind us. While the customs officials had been making their inspection, a Venetian pilot had come aboard to navigate our safe passage through the treacherous mudflats of the lagoon.

Captain Ratsey ran a well ordered ship, issuing a series of quiet, measured instructions to his officers who bellowed them across the decks and up into the rigging. The crew were competent and nimble enough: scaling the shrouds and crossing the ratlines, unfurling and trimming the sails, and keeping the decks in order. Edward and I, along with Lapthorn, stood upon the poop deck as we sailed out from the lagoon and into the Adriatic, passing a colourful procession of ships and boats sailing towards the city. I kept one eye astern, lest we were being followed.

As the *Pride* worked her way southwards, Edward and I took to our books to pass the time. When the weather was fair, we would sit out on the poop deck, our backs against the bulwark and our books upon our knees. Edward began to read Grotius's *On the Law of War and Peace* and I started *On the Truth of the Christian Religion*.

When the weather turned inclement we retired with our books to the cramped confines of our cabin. Sometimes the churning of the waters below would make reading unbearable and at those times we would while away the hours in conversation. We would talk about what we had read and debate the finer points of Grotius's arguments, such as the rationale for holy war, upon which, it escaped neither of us, the existence of the Order of St John now depended.

That evening we were again invited back to Lapthorn's cabin and indeed that became the pattern for every evening during our voyage aboard the *Pride*. We would accept the invitation to the merchant's cabin and, once the meal was served, the taciturn captain would join us. Of course, the food became less fresh and more salted as we made our way south, but the wine continued to flow from Lapthorn's personal collection in the hold with no reduction in quality or quantity.

During these meals, Edward regaled our hosts with tales of the *corso*. Lapthorn was captivated by the descriptions of scimitar-wielding janissaries and knightly acts of heroism, mopping his forehead with a handkerchief and punctuating Edward's monologues with exclamations of wonder. The captain paid close attention to Edward's accounts of the handling of the ships and the tactics of the Order and of the enemy; Ratsey's detailed questioning on those topics were often his only contribution to the evenings' discussions.

For our part, Edward and I probed the merchant and the captain for news from England. Lapthorn was only too happy to oblige but his accounts were patchy and vague. He preferred to talk about his family, especially his three beloved children: two boys and a girl. The glass ornaments upon his shelves were gifts for them and his wife. Captain Ratsey was much less forthcoming but, on the occasions when he did speak, was precise in his information, with a meticulous eye and ear for detail.

There was also much talk of developments in Europe. Through these discussions, I came to understand that the struggle for La Rochelle, between Richelieu's army and the protestant Huguenots, was part of a broader set of tensions and conflicts flaring and raging across Europe. Christians were committing the most barbaric acts of savagery against fellow Christians, and all in the name of faith. Edward was not shy to point out that, all the while, the greatest threat to Christendom was gathering strength in the East.

As the evenings sank into a pattern of supper and discourse, so the days fell into a routine of reading and conversation, on deck and in the cabin as the weather dictated. Away to our starboard, day by day, the long flank of Italy rolled by and the heat intensified.

Reading Grotius's book was hard work at first and I remembered the chidings I had received years ago from my schoolmaster about my lack of aptitude for Latin. But with little else to divert my attention and under Edward's tutelage, I began to read more fluently, which made it easier to follow the author's meaning and improved my answers to Edward's challenging questions. When, as often happened, it all became too much, I would return to reading *Othello*, which became well-thumbed over the course of the voyage.

My requests to Edward for help on points of translation whetted his appetite to hear of Grotius's arguments. The author had much to say on the imperfections, as he saw them, in the Jewish and Islamic religions – seeking to establish logical flaws in their articles of faith. There were also pages and pages of reasoning on the folly of wars between Christians. This provided an erudite backdrop to our meal-time discussions about the many fronted war between Catholics and Protestants, which ranged from the machinations of Cardinal Richelieu, to the warmongering of King Christian of Denmark, to the tactics of the Emperor Ferdinand's generals, Tilly and Wallenstein.

Sometimes, when we were alone, Edward asked me more about my time in Algiers. I suspected that his interest had been piqued by

Grotius's writings on Islam. In any case, Edward enquired into the nature of life in the city with a renewed interest that extended well beyond the details of its defences. At first he clearly expected me to list a catalogue of horrors so long that it spilled out over the walls of that 'nest of vipers', as he called it.

While I was not slow to describe the low points of life in Algiers, I was also quick to identify the parallels I had encountered in Christian lands – like the stinking slave house in Malta – and to demonstrate the better aspects of life in Algiers, many of which were embodied in my late master. Indeed, I took pains to set out where I saw the Ottoman ways as superior to those I had encountered in Christian lands, which left Edward more bemused than outraged. I learned when to draw the line and to stay my tongue from the colour that flushed in his cheeks.

For a good while, Edward's reaction was to dismiss my points as nothing but an apology for the infidel: deeply ingrained was his loathing. But I did not waver from my views and, as long days drifted by in reading and conversation, Edward began to concede that not everything Islamic or Ottoman was by definition bad, though this was an idea that seemed to wrestle with his most fervent beliefs. I came to understand that his whole life had been constructed around the imperative to resist the advance of 'the Turks' to the bitter end. The newfound chink that I had discovered in his armour made me more willing to recount further aspects of my life in Algiers, things I had never told him before: the small human touches as well as the finer points of the administration. Once I even mentioned my prospective marriage to Aisha, an Ottoman bride. I wondered whether I had gone too far. Edward, sucking on his pipe as he listened, pulled a frown but did not erupt as once he might have done. 'It seems to me that you were cut from a strange cloth, Tom,' was his only, cryptic comment.

By the time we had rounded the heel of Italy and ventured out into the Ionian Sea, I had become confident in my view that too much blood was spilled on account of religious differences, and I said as much to Edward. It was a thought put in my mind by the learned Grotius, but one which I had extended well beyond his intended limit to encompass all religious conflicts, not just those between Christian factions. Edward could never be reconciled with such a view, but he did not dismiss it out of hand. Instead he acknowledged our difference of opinion: 'I understand your reasoning, Tom, really I do,' he said, 'but as for me, well – as the prophet Jeremiah taught us – a leopard cannae change his spots.'

At Sicily, we acquired an escort in the shape of another English merchantman, the *White Lady*, departing Syracuse on her voyage home. Captain Ratsey knew her captain of old and the prospect of company as we crossed the dangerous waters off the Barbary Coast lifted the spirits of all on board.

In the event, our voyage westward through the Mediterranean was uneventful. Captain Ratsey and his counterpart aboard the *White Lady* were experienced enough to keep well out of sight of land until the last possible moment where the Straits of Gibraltar drew the coasts of Africa and Europe close together. We raced through the straits, every sail unfurled, every gun port open. I stood beside Edward on the poop deck, both of us fully armed, Edward with his new spyglass to his eye, surveying every passing bay and inlet for skulking ships. If there were any there then they did not select us for their prey.

I remembered the heaving, purple-grey swell of the Atlantic from my original voyage south as a captive aboard the *Sword*. It was not something that I cared to remember. The *Pride* and the *White Lady* pitched and rolled between the shifting walls of water. The clement winds of the Mediterranean gave way to fierce, cold gales that tore at the sails and sent showers of foam across the decks. As we sailed north, the captain attempted to keep the coast of Portugal just beyond the horizon, though on occasion we would catch a glimpse of a distant headland. 'Out of sight, out of danger,' was his motto.

Edward and I were grateful to be able to while away those days in our cabin, only surfacing for air when gripped by sea-sickness and for our ritual supper in Lapthorn's cabin. By now we had each completed our respective first tomes of Grotius and exchanged them. In truth though, we had discussed so much of each other's texts as we had gone along that starting to read *On the Law of War and Peace* was like reuniting with a well-known friend.

We were happy to leave the struggle for mastery over the elements to the crew, who seemed capable enough – a coarse collection of Englishmen, drawn from all along the south coast. There were some younger than me, with whom I established friendly acquaintance. They reminded me of Jack, the cook aboard the *Sword*, carving out a life of adventure upon distant and dangerous waters, the envy of their friends back at home.

We pressed on northwards, Edward counting down the days, his anxiety growing. It was the fifteenth day of August by the time we sighted Cape Finisterre, the north-western tip of Spain. According to the cipher, this meant that we only had one week left to reach our destination in time to save Buckingham and we still had many leagues ahead of us. This date was also the one ordained for the assassination of the Duke of Mantua. We could only hope that he had received and heeded our warning.

We switched to a north-easterly heading across the Bay of Biscay, where once Murat Reis had hunted down the unfortunate *Santillana del Mar*, so close to her home port. I wondered at the fate of those poor souls on board, many of whom I had seen sold off into captivity in the slave market of Algiers. Some would doubtless have been ransomed by now; others would be seeing out their days under the harsh Barbary sun. Some would already be dead.

On some days, as we crossed the great bay, the gusting winds would die away to a whisper. At such times, Edward would prowl the quarter deck, clenching his fists and kicking at the bulwark to vent his frustration. To him the prospect of coming so far only to be thwarted by a lack of wind was unbearable. He would mutter obscenities about the folly of dispatching us first to Italy, to warn the Duke of Mantua, when common sense would have split the tasks and sent us, or another knight, directly to England. 'I grant you the Grand Master has more wisdom than almost any man,' Edward fumed, 'but this is sheer idiocy. I knew it was wrong from the outset.'

I found myself counting down the days for a different reason. Of course, I too was keen to complete the mission we had embarked upon in Malta. Much more than that though, I was counting down the time until my eyes should alight once more upon my home. Often I could think of little else, something that I considered strange given that I had, of necessity, put thoughts of home to the back of my mind during my life in Algiers. But now home – my real home – was drawing closer and the thought of being there caused my heart to race.

I unearthed a deep longing to see my mother again, if only she yet lived; a feeling that had lain suppressed for so long within me. Of course I was keen to see my sister too, and wondered what she would now be like as a young woman. But the thought of being reunited with my mother was what brought secret tears to my eyes along with a confused mixture of excitement and dread. My fear was that she might already have departed this fragile life so that our reunion would be at her grave.

When my mind lingered on such a dreadful thought, I wondered why on earth I had forgone my chance to escape? It would be my own fault if I arrived too late, if my mother had already passed away, her body emaciated by the grief of all she had lost. I should have joined Will in that boat at the quayside and been home months ago. What had happened to me to make me forfeit my chance to return to where I belonged? How could I have thought it better to stay than to go home? And then I reminded myself that Fortune had smiled on me in Algiers. I had been blessed with a kindly master, a good, purposeful life and a promising future, a future that had been shattered by that twist of fate that had seen our ship captured by the Order of St John.

In this way, my conflicting thoughts resembled the vagaries of the wind, sometimes gusting towards home, sometimes listless or even twisting around into a headwind. In the end, just as the *Pride* finally crossed from the Bay of Biscay into the English Channel, so my mind finally resolved that, while I had benefited from my time abroad, home was where I belonged. That resolution restored a sense of calm within me that matched the calming of the waters around us.

This peace of mind gave way to joy in my heart when I first saw the coast of England. We had been summoned to the quarterdeck by the joyful shouts that started up in the crow's nest, rippled down through the rigging and permeated through the hatchways to the lower deck, until the very timbers of the ship were vibrating with a chorus of elation. At first the land was no more than a dark line upon the horizon but, little by little, low, green hills emerged from the sea. I joined in the happy shouts of the crew, embracing and shaking hands with at least a dozen of them.

That was on the afternoon of the twenty-first day of August and the height of my elation was matched by the depth of Edward's relief at the prospect of reaching our destination on time. The captain had informed us that we would anchor overnight off the coast of Devon and that we should be in Portsmouth before nightfall on the following day.

Chapter 20: Portsmouth

We sheltered for the night in Tor Bay, weighing anchor at dawn to begin the final leg of our voyage. The summer sun beat down upon us but without the unrelenting ferocity of the Mediterranean. Soft, white clouds swept across the sky on a wind that carried us forward at a good rate of knots. We crossed the broad expanse of Lyme Bay and, by noon, had reached Portland Bill where a beacon had been placed high upon the headland to warn ships of the treacherous tidal race below.

After Portland, we hugged the coast of the Isle of Purbeck, its white cliffs interrupted by narrow gullies or chines. Fields of undulating corn and grass lined the cliff-tops. I could smell the sun-baked sheaves of the corn. I could see men tending their livestock, close enough to call out to. At times the coast was so near that I was tempted to dive into the inviting water and swim to shore.

So it was that I found myself at the bowsprit of the *Pride of Rye*, sea spray stinging my eyes, as we rounded a headland to be confronted by a glistening expanse of water. Through the haze a line of cliffs emerged in the distance: a low reddish strip in the south rising to great white precipices in the north, all topped by rolling downs of green, tinged with the yellow hues of summer. It was the unmistakable sight of the Isle of Wight, my island. If only Edward had been at my side then I could have borrowed his spyglass to survey the western coast of the island; I might even have been able to spot the steeple of the church in my own village. But Edward was astern, willing the *Pride* on towards our destination.

It was at this point that we parted company with the *White Lady*. She bore south to round the bottom of the island, and from there to continue her way along the south coast and round Kent towards London. There were shouts of farewell across the widening stretch of water between the two ships until the shouts from the *White Lady* faded out of earshot and only the cries of the encircling gulls remained.

Aboard the *Pride*, Captain Ratsey bore north-west, skilfully navigating around the western tip of the island, where the massive chalk walls culminated and then crumbled into an array of tooth-like rocks. The locals call them 'The Needles' after the spindly chalk tower standing proudly in their midst. Beyond them, the sea funnelled into the Solent, the channel that separates the island from the mainland. Only an experienced captain, familiar with these waters, or a fool-hardy stranger would have chosen that route in favour of the safer, longer route around the southern tip of the island.

On board, every man in the crew who was not involved in sailing the ship was busy preparing her to dock. The guns were tied fast to the sides. Hammocks were stowed away and each man's chest was packed and ready. After dinner, the galley was given a final clean, under close inspection from the bosun, and the lower deck and main deck were scrubbed to the rhythm of joyful shanties. I packed my few possessions into Edward's sea chest.

'Heaven knows when I'll have need for this again,' I said as I folded my hammock.

'Aye, it's all right for you,' said Edward. 'Think of me as I'm being buffeted by the waves on my voyage back while you've got your feet up at home.'

On our port side, we sailed close to the mainland shore, where the ancient trees of the New Forest reached down to white shingle beaches. The shoreline ended at the broad inlet of the Southampton River, which flowed away to the north behind a long spit of sand. Now it was my turn to point out the features of the land to Edward, who surveyed the terrain through his spyglass with interest.

On our starboard, the shore of the island unfurled. I saw and I remembered a series of harbours and inlets: first Yarmouth, then Newtown, and then the River Medina, bisecting the island and spilling out into the Solent between the West and East Cowes. Thereafter the island's coast fell away to the southeast, concealing the clandestine waters of the Meade Hole and beyond that the creek at Wootton and the tidal sands of Ryde.

It was a glorious late afternoon on the twenty-second day of August when we finally arrived at our destination: more than three weeks after we had set sail from Venice and only one day ahead of the fateful date in the cipher. A narrow channel, invisible at a distance, formed the maritime gateway to Portsmouth. We sailed out of the Solent and into the channel, each side guarded by a squat stone fortress, bristling with guns. The channel opened out into a large natural harbour in which dozens of ships lay at anchor, both men-of-war and merchantmen. A flotilla of smaller boats plied their trade among the ships and between the quays on either side of the harbour.

The *Pride* rounded a short neck of land on our starboard and the helmsman steered her into an inner harbour that doubled-back towards the town. Bustling quays lined the cramped waters. As the crew dropped anchor, Edward settled our bill for the voyage and we said our farewells to Captain Ratsey, who spared us only a moment for a reluctant handshake, and to the smiling Linus Lapthorn.

'I wish you a safe return from the campaign in France, Master Tom,' he said. 'You teach that Richelieu a lesson.'

'I'll do my best,' I replied, blushing.

The tender of the *Pride* was lowered into the water and we clambered down into it with our possessions. A boatman rowed us the short distance to a spit of land that stretched out like a breakwater, protecting the small inner harbour. This narrow stretch of shore was crowded with boats and mariners. We beached and disembarked, leaping from the prow to keep our shoes clear of the waves. My shoes crunched the shingle; it was the first time I had felt English land beneath my feet in six long years. The boatman carried Edward's chest on to the beach before pushing the tender off into the harbour and rowing back to the *Pride*.

A cluster of ramshackle buildings huddled above the beach; we headed towards them. The two nearest buildings were both inns. They spewed people and noise from every window and door.

'I guess here is as good a place as any to look for lodgings,' said Edward glancing up at the inn on our left.

I looked at him with a raised eyebrow. He allowed a drunkard to stagger out from the inn before entering, pulling his chest behind. I followed. Inside, the inn was packed with idling men in different degrees of drunkenness. Some lolled at the bar. Others slouched at tables. Edward called the innkeeper over from the taproom. A bald, pot-bellied man with sweat on his brow and filth on his apron, the innkeeper eyed us as he ambled between the tables.

'You look like a thirsty pair of gentlemen,' he said.

'Thirsty, yes, but first in need of lodging,' said Edward.

'You and the whole of the King's army!' the innkeeper replied.

'Aye, but we can pay you,' said Edward.

'A good point sir. Up front?'

'If that's what it takes.'

'Well now,' he said, wiping the sweat from his brow, 'I think I might have just the room for you.'

He led us up narrow wooden staircases to the second floor. Each step creaked as if in a desperate struggle to bear our weight. Half way along a landing he opened the doorway into a small, dingy room with a single bed. He opened the shutters to let in the light. It did little to increase the room's appeal.

'Is this all you've got?' asked Edward.

'It ain't all I've got, sir,' the innkeeper replied, labouring for breath, 'but it is the best I've got available at the present. The town's bursting at the seams. You can try your luck elsewhere but I doubt you'll find anything better, if at all.'

'And how much are you asking for this hovel?' asked Edward.

'Since I can see that you are both worthy gentlemen, I will not take more than a shilling each a night from the both of you.'

'A shilling each?' exclaimed Edward. 'I could rent a decent room for a week for a shilling.'

The innkeeper shook his head. 'Begging you pardon, sir, not in Portsmouth you couldn't.'

Edward paused as if weighing up his options. 'Very well; I'll give you a shilling and sixpence a night for the two of us and not a farthing more.' He stared at the innkeeper, his palm moving to the hilt of his sword.

The innkeeper's eyes seemed to protrude a little. 'Right you are, sir,' he said. 'And how many nights do you expect to stay?'

'As few as possible,' replied Edward, turning his back on the innkeeper and looking out of the window. 'Now pour us two tankards of ale and lay on the best meal you can muster. And be quick about it.'

The innkeeper coughed in the doorway. 'Begging your pardon again sir but, as I was saying, it's payment in advance.'

Edward spun round and with a scathing stare handed over four shillings from his purse. 'That should cover us for now.'

The innkeeper's podgy fingers grasped the coins. He inclined his bald head, beaded once more with sweat, before retreating through the doorway on to the landing.

'One more thing,' Edward shouted after him.

'Yes, sir,' the innkeeper hurried back and stuck his head back through the doorway.

'They say the Duke of Buckingham is hereabouts. Is that so?'

'Why yes sir, the whole town knows that he's staying in Captain Mason's house at present.'

'And where might one find Captain Mason's house?'

'It's in the High Street. It's the house that's known as the Greyhound.'

'Funny name for a house,' I said.

'Ah yes. It used to be a tavern, you see. You'll find it at the far end of the High Street.'

'That will be all,' said Edward.

The innkeeper withdrew once more, creaking stairs marking his descent.

Edward sat down on the bed. I opened the window to dissipate the smell of damp and took in the view, which looked out over the small inner harbour where the *Pride* was at anchor. A handful of warships jostled for space. They were taking on supplies from the boats that crossed back and forth from the quayside and from the beach upon which we had landed.

'We should seek an audience with the Duke as soon as possible,' said Edward. 'But I'll be damned if I'll do anything more without a good meal inside me.'

'It's tomorrow, isn't it?' I said. 'The day mentioned in the cipher.'

'Aye. Tomorrow's the twenty third day of the month. It could be an interesting one for His Grace the Duke.'

'Do you know him?'

'Me? No. My brother knew him. They were both at the court together, both favourites of the late King James, or so I gather. Anyway, my brother's been dead these last two years.' Edward's voice faltered and he looked away for a moment. 'Come on,' he said with a sigh, 'let's see how that swindler of an innkeeper is doing with our supper.'

We went down to the main room of the inn. The innkeeper had cleared away a drunkard from a table and had set two frothing tankards upon it. He gestured towards the table in a fawning manner as we approached.

We each took a stool and sat down. Edward extracted his pipe from his pouch, which Lapthorn had insisted on replenishing with his finest Virginian tobacco before we disembarked from the *Pride*. I took a swig of ale and couldn't help but listen to the various conversations swilling around the inn, keen for news of England, news of home. In truth, I heard little of interest. Most of the talk was of women and money or the lack of them. The innkeeper brought us roast mutton and some bread; I delighted in the sensation of succulent, unsalted meat in my mouth. After the meal, Edward lit his pipe and put his feet upon a stool and belched. He stared at the dishevelled men loitering about the inn, as if inviting them to challenge him. None of them had the energy or the inclination.

'That's better,' said Edward, banging his empty tankard down on the table and wiping his mouth with the back of his hand. 'Drink up laddie, we need to find the Duke.' He finished smoking his pipe and strutted out through the doorway.

We headed into the town along a make-shift street that led from the shore through an open gate in the town's perimeter wall. On our right loomed the large, round tower guarding the narrow entrance to the harbour. Beyond the gate the town bustled with activity. It was a town preparing for war. Every nook and cranny was crammed with goods or people. Men and boys and donkeys with carts carried supplies in an unending procession towards the harbour. Women went briskly about their business, underpinning the war effort.

We made our way against this tide for a short distance until we reached the massive square tower in the harbour wall. It stood at the end of a wide paved street leading into the heart of the town. Edward caught the arm of a youth pulling a small cart and asked him whether the paved street was the High Street. The lad replied with an indignant scowl that it was, wrestling his arm free before continuing on his way.

The High Street was lined with shops, taverns and fine houses, most built of brick on the ground floor with timber-framed upper rooms balancing precariously above. Here the hordes of mariners and tradesmen rubbed shoulders with elegant gentlemen and ladies. On our left we passed a large church with a tall central tower crowned with a weather vane.

Further down the street we saw a gathering of perhaps three score men around the doorway of a house. As we neared, I could see that a man was addressing the crowd. He stood in an elevated position, so that his head and shoulders were visible above the throng. Even from a distance and with such a limited view, I could see that this man's looks were striking. His hair fell in rich, brown curls to a wide ruff and he sported a finely shaped moustache and beard. His dark eyes darted around the crowd, holding the gaze of each man for a second or two, before moving on to the next.

'Hello, what have we here?' Edward muttered over his shoulder as we approached. 'I reckon we've found our man.'

As we arrived at the periphery of the crowd, I soon gained a sense of the conversation that was flowing back and forth between the crowd and the elegant man on the doorstep. They were demanding their wages and asking variations on a theme of how they were going to provide for themselves, let alone for their families, without pay.

'We ain't been paid for weeks!'

'You promised us we'd get our money.'

'How am I supposed to support my family without my wages?'

'Bet you're not short of a shilling or two yourself!'

The gentleman on the doorstep was reassuring them in an eloquent, unruffled tone that their wages were on their way. 'Be patient for just a little longer. Parliament has agreed to pay you all everything that you are owed. No less a person than His Majesty the King himself has given me his personal assurance that his loyal subjects will be paid their dues.'

Having said his piece, the gentleman told the crowd to return to their business. As he retreated inside the doorway a man next to me shouted: 'You're all fine words, but where's the money?'

'He's all talk. He ain't got no money!' cried another man.

There followed a general chorus of heckling and jeering but the door had already closed and the crowd began to disperse in small groups of grumbling discontent.

Edward strode towards the closed door, the last of the disgruntled men parting to make way for him. He banged the knocker. After a short delay, the door was opened by a well-dressed manservant, who looked Edward up and down from the doorstep, his gaze seeming to linger on every stain and crease on Edward's careworn attire. Edward cut short the visual interrogation.

'I am Sir Edward Hamilton, Knight of the Order of St John, and I would speak with the Duke urgently.'

The manservant rolled his eyes and responded in a thin, oily voice. 'His Grace is not receiving at present.'

Edward grabbed the servant by his doublet with both hands, so that his starched ruff was forced upward and pulled him down from the doorstep to ground level. Edward now towered over him.

'Now listen. I have come here as the emissary of His Serene Highness the Grand Master of the Order of St John to speak with the Duke. Pray tell your master that I would like an audience with him at his earliest convenience.'

The look in the servant's eyes had turned from curious condescension to outright fear. Edward released his grip and the man recoiled into the house, rearranging his clothes as he fled. Edward tapped a boot upon the doorstep. I waited a yard behind him.

A minute later, I heard the ring of footsteps striding down the hall; it was another man who now appeared in the doorway. His attire identified him as a gentleman, a military officer. His left hand rested upon the hilt of his rapier as he took the measure of Edward.

'Sir Edward. I am Captain Mason, and His Grace the Duke is a guest in my house.'

'Good, I have urgent business with the Duke.'

'So I am told, but I regret to say that the Duke has retired to his chamber to rest and has expressed his particular desire not to be disturbed. If you like, I could request that he grant you an audience at the earliest opportunity – which would be tomorrow morning.'

'Tomorrow morning may be too late. The Duke's life may hang on the news I bring,' Edward replied without concealing his impatience.

There was a look of surprise on the captain's face. He played with his moustache for a moment as he considered his next move. 'I see. You had better come in.'

The captain led us along a hallway and into a spacious, oak-panelled room overlooking the street. He offered us both a seat but we declined.

'Sir Edward, pray tell me your news so that I may relay it to His Grace at the first opportunity.'

'With respect, I am instructed to pass my message directly to the Duke himself to ensure that it reaches him.'

'I can assure you, that while His Grace is a guest in my house, his safety is my utmost concern, particularly in these difficult times.' Captain Mason glanced through the window on to the street, as if expecting to see the crowd reassembling.

'I do not doubt you, Captain, and I would be happy for you to be present when I convey the news, but my orders are such as they are. The Duke's life is in imminent danger and I must warn him of the specific intelligence I bring.'

The captain again twisted the end of his moustache for a few moments between his fingers before responding. 'Wait here gentlemen.'

He left the room, closing the door behind him. I heard his boots climbing a staircase to the first floor, followed by a knock upon a door. All further sounds were lost amid the general commotion of the household. Edward paced up and down, stopping once to brush off some dirt from his cloak. The loud, continual ticking of a clock in one corner of the room seemed to burden the passage of time. I inspected my own outfit. Despite being cleaned at the priory it was now a lacklustre imitation of the one I had purchased in Malta. I did my best to smarten myself up.

At length, I heard footsteps approaching outside the door. The captain reappeared followed by the gentleman whom we had seen addressing the crowd earlier and two armed menservants. The captain made the formal introduction: 'Sir Edward Hamilton, Your Grace, a Knight of Malta.' Edward gave a low bow towards the Duke, and I followed suit.

The Duke was even more handsome close up. He was as tall and as strong as he was good looking. His glossy hair fell down to his embroidered ruff; a silken sash ran over one shoulder and across his chest. His right hand fingered the jewelled hilt of his rapier as he glanced at me and eyed Edward. He held his left hand to his trimmed beard as if deep in thought.

'Hamilton, did you say? Still that is of no consequence here,' he muttered to himself, then continued in a full but drawling voice. 'I'm tired. This had better be worthwhile.'

'Your Grace, I come here as at the request of His Serene Highness the Grand Master of the Order of St John of Jerusalem.'

The Duke waved his hand in a circular motion, bidding Edward to proceed to the point.

'I bear news relating to Your Grace's personal safety.'

'Sir Edward, this is a time of war. My safety can never be assured. Danger and death are forever stalking me and there but for the grace of God go I.' He sighed, as if to convey the noble resignation with which he bore his fate.

'I bring news of a specific risk, Your Grace.' Edward continued unfazed. 'You may know that a century ago, a member of your most distinguished family, Grand Master Philippe Villiers de L'Isle-Adam, led our Order safely from our ancient home in Rhodes to our new home in Malta, from where we have been able to continue our holy war against the infidel.'

I saw the Duke's eyes widen a little. Edward had gained his attention.

'Our Order has not forgotten the debt of gratitude we owe to your noble family.'

The Duke nodded, accepting the gratitude.

'Consequently, when the present Grand Master learned of a direct and specific threat to Your Grace's safety, he dispatched me to warn you of it.'

'And what is the nature of the threat?' asked the Duke. 'I had a mob outside my door not half an hour ago but I had no fear for my personal safety.'

'The threat comes from France, from Richelieu.'

'*Quelle surprise,*' the Duke muttered, feigning astonishment.

'Some weeks ago, I was passed a paper containing a cipher by a friend of the Order in Paris. When this was deciphered by my friend Master Cheke—,' he paused to nod in my direction, 'it revealed a French plot to assassinate both yourself and the Duke of Mantua.'

'May I see this cipher?' Captain Mason interjected.

'Yes. Tom, if you would be so kind.'

I retrieved the paper showing both the original cipher and its decryption from my inner pocket, unfolded it and handed it to the captain. I watched his eyebrows rise as he read its content.

Edward continued. 'This secret information, which at least four men have now lost their lives for, identifies a specific date for the assassination: tomorrow. This is why I pressed for an audience today.'

'I am grateful for your efforts, Sir Edward,' said the Duke.

'Is Richelieu aware that you have uncovered his plot?' asked Captain Mason.

'I think not,' Edward replied. 'We dispensed with two of his agents who were on our tail in Venice. I do not think it possible for word of their fate to have got back to Richelieu in time for his plan to have been altered. We ourselves have only this day stepped off a ship from Venice. So it is reasonable to assume that the assassin is already in the vicinity and poses a mortal danger to your Grace's person. Unfortunately, we do not know who the assassin is.'

'Indeed, that is a pity,' said the Duke, 'for I am not one to cower indoors until such a threat has passed.' He banged a fist against one of the oak panels in the wall. 'We have much work to attend to tomorrow as the fleet will set sail for France in a matter of days. So I shall continue to go about my business. I will not be daunted by this underhand threat from that dog of a cardinal. I will though be on my guard, thanks to your noble efforts and the Grand Master's kind consideration.'

'Your Grace, is that wise?' Captain Mason intervened. 'Could you not pass the time in seclusion for but one day or visit the King in Southwick?'

'My dear captain, your concern for my safety is deeply appreciated, but I see little merit in disappearing from the scene for a day. If the assassin is indeed here, and I don't doubt the integrity of this intelligence, then surely he will wait for his moment to strike whether that be tomorrow, or the next day or the next day. If I were to step back from our preparations and think only of my own safety then I would be playing straight into Richelieu's hands. Each day his stranglehold on La Rochelle grows tighter and the risk of our arriving too late increases.' He walked over to the window overlooking the street, gazing out as if surveying the battle preparations. 'No my friend, I must press on, though I shall seek to avoid any unnecessary risks and I will trust in your ability to keep an eye out for the would-be assassin before he gets his chance to practice his handiwork upon my person. And with these fine fellows in town—' he turned his head and his dark eyes flashed towards Edward and me '— I am sure that I will be in safe hands.'

The captain frowned, but said no more.

'Now gentlemen,' the Duke continued, 'I thank you sincerely for your pains. I place my household at your service and send my most heartfelt thanks to His Serene Highness the Grand Master, for now I must retire to my chamber. Oh, and please tell no one else about this plot, it would do no good for morale.'

His lips twitched in a thin smile as he turned with a flourish and swept out of the room. His two menservants followed. We were left alone once more with the captain.

The captain closed the door to the room and turned to speak to us. 'I fear the Duke pays too little heed to his own safety,' he said.

'Do you know his plans for tomorrow, and are they widely known?' asked Edward.

'Yes, on both counts. Tomorrow morning, as usual, he will receive a host of people and hear their various petitions.'

'Where will he do that?' asked Edward.

'Here, in this room. He will sit on that chair and the people will come forward as they are called to speak with him.'

'And after that?' asked Edward.

'After that, he will do what he usually does, take dinner and then go and inspect the preparation of the fleet and the army before retiring for the afternoon and taking supper here in the evening.'

'Is there anywhere specific that he is due to go tomorrow?'

'No, not that I'm aware of. He will dine in one of the taverns as takes his fancy and will visit whatever aspect of the preparation has caught his attention.'

'But he could be followed?'

'Undoubtedly,' replied the captain.

'What do you think Tom?' asked Edward.

Surprised to be asked my opinion, I said the first thing that came into my head. 'If I were an assassin then I would strike where I knew I would find the Duke.'

'You mean here, in the morning?' asked Edward.

'Yes, or in the evening, since he is known to retire here. If the assassin is not already part of this household then I presume it would be easier for him to gain access during the morning when the Duke is receiving guests?'

'Yes, indeed,' replied the captain. 'In the evening, I could have some of my most trusted men stationed outside the Duke's door. But in the morning the Duke is generous with his company and tends to receive any gentleman who seeks an audience with him.'

'Then could you remove all weapons from those seeking an audience?'

'Of course,' Captain Mason replied.

'And could the three of us and his menservants be here in the room, standing guard?' I asked.

'Yes, since you have gained the Duke's trust, I was thinking along similar lines myself, if you would be good enough to assist us in this way,' said Mason.

Edward and I both nodded our assent.

'Right, let's adjourn until the morning,' said Edward, 'and I would suggest that your men keep a close watch on the Duke this night too. At what time should we come in the morning?'

'Be here before nine o'clock. Tell whoever answers the door that I have sent for you and that you should be brought to me immediately.'

'Agreed,' said Edward.

We left the house and wandered back through the town towards our inn. Our return was noteworthy only because Edward stopped along the way to purchase a new cloak from a shop on the High Street, opposite the great church. It was in the fashion worn by many of the officers that I had seen parading through the town. My initial thought was that Edward had been stung by the condescending look from Captain Mason's servant, but he soon put me straight. 'I stick out like a sore thumb with the insignia of the Order on my cloak. This should help me to blend in a little.'

That evening we ate and drank among the waifs and strays who found company and sustenance in our inn, which was located on the spit of land that the locals called the Spice Island. The beer flowed and the shanties followed but the mood in the place was a touch subdued. I guessed that there was neither enough money nor expectation about the forthcoming campaign to truly buoy the drinkers' spirits. I enjoyed the taste and texture of the fresh food and washed it down with plenty of ale – as did Edward, even though he complained that it was rancid.

My feet were unsteady as I climbed the creaking stairs to our room. As I lay down to sleep upon a coarse blanket, the hard wooden floorboards beneath me felt as though they rolled with the waves aboard ship. Edward snored like a horse as he slept fully clothed upon the bed.

In the morning, Edward woke me early. My body ached all over. He had the innkeeper send us up some bread for breakfast and a pail of water to wash ourselves. After we had washed and dressed, Edward checked over his pistols and insisted that I do the same with mine. Once he was satisfied he donned his new cloak. 'It's time to go to work,' he said.

We left the inn and retraced our steps through the awakening town to Captain Mason's house. The oily manservant who again opened the front door led us, without hesitation, through to the oak-panelled room in which we had met the Duke the previous evening. Captain Mason joined us moments later. He informed us that he had registered an early success that morning in persuading the Duke to wear his breast-plate, something which he was loth to do.

We decided that we would spread out around the room during the period when the Duke would be receiving petitions, which was expected to last for an hour. The captain would stand by the window, Edward would hover near the door, while I would take up a position beside the wall opposite the door. The Duke's menservants would, as was customary, stand at each side of the Duke's chair. In that way we would have the four walls of the room covered and would be able to keep a close eye on the petitioners, who should in any case have been disarmed upon arrival.

The first petitioners arrived at around nine o'clock and began to assemble in the room, awaiting the arrival of the Duke. The air in the room became close with their hushed murmuring. During this time Edward and I tried to look inconspicuous, like another pair of petitioners, waiting in the corner beside the grandfather clock.

After half an hour, once the room was full – I counted fourteen petitioners in all – the Duke swept in. A hush descended as the people parted and he processed the short distance across the room, scenting the air with his perfume. He sat down upon his grand chair, flanked by his servants and an equerry. There followed a brief jostling for position as the petitioners edged towards the Duke while affecting to maintain a respectable distance. Edward and I used this opportunity to take up our agreed positions. In the event, the room was so crowded that my position afforded me only a limited view but I was nevertheless able to hear much of the Duke's conversation.

The equerry had been taking a note of the various petitioners as they arrived at the front door and had placed them in order on the paper that he held out officiously in front of him. He called forward the first petitioner, one Mr Marriott, a farmer from the village of Rowner, on the other side of the harbour, who was seeking payment that he was owed towards the cost of billeting Buckingham's troops. The Duke thanked the farmer for his contribution towards the war effort and told him that Captain Mason would see that he was duly compensated. The equerry made a note of the outcome and then summoned forward the next petitioner.

The other petitioners followed in turn and some recurring themes emerged: most were asking for payment of monies owed to them; some were asking for justice to be served on some of the Duke's errant troops; and others simply had something to sell in support of the war effort. On most occasions, the Duke would refer them to Captain Mason, who I soon gathered acted as his quartermaster: in charge of supplies, finances and the general organisation of the war effort.

I kept an eye as best I could on each of the men that approached the Duke. I also tried to survey the men who were waiting on my side of the room. This became a little easier as the crowd began to thin once several of the petitioners had departed.

It was while I was glancing around the men at the rear of the room near the window that a glint of metal caught my eye. It was there and then it was gone, which caused me to wonder whether my eyes had deceived me, whether it was only my imagination at play.

The flash had seemed to come from the waist of a man at the back of the crowd of petitioners. I focussed my attention on him and noticed that he was alternating his weight between his feet. His breathing appeared shallow. His fingers fidgeted with the hem of his cloak, which was clasped at the front with a brooch. My attention was rewarded. I saw another flash of metal, much clearer this time. His fingers had dislodged enough of his cloak to reveal, for a fleeting moment, what looked like part of a blade tucked into his waistband.

My eyes were now fixed upon this man, whom I put in his forties. He was of slender build, with red hair that fell down in locks to his shoulders. He wore a wide-brimmed hat that shaded his face, preventing me from gaining a good view of it. I tried to catch either the captain's or Edward's eye but to no avail. From that moment, everyone else dimmed out of focus, as if this man were the only real person in the room. I watched him edge forward, closer to the Duke, as the current petitioner's audience ended. My pulse quickened.

The equerry called another petitioner forward and the red-haired man filled the gap vacated, so that he was now only six feet away from the Duke with only the lone petitioner standing between them. Transfixed, I registered every move, every breath of the red-haired man. In the background, the petition droned on in a similar fashion to those that had gone before: a claim for payment owed for billeting. It seemed destined to be dealt with in the manner of its forerunners. The red-haired man continued to fidget. I saw him craning over the shoulder of the petitioner, surveying the Duke, perhaps looking for the best place to strike.

My heart began to beat so hard that I thought it must be audible to everyone in the room. Again I tried to catch Edward's eye but he was watching the Duke. The situation felt unreal. I began to panic about my next move: would I hesitate, as I had done outside the ambassador's house in Venice? But then I doubted once more what I had seen – perhaps all I had seen was the flash of a buckle on an innocent petitioner come to resolve his grievance. Then I thought of his fidgeting, but reasoned that I too would feel nervous before presenting my petition to such a great man. Then I recalled the cipher, the purpose of our mission. The current petition concluding, the petitioner about to depart, the red-haired man about to have a clear route to the Duke, I had to act at that moment or not at all. I trusted my instinct.

'Stop!' I shouted. I saw the man's face contort as his right hand darted across his waist to grasp the concealed blade. He brandished his pale blue eyes at me for a second then fixed them back upon the Duke.

I threw myself at the assassin. As I did so, he pulled out his dagger and dashed towards the Duke. I grabbed at him, catching his right arm in one hand and his cloak with my other hand. But he was strong and he escaped from my grasp with a thrust of his right elbow that sent me crashing headlong to the floor, still clutching his cloak. Far from impeding him, the cloak was ripped from around his shoulders, freeing him to advance upon the Duke. I was now powerless to intervene and could only watch the next split seconds unfold from my prone position.

'Die you murderer!' the assassin screamed as he leapt forward, his right arm raised, the dagger pointing down towards the Duke's exposed neck. The Duke only had time to raise his left arm in an attempt to parry the blow. He remained rooted to his chair. His menservants were unsheathing their rapiers but were too late to protect him.

The next thing I heard was a deafening explosion that shook the panels of the room. In that same instant the assassin was thrown sideways towards the wall where I had just been standing. I smelt the acrid smoke of gunpowder. I glanced over to see Edward, still pointing his smoking pistol at the place where the assassin had stood ready to strike but a moment before.

After that there was pandemonium in the room. People were rushing for the door, hastened on their way by the captain who was bellowing 'Out, out!' and ushering the Duke to safety elsewhere in the house.

I staggered to my feet, leaving the assassin's cloak splayed across the floor. Meanwhile, Edward ignored the captain's instructions and strode across the room towards the assassin. He placed his pistol back into his waistband and drew his rapier. The assassin lay on his side, his knees tucked up so that he was curled almost into a ball. His hat had come off and his face was turned down towards the floor.

'Got him in the heart,' Edward muttered to me as he prodded the man with his boot, his rapier poised to finish the job. He rolled the assassin on to his back. I had expected him to be dead but I heard him groan. The locks of his hair had fallen across his face and his right arm lay limp at his side with the dagger a few inches away from his outstretched fingers. A dark stain was growing on the front of his doublet.

Edward kicked the dagger away, sheathed his rapier and knelt down beside the man. 'So who are you then?' he said as he pulled him up by his doublet so that his back was propped up against the wooden panels of the wall. Edward shook him and his red locks fell away to reveal his gaunt face, the lifeblood ebbing from it.

I was surprised to see Edward's head jerk backwards, as if he were shocked by the sight. Then he seemed to regain his composure and uttered a few words. I listened, though the words that followed were hard to make out against the din continuing outside the room. I noticed that Edward's voice had now fallen to a whisper. 'Why?' I heard him asking.

I couldn't hear the man's response, which was mouthed rather than spoken, but I sensed that Edward had heard it. I drew nearer to come within earshot. The man was choking. He coughed up blood and murmured something else but I struggled to hear it.

'When?' Edward demanded.

I didn't hear the reply. The assassin's eyes rolled backwards, their lustre gone. Dark blood continued to seep through his doublet.

'The Lord bless you and have mercy on your soul,' Edward whispered, releasing his grip on the man's doublet. He raised himself on to his feet and cast his eyes upwards, muttering: 'The gods look down and laugh at this unnatural scene.'

Captain Mason rejoined us. He gave the assassin a heavy kick in the ribs. There was no reaction at all.

'Did you get anything out of him?' Mason asked Edward.

'Not much; I got him to admit that he was in Richelieu's pay. A French spy.'

'So your intelligence was spot on,' said the captain. 'We are greatly indebted to you.'

'I was just doing as I was instructed by the Grand Master.' Edward's tone was flat. He continued to look down.

'Well the Duke will, I am sure, wish to reward you, both of you, for your service.'

'You are very kind but that won't be necessary,' said Edward. 'Our work here is done and we have business to attend to elsewhere.'

There was a firmness to Edward's statement that the captain did not seek to contend with. For several moments all was still and quiet in the room.

'Where are you bound for?' asked Mason.

Edward looked at me, as if to deflect Mason's attention towards me.

'Tom, here, is long due a return to the Isle of Wight,' he said.

'Oh really, whereabouts?' asked the captain.

'Mottistone,' I answered.

'Mottistone,' Mason repeated, twiddling his moustache. 'Now there's a coincidence. That's the manor of Robert Dillington, isn't it? Or I should now say *Sir* Robert Dillington.'

'That's right,' I replied, 'though he was not a knight when I left.'

'Indeed not, he purchased his knighthood from the Duke but three days ago. I settled the finances myself.'

'Peddling knighthoods: now there's a sorry state of affairs,' said Edward.

'Well, as you've heard, Sir Edward, we have many bills to pay, and we need to raise the money one way or another, or we'll have a mutiny on our hands. Selling titles is one way to raise funds, I'm afraid.'

'If selling titles is one of the ways, I dread to think what the others are.'

'Parliament has not been generous in its support of the war, Sir Edward. Sometimes we must endure necessary evils for the greater good.'

The captain's response did nothing to lessen the disapproval etched on Edward's face.

'Robert Dillington is a close friend of my family,' I said, seeking to lighten the conversation. 'He has shown us great kindness through difficult times. Do you know if he is still here in Portsmouth?'

'No, I don't think so. I didn't speak to him much, he was too busy ingratiating himself with the Duke and I was attending to the paperwork but I do recall that he said something about heading back the island to be married this very weekend. He had been waiting for his knighthood to be bestowed before he tied the knot. I do remember the Duke commenting that Sir Robert had done well to land himself such a young bride.'

'Well I'm sorry to have missed him, but I shall hope to catch up with him soon, and to share in his good fortune,' I replied.

'Come, Tom,' said Edward. 'Let us get back to the inn. Captain, I trust that you will put things in order here?'

'Yes, of course. We won't want news of this to spread. Much as I'd like to proclaim that we've foiled Richelieu's cowardly plot, I wouldn't want this to give others the same idea. I'm less assured about the continued goodwill of the populace than His Grace is. I have already asked the Duke's equerry to tell those present this morning to keep what happened strictly to themselves, or risk the Duke's extreme displeasure.'

'Well you can be assured that we will do the same. The Order would not want it to become known that we had crossed swords with France.'

Mason nodded in understanding. 'Then, I wish you Godspeed,' he said.

'Thank you,' Edward replied. 'Come on Tom, our work here is done.'

Chapter 21: Chance Encounter

The morning's events cast a long shadow over Edward. He trudged in silence from Captain Mason's house back along the High Street towards the inn. I was at a loss to explain why the death of an assassin had so affected him; after all, I had seen him despatch Richelieu's agents in Venice and my fellow voyagers aboard the *Dolphin* without a flicker of regret or remorse. Indeed, his eyes would light up when he recounted such events from the past, which he often did to anyone who cared to listen.

We exchanged not a word until we had passed through the town gate on to the Spice Island and approached the inn. I continued to ponder what had happened. At last I could hold back no longer and broke the silence.

'You knew him, didn't you?'

Edward made no answer.

'The assassin, I mean.'

'Aye, I did,' Edward replied.

'Who was he?'

Edward looked at me with doleful eyes but did not respond. I left the question hanging. Before we entered the inn, Edward went down to the shore. He rinsed his hands in the low waves, foam running over his boots. He ran his wet hands through his hair and over his face.

I saw that the *Pride* was still at anchor in the inner harbour. The quayside beyond her was a hive of life, swarming with people about their business, all ignorant of what had just happened.

Edward made his way back inside the inn. Although it was not yet noon, the crowded main room was already in full voice: drunken sailors were lifting the low rafters with their bawdy tales and songs. All the tables were occupied but Edward spied a man asleep at a table in a corner and pushed him off his stool on to the floor, taking the stool for his own. The man, stirring from his stupor, was about to remonstrate but took one look at Edward and thought better of it. He sidled away rubbing the back of his head. Edward banged his fist upon the table and the innkeeper came running over.

'Two tankards of ale,' Edward demanded, 'and make sure it's better than the last lot of bilge water.'

The innkeeper scuttled away while Edward sat at the table reloading the pistol he had fired at the assassin.

We each drank our first tankard, Edward much faster than I. He ordered two more and prepared his pipe while I finished my first ale. Our lack of conversation felt awkward. The question of how Edward had known the assassin and why he had been so unnerved by what had come to pass was still burning in my mind. It was more out of concern for Edward than curiosity that I sought an answer.

'Had you seen him before in Paris?' I ventured. I spoke in a low voice, but such was the noise in the inn that no one, or at least no one sober, could overhear us. I wondered whether Edward would reply to my question this time. There was a delay before his eyes dipped in confirmation.

'Aye,' he replied, 'I knew him from there and many other places.'

'Was he one of Richelieu's men then, or some connection to the Order in Paris?'

Edward looked at me again, pain etched in his grey eyes. 'No, he was one of my brother's men. His name was James Hamilton.'

I said nothing in response and Edward must have sensed my incomprehension.

'He was one of my own family, of my own blood. And I shot him like some heathen dog.'

Neither of us uttered a word for the next few minutes, in a tacit agreement that lasted until the final drop in Edward's tankard had been drunk. In my mind I was mulling over how it could be that Edward's own family was embroiled in an assassination attempt. I was sure that Edward had known nothing of such a connection in advance, or at least I thought I was sure. It made me realise how little I actually knew about him, for all the time that we had spent together. What I knew of his past was only what he had chosen to tell. Edward lit his pipe, engulfed in his thoughts.

I let him finish his pipe then I asked him: 'Why did he do it?'

He stowed his pipe in his tobacco pouch, keeping his eyes fixed on that task.

'I told you before, didn't I, that my brother had died some years ago?'

'Yes, you said he was a Marquess.'

'Aye he was that, and a rising star at the court by all accounts. Still, he was cut down in his prime. He died in London.'

'Does that have something to do with this?' I asked, presuming that it did.

'Back there in the house, with almost his last breath,' Edward's face contorted in a grimace, 'James told me that Buckingham had my brother poisoned. That's how my brother died, in agony. And, by some bitter twist of Fortune's wheel, it was I who prevented James from avenging my brother's death.' He raised his eyes to the ceiling and muttered as if in prayer: 'Oh, call back yesterday, bid time return.'

After a respectful pause, I continued. 'So James wasn't working for Richelieu then?'

'Maybe, maybe not. I have learned that life is seldom straightforward; it's murky and it's complicated. Perhaps James had a dual motive. He certainly spent a lot of time in France. Perhaps Richelieu knew he'd be up for it. We'll probably never know now.'

The innkeeper brought us over fresh tankards, crashing them down so they splashed across the table. Neither of us cared. Our conversation ceased until the innkeeper had left us. I ran over the shooting and its aftermath again in my mind.

'He told you something else, didn't he?' I said.

'Aye.' Edward stared into the depths of his tankard.

'He told you something else had happened, or was going to happen?'

'Not much gets past you, does it Tom?' There was bitterness, perhaps even a threatening tone in his reply. He opened his tobacco pouch again and began to refill his pipe.

'He told me that there would be another.'

'Another assassin?'

Edward didn't answer but finished preparing his pipe. I took his silence to be confirmation.

'When?'

'Today, tomorrow; he wasn't clear.'

'But you didn't warn Captain Mason?'

'No.'

'So what are we going to do about it?'

He looked right at me, ferocity burning in his eyes. 'Nothing. We'll be on our way at the first chance we get, just like I told the captain.'

'Nothing?' I half shouted, feeling my cheeks flush.

'Aye, you heard me right.' His back straightened.

I sat in stunned silence, struggling to contain my anger. I wanted to remind him of the task that the Grand Master had assigned to us. A friend of the Order had paid with his life for providing Edward with the intelligence to save Buckingham. Our task was to help avert the Duke's assassination. If we knew that he was again in imminent danger then we must at least warn him. A quick message to Captain Mason would suffice; we need do no more than that. But Edward knew all this. He bore the weight of his vow of obedience to the Order. I sensed that a change had come over him. At this moment, the interests of the Order were secondary to those of his family.

The influence of the ale and the noise all around us was in no way conducive to clear thinking. I questioned my own position. *Did I not have any say on this matter? Was I merely Edward's servant? Was I not a loyal subject of this country? Did I not have a moral duty to save a man's life? Would his blood be on my conscience if I failed to act?* These thoughts and many more whirled around my mind. How I now regretted my curiosity: far better that I had never discovered those final words of the assassin.

I sat in a dismal reverie, resting a shoulder upon the wall as I weighed up the arguments. Meanwhile, the happenings in the inn passed me by. I was not aware of Edward ordering us some food from the innkeeper and more ale.

The more I thought, the less I perceived the right and proper course of action. In my heart, I felt that the right thing to do was to stand by Edward. That sentiment outweighed any notion of duty to my country or her leaders, the country that I had returned to but yesterday, the country that had forsaken me during my years of captivity. Nor did I feel any personal allegiance to the Order and the will of the Grand Master. Instead, what weighed most upon my conscience was allowing a grievous crime to be committed, indeed of being complicit in such a crime by inaction. But then, I reasoned, this was a time of war, and war claimed many a good life. And I doubted whether the Duke had spared much consideration for the lives of his men in pursuit of his own interests, sending them in their thousands to a watery grave or to be butchered upon the field of battle.

The steaming bowl of mutton stew placed in front of me restored my senses somewhat. I focussed back in on my surroundings. Edward ate his stew in silence, save for the occasional slurp as he ladled it into his mouth. I felt too uncomfortable to meet his gaze and my attention drifted across to the table nearest to us. A couple of old tars were filling themselves with the same stew and engaging in hearty conversation. I fixed upon the one who was facing me. He had a pock-marked face and wore an earring. As I watched him talking and eating, I fancied I had seen him before, that I knew him from somewhere. I discounted the idea that he was one of the crew of the *Pride*, many of whom must have been in town at that moment. My memory of him was more distant. I was struggling to place him, but I felt I had known him long ago, when the years had not weathered him quite as much as now.

I watched him as I supped my ale. He laughed raucously at some joke told by the other tar. It was at that moment that I remembered. I was almost sure that he was old Jeffers, one of the crew of the *Sword*, the one who had called me 'Powder Tom' in jest, though I had never established why. He had said it was something to do with my bounty, which I never understood. I caught his eye, causing a faint glimmer of recognition to play across his brow. He turned away but my suspicions of our prior acquaintance had been confirmed.

It was then that Edward noticed that I was staring at the man. 'What's with that fellow over there?' he asked.

'Oh, nothing really,' I replied. I was about to let the matter rest when I figured that it was good to have Edward conversing once more on a different subject; so I offered a little more information. 'He was one of the crew on a ship I sailed on once.'

'Which one?'

'The *Sword*, the *Saif al Din*,' I replied without thinking.

'You mean he was a sailor on an infidel ship? A corsair?' Too late I realised what I had started.

'Yes.' I replied.

Edward brought his tankard crashing down upon the table.

'Then of all the scum in this hell hole of a port, he'll be the worst.' His words were so loud that everyone in the inn heard them. 'He's a bloody *renegado*, with the blood of Christian men and women on his hands, I'll vouch.'

Jeffers cast an alarmed look in our direction.

'Are you looking at me, you scumbag of filth?' Edward shouted as he stood up, sending his stool sideways across the floor.

Jeffers averted his eyes, as if engrossed with his stew. In truth, I did the same. It was so long ago that I had long since lost any desire for retribution against Murat Reis and his crew. My life had moved on in the intervening years and though I still felt a keen sense of loss, I felt no regret. Moreover, things were about to be set right: I was going home. Edward, however, was not in the mood to let it go.

'Aye, you. I'm talking to you, you filthy dog of a *renegado*. Had your fill of attacking Christians, have you? Come back to enjoy the quiet life in your dotage? Does everyone here know your dirty secret?'

I looked up to see Edward reaching Jeffers's table. He had removed his cloak to display the black habit of the Order with the white, eight-pointed star emblazoned across the front. Both Jeffers and his companion were staring up at Edward, fear etched in their wide eyes. I got to my feet, expecting trouble.

Edward confronted Jeffers's companion first. 'Get lost, unless you're a *renegado* too?'

The man was only too happy to vacate the table. He scurried away to what he considered to be a safe distance, but continued to watch developments from the other side of the room.

Edward grabbed the man's stool and sat down, so that he was face to face with Jeffers.

'My friend here, tells me that you were aboard the infidel ship that captured him?' Edward continued to speak in an elevated voice so that the people around could hear the accusation.

Jeffers remained silent for a few seconds, as if considering his options, whether to deny everything or to plead guilty and face the consequences. 'I don't know what you're talking about,' he replied at length. 'I've never laid eyes on him before.' He glanced up in my direction, though he could not look me in the eye.

'Well, you know there's a very quick way to prove one way or another whether you're a man of your word or a *renegado*,' said Edward.

Jeffers looked around in desperation, as if seeking benign intervention from elsewhere in the inn. No one came to his aid. An anxious quiet had descended as, all around the room, onlookers waited to see how this argument would be settled. Doubtless there were many amongst them who were relishing the prospect of seeing a good fight. I walked over and stood behind Edward, watching his back.

Jeffers stood up. 'You're a mad man. Spare me your ravings. I've got things I need to do.'

Edward shoved the table forward so that it rammed into Jeffers's thighs sending him toppling on to the floor, his half-drunk tankard following him down. When he returned to his feet, mopping the beer from his face with his sleeve, he found Edward's pistol pointing straight at his chest.

'So now you would murder me! For the Lord's sake, it's plain for all to see that you're a mad man, a killer. You should be locked up.' Jeffers's eyes darted around, pleading for support.

My right hand moved to the hilt of my rapier as I likewise surveyed the room. No one came to Jeffers's rescue.

'Well you're right that I'm a killer,' replied, Edward, still seated with his pistol in his outstretched hand. 'Indeed, I've already killed a man today, but believe me, killing you would give me far more satisfaction.'

'See, he admits it; he's a killer!' Jeffers shrieked.

'And why shouldn't I put a bullet through you?' asked Edward. 'Since you were complicit in the kidnapping of this man behind me when he was just a boy, complicit in aiding foreigners to commit such a crime on English soil against one of the King's loyal subjects, you committed an act of treason. And you know what the punishment for treason is, don't you? My bullet would only be sparing you from a more drawn out execution. Or maybe I will hand you over to the Duke instead, who'll have you lynched before the day is done, I'll wager.'

'Well it's your word – a self-confessed killer's word – against mine, a god-fearing and loyal subject, so I reckon I'll take my chances with the Duke, and I'll prove to him that you've got the wrong man.'

A murmur rippled round the room. I feared that Jeffers might have succeeded in kindling support.

'It's my word too, Jeffers,' I said with as strong a voice as I could muster, 'and I say you're as guilty as sin. If you want to prove your innocence, all you need do is drop your breeches. We've plenty of witnesses here who'll be able to see for themselves.'

There were snorts of laughter around the room but they soon died away. Jeffers stood motionless. I appreciated how the wheel of Fortune had turned. Where once Jeffers had laughed at a helpless, captive boy, now I had turned the laughter upon him as he stood helpless and ensnared. It filled me with no pleasure.

Edward stood and motioned with a tilting of his head towards the door. 'Right, out you go. You've an appointment with His Grace's hangman.' To add to the sense of urgency, or perhaps to pacify any potential dissent among the onlookers Edward pulled out his second pistol so that he held one in each hand. To add to the effect, I retrieved mine from my breast pocket.

Jeffers looked at Edward's pistols, glanced at his face, and then skulked towards the door, raising his eyes only once from the floor in a final bid to attract support from his fellow drinkers. None came. Edward pressed a pistol into Jeffers's back and we followed him outside into the street.

'Now, walk towards the gate,' said Edward, 'run and you're a dead man.' We followed a couple of paces behind, our pistols levelled at his back.

As we neared the gate in the town wall, Jeffers stopped in his tracks and turned to face us. A broad smirk played upon his lips.

'All right, so you found me out,' he said.

'Save your breath, leper face,' said Edward, gesturing with his pistol to continue moving forward.

Jeffers stood his ground. 'You never did find out why you were taken, did you Tom?' There was a laughing malice in his voice.

I stared at him unmoved, believing these to be nothing more than the desperate antics of a condemned man.

'If you turn me in, then my secret will go to the grave with me.'

'I could live with that,' I said.

'I know it all, I remember it all. Why we took you but left your sister and mother; why we took those other two brats and killed their father. Oh, there is so much that I could tell.' He smirked again, then turned and sauntered away until he was almost at the gate in the town wall.

Losing control of myself, I ran up behind Jeffers and punched him as hard as I could in the side of the face so that he was sent sprawling upon the dried mud in the shadow of the wall.

He picked himself up, dusting himself down and feeling his right cheek for blood.

'That really got to you, didn't it, Powder Tom?' He spat the words at me.

I grabbed the collar of his tunic with both hands and hurled him back against the wall a few yards along from the gate. His face was only a couple of inches from mine. I could smell his rancid breath.

'If you know something, you'd better tell me now, so help you God,' I shouted.

Jeffers grinned, spat blood on to the ground beside me, then glanced towards the gate. As he seemed to have expected, or doubtless had the canniness to plan, our scuffle had attracted the attention of the guards at the gate, three of whom came out to investigate what was happening. They saw me holding Jeffers up against the wall, saw Edward with both his pistols drawn.

'Put down your weapons, all of you,' shouted the sergeant of the guard. His two men raised their muskets and pointed them in our direction.

Edward put his pistols back into his waistband.

'I said put them down,' cried the sergeant.

'This one's got a pistol too,' wheezed Jeffers. I tightened my grip and pressed him harder against the wall.

Edward turned to the sergeant and said in a commanding voice, 'Guard, send for Captain Mason immediately. Tell him that Sir Edward has another traitor for him, and that this one's still alive, for now.'

The sergeant hesitated.

'Do it now,' Edward shouted, 'or you and your men will be out of work before nightfall.'

The sergeant withdrew, instructing his two men to keep us within their sights while he sent for the captain.

It was stalemate, and we all stayed where we stood. Jeffers grinned at me, goading me.

'It is to your misfortune,' I said to Jeffers, 'that Captain Mason is greatly in our debt, thanks to the last traitor we dispensed with. It was a good try, but your luck has run out. Speak now, of what you know, or it will be the worse for you.'

'No chance. If I tell you what I know, then I want my freedom,' Jeffers replied.

'And why should we grant you that? You deserve your punishment.'

'Because you really do want to know and you may yet need me alive.' His tone had become snide.

'Well then, speak fast; you have until the captain arrives. I make no promise as to your freedom.'

I loosened my grip on his tunic and stepped back to give him a little space. I expected him to blurt out some details about the ways and means of Murat Reis. Instead, his opening words caught me like an unexpected blow to the midriff that knocks the wind right out of you.

'It was all Dillington's work.'

'Robert Dillington?' I asked in disbelief.

'The very same. He was behind it all. And I can swear to as much in court, which is why you need me alive. I was there. I witnessed it all.'

I did not believe it, or rather, I could not bring myself to believe it, but I still said: 'Tell me more.'

'Not until you have sworn that you'll let me go, that I shall have my freedom.'

In hindsight it was fortunate that this decision had fallen to me. Had it fallen to Edward then I have no doubt that he would have skewered Jeffers to the town wall there and then rather than contemplate letting him go free. But as things stood, the decision was mine and there was only one option I could take.

Jeffers must have read this in my eyes. 'Swear it, so that everyone around can hear,' he said, gesturing to the guards still pointing their muskets at us.

'I swear it, as Sir Edward here is my witness, but you must tell me all you know.' I heard Edward mutter something but he did not intervene.

'Good, clever lad,' said Jeffers with a release of breath. He was clearly more relieved than he wished to let on. His tone remained snide. 'Yeah, I'll tell you everything. Like I was saying, Dillington was behind it all. Back in the day, he made his money through smuggling. That's how he got his fortune.'

'So you're saying he's a smuggler, well so are half the gentlemen on the Isle of Wight, I'll wager. What's that got to do with anything?'

'Be patient, Powder Tom, and I'll tell you. Smuggling gave Dillington plenty of contacts, from doing the runs across the Channel. That's how he first met up with old Jan Janszoon.'

I mouthed the name. It kindled a vague recollection in my mind.

Jeffers continued. 'Those were in the days before Jan Janszoon became known as Murat Reis.'

'Dillington knew Murat Reis?' I asked. Incredulity now vied with my need to know the truth.

'Yes. The Meade Hole, that's the anchorage where they used to meet up, to discuss cargos and such like. I was there many a time, not far up the Solent from here.'

'I know it,' I said.

'One day, word goes from Dillington to Murat Reis that he wants an unusual bit of business doing for him. He wants some people kidnapped and killed.' Jeffers sniggered, as if relishing the story.

'Go on,' I said.

'Well, old Murat is up for it if the price is right. In return he wants gunpowder, cos he knows that the powder from the King's docks in Portsmouth is much better than the stuff you'll find in Barbary. And he knows that Dillington and his men can get hold of it.'

'Yes, that makes sense,' I said to myself. I was only half listening now as my mind digested the information and pondered what it meant.

'So Dillington gives him precise instructions: when to come; which houses to go to; who to take, and who not to touch; where to find the gunpowder and so on. It was all written down and agreed. Dillington even drew him a map.'

'And Murat stuck to the deal?' I asked.

'To the letter,' Jeffers replied. 'There's honour amongst thieves and, like I say, those two went back a long way together. That's why we left your sister and mother, though there was many of us who'd happily have brought them along too. Murat personally saw to that.'

'Yes, I remember,' I said, trying to take it all in, picturing Murat Reis with his lantern at the foot of the stairs in our cottage, orchestrating proceedings. 'But why would Dillington want me gone, and why the Leigh children?'

'Well, I know this cos I was there when Dillington and Murat agreed the deal and, God's truth, Murat asked the very same question. Dillington wanted those other children gone and their father dead because he wanted their land and that pig-headed farmer wouldn't sell it to him at any price. Fine bit of land, apparently, great views across the sea, and easy access to the beach.'

'Handy for smuggling,' I murmured.

'And as for you, we kidnapped you rather than killed you there and then cos Dillington wanted it that way. He reckoned it was less suspicious to have you taken than to have you murdered in your bed, and he wanted to spare your mother and sister from the sight too, bless him. Still, he was more than happy for Murat to lose you at sea, should the opportunity arise. But old Murat, he knew you'd be worth something at the market, so he kept you alive.'

'But why did Dillington want to do away with me? I had no land or riches to my name. I had no quarrel with him, I was just a boy.'

'Oh, you had something that Dillington wanted all right. He had already set his sights on marrying your sister, Elizabeth I think her name is, when she was of an age. And he wanted to make sure that you, as her older brother and the proper heir to the manor, would never be able to spoil his plans.'

'Wait, you said he's planning to marry my sister?' My head was spinning. There was too much to take in and it all seemed unreal. I glanced at Edward behind me. He was following the conversation with a frown etched deep into his forehead.

Jeffers nodded with enthusiasm, delight in his eyes.

'And what do you mean, the 'proper heir'? Dillington bought the manor estate fair and square from my family after my father's death. He even supported my mother, saving us from destitution.'

Half of me now suspected that Jeffers was peddling a pack of lies to save his own skin; but the other half realised that he spoke the truth. I was beginning to doubt much of what I knew, or thought I knew, about my own past.

'But why did you have to sell the estate?' Jeffers asked, twisting the knife.

'To cover my father's debts.'

'And how did your poor father rack up those debts?' Jeffers asked, mimicking concern.

'Because his ship was lost at sea,' I replied.

'Lost at sea? Ah, now let me think, the *Mermaid* wasn't it?'

My eyes opened wide, confirming to Jeffers that he had correctly remembered her name.

'Oh, she made a fine prize, she did,' laughed Jeffers. 'It was all arranged between Dillington and Murat Reis.'

'But Dillington was a partner in that ship, he invested his own money.'

'I daresay he did, and that he saw a very good return on that investment – unlike your father. Dillington always had a good head for business.'

I turned away for a moment, trying to suppress the tears welling in my eyes.

'But Dillington told my father to invest in that ship and to borrow to increase his investment.' I spoke as much to myself as to Jeffers.

'I bet he did; all the more for him to lose.' Jeffers wore a grin from ear to ear of his pock-marked face.

'And it was those debts that broke my father and sent him to an early grave,' I muttered.

Edward placed a hand upon my shoulder. 'Come, Tom,' he said. 'I think you've heard enough from this villain.'

I turned to face Edward, tears laced with anger were streaking my cheeks. I allowed my head to bury into his shoulder and he put a strong arm around me.

'I trusted him,' I sobbed, 'we all did.'

Behind me, I heard Jeffers ambling away towards the guards at the gate. 'You're going to love having Robert Dillington as a brother-in-law, ain't you?' he shouted, sniggering as he went.

I couldn't move, couldn't speak.

'It seems to me,' said Edward, 'that you have a score to settle at home.'

I gave no answer and stood there numb as Jeffers's revelations sank in.

My dark thoughts were interrupted by the sound of hooves approaching the gate from the town. I turned, wiping my eyes to see Captain Mason dismounting. He passed his horse to one of the guards at the gate and approached us on foot, accompanied by the sergeant.

'Sir Edward, you sent for me,' he said, 'something about another traitor.'

'Aye Captain, we thought that man was a treacherous renegade,' Edward motioned towards Jeffers, who was watching us nervously from beside the gate, 'but he has pointed us in the direction of the true villain.'

'And who is that?'

'Your friend Robert Dillington,' said Edward, 'and we owe him a visit.'

The captain looked confused. 'Then there's no need for action here?'

I took a final look at Jeffers, watched the fear return to his eyes. I knew that, just at that moment, I held that smirking, unrepentant villain's life within my hands.

Edward looked to me to respond.

'No captain,' I said, 'we have no further business here.'

The captain shook his head in bewilderment or annoyance and was about to walk back towards the gate when Edward asked, 'How fares the Duke?'

'He's undaunted,' Mason replied. 'In fact he's meeting with some officers from the army as we speak, come to plead for money to pay their men, no doubt. So I'd better head back to keep everything in order.'

'Of course,' said Edward.

From the gate there came the sound of more hooves approaching at speed. This time the horse proceeded through the gate, its rider – a young army officer – looking around, as if to find someone. He spotted Captain Mason and dismounted.

'Captain,' the officer said, struggling for breath.

'Yes, Sturton, what's the matter?'

'It's the Duke.'

'Why, what's he done now?' asked Mason.

'He's been stabbed. He's dead.'

Chapter 22: The Island

Captain Mason grabbed the reins from the officer and swung himself up into the saddle. Without a word of farewell, he galloped off through the gate trailed by clouds of swirling dust. Sturton, the young officer, ran after him.

'Should we go too?' I asked.

Edward shrugged his shoulders. 'What good would that do? What's done is done. The bloody dog is dead.'

'They may need our help.'

'They've got half the English army here; I'm sure they can manage without us.'

'But we've got to do something.'

'Aye, I'll tell you what we've got to do. We've got to get our things and find a boat to get us out of town before they shut the whole place down and start locking up anyone suspicious. I don't want to be here when that happens.'

I hesitated; Sturton's news had stunned me. Edward grabbed me by the arm and pulled me towards the inn. The pain from his grip brought me back to my senses.

Back at the inn, the air was still thick with the excitement stirred up by our confrontation with Jeffers. The singing had stopped and had been replaced by a cacophony of heated conversations. Our entrance cut these conversations short and we attracted glowering stares from around the room.

'What you done with Jeffers then?' It was the old tar who had been sitting with him who shouted at us from a safe distance.

Edward flashed him a withering look and forced his way through to the back of the inn where the staircase led up to our room. I followed him, imagining a dozen daggers piercing the flesh of my back.

Edward set to work flinging his belongings into his chest. Behind us, I heard footsteps on the stair, accompanied by puffing and wheezing. The innkeeper appeared at the open door.

'It's not such a bad thing that you're leaving,' he said. 'I don't want no trouble and there's a lot of folk downstairs who ain't so happy with what you just did to old Jeffers.'

'Not so happy, eh?' said Edward over his shoulder, not bothering to turn round. 'They should keep better company.'

'We're leaving now,' I added.

'Well, you're all paid up,' replied the innkeeper, relief evident in his bulging eyes.

'All paid up,' replied Edward, turning to flash the innkeeper a thunderbolt stare. 'You brazen thief! We've more than paid for our lodging. Still, I don't have time to waste haggling over pennies with the likes of you. We've already dallied far too long in this cesspit.'

Edward pulled the chest along the floor, elbowing the innkeeper out of the way, before hauling it down the stairs in a series of thuds that shook the timbers of the inn. I kept my eyes on the innkeeper as I brushed past him and followed Edward down.

'I hope there'll be no more trouble,' the innkeeper shouted after us.

'Trouble?' I said, glancing back up the stairs. 'You can be sure of that.'

We pushed our way out of the inn and walked the few yards down to the narrow stretch of shore. The chest scraped over the shingle. Several boats had been pulled up on the beach; some were being loaded with goods, others were in the midst of unloading.

Edward stopped hauling his chest and looked towards me, red-faced and breathless. 'You're the local round here,' he said. 'Find us a boat over to your island.'

Despite my anger at this rough treatment, I decided to humour him. I passed a couple of empty fishing boats and found a sober-looking man sat on the side of a small, single-masted skiff, smoking a pipe.

'Can you take us over to Ryde on the island?' I asked.

The man pulled a face, said nothing but looked me up and down, taking another draw on his pipe.

'We'll make it worth your while,' I added.

'Will you, young master? See I'm just about done for the day and was looking forward to putting my feet up with a tankard of ale for company.'

'A shilling for your pains,' I said.

He puffed nonchalantly on his pipe, though his eyebrows betrayed his interest. 'Call it two shillings, and you have yourself a boat.'

'Agreed,' I said and beckoned to Edward, who dragged his chest across to join us.

'Here, give us a hand to push her off,' said the man, tapping the smouldering tobacco out from his pipe.

We pushed the boat out over the waves breaking upon the shore, heaved the chest in and clambered aboard, Edward cursing the water that had seeped into his boots. We sat down upon the low, damp bench at the bow. The boatman sat in the middle of the boat with his back to the mast, facing the stern. He placed the oars in the rowlocks and with a few strong strokes pulled us out into the main harbour. He twisted his head around every few seconds so that he could pick his way through the multitude of boats ahead of us.

Over at the town wall I could see the guards closing the gate that opened on to the Spice Island. I made out the figure of Jeffers outside the gate; he was in conversation with a group of soldiers and pointing towards the inn. The soldiers began to march along the short road towards the inn and the beach from which we had just departed.

Our progress along the narrow channel separating the harbour from the open waters of the Solent was desperately slow. The tide was flowing against us. On our port side there was activity on the wall that linked the round and square forts. Men were running along the ramparts. I cast a nervous glance towards the fort on our starboard; Edward was alert to the danger too. I offered a silent prayer as we inched through the lead-grey waters between the forts and their menacing guns. We would be an easy target.

After what seemed like an hour, but was probably less than a quarter, we made it out into the Solent. Beyond the protection of the harbour, our skiff bobbed like flotsam upon the untamed waves. The boatman drew in the oars, hoisted the small sail upon the mast, and moved to the stern to work the tiller.

We advanced under our solitary sail, seeking to make the most of the south-westerly wind that blew towards us from the island, whipping the waves into a spray that doused us at regular intervals. I tasted the salt on my lips and felt it caking my cheeks, which were already stinging from the brisk wind. The boatman worked to windward, sailing close-hauled so that the boat moved in a zigzag fashion and the wind came at us from one side then the other. I often glanced back at the entrance to the harbour, in case any vessels had been launched in pursuit.

Ahead of us, across the Solent, a wide expanse of sand edged closer. I remembered that these treacherous sands had been the undoing of many a poor soul caught out by the rapid, merciless advance of the swirling tide. Beyond them rose the dark green mass of the Isle of Wight. Nestling at the shore was a cluster of dwellings marking the small village of Ryde, towards which our boatman steered.

'How far is it across the island to your village?' asked Edward. He seemed calmer now that we had left Portsmouth behind and spoke in a low voice so that the boatman would not overhear us. The incessant flapping of the sail made sure of that.

'To Mottistone: fifteen miles, maybe more,' I replied.

'And it makes sense to travel across land rather than to go around by boat?'

'Yes, I think so. We should be able to hire horses and cover the distance quicker over land. It might take us a whole day to sail around, particularly into this wind. In any case, I don't think even your powers of persuasion would coax this fellow to sail us there tonight.'

'Where shall we stay the night?' asked Edward.

'Depending on our progress, I think we should find an inn at Newport, near the centre of the island.'

'Aye, we should head there tonight. Who's in charge of this island by the way?'

'Well, I suppose there's the governor, who lives up at the castle in Carisbrooke, not far from Newport.'

'Should we pay him a visit, and let him know what this knave Dillington has been getting up to?'

I didn't answer straight away. With all the tumultuous happenings that day, I had given no thought to how we would deal with the situation that would unfold when we reached the island.

My mind had been chewing over Jeffers's revelations, trying to come to terms with them. One thing I knew was that I had to tell my sister what I had learned about Dillington, which I hoped would put a stop to their impending marriage. Since today was Thursday, assuming Captain Mason was right that the wedding would take place at the weekend, we would have time to work up a considered plan of action on our ride over to Mottistone in the morning.

'Yes,' I replied, once I had digested Edward's question, 'we could call in at the castle and speak to the governor.'

Our boatman knew these waters well. He sailed along a shallow channel between the sand flats until the boat grounded and we could sail no closer. Edward paid him his two shillings and we helped him push back off into the water. We crossed the remaining stretch of sand, a couple of hundred yards, on foot. Edward dragged his chest behind him, leaving a trail that wended its way right back into the sea.

It was late afternoon when the sands gave way to grassy earth and I set foot once more upon the firm ground of the island, my island, from which I had been taken six long years ago. I had a strange feeling inside me: as if something that had been wrong for a long time had now been put right. I could not say that I shed tears of joy, it was not like that, but something stirred within me.

We reached the huddle of fishermen's cottages and made for a coaching inn that lay beyond them in a lane rising up from the shore. This inn was a regular staging post for travellers making the crossing to and from the mainland. There were stables at the inn and Edward hired us two fine mares. He took the larger one, which was chestnut brown; mine was white with a black nose and, by good fortune, a pleasant temperament. Edward also hired saddle bags, into which he transferred most of the contents of his chest, which he left in the safekeeping of the innkeeper.

We were keen to reach Newport before nightfall and departed without delay, riding up the lane side by side. In no time we were clear of the village and into farmland, a patchwork of golden fields criss-crossed by tall hedgerows. I listened to the birdsong, which rekindled memories of the sounds of home. I recognised the trees, clad in their late-summer vestments. I breathed the air, which was thick with the half-forgotten smells of my childhood: from the hedgerows came the scent of wild garlic and from the fields came the smell of warm hay, stacked and ready to be brought in for winter.

I led the way, following lanes that meandered across flat, open farmland towards a grassy ridge with a procession of trees lining its top. This, I knew, was Arreton Down; we could ride along its spine towards the centre of the island.

On reaching the top of the down, we rode west towards the sunset, which was enflaming the sky in hues of pink and red and amber. The land tumbled down on either side of our path. On our left the coast of the island curved round in a graceful arc towards the south. On our right we could look back across the Solent towards Portsmouth, with its thick stone walls and protected harbour, a pool of molten gold. The ridge eased down at its western end so that, as dusk began to close in, we reached more level ground and joined a road that wended its way through a shallow valley.

Not long afterwards, we crossed the River Medina, which bisects the island from north to south, and reached the town of Newport. I knew the town well from my childhood. My old school was here; I wondered what my old school-friends would think if they could see me now. We rode up past the quay into the centre of the town. Here the buildings were of brick and stone, their roofs neatly thatched. The streets formed a tight grid reminding me, in a small way, of the great lattice-work of streets in Valletta. Edward did not appreciate this comparison.

The sky had darkened to a deep blue by the time we dismounted. We sought accommodation for the night at an inn under the sign of the Bugle. A stablehand led our horses away. The innkeeper, a sour looking fellow barely as old as me, showed us to a comfortable room on the first floor with two welcoming beds and a view over the town's main square. I could have gone to sleep there and then, but Edward persuaded me to come downstairs for supper. We found ourselves a table and, as I was saddle sore, I eased myself on to a stool. The lanterns creaked as they swung from the low beams overhead; the windows were open to let in the mild night air.

Edward ordered a pitcher of the finest ale, from the same lad who had taken our horses to the stable. I suspected that there was only one sort of ale in the inn, which duly appeared, dark gold and frothing. We dined upon roast ham that night, served with an array of vegetables that I welcomed as forgotten friends: carrots and turnips, cabbage and sprouts.

Our fellow diners and drinkers were a motley collection of townspeople and farmers. The atmosphere was less raucous and altogether more convivial than that in the Spice Island inn. I spotted the innkeeper, now less down in the mouth but more flushed in the cheek, sitting at a table in the corner and drinking tankard after tankard at the loud encouragement of his fellows.

Edward seemed more at ease, though he remained pensive. When he had finished his meal he put his right boot upon a stool, took out his pouch and his pipe and pushed a pinch of Lapthorn's finest Virginia tobacco down into it. He lit the pipe and smoked it, consumed by his thoughts.

After his final draw on the pipe, he turned to me with a glint restored in his eyes. 'What do you say to paying the governor a visit in his castle this evening? You said it wasn't far away.'

At this point, I confess, I was looking forward only to the prospect of a good night's sleep in a proper bed. I wondered where Edward found the stamina to go on, particularly after the day we'd had. He seemed to be possessed by an indomitable spirit, an irrepressible capacity to persevere, even when pulled down into the depths of adversity. As for me, my tiredness tempered my reply. 'Could we not call in on him tomorrow morning? The castle's about a mile away. But it's more or less on the way we're going to be riding in the morning.'

'Aye, we could. But I fancy we'll more likely catch him at home at night.' Edward beckoned the stablehand over. 'Boy, do you know the governor of this island?'

The lad hesitated before nodding, surprised by the question.

'I take it he lives up in the castle?' Edward continued.

'In Carisbrooke,' I added.

The lad nodded again.

'And now tell me,' said Edward, 'if we were to go and pay him a visit this evening, do you think we'd find him at home?'

The lad paused for a moment. 'Well on most days I have to say that I wouldn't know, sir. But I fear on this night you'll not find him there.'

'How do you know that?' I asked.

'Because most of the gentlemen on the island have gathered for a party this evening, and I reckon he'll be there too.'

'Och, that's a shame, but it can't be helped,' said Edward, indicating to the lad that he could go, but only if he brought us another pitcher of ale.

I breathed a sigh of relief that my bed would now be not so distant a prospect. As Edward smoked another pinch of tobacco, I sat and listened to the conversations around me, picking out the names of people and places, many of which I knew.

As the night drew to a close most of the townspeople and farmers departed leaving only the small group at the table in the corner who were propping up the innkeeper. Edward and I took ourselves up to our room and I delighted in sinking my sore and weary body into my bed. I was asleep within moments.

In the morning I woke early, gripped by nervous excitement at the prospect of returning home. I could think of little else but whether I would find my mother still alive and if so, how she – and my sister – would take to my sudden reappearance after all this time. I thought about what I should say when we met; what words could possibly capture my happiness and my regret?

I persuaded Edward to accompany me down for an early breakfast. This was served by a friendly old spinster with a stout frame and a ruddy complexion, who waddled among the tables with a linen cap on her head and an apron over her dress, balancing enticing plates of food. When she brought ours to the table – a fine spread of bread, bacon and eggs – Edward struck up conversation.

'It's small wonder that the master of the house isn't serving the breakfast this morning,' he said with a chuckle. 'He looked a little worse for wear last night.'

The woman's face turned serious. 'Poor man,' she said, 'his sweetheart is to be married to another this very morn. It's the talk of the island. Most of the gentlemen and ladies from round these parts will be there.'

Edward made a sympathetic expression as he pierced a thick rasher of bacon with his fork.

She leant in close and lowered her voice. 'To rub salt into his wounds, we all know that the bride – a lovely sweet thing, poor dear – would rather be here with the young master than stuck out in the back of beyond in that cold manor house with an ageing husband. Well, it's just not right, is it?'

She could tell that she now commanded our complete attention. Relishing being our source of information she reduced her voice to a whisper. 'There's some who say that by rights the manor should be hers anyway, not his. Still, as you saw last night, the master's friends were helping him to, well, you know, get over it. And he's a fine-looking man so I'm sure he'll find someone else someday.'

'You mentioned a manor. Which one would that be?' I asked, though I already knew the answer.

'Why that would be Mottistone Manor,' she confirmed.

Edward and I exchanged a glance. 'Is that where the governor was last night then?' I asked.

'Oh, yes, I should think so: him and most of the important gentlemen from hereabouts. Master, I mean, *Sir* Robert Dillington invited all of them; still there's some real gentlemen round here that won't give him the time of day.'

Edward and I sat in stunned silence for a moment.

'And you say the wedding is today?' Edward asked.

'Oh, yes. Like I say, it's the talk of the island. It's this very morning, if I'm not mistaken.'

'Out at Mottistone?' I asked, already rising to my feet.

'Yes, that's right,' she said, now looking perplexed.

Meanwhile Edward had reached into his purse and was putting some coins on the table. 'This one's for you,' he said. 'Give my commiserations to your master and tell him that you never know when Fortune's wheel will turn in your favour. Time and the hour run through the roughest day.'

'Thank you, sir. I can imagine this'll be his roughest day all right. But won't you be having any of this breakfast?'

Edward tore off a piece of bread and stuffed it into his mouth, passing the rest to me. 'Thank you, this will more than suffice. You have been most kind. We have a wedding to attend. Tell the stable lad to prepare our horses without delay.'

We took the stairs two at a time.

'What time do you hold weddings in this part of the world?' Edward asked.

'I don't know,' I replied, 'ten o'clock, maybe, eleven. She said it was going to be in the morning.'

'Then we'd better get there fast. I reckon it's already past eight.'

We donned our sword belts, bundled our possessions into the saddle bags and flew back down the stairs. As we burst out of the inn Edward bellowed for the stable lad, who came running round the side of the building a few moments later holding the bridle of each of our mares.

We fixed the saddle bags and mounted the horses. 'Follow me,' I shouted as we clattered down the narrow main street, a cluttered thoroughfare in which pigs and chickens roamed. We passed a series of shops and workshops in rapid succession: coopers, weavers, tailors, candle-makers, cobblers and bakers. Many were opening up for the day's business, their wares being set out on stalls in the street. In our haste, one of my mare's hooves caught the leg of a stall, sending it toppling to the ground and eliciting vehement curses from the shopkeeper. I didn't look back.

Once through the gate that marked the end of the town, we broke into a gallop, passing around half a mile of farmland before we reached the village of Carisbrooke. The castle loomed on the hill to our left; the mighty stone towers of its gatehouse disappearing into the morning mist. I pointed it out to Edward as we passed, allowing our horses to draw level for a moment, though barely slowing our pace.

'I take it we're not stopping,' he called out.

'I reckon the governor will have stayed overnight out at Mottistone or thereabouts,' I shouted back.

'And even if he didn't,' Edward replied, 'it looks like he's a friend of Dillington. If that knave's got powerful friends then we'll need to be on our guard.'

It was a sobering thought and one that had not escaped me. I dug my heels in to the flank of my mare, feeling her sweat soaking into my breeches. We pressed on, following the road, which wound like a serpent of dried mud through the wooded valley of Bowcombe. The ground ahead climbed up in a series of ridges. Unrelenting we spurred our horses on; they whinnied and shivered from the exertion. The stamping of their hooves reverberated through the still air. Behind us the dust flared upwards.

Had we been travelling at leisure then we would have remained on that road as it skirted round the higher ground. But time was not on our side; the sun was climbing ever higher and every minute, every second that passed might be the one that made us too late. Instead I led the way up narrow lanes and twisting paths through gorse and bramble to the higher ground, along ways I had trodden a hundred times as a boy, now spreading out ahead of me like unfolding memories.

Up on the high ground the going was firm. White chalk shone through the balding turf. From here, the western half of the island unfurled to the north – where the great forest of Alvington stretched right to shores of the Solent – and swept out to the south, across an undulating patchwork of fields and low, wooded hills. The edges and contours of the landscape were softened by the lingering haze. Beyond the fields, the coast curved round in an arc of coloured, crumbling cliffs and narrow chines. And over the cliffs lay the unending expanse of sea, sparkling like a million diamonds.

As we pressed on, I heard the single chime of a church bell come drifting up through the haze. I recognised its tone, which resonated right into my heart. It rang again, another single note. It was the peal of the church bell that I had heard countless times in my childhood, calling the faithful or marking some other event in the life of my village. As our horses galloped across the close-cropped turf I pictured the squat steeple of the parish church with its solitary bell. Another chime, and another, and I realised that the bell was ringing to announce the start of the wedding service, to usher the guests to their pews.

'Do you hear the bell?' I shouted to Edward, as he rode beside me.

'Aye, I hear it.'

'It means the wedding is about to begin.'

'Then we had better ride harder.'

He spurred his mare to exert yet more effort and edged ahead of me, small white clouds rising in the wake of her thundering hooves. I pressed my heels hard into the flanks of my mare to keep pace. We raced along the ancient way that lined the top of the down, between yellow-flowered gorse and short trees that had been twisted and disfigured by the westerly winds. Louder, closer, the church bell continued its slow succession of chimes. There was no joy for me in its tolling but rather a deadened, hollow ring. And then the chimes ended, and I knew what that must mean: the wedding had started.

We reached a junction where a grassy path veered off and down to the left between the gorse bushes. I knew that Mottistone now lay beneath us. The path from the top of the down was steep and winding, perilous at the speed we were riding. On more than one occasion my mare lost her footing as the path careered downwards.

It was during this rapid descent that I laid eyes once more upon my village. I knew in that moment, from the pit of my stomach, that whatever Algiers had become for me, it had never been my home. I saw the familiar knot of cottages clustered around the village green with the well at its centre. Watching over the green, perched on a low rise, was the small stone church, pressed close to the ground as if ducking below the gusting winds. Only its short steeple and broach spire seemed tall enough to brave the elements. The bell in the steeple was now silent and still. Close by on our left, nestling snug and half-concealed against the flank of the down, was the manor house that had been home to my family for centuries. Bright stone walls gleamed beneath its tall chimneys and slate roof. Our path led past the ancient Longstone and down along the edge of the manor garden before emptying into the road right in front of the church.

The road was deserted. Everyone from the village must have been crammed inside the small church. There was no one about to see our unseemly arrival. We dismounted and tethered our mares to a post beside the lychgate. My fingers were trembling, either from exertion or from nervous excitement or both. I hated not knowing what was about to happen; not knowing whether I was going to meet my mother again; not knowing how we would confront Dillington and what would happen to the wedding. Inside the church a multitude of voices broke into song.

'So, what's our plan?' I asked, struggling to regain my breath. My stomach was churning so much it felt like I was about to retch.

In our haste to arrive at the church there had been no opportunity for conversation or crafting a plan.

'Well, it looks like we're out of time for fancy plots,' said Edward, straightening his sword belt.

He rummaged in his saddle-bag and pulled out his new cloak, throwing it over his shoulders.

'For God's sake,' I muttered to myself, 'this is no time to be worrying about your attire.'

'I say we head right in and confront the knave,' said Edward, giving the saturated flank of his mare a pat.

'And what happens after that?' I asked, recalling our decision to be careful.

'After that, we'll just have to think of something,' said Edward.

We walked through the churchyard. My heart was pounding, my mouth dry, my senses heightened. I felt fear as well as excitement. Sweat prickled in the pores of my skin. I couldn't help but glance at the headstones that we passed, particularly the newer ones. I was looking at the names that were etched into them, looking – I admit – for my mother's.

We rounded the short tower at the front of the church and arrived at the porch. The old studded door to the church was wide open; the psalm came booming out. We took the opportunity to slip inside while the congregation was still in full voice and took a place in a pew at the back, next to the door. An old couple, dressed in their best clothes, squeezed along the pew to make room for us, tutting. A few others turned their heads and glanced at us, doubtless assuming we were late-coming guests; otherwise our entrance seemed to have gone unnoticed.

The church was so full that we had been lucky to find any space in the pews. I had a reasonable view up the short nave, which was divided into three aisles by stone arcades. The central aisle continued up into the chancel and there, before the altar rails, stood two figures, their backs to the congregation, their heads turned towards the vicar on the altar. On the right stood the groom, tall and thin, his hair falling lank to his shoulders, greyer than I had seen it last. It was the figure of Robert Dillington. On the left was the bride, in a veiled white dress; I could not see her face. The sunlight flooding in from the large square window above the altar gave her dress an ethereal quality.

My pulse raced and my mind whirled. *We were too late; we must have arrived too late.* I looked around for any sign of my mother but to no avail: the church was too crowded and everyone had their backs to me.

The congregation finished singing the psalm and the vicar stepped down from the altar, crossing the chancel to the carved wooden pulpit overlooking the nave. From here he surveyed the congregation imperiously. It was the same vicar that I remembered from years ago, only plumper and more shrivelled; the one who had railed forth with such vitriol against the heathen Turk. He cleared his throat and a whispering hush descended upon the church.

346

'And now,' he said in his pompous tone, 'we come to the solemnization of matrimony. I can duly confirm that the banns of marriage were read out these past three Sundays in accordance with the accustomed manner. Please be seated.'

The congregation sat down to a chorus of coughing and whispering as the vicar walked with affected gravity back to the altar. The tightness in my chest eased a little. There was still time but I had no idea how we would make use of it. I glanced at Edward but his face was inscrutable, his eyes fixed on the altar, his jaw set.

From his elevated position the vicar looked out over the bride and groom and across the serried rows of pews. He took a deep breath. 'Dearly beloved, we are gathered together here in the sight of God, and in the face of this congregation, to join together this Man and this Woman in holy Matrimony; which is an honourable estate, instituted of God in Paradise, in the time of man's innocence...'

Edward elbowed me in the side.

'That's Dillington then, the groom?'

I nodded.

'I'm going up there,' he said, 'to confront him before they exchange vows.'

I nodded again, my throat too dry for words.

'Watch over the door, and await my signal,' he said.

An old woman in the pew in front turned round and looked daggers at us.

The vicar continued to drawl: '...and therefore is not by any to be enterprised, nor taken in hand, unadvisedly, lightly, or wantonly, to satisfy men's carnal lusts and appetites, like brute beasts that have no understanding; but reverently, discreetly, advisedly, soberly, and in the fear of God; duly considering the causes for which Matrimony was ordained...'

On my left, Edward was looking down, giving his pistols a final check. I heard him muttering to himself: 'Wait for it, wait for it, here it comes.'

'...Therefore if any man can show any just cause, why they may not lawfully be joined together, let him now speak, or else hereafter for ever hold his peace.'

The whispers from the pews gave way to an agonising silence. I wondered what Edward was waiting for but just as the vicar seemed about to resume proceedings, Edward stood up and kicked the foot of the pew in front so that the loud thud reverberated through the church. More than a hundred pairs of surprised eyes turned towards him. He began to walk in a measured pace up the aisle towards the chancel. His boots rang out upon the stone floor, echoing in the rafters that arched like an upturned hull above the murmurs of the congregation. His gaze was fixed before him. I suspected he was giving Dillington an unflinching stare.

When Edward reached the end of the nave he side-stepped the bride and groom standing isolated in the chancel and proceeded right up to the altar, eliciting gasps from some members of the congregation. The vicar turned with a look of outraged astonishment towards him.

'Well, sir, do you know of any impediment?'

Edward raised one hand with an open palm to silence him.

In the chancel, Robert Dillington stepped towards Edward. The elevation of the altar above the chancel only heightened the difference in stature between the two men. Edward exuded power. The sunlight streaming through the window seemed to radiate from him as he stood and faced down the entire church.

'Friend, you are welcome to my wedding, but I fear I know you not.' It was the voice of Dillington, loud and confident so that all should hear him.

With a theatrical gesture, Edward unclasped his cloak and let it fall upon the altar about him, revealing the white cross of the Order of St John emblazoned upon his black habit. A wave of gasps and mutterings rippled across the congregation.

'You may not know me,' said Edward, in a commanding tone, 'but I know you, Robert Dillington, for what you are.'

'Then you should do me the courtesy of addressing me by my title.' There was unconcealed anger in Dillington's voice.

'By your title? You mean that piece of paper that you pawned from Buckingham?' shouted Edward, laughter in his booming voice.

'It is a title good and proper. And if you insult me further I shall have you removed from this church and duly punished.'

'By my reckoning, you need to be dubbed by the king to become a knight of the realm not merely to purchase a piece of paper. It's a shame that Buckingham now lies dead, else I might have asked him to rescind your title, on the basis of what I know about you.'

The news of Buckingham's sudden demise provoked an unrestrained outburst across the congregation, doubtless the effect Edward had intended. The vicar rushed across the chancel to his pulpit to restore a semblance of order, both his plump hands waving in the air. 'Ladies and gentleman, contain yourselves please. Remember, this is the house of God.'

A degree of quiet returned and the vicar turned to face Edward. 'Now sir, I know neither you nor your purpose here but you have succeeded in disrupting this holy ceremony. I ask you one final time whether you know of any reason why these two may not marry?'

'Aye, as a matter of fact I do,' replied Edward. He walked in measured steps towards the pulpit, brushing past Dillington as he went. Taking up a position adjacent to the pulpit, Edward addressed the congregation, making the vicar an irrelevant side-show.

'I am Sir Edward Hamilton, Knight of the Order of St John of Jerusalem, of Rhodes and of Malta; eldest son of the late Marquess of Hamilton and Earl of Arran, and cousin of His Majesty the King.'

During the deliberate pause that followed the vicar seemingly recalculated where his interests lay and retreated a few deferential steps giving Edward access to the pulpit. Edward stepped up in a purposeful fashion, his grey eyes roaming across the congregation, daring anyone to oppose him. Then he removed both of his pistols and balanced them upon the top of the pulpit, in full view of the congregation, each one rattling against the varnished wood as he placed it down.

'Oh no,' I muttered, 'what are you doing?' I sensed a panic emerging across the congregation and spotted a couple of men reaching for the hilts of their rapiers. Fortunately, most of the men in the congregation appeared unarmed.

'Men, bar the door,' Edward shouted. I took my cue and darted round the end of the pew to push the door of the church closed with a bang that echoed down the nave. I saw nervous glances around the church from confused faces wondering how many men Edward had at his command. Then he continued, gripping the top edges of the pulpit in each hand as if he were actually the vicar giving his sermon.

'Be at peace, everyone, for my purpose is only to make it known to you what I have come to learn about this man, Robert Dillington, who stands before you.' This prompted a murmuring from the pews but Edward's voice boomed above it.

'As you can tell by my habit, I am a sworn enemy of the infidel, and an enemy of any man in league with the infidel. Such a man stands before you now. But worse than that, this man is a traitor to his own country too.'

'This is preposterous,' shouted Dillington, 'whatever you think you know you may keep till after this ceremony has concluded so that we may settle it like gentlemen.'

Dillington turned and said something to the bride before walking over to the chancel step to face the congregation and shouting, 'Come on, let's get him out of here.' He beckoned to various men to come up to the chancel to assist him. I saw his pale blue eyes smouldering with rage, his sharp features, which I had once associated with intelligence, now conveyed his ruthlessness. His beckoning gave rise to shouts in his support from various members of the congregation.

Our position was fast becoming untenable. My fumbling fingers felt for the pistol inside my doublet, though I didn't know what use I could put it to.

Edward's voice rang out loud and clear from the pulpit. 'What I know may indeed prove to be an impediment to your marriage. For I do not believe that you have permission to marry this lady.'

The spot in the chancel where the bride had been standing was now empty. She had retreated to the front pew on the left of the nave, outside my field of vision.

'And whom should I require permission from, pray tell?' shouted Dillington, his voice now laced with sarcasm. 'Her father is dead and her brother is gone these many years and sure to be dead too.'

There were now more shouts of agreement and support for Dillington from across the congregation. Men began to muster with intent in the central aisle: half a dozen, then ten, then a dozen.

'You lie,' shouted Edward, 'for, her brother is not dead, but was taken into captivity by Barbary corsairs and yet lives; taken into captivity because *you* ordered it.'

'You're a lunatic,' cried Dillington above the gasps from the pews. He appeared to be sizing up his support in the aisle but was not bold enough to make the first move towards the pulpit, doubtless for fear of Edward's pistols. He addressed the congregation, his voice impassioned, his finger pointing at Edward. 'It is his word, the word of a lunatic, against mine, an honourable gentleman.'

The situation reminded me of the confrontation with Jeffers the day before in the Spice Island inn, only now the stakes were raised and the onlookers looked ready to side with the villain. The men in the aisle began to move forward in numbers into the chancel. I saw Edward cast them a concerned sideways glance. He could not hope to fend off such a mob if it came to a fight. We were hopelessly outnumbered. I had to act now or all would be lost.

'It is my word too,' I shouted, taking up a position at the far end of the aisle. Everyone's attention was suddenly drawn round to me. The firmness in my voice surprised me, for my fingers were still trembling, my stomach turning somersaults, my breathing shallow and fast. 'For I am Thomas Cheke, the very same, whom Robert Dillington had kidnapped and cast into slavery.'

At this, the whole church erupted. People jostled each other to get a clear sight of me. Some gaped, some put their hands to their mouths. Others gasped and cried out 'Can it be true, is it really him?' and other such questions of doubt and exclamations of wonder.

I sensed that the tide was beginning to turn in our favour; I was determined to make it ebb faster. I had to bawl out my words to make myself heard above the commotion in the pews. 'And it was not just me. It was George and Catherine Leigh, you had them taken as slaves as well, didn't you?'

My outburst unleashed another wave of unrest that surged across the congregation. I now saw fear in Dillington's eyes. On my left, a couple of pews in front, there was some pushing and cursing as a man forced his way into the aisle. To my shock I recognised him as Henry Leigh, the father of George and Catherine, the man whom Murat Reis's men had left for dead at the doorstep of his own farm. His hair had greyed and his face had become sallow but he still had the frame of an ox.

'Is it true?' he roared. His crazed eyes fixed on me, imploring me to confirm it. 'Is it true that *he* ordered it?' He thrust a finger in the direction of Dillington, once more standing isolated in the chancel. The mob who had assembled in the aisle were retreating back into their pews.

'It is true,' I shouted. 'And we can tell you how he did it, and why he did it. But know this: that man in the pulpit there, Sir Edward Hamilton, has now paid the ransom for your children's safe return, while that knave Dillington ignored every desperate plea for help.'

'Lies, lies, all lies,' shouted Dillington, but conviction had now given way to desperation in his voice. His pale eyes were now focussed on the huge, muscular frame of Henry Leigh lumbering towards him up the aisle. He turned to his left side and shouted: 'Governor, do something to restore order. Put a stop to this slander.'

In response to Dillington's plea, a well-dressed man, who had not thus far taken any visible part in the proceedings, stepped forward from the front pew, right beneath the pulpit. His cloak was pushed to one side, exposing his hand upon his rapier hilt. He stood between Dillington and Henry Leigh.

'Henry, stop there.' He spoke in a calm, confident voice, holding his left palm up to stop the farmer's advance. A degree of quiet returned to the congregation as people strained to hear the governor's words.

'Now listen, everyone, the truth will out, of that I have no doubt. But it will be done properly, not in some brawl inside God's holy place. It looks to me like today's ceremony is at an end, so I demand that we all keep our heads and make our way peacefully outside.'

Though the governor's words may have had the desired effect on the greater part of the congregation, who began to file towards the door, Henry Leigh would not, I am sure, have heeded any man's words in such circumstances. He pushed past the governor, who made no further attempt to stop him, and into the chancel where the petrified figure of Robert Dillington awaited him. With a mighty swing of his right arm he smote Dillington full in the face. I lost sight of the villain as he collapsed backwards on to the floor of the chancel. My view was blocked by the members of the congregation who were now flooding towards the door to exit the church. I walked ahead of them, opened the door and stepped out through the shaded porch into the bright churchyard.

The congregation poured out of the church in all their flustered finery. Most of them cast me curious looks as they passed, some tutting, others muttering. Many of the faces I recognised: older, but still the same. Some of the locals shook me by the hand but I barely noticed them. My attention remained fixed on the porch and the people passing through it. I was looking for one person in particular; hoping, praying that she was still alive. And then she came. The sheer panic in my mother's face melted into joy as her eyes found me. 'Tom, my Tom, you're alive.'

She rushed towards me and took me in her arms, frailer now than I remembered her. She held me, her body heaving as she reached up to kiss me. Tears were in her eyes and on her cheeks. They filled my eyes too.

'Robert told us you were dead; he said he had word that you were all dead.'

'It's all right. Everything's going to be all right now,' I said.

We stood there for a minute, the two of us, as the remnants of the congregation streamed past. In truth I no longer noticed them. I rested my chin on her shoulder. Beside me, a blue-winged butterfly alighted on the soft lichen of a headstone. It paused for a moment then flittered on.

My sister was one of the last to leave the church. Her veil was now pushed back to reveal her face, almost as white as her dress. She had blossomed into the woman I had imagined her to be, though her eyes were reddened by tears. She came and joined in our embrace.

'Tom, you've come back,' she said.

Epilogue

So it was that I returned to the island, my arrival almost as dramatic as my departure had been. But my reunion with my mother and sister in the churchyard in Mottistone is not the right place to end this memoir. There remain loose ends to my story that I feel obliged to tie, so that you may understand what has become of my life now that Fortune's wheel has come to a rest.

After the abortive wedding, my mother, Elizabeth and I returned to the family cottage, a short walk down the lane from the church. It was the same cottage that I had been taken from on that fateful night six years before. How different it looked from my last memory of it: the shutters were wide open, allowing the sunlight to stream in. The crockery and ornaments were neatly arranged on the dresser. Vases of cut flowers filled the room with their sweet scent. The furniture had been set out to receive wedding guests, though the principal festivities were to have been held at the manor.

I did not know at first how Elizabeth would take to my ruining her wedding day. She was quick to allay my concerns when I broached the matter. 'Oh Tom,' she said, 'have you forgotten me so completely?'

Elizabeth explained that she had agreed to marry Dillington under duress. Having given up on winning her hand by fair means, Dillington had resorted in the end to a 'rough wooing'. He had threatened to bring destitution upon my mother and Elizabeth if she failed to take his hand. My mother knew that her current manner of living depended on Dillington's continued generosity, without which she could not afford to pay the rent. Elizabeth had come to understand that too. Her true love was, as we had been informed, the young landlord of the Bugle Inn at Newport, whose sullenness I could now forgive, under the circumstances.

Edward told me afterwards that Robert Dillington had left the wreckage of his wedding by the side door of the church, with a bloodied nose and fewer teeth than he had woken with that morning. From there he must have scuttled back into the manor house, for I saw nothing more of him that day or for many thereafter.

Edward followed us to the cottage, leading the horses, but not before he had given the governor a full catalogue of Dillington's crimes and had received the governor's assurance that Dillington would feel the full weight of the law. I greeted Edward at the front door of the cottage. We both had to stoop to enter.

'You put on quite a show back there,' I said.

'Och, the occasion demanded it.'

'I thought it was touch and go for a while.'

'Nonsense; I had everything under control.' Edward laughed.

'You certainly gave a fine sermon.'

'Well, I am a man of the cloth, so to speak.'

'And a cousin of the king?' I raised an eyebrow.

'Aye, a distant one,' he replied with a wry smile. 'At that particular moment, I felt the need to impress the congregation, and they weren't to know any different.'

I made the introductions between Edward and my mother and sister. My mother made a fuss over him and sat him in our best chair. We were soon joined by Henry Leigh and his wife, Martha, desperate for news of their children. My mother told me afterwards that she saw a flame of hope rekindled in their eyes that day, a flame that had died out years ago. I told them what I knew of their children's lives in Algiers, glossing over some of the rougher edges. I reassured them that George and Catherine were in good health, described where they lived and such details that came to mind, which were few in Catherine's case.

My news was greeted by the Leighs with a mixture of happiness and pain, but they left with the prospect that the ransom might yet secure their children's freedom, that they might lay their eyes and hands upon them once more.

The ending to their story – as with so much in life – turned out to be a cup of joy laced with bitter aloes. Within a month of my arrival, George returned to the island, and with him he brought hope and a future back into his parents' lives. More than that, over the next few months he set to work transforming his family's farm, employing new practices that he had learned in Algiers. As Edward was fond of saying: 'sweet are the uses of adversity'.

As for George's sister Catherine, fate had set her life upon a different course. When given the choice, and I believe that it was freely given to her, Catherine had chosen not to return to England. Her life was in Algiers now, and in her eyes it must have seemed a good one. I could understand her thinking. George tried his best to reassure his parents that their daughter was happy and well but they were unable ever to reconcile themselves to her fate. They still wait for the day of her return.

George was not the only one of my fellow captives in Algiers who journeyed to the island. Before the year was out, Will undertook the voyage along the coast from Devon to my home. He had come to fulfil the promise he had made to me on the quayside at Algiers, to tell my mother and sister that I was alive and well. So he had quite a surprise when I opened the front door to him in Mottistone.

'You could have saved me the bother of coming all this way,' he said, his eyes brimming with unexpected joy.

Will and I walked over to the Sun Inn at neighbouring Hulverstone and much mirth we had reminiscing about our lives in Algiers. I was glad of the opportunity to share such memories because George, with whom I might have exchanged many a tale, would never speak of the place. Will and I drank to the health of old Jacob and Silas who, for all we knew, were still seeing out their days under the warm North African skies.

As for Sir Robert Dillington, remarkably perhaps, he kept his title, his ill-gotten property and his freedom – despite the governor's previous assurance that he would feel the full force of justice. Apparently there was not enough hard proof of his complicity in the kidnapping: certainly Jeffers – our key witness – was nowhere to be found in Portsmouth. George and I reckoned the real truth was that the governor was himself up to his neck in smuggling, and that preserving Dillington's freedom was the price that the governor had to pay to ensure that Dillington kept his mouth shut. Nevertheless, Dillington did endure some constraint on his freedom, becoming largely a recluse inside his manor houses – he owned several - while on the island, fearful perhaps of another encounter with old farmer Leigh or embarrassed by his newly crooked nose and gap-toothed smile. Moreover, Dillington's reputation was ruined in the village and across the island, for word had spread of both his crimes and his humiliation and rumours need no hard proof to stick. His punishment, rather like Mehmet's in Algiers, was to be denied the one thing he craved more than anything in life having already amassed a fortune – status, in particular, the high regard of the local gentry.

As for Edward, after a week at the Sun Inn at Hulverstone, in which he had taken up temporary residence, his feet were itching. On a fine, early September morning, I rode back with him to Ryde to return the horses, collect his chest and see him aboard a boat back to Portsmouth. From there he planned to make his way up to London and thence back to Malta. It was a sad farewell as I embraced him for a final time there upon the wide sands; I even thought I saw his eyes moisten. But that was not the last I heard of him.

As for me, I attempted to settle down in Mottistone and to resume my former life; but it could never be again as it used to be. A childhood home pulls on the heart-strings but, for better or worse, my horizons were now too broad to eke out my living in a rural village. In any event, we could not stay in our old cottage. My mother would pay not a farthing more in rent to Dillington now she knew the part he had played in her husband's ruin and my kidnapping; and for his part Dillington would have had us evicted at the first opportunity had he not feared for his own safety in the village as a result.

So within a matter of days we had moved to a cottage belonging to the Leighs a little further down the lane, towards the sea. I was grateful for my old bed, which we took with us but now seemed so small, and glad of a settled roof over my head. I had a table and chair set up in my room, beside a window that looked out across the Leighs' fields to the sea.

I enjoyed living with my mother and sister again but this arrangement lasted for only three short months. That was all the time that it took for another marriage to be arranged, the bridegroom of course being the innkeeper of the Bugle Inn. This wedding was a joyful ceremony in St Thomas's Church at Newport. It was my privilege to give Elizabeth away. I remember exchanging nervous glances with her when the vicar asked whether anyone knew of any impediment to the marriage; happily, there was none. Elizabeth left us to take up residence as the landlady of the Bugle and a fine one she has become. She relishes her life – even if it is not one that many would deem fitting for her gentle birth.

My mother and I remained in the Leighs' cottage in Mottistone and it was there during the months that followed that I put pen to the pages you have been reading. Many candles were consumed as the days grew short and I laboured into the early hours. I wrote in haste while my memories were fresh. I did not seek another employment, though I often helped out on the Leighs' farm. Edward had left me with enough money to see me through a year or two on a modest living. He assured me it was only my fair share of the prize money earned on the *Gloriosa* but I knew that all of that and more had been given to Simeon Azzopardi in Valletta for George and Catherine's ransom. Instead I attributed the gift to Edward's unfailing generosity. I have therefore dedicated this memoir in part to him.

Edward had one more surprise in store for me. A few days before Christmas I received a parcel. It had been conveyed aboard a ship that had arrived in Southampton from Malta. Inside the parcel was a short covering letter from Edward. In this letter he described his new lodgings in Valletta – no longer in the French *auberge* – and recounted the unfortunate and abrupt end to *Fra André's* position as the Grand Master's secretary. He also informed me that the old Duke of Mantua was alive and well, much to Richelieu's chagrin and to the benefit of the Order.

The substance of the parcel consisted of two items. The first was a deck of worn playing cards. I recognised them at once as those that Jack had given me as I departed from the *Sword* into my life of servitude. They were the ones with which I had played during long, hot evenings with Pierre and Joaquin in my old master's house in Algiers. I had left them of necessity with my other possessions at the inn in Birgu as we fled from Richelieu's men.

The cards brought a tear to my eye, but that was as nothing compared to the main contents of the parcel. I unwrapped it from a cover of silk. It was the Koran that my old master had bestowed on me as a mark of his faith in me, and which he had himself owned as a child before me. I have dedicated the other part of this book to the memory of Ibrahim Ali, in return for all the kindness and opportunity he afforded me and in recognition of his nobility, wisdom and humanity. If only, I thought, he and Edward could have met in a different time and in a different place, they would have got on; they would have enjoyed each other's company. But that was not the world into which Fortune had cast them. However, the fact did not escape me that Edward had taken pains to return my Koran to me: a year earlier and, I was sure, he would have thrown it into the fire and stamped upon the embers.

At the turning of the year, when it became clear that Dillington would never meet true justice, in this world at least, I left the cottage and moved to the new town of Cowes, at the northern tip of the island. I rented a small house near the harbour from where I could watch the ships navigating the Solent, some coming to load and unload their cargos at the quayside. My new location had the benefit of being not too far from Newport, to where my mother had relocated to be near my sister. It was a foothold on the island, but it faced out to the sea and to broader horizons. I liked that.

In Cowes I set myself up as a merchant. I rented some space in a warehouse on the quayside and invested the money I had left from Edward as part shares in the cargos of ships sailing from Southampton and Portsmouth, including on Linus Lapthorn's ships sailing to and from Virginia. In this way I have been able to put to good work all the skills in trade and finance that I acquired in Algiers. I am sure that my old master would have approved.

From a modest start, I am beginning to make a good living, though one that is forever subject to the vicissitudes of Fortune. Often I sit upon the quay, watching the tides ebb and flow. I like it best when the sun is setting over the western reaches of the Solent and the twilight encroaches. I contemplate the wide world beyond these shores. Sometimes, when night falls, I retreat to the bedroom in my little house and I sit, as I used to do, reading verses from the Koran, imagining Joaquin and Pierre laughing as they play at cards beside me, the Frenchman perhaps with a glass of cognac in his hand. At these times I give thanks to God's Providence for the life I have led and the people I have known, and I ponder the next turn of Fortune's wheel.

Thomas Cheke Esq.
Cowes, Isle of Wight.
AD 1629

Endnote

Having followed the journey of Tom Cheke from his fearful awakening in Mottistone, through Algiers, Malta, Venice, Portsmouth and then back again to the Isle of Wight, readers would be justified in wondering how much of his memoir can be verified as historical fact and how much was exaggerated or even fictional. In bringing Tom's memoir to the public's attention, I felt duty-bound to investigate the credibility of the people and happenings that unfold in the memoir as part of my broader editorial responsibilities.

The facts in Tom's memoir are relatively straightforward to establish where they relate to people, places or events in Britain, but they become more difficult to verify in Venice and Malta, and harder still in Algiers. Nevertheless, it is possible to piece together a number of important facts across the whole span of Tom's journey. In terms of people on the Isle of Wight, I have verified the personages of Tom, his sister and mother, and his Cheke ancestry, including his forebear, Sir John Cheke, who was tutor to King Edward VI at Cambridge and a notable classical scholar in his time. Tom's father did indeed die young, after which the records verify that Mottistone Manor was sold to Robert Dillington, who – according to the acclaimed diaries of the contemporary islander Sir John Oglander – had amassed his fortune through avarice.

As for Dillington, we know that he purchased his baronetage from the Duke of Buckingham in 1628, was a Member of Parliament in 1654-55 and lived to a ripe old age (almost 90). His alleged connection to the smugglers operating out of the Meade Hole – identified with Osborne Bay – is understandably hard to prove, as the Governor of the island is said to have argued. You can find the raised tomb of the wife of another Robert Dillington (son of the Robert Dillington in the memoir) inside the parish church at Mottistone. Of course there is no record of Dillington senior's wedding to Elizabeth Cheke in the parish records as the vicar thankfully never concluded proceedings. The Cheke ancestral records confirm that Elizabeth did go on to marry the landlord from the Bugle Inn in Newport.

Of the Leigh family I found no precise record, though there is ample evidence of the Leighs being a notable land-owning family in both Mottistone and the neighbouring parishes around this time.

That leads naturally on to the credibility of the account of Tom and the Leigh children's kidnapping by Murat Reis the Younger, a native Dutchman formerly known as Jan Janszoon. The deeds of this villain of the high seas have been well documented, given the gaping wounds they inflicted on societies as far afield as Ireland and Iceland. It is worth noting that Murat lived to a grand old age, even surviving capture by the Order of St John in 1635, from whom he escaped after five years' captivity. (It is also noteworthy in passing that Murat's descendants are said to include some of the most distinguished families in both England and America, notably the Spencer-Churchill family, headed by the Duke of Marlborough, and the Vanderbilts and even Jackie Kennedy and her children with John F Kennedy.)

What is less well known, amongst the general population at least, is the extent of raiding by Barbary corsairs along the southern coast of England. There are accounts, for example, of peasants being carried away while out harvesting on the Isle of Wight, and more daringly whole towns being plundered, such as Poole in Dorset – whence Jack claimed to have been taken – and Looe in Cornwall. Most audacious of all, perhaps, was the establishment in 1627 of an Islamic republic (of sorts) by Murat Reis and his corsairs on the island of Lundy in the Bristol Channel, which took years to dislodge. During that time the Ottoman flag few within sight of the British mainland.

In terms of the specifics of Tom Cheke's abduction, given the clandestine nature of the affair, it is not surprising that I found little by way of corroboration for Tom's own account of his kidnapping. Suffice it to say that such an abduction would not have appeared extraordinary in its time and place, though the precise nature of the raid and the payment in gunpowder make it possibly unique. (It should be noted however, that there are contemporary accounts of British naval gunpowder from Portsmouth being smuggled away to the Barbary ports where it fetched a good price owing to its superior quality.)

As noted above, Tom's life in Algiers is hard to substantiate, particularly for one such as I, unfortunately illiterate in Arabic. Suffice it to say that some facts and personages are credible. For example, Ali Biçnin appears in historical records as a renegade Venetian known in his native tongue as Picenino. (Ali Biçnin was the key witness in the trial of those involved in the currency fraud and the builder of the expensive mosque in Algiers, which still stands today and has recently been subject to extensive restoration.) The English Consul, James Frizell, was also verifiably active in Algiers around this time.

With respect to Murat Reis's smuggled haul of silver bullion and the subsequent currency fraud, I was able to verify that the silver coinage in Algiers was indeed debased during the years when Tom claims to have been resident in the city. This debasement has been linked by historians to an influx of silver resulting from the capture by Barbary corsairs of numerous Spanish galleons laden with silver bullion on their return voyages from the New World.

Of Tom's master in Algiers, Ibrahim Ali, I found no specific match – though the name appears common in the relevant period as indeed it is today. The positions that he held – such as *Hazinedar*, which Tom refers to as the Grand Treasurer (though we might understand it better as a role similar to that of Chancellor of the Exchequer or Minister of Finance) – certainly existed, as of course did Sultan Murad III and his hundred offspring, of whom Mehmet, the errant *Gümrük Emin* or Controller of Customs in Algiers, is claimed to have been one. (By Tom's time in Algiers, the Ottoman throne had passed through several hands to Murad IV.)

Once Tom had been captured by Sir Edward Hamilton and delivered to Malta, the facts of his story become easier to corroborate, helped no doubt by the many Anglophone records and histories of that country. Certainly, the Grand Master of the Order at the time, Antoine de Paule, is accurately referenced (as, notably, are the feats of his distant predecessor, Grand Master Philippe Villiers de L'Isle Adam, whose loose family connection to the Duke of Buckingham precipitated Edward and Tom's voyage back to England.)

Edward Hamilton is a harder person to pin down historically. The Hamilton family records appear to indicate that he died in childhood. At that time, however, Edward's father was in exile in France, his estates in Scotland were forfeit and he was dabbling in recusancy (i.e. reverting to the Roman Catholic faith). Under such circumstances, it would have been entirely reasonable to pledge his son to the Catholic Order of St John at an early age, but later to regret that decision as his family returned both to Scotland and to the Protestant fold with their former estates restored. Under such circumstances, the young, distant Catholic son of the first Marquess of Hamilton would have been an embarrassment best swept under the carpet.

Adding some firmness to this speculation, Edward is not the only example of hard-to-trace Scottish nobility within the ranks of the Order of St John at this time. My research has found that a scion of the noble family of Ross, Sir David Ross of Broadford, was a Knight of Malta and a broad contemporary of Edward.

It is noteworthy also that the untimely death of Edward's younger brother, the second Marquess of Hamilton, was indeed reckoned by many to be the result of poisoning – on the orders of the Duke of Buckingham. Some years after the event, a doctor who had been involved in the case gave evidence to that effect, providing the Hamilton family with a clear motive to exact revenge and explaining why the news had not reached Edward until the fateful day of the assassination.

As for Cardinal Richelieu and the cipher, this must have been such a closely guarded secret of the French state that it is hardly surprising that it cannot be corroborated by historical records. What we can surmise, however, is that Richelieu would have loathed Buckingham following the turncoat Duke's change of sides in the struggle between France and the Huguenots at La Rochelle. In terms of Richelieu's other alleged victim, Charles I - Duke of Mantua, it is true that he believed himself to be the King of Constantinople, and therefore the natural enemy of the Turks and ally of the Order of St John. There was good reason for the Cardinal to want Charles replaced with his more compliant son, which could have eased Richelieu's problems on France's eastern front.

I found no records of the dead French agents in Venice, nor of the death of Marco, the young Knight of the Order, which was just as Edward had intended. Nevertheless, the Order's prior in Venice, Nicolò Cavaretta – the former Admiral of the Order's fleet – is readily verified. The priory still stands, its garden a rare (and private) oasis of greenery in *la Serenissima*. There is evidence that the Mantuan ambassador did indeed keep a house in Venice at this time, though I was unable to verify its location from Tom's account or other sources.

In Portsmouth, the circumstances of the Duke of Buckingham – George Villiers's, untimely death are well documented. His ultimate assassin, John Felton, was a disgruntled army officer, though rumours of a French plot were rife, and may well have inspired Dumas's fictional account of the assassination in *The Three Musketeers*. What is clear is that Buckingham died in Captain Mason's house, which was known as the Greyhound and still stands to this day, albeit in modified form, in Portsmouth old town.

The final question that the astute reader may have pondered is why Cheke did not publish his memoir and instead left his manuscript to gather dust? In response, I can only offer my own speculation, which is that the contents of Cheke's manuscript were too sensitive to risk publication, particularly in view of the international politics of the time. Publication would have been perilous for both Tom and Edward – not least as the memoir implicates them in the deaths of three men in Venice. It would also have been detrimental to the Order of St John, especially in its relations with France. Moreover, Tom's clear respect for Islam would have been both controversial and dangerous in what was a highly intolerant time. He could therefore have been forgiven for playing it safe and keeping his memoir under wraps for at least a while. His ultimate intention for his manuscript remains an insoluble mystery. I hope that I have done it justice.

DJ Munro
Edinburgh
2015

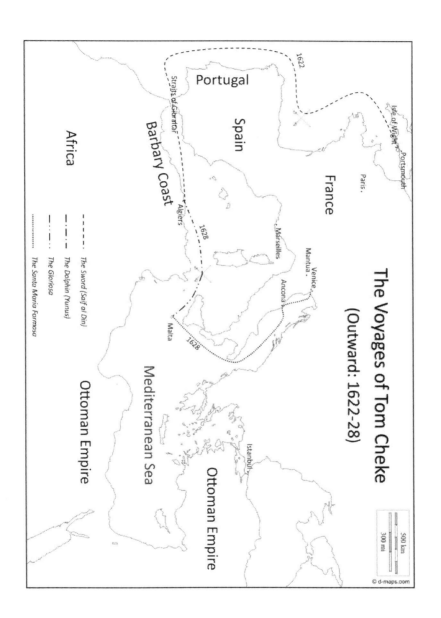

The Voyages of Tom Cheke
(Outward: 1622-28)

- - - - - - The Sword (Saif al Din)
- · - · - · The Dolphin (Yunus)
- ·· - ·· - The Gloriosa
············· The Santa Maria Formosa

Portugal
Spain
France
Africa
Barbary Coast
Straits of Gibraltar
Algiers
Marseilles
Venice
Mantua
Ancona
Malta
Paris
Portsmouth
Isle of Wight
Istanbul
Ottoman Empire
Mediterranean Sea
Ottoman Empire

1622
1628
1628

500 km
300 mi

© d-maps.com

Further information

Thank you for reading *Slave to Fortune*. If you're interested in discovering more about Tom's world then you can learn about the colourful people and places that he encountered during his travels at www.slavetofortune.com.

Take a look at some wonderful old maps, read about the various ships Tom sailed upon and discover fascinating historical insights relating to the book.

There are special features on a range of topics including:

- The Order of St John (Knights Hospitaller)

- Glimpses into 17th century English life

- Particular areas of interest for American readers; *and*

- Parallels between the novel and Robert Louis Stevenson's masterpiece: *Kidnapped*.

There's also an opportunity to see if you can 'crack the code', to leave a comment and to read what others have said about the book.

If you liked *Slave to Fortune* then please consider giving it a review on a site like www.goodreads.com or www.amazon.com. It only takes a couple of minutes – even if you've never done it before.

You can also 'like' the book and stay in touch with any news and reviews on Facebook.

Thank you and best wishes,

DJ Munro
www.djmunro.net

Printed in Great Britain
by Amazon

49193245R00218